SCHISM

BRITT HOLEWINSKI

DELIRIOUS PIXIE

143 Cadycentre, #158

Northville, MI 48167

ISBN-13: 978-0-9883007-5-0

ISBN-10: 0-9883007-5-3

Printed in the U.S.A.

Cover design by DKD

Book design by Ally Khristova

Author photo by Maria Rock

Prologue

*T*he two young men moved quickly under the cover of night, the summer air thick with humidity. Sweat trickled down their foreheads and spines as they scurried through the trees with only the single flashlight to guide them. A new moon made the darkness complete—a rare advantage for them.

A year separated them, but both ran at the same speed, the elder had longer strides while the younger kept up with a quicker gait. Armed, they each carried loaded rifles. The younger one pressed the button on his watch to activate the light; the green glow revealed thirty seconds left on the clock.

Twenty-nine…twenty-eight…

They were fugitives, but revenge was worth the risk. In less than thirty seconds it would be done.

Twenty…nineteen…eighteen…

Their truck was just a hundred yards away. Both were out of breath, but they pressed on.

Nine…eight…seven…

They finally cleared the trees as their feet left the grass and struck pavement. The older one reached into his back pocket and managed to grab his keys while maintaining speed.

Three…two…one…

The explosion was loud, and a ball of fire lit up the night sky behind them as they paused a split second to look. It was done, and there was nothing left to do except drive—and drive fast. They reached the truck and scrambled inside. The ignition mercifully fired up on the first try, and a moment later, they vanished on the highway.

Chapter I

*A*ndy's eyes fluttered open as the first light of dawn entered her bedroom. Waking up naturally, without any noises or lights from electronic devices, was one of the few benefits of life after the virus. She sat up and looked over at the other side of the bed. It was empty, but the sheets were rumpled and still warm. She stood up slowly. Her feet ached and her back throbbed. She moved to the window and opened it, allowing the cool air to enter. Closing her eyes and placing her hands at the base of her spine, she took a deep breath and arched backward as she greeted the day with the same recurring thought: *My name is Andrea Christensen. I am one of the oldest people in the world.*

Andy Christensen grew up in the suburbs of Chicago. At thirteen, she and her mother were involved in a horrific car accident. The oncoming SUV slammed into their car on the driver's side and while Andy escaped with a few bruised ribs and minor scrapes, her mother was instantly killed.

Devastated, Andy stumbled through the remainder of the school year, walking the corridors like a zombie. Her father abandoned his medical practice and moved them to Bermuda. He had an old college friend who owned a house there and offered a place for them to stay for the entire summer. The tiny, secluded island was a place of refuge.

Andy's father spent most of his days fishing and reading in a beach chair before sunset, while Andy wandered the island seeking any adventure of interest to a thirteen-year-old. It was then when she met Morgan and Charlie Pemberton. The siblings were born and raised in England. They lived in Oxford—their father a history professor at the famous university, while their mother worked as a nurse. They had rented a house on the beach for the entire summer.

Just a few months younger than Andy, Morgan was tall and willowy with wavy, chestnut hair and pale skin. She was a soft-spoken girl who had studied ballet for ten years. "Not long after I learned to walk, I was already twirling around and doing pirouettes," Morgan remarked. Her brother Charlie was a genius in the very literal sense of the word. His mind was simply a wonder to observe. Words like "magnanimous," "exacerbate," and "contemptuous" wove through his sentences with remarkable ease. Three years younger than his sister, he was tall, wiry and pale with brown hair and light brown eyes.

The three became quickly inseparable. A born adventurer, Andy tried anything—from diving off rocks to swimming fearlessly with dolphins and sea turtles that came near shore. Charlie, being nearly as fearless, would follow along, but Morgan was more timid and would often sit on the shore and watch.

As these sun-soaked days passed, the sting of her mother's death slowly began to wane, and when Andy wasn't wandering off with her friends, she would join her father for a few peaceful moments fishing off the pier near their vacation house. One day her father caught a large grey snapper, and as Andy watched the smile spread across his face as he reeled the hapless fish in, she realized that it had been months since she'd seen him look so happy.

24 June 2017

The thirty-first day on the island, Andy woke up later than usual. Judging by the quiet in the house, she assumed her father was already out fishing and she was alone in the house. But as she headed downstairs to the kitchen, she saw Morgan and Charlie sitting at the kitchen table. They were eerily silent.

Still groggy from sleep, Andy rubbed her eyes before realizing her friends were crying. "What's the matter?" Neither could manage an answer as Morgan let out a choking wail. Startled, Andy turned to Charlie. "What's happened?!"

"They're sick…they have that virus…the one everyone's been talking about," he gasped in desperate bursts.

"Who's sick?!"

"Mum and dad...people are dying from it," he whispered.

It had been all over the news the past few days: a virus that had accidentally been released from some lab on the East Coast of the United States. But listening with the ears of children, the details of the situation had been quickly forgotten once Andy and her friends stepped outside and into the ocean.

But now seeing the look on their faces, she became gripped with fear about her own father, and without a word, she bolted out the front door, her feet moving so quickly that they barely made contact with the ground.

The pier was about a hundred yards away from the house. Andy tried desperately to see if her father was at the end of it. Without a single cloud to shadow it, the sun, already strong and steady, forced her to squint. A rush of relief flowed through her when she saw him sitting at the pier's edge, and she slowed her pace as she approached him.

He turned to her, his face incredibly pale despite all the hours he'd spent in the sun. "Honey...I'm not feeling so well..."

He could barely stand up, and Andy had to help him up to his feet.

Two days later, her father was dead.

꒰ঌ❦໒꒱

The days and weeks that followed were terrifying. The once-tranquil island of Bermuda rapidly transformed into an isolated prison of chaos and fear. The virus that had been reported on the news was far more serious than anyone could have imagined...and far more deadly. It was an airborne contagion with an incubation period of ten to fourteen days. Infected people could be walking around for two weeks without showing any signs of being sick, all while spreading the virus to next-door neighbors or to strangers traveling from across the globe. Once the symptoms appeared, however, certain death occurred between two and four days.

And there was no vaccine.

Before the televisions went silent, the last news reports suggested that the release of the virus was accidental and had occurred at the Center for Disease Control in Georgia. The origin of the virus, however, remained a mystery. Within several weeks, over six billion people world-wide were dead.

Despite its virulence, there was one particular group who was completely immune to the virus: children. Anyone older than the pivotal age of thirteen or fourteen perished. This made Andy and Morgan amongst the oldest survivors on the island.

The majority of the ten thousand surviving children lingered in either

Hamilton, the capital, or in the northeastern town of St. George. Andy's vacation home, where she now lived with Morgan and Charlie, was situated on the more remote southwestern side of the island. This physical distance from the cities and other survivors was a welcome separation, as thousands of corpses littered nearly every house, street, and building across the island.

Within days, the stench of rotting flesh had become unbearable. The mere sight of death itself had become maddening. In the beginning, they buried each body in the ground, but after a week, digging fresh graves became too exhausting and cremation was the only sane solution, although creating a human bonfire seemed to approach a new level of depravity. At first, they speculated about the lives of every person placed into the fire, but after a while, they stopped wondering. The emotional detachment was necessary; otherwise, it would have been too much to bear. Soon the smell of decay diminished.

Their parents received better treatment. Morgan and Charlie chose to bury their mother and father under a large, flowering tree on the edge of one of the island's many golf courses. For her father, Andy chose the ocean as his final resting place. After placing a daisy-chain of flowers around his neck, she placed his body in a small boat with her friends' help. Then she turned on the motor and let the boat head out to sea. She watched with tears as her father disappeared over the horizon.

Once all the grocery stores and markets were emptied, food became an issue. Initially, Andy and her friends had gathered enough boxes and cans of food to completely cover their kitchen floor, but this lasted only a few months. Out of necessity, they learned to fish and grow food. It turned out that Andy was a natural at fishing; her talent kept her and her friends alive. Growing vegetables, however, was much harder to master, but fortunately the soil beneath the same golf course where Morgan and Charlie's parents were buried proved to be both fertile and forgiving. By the time the canned vegetables ran out, their garden had yielded just enough to get by.

That first year was the most difficult. When not guarding their home and food from other hungry survivors, there were storms to contend with. Two hurricanes pummeled Bermuda in August and September, each gradually destroying the roof of their home. The flimsy plastic sheeting they used to cover any holes did little to keep sun and rain from entering uninvited. Then illness plagued them at some point—everything from the common cold to dysentery. On Christmas day,

Andy vomited so much that she half-expected her insides to come out as Morgan and Charlie initially feared she might have the same virus that had killed their parents. But she soon recovered.

As other survivors throughout the island starved, vicious fights broke out every day over a couple of cans of food. Inevitably, the older survivors formed what could only be described as gangs. Controlled by older children, much of the mischief was carried out by the younger members who stole food and supplies from other gangs as well as hapless children. Fortunately, these gangs kept to their own neighborhoods and rarely roamed toward the west end of the island. On the rare occasions when they strayed too close, Andy and her friends remained fortified inside their home until the threat moved on. They armed their home with a sufficient stock of guns and ammunition, which were found after extensive scavenging of neighboring homes, buildings, and the nearest police station. Andy and Charlie practiced their marksmanship by targeting sea gulls on the beach, and anything they killed usually became supper. At first, the power of a gun was intimidating, but their comfort with the weapons gradually increased. Morgan hated guns, but she forced herself to learn to use one just in case.

Chapter II

*A*ndy looked in the mirror and suddenly realized that she was no longer a child. Five years had passed. Now eighteen, her long blond hair—nearly white from years in the sun—framed a face that had become more oval in shape over time. Her bright green eyes sparkled not with the carefree air of youth but with the wisdom of age beyond her years. And despite the years of living on a meager diet, Andy's hips and chest had swelled just enough to create an hourglass figure. These changes, however, were imperceptible to her. She only saw the muscles in her shoulders and arms from swimming in the ocean, and the calluses on her hands from fishing and gardening.

Morgan, meanwhile, grew both taller and more beautiful. With her delicate features and high cheekbones, she resembled the models plastered on the pages of the tattered women's magazines that she and Andy had skimmed through millions of times.

"With your looks, you could've been one of these women," Andy often told her friend, who would laugh and say, "Why would I want to be one of them? All they do is stand there with weird looks on their faces."

"I know that. I'm just saying that you're as pretty as they are."

"Thanks. So are you."

As usual, Andy would scoff at this and quickly change the subject. The truth was that both girls had become attractive women in their own right.

Charlie had grown a foot taller, and his voice deepened with the onset of adolescence. Now a good-looking young man of fifteen, he had emerged from the typical awkward phases of a boy's early teens into to a teenager full of confidence and desire for adventure. He proved to be a terrific athlete, and over the years he and Andy would race each other swimming along the shore. During the first three years, she remained victorious, but around Charlie's fourteenth birthday, he finally matched her speed, and by the fifth year, Andy was the one trying to keep up.

"I need to face it. I don't think I'll ever be able to beat you again," she said breathlessly one morning after another defeat in the ocean.

"Aw, you're fast, Andy...for a girl," Charlie teased, provoking a large splash of saltwater in his face.

"Oh, yeah? Well, if I *were* a boy, I'd beat you every time!"

Along with his athletic skill, Charlie's mental knowledge expanded enormously over the years. He read extensively, and his days were often spent learning practical things like fixing car engines or hooking up a generator to their home. But it was sailing that became his passion. Using an abandoned sailboat left at a nearby pier, he could maneuver around the island with expert skill.

Charlie's love of sailing pleased Andy, for she knew the day would come when leaving Bermuda would no longer be a possibility but a necessity. Though they had managed to stay alive for five years, the gangs' methods for controlling the island's food and water supply had become more punishing, and the resulting violence had crept closer to their home. On more than one occasion was Andy was forced to use her gun to deter trespassers. It was no longer a question of *if* but rather *when* extreme measures would need to be taken.

The night everything changed, Andy was busy mending the bloody leg of a boy who had taken a nasty spill down a rocky slope near his home. Using medical skills inherited from her father, who had been a surgeon, she stitched up a deep gash on the boy's kneecap.

While finishing the final stitch, Charlie appeared. "Have you seen Morgan? I can't find her anywhere, and I need to ask her something."

"She's at school. English class," Andy replied as she dabbed the boy's leg with disinfectant. "She should be back any minute."

Morgan had been teaching English for the past two years. She viewed it as a way to give the children she taught some structure and sense of accomplishment in their otherwise chaotic lives.

"That's right. I forgot," Charlie replied and left Andy alone with her patient.

An hour later, Morgan still had not returned. Outside, the darkness of a moonless sky enveloped the island. In the kitchen, Andy paced back and forth across the floor while Charlie sat huddled in his chair with his knees hugged to his chest, making him look ten years old again. Neither spoke; both were consumed with worry.

In a sudden flurry of movement, Andy grabbed a flashlight from underneath the sink before dashing upstairs to retrieve a pistol from the lockbox in her bedroom. When she returned to the kitchen, she began loading the gun. "I'm going to look for her. Stay here, and if anyone comes, grab the shotgun."

Charlie glanced from Andy to her pistol and stood up. "I'll get it now," he said and retrieved the large weapon from the small closet by the front door. Andy despised the shotgun because of the large bruise it left on her arm every time she fired it, but Charlie was now strong enough to suppress its fierce recoil.

"I should be the one to go look for her," he said. "She's my sister."

"But that's why *I* should go look for her. I'll be thinking more clearly than you."

Charlie opened his mouth to protest, but stopped before saying, "Fine. I'll guard the house."

Andy began making her way toward the school. Even with the flashlight's wide beam, the road was pitch-black. She moved as quickly as possible, both out of concern for her own safety and the urgency to find her friend.

There was no sign of anyone when she approached the school. The classroom Morgan most often used was empty, except for a young girl sitting on the dingy floor in the back corner. No more than six or seven years old, she was curled up in a terrified ball of gangly arms and legs. Slowly, Andy tucked the pistol behind her back so as not to frighten her.

"Hey, sweetheart. What's wrong?"

Streaks of tears glistened on the girl's cheeks. Between sobs, she managed to blurt out, "They took Miss Morgan!"

Andy felt her stomach plunge. "Who—who took Miss Morgan?"

The girl could only shake her head as tears streamed down her face. Andy tried her best to remain patient. "Please, honey, you have to tell me where they took her. I need to help her."

"They—they took—her to—the bathroom. And then—and then they—locked the door!" The girl choked for breath as the blood in Andy's ears began to pound.

"Some—some of the boys try—tried to open the door—but they—couldn't!"

The girl began to shake uncontrollably, and Andy jumped to her feet and bolted into the hallway. The door to the women's room was locked. She withdrew her gun, chambered a round, then aimed at the keyhole and fired. The bullet ripped through the lock, and she kicked the door open. The room was dark, and once she aimed her flashlight inside, it took a moment to register what she saw, and when she did, she vomited in the nearby sink.

Morgan lay on her side in a crumpled heap on the bathroom floor. Naked from the waist down, her thighs and torso were covered in fresh bruises. Her left eye had already swollen shut, and blood ran from her nose to her mouth. Through the intense beam of light, Andy could see that she was unconscious but still breathing. She crouched down and slowly lifted Morgan's T-shirt, then gasped in horror upon discovering more bruises on her back and ribs.

God, what have they done to you?

Opposite the door was a window with missing panes, providing a clear indication of how the assailants managed to leave the school while keeping the bathroom locked. It wasn't enough for them to beat Morgan within an inch of her life, but they had to make it difficult for anyone to find her.

Dazed, Andy attempted to put Morgan's underwear back on but they had been torn apart. Stifling another wave of nausea, she reached for Morgan's jean shorts laying a few feet away and carefully slid them onto her friend. Then, with every ounce of strength she had, she hoisted Morgan off the bathroom floor and flung her over her shoulder and carried her home.

Morgan's physical condition, though horrific to behold at first, slowly healed. Some stitches and antibiotics ensured a full physical recovery while sleep took care of the rest. Soon her bruises lightened from purple to yellow, and the swelling receded. Her emotional wounds, however, would need much more time. She would cry for hours on end, then suddenly stop and stare out her bedroom window toward the endless ocean for an hour or two. Her appetite had vanished, and Andy and Charlie's mutual urgings for her to eat went ignored, while her tranquil and generous nature had transformed into one of heavy silence.

For days, neither Andy nor Charlie knew how to act around her. They tried being supportive, but that only seemed to irritate her. When they tried to pretend as though nothing had happened, it only compounded her depression. About two weeks after the horrible incident, Andy and Charlie had a serious discussion alone in the kitchen. It was Charlie who suggested leaving Bermuda, and Andy agreed. It was time to go. What had happened to Morgan had tainted their home that even the little joys like watching the sun set beyond the ocean or swimming among the fish had lost their splendor. When Andy brought up their idea to Morgan, tears of relief quickly filled her eyes. She nodded weakly but said nothing more.

∘⊰♦♦⊱∘

The United States was the only realistic destination. At a distance of six hundred miles from the shores of North Carolina, Bermuda's location offered few options. Though Charlie was confident in his sailing skills, he admitted that the six hundred mile journey would be a huge challenge.

"I may overshoot Cape Hatteras by more than a few kilometers. And if the weather's bad, we may land somewhere north of Nags Head or somewhere south into Cape Lookout," he warned.

"I'll just be glad if we hit land that's somehow connected to America," Andy replied as she followed along with a map.

The two of them did most of the packing while Morgan continued to recover. Her mental condition remained fragile, and Andy worried how she would handle the voyage. Would she have the strength to save either her brother or her if one of them fell overboard? What if she fell overboard herself? Would she have the will to swim and save her own life?

When she cautiously voiced these concerns, Morgan's brusque reply was, "I was raped. If I can live through that, I can live through anything. I just want to leave this island forever and never return."

Andy let the matter rest.

Few items were taken for the journey. Besides sufficient supplies of food, water, clothing, and medicine, Andy brought along her collection of medical journals and pistol. Charlie took his favorite books, sailing tools, and the shotgun. Morgan, however, brought nothing more than her clothes and shoes. Amazed how five years of living could be condensed into a few hours of packing, they closed the beach house for the last time and departed.

The sky was beautiful that morning and the wind perfect for sailing. They got off to a quick start as Bermuda disappeared over the horizon.

As she gazed westward, Andy wondered what her home—her country—would be like.

It was her nineteenth birthday.

Chapter III

They reached the outer shores of North Carolina after five days and nights at sea. Dehydrated, seasick, and exhausted from restless sleep, all three collapsed onto the sand under the sun until their equilibrium returned and their stomachs stopped churning. With their balance regained, they turned their focus inland.

With the sailboat securely anchored, they walked north along the shore to determine where exactly they had landed. After a mile, buildings materialized in the distance. Leading the way, Andy headed toward the buildings until reaching what appeared to be the main road dividing a small beach town. Derelict homes and storefronts just one bad storm away from crumbling to the ground were scattered along the road. Another quarter-mile further, they approached a tilting sign that read 'Salvo.'

Charlie retrieved a folded map labeled 'Cape Hatteras National Seashore' from his back pocket and found the town of Salvo. After a quick mental calculation, he pointed out their location. "We're here, about fifty kilometers south of Nags Head, which is…" He traced the map with his finger, "…here. From there we can take the bridge on this road…I-64…over to the mainland. Or this road…158." Charlie shrugged. "I guess it all depends on where we want to go from here."

Andy squinted at the map, shading her eyes from the summer sun. "Fifty kilometers? That's what, about thirty miles? We're not walking thirty miles." The journey at sea had taken its toll on Morgan, and the yellow bruising around her eye on her otherwise pale face now gave her a deathlike appearance. "We can either hope to find a car in town or go back to the boat and sail north along the coast."

"I don't think I can spend another minute on that boat," Morgan uttered weakly and pleaded with her eyes. "I'm sorry, but I know I'll get sick again."

"Okay, then we'll just have to find a car and some gas," Andy replied in her most reassuring voice. She then exchanged her pistol for the shotgun in Charlie's hand and nodded toward a rickety wooden bench on the other side of the road. "Wait there while I take a look around."

As Andy watched them cross the road, she couldn't help but notice how frail Morgan looked. Already a thin girl, her weight had clearly dropped since her attack.

Salvo was nothing more than a hollowed-out ghost town swept away by wind, sand, and time. The beach homes and restaurants that had once received proper care and attention now showed all the obvious signs of abandonment: peeling paint, broken windows, and cracked sideboards. After a few blocks, Andy stumbled across two human skeletons lying on the sidewalk, partially covered in tattered clothing, and skirted around them.

"Where is everybody? Are they all dead?" she muttered aloud after several blocks. She came across a few cars but no keys. She tried hotwiring them, a skill Charlie had taught her, but the batteries where dead. Andy soon gave up and returned to her friends.

"No luck," she reported. "Not that I'm surprised. Anyone passing through this place in the last five years probably snatched up any running car long ago."

"Then let's head back to the boat," Charlie suggested. "Morgan, I know you're not feeling well, but we don't really have another choice."

Though hardly excited by the idea of returning to the boat, Morgan understood.

Unfortunately that afternoon, an uncooperative wind worked against their sails, and it took more than half a day to reach Nags Head, thirty miles to the north along the Outer Banks. By sundown, they anchored the boat and chose to remain onboard another night.

The sun rose to a clear sky the following morning. Groggy, Andy crawled out of her tiny bed and checked on the others in the second bedroom below deck. Morgan was snoring like a log, but Charlie was beginning to stir.

Andy crept toward the side of his bed. "Wake up, sleepyhead," she whispered.

"Err…nooo," he groaned and rolled away.

She gave his shoulder a nudge. "C'mon…time to get the sails up. The winds look good."

Charlie rubbed his eyes open and looked over at his comatose sister. "Probably just as well. Her snoring was non-stop last night." Sitting up, his short brown hair stuck up in the back like feathers. "I should've told her to go into your room."

Laughing at the sight of Charlie's hair, Andy followed up the narrow ladder to the deck.

The conditions for sailing proved far better than the previous afternoon. As the vessel reached the coastal border between North Carolina and Virginia, Charlie asked Andy how far north she planned to go. She looked at their map and understood exactly what Charlie was asking. The mouth of the Chesapeake Bay was approaching. If they were intending to go to Washington DC or Baltimore, they should sail up the Bay. If Philadelphia or New York was their destination, they would need to continue along the Atlantic Coast.

"We're going to Washington," Andy said.

"Why there?"

"It's the capital. Why not start there?"

Charlie saw no reason to argue. He'd never been to the United States. "That'll take a couple of days to get there if we sail the whole way," he replied while examining the map.

"Well, it's either this or keep looking for a car that works. And has gas."

Charlie turned back to the ladder. He was thinking of his sister.

"We can dock at Virginia Beach and look again," Andy offered, reading his mind.

The sailboat reached the eastern side of Virginia Beach by late afternoon. As they walked along the shore and passed several beachfront hotels, they discovered that the coastal city appeared to be just as deserted as the Outer Banks. Heading inland, they found many cars and trucks in the parking lots of empty restaurants and stores, but after using the stock of the shotgun to break the windows of each vehicle, they found that none of the engines would start. Discouraged, they returned to the sailboat and prepared to spend another night onboard.

When Andy woke up the next morning, she found Charlie already raising the sails. "You're up early."

"Figured we should get moving. The weather doesn't look promising."

Andy turned west and gazed up. The clouds were low and gray. Frowning, she pulled on her rain jacket as Morgan appeared from below. Immediately seeing the sky, she helped her brother hoist the remaining sails while Andy undocked the boat.

Rain began to fall as they passed over the westernmost tunnel of the Chesapeake Bay Bridge-Tunnel, but the winds propelled the sailboat up the Bay faster than predicted. As the storm quelled hours later, the mouth of the Potomac came into view. Still, it was hard to tell exactly where they were.

"There're too many of these stupid inlets!" Andy yelled while shoving the map aside.

"This has to be it," Charlie decided.

"How do you know?"

"Based on the distance we've travelled today, this has to be the Potomac."

"So why don't we dock and see for sure?" Morgan suggested.

Upon finding a large enough pier, they anchored once again, and after walking inland almost a mile, they discovered through various street signs that they were in a town called Reedville.

Charlie retrieved the map from his back pocket. "Ha, I was right!" he exclaimed and pointed out where they were.

Morgan spotted a pickup truck parked on the side of a nearby road and wandered toward it. The handlebars of several bikes were visible over the side wall of the truck bed. She peered in at the driver's side, but the tinted windows prevented getting a good look. She tried the door handle and it opened. "Bloody hell!" She jumped back and covered her face.

Andy and Charlie ran towards her. Arriving first, Andy took one look inside the truck and recoiled. Morgan was already yards away, retching into the grass. Andy rushed over to her and pulled her long hair away from her face.

Meanwhile, Charlie inched toward the truck, his face contorted in an expression of horror. With one hand, he covered his nose. A horrendously decomposed body sat in the driver's seat, the seatbelt still buckled over what remained of the person's lap. It wasn't a virus victim; there would have been nothing but the dry bones of a skeleton. This was a more recent death. Maggots crawled in and out of the mouth, nostrils, and other orifices. The state of decay of the corpse was such that Charlie could not determine its sex. Looking down beyond the torso, he noticed something else. "It's got no legs!"

"What?" Andy called back. She returned to the truck and peered inside. Sure enough, there was nothing hanging below the edge of the seat. There was, however, a large pool of dried blood on the floor mat and a single shell casing from a bullet stuck to it. Pinching her nose, she reached inside and picked up the shell with her free hand while careful to avoid touching anything else.

"Maybe he—or she—killed themselves?" Charlie guessed.

"But how can you drive without legs?"

"Maybe a wild animal got inside after…it was already dead."

Andy made a face at the gruesome suggestion and noted the open window in the back seat on the other side of the truck. "Something could've crawled in, but it wouldn't have eaten the leg bones too."

By now Morgan had recovered and was examining the contents in the open truck bed. "There's four bikes back here. And a tire pump. And a gun of some kind," she reported.

"Excellent!" Andy yelled back. "At least we won't have to walk everywhere. Are there any bullets?"

"Yeah, looks like a few boxes."

"Great. Now if only this truck starts and there's gas, we're in business."

"Andy, I'm not riding in a truck that's had a dead body rotting inside!" Morgan protested.

Ignoring her friend, Andy looked around and spotted a large tree branch resting in the grass by the road. She retrieved it and entered the truck through the passenger's door. Using the thick end of the branch, she pushed the corpse out of the truck with a mighty shove as Charlie jumped out of the way before it hit the ground. She tossed the branch outside and leaned in further to discover that the keys were in the ignition. "It's a stick shift. Charlie, press down on the clutch."

Stepping around the corpse, he grabbed onto the doorframe and compressed the pedal with his right foot. Andy put the gear was in neutral and turned the key. After a lengthy turn over, the engine started. Her eyes immediately searched for the fuel gauge. "Thank God! There's more than half a tank!"

"Yeah, and a bloody mess on the seat." Charlie was looking down at where the corpse had been. The seat was covered in dried blood and looked as though it had been slashed with a blade many times.

"Oh, you big baby. We can cover the seat with a towel."

Charlie grimaced but couldn't deny the stupidity of passing up a functioning vehicle with more than a hundred miles of gas in it because of a little blood. "Okay, but you drive."

"And I'm sitting in the back," Morgan declared.

"Fine," Andy conceded.

"What about the boat?" Charlie asked with concern. "What if this truck dies fifty kilometers down the road?"

"Well, then we can either bike back, or we'll find another car or something. But we can't stay on that boat forever."

Morgan and Charlie looked at each other, uncertain.

"We can always come back, okay?" Andy reassured while examining the sky. Nightfall was approaching. "It's too late to drive anywhere now, and since it doesn't look like anyone's coming by to steal our boat or much else, let's head back for the night. We'll leave first thing in the morning."

"Okay."

Before heading back to the boat, Andy glanced down at the corpse and wondered again about the missing legs but only for a moment. Just another dead body amongst the thousands she'd seen.

The smell of bleach had replaced the smell of human decay. Morgan had insisted on purging the truck of bloodstains and melted flesh and spent the first hour of the new day scrubbing the seats while Andy and Charlie unloaded their things off the boat.

Andy drove the entire way to Washington DC the following morning. There were just a few cars stranded in the middle of the highway as the city drew closer, but soon they increased to such a number that she was forced to weave between the vehicles, treating the highway like an obstacle course. At one point when the road became completely blocked, she rammed her way through them. Some of the abandoned cars were like coffins containing a skeleton or two, while others sat empty. The congestion worsened at the Capital Beltway that encircled the city. It was as though the virus had struck every driver dead at the exact same moment during the peak of rush hour traffic. A horrifying moment frozen in time.

"Charlie, get me off this road!" Andy cried in frustration.

Charlie deftly found their location on his roadmap. "Take this exit," he pointed. It was a sign for another highway.

"Okay." She pulled off the Beltway and onto I-395 where conditions improved. Her palms began to sweat as they crossed the Potomac River. She felt like they were becoming more and more trapped the closer they got to the city limits.

"Are you sure we want to keep going?" Morgan asked as though reading her friend's mind.

Andy didn't answer. She wiped each hand on her jean shorts.

"We've come this far. Might as well keep going," said Charlie, trying to remain upbeat.

Off to her left, Andy saw the Washington Monument. "Charlie, can you get me there?" she said, gesturing toward the gray obelisk jutting sharply into the skyline.

He nodded and reexamined the map.

Morgan pressed her head against her window and stared at the monument. "At least it's still standing," she murmured.

When they reached the monument, Andy parked in front of the overgrown lawn surrounding its base. Morgan and Charlie followed as she walked toward the monument. The entire area was disturbingly quiet; not a soul or sign of life in sight.

Within yards of the visitor's entrance, Andy stopped dead in her tracks. "What the—?"

The land where fifty American flags had once encircled the monument, flying proudly, was now covered in shredded pieces of fabric and flagpoles bent askew, some nearly horizontal. Graffiti covered the bottom few yards of the monument's surface; mostly words and phrases that she could hardly decipher. Though the rest of the monument was devoid of graffiti, being too high for anyone to reach, the marble was dull and dingy.

"Who would do this?" Andy's face was contorted into an expression of disgust.

Morgan and Charlie moved behind her. Though not as affected by the sight, they were nonetheless disheartened by what they saw. The damage represented a lack of civility and respect. After traveling a thousand miles by land and sea to flee violence and chaos, they seemed to have stepped right back into it.

Morgan placed a hand on her friend's shoulder. "Come on. Let's go."

But Andy didn't move. She could only stare back at the monument. "I thought if anywhere could…" she began hoarsely but didn't finish.

A moment later, her thoughts were interrupted by the harsh crack of gunshots in the distance. All three of them frantically looked around, but Charlie was the first to see it. "There!"

Midway along the National Mall toward the Capitol Building, a small cluster of people scurried about shooting off guns, either at one another or others hiding out of sight. Andy remained rooted to the ground and watched in disbelief. Only when the far-off figures began to grow larger did she make a move and shout, "Get back in the truck...now!"

They raced back to the vehicle. Andy started the engine and steered north onto Fifteenth Street and across Constitution Avenue. In the back seat, Morgan glanced anxiously through the window to her right. The figures appeared to be getting closer.

"I think they're following us. Move faster!" she urged.

"I'm trying!" Andy yelled as she weaved through more cars blocking the road and cursed herself for picking the wrong direction. But no direction was clear.

"How many are there?" Charlie asked fearfully.

"I don't know...eight?" Morgan answered.

Another series of gunshots rang out. When a bullet struck the rear windshield of a car next to them, Andy drove over the curb in a desperate attempt to move faster. The maneuver caused the truck's front left tire to blow. Losing control, Andy ran into the side of an SUV. She tried backing up, but it was futile. They weren't going anywhere.

"No!" Andy shouted and punched the steering wheel. Thinking quickly, she called back to Morgan, "Hand me the rifle and bullets."

"What are you going to do?"

"What does it look like?"

Morgan did as instructed. Meanwhile, Charlie grabbed the pistol resting beside the parking brake as Andy loaded the magazine of the rifle. Her fingers were trembling.

"God, I hope this thing works!" She looked back at Morgan. "Get down on the seat."

Morgan flattened herself in the backseat as Andy and Charlie crouched down.

"If they shoot again, fire back," she whispered to Charlie. They held their breath as the figures approached. Andy counted six of them. Two raised their own guns simultaneously and let off another round of shots. Several hit the back of the truck and the rear windshield. Morgan screamed and covered her ears.

Acting solely on instinct, Andy kicked open her door and sprayed a long round of bullets toward the pursuers. She tried to aim but everything became a blur. Meanwhile, fear paralyzed Charlie, and he remained tucked into his seat.

It wouldn't have mattered had he fired back; most of Andy's bullets struck the small crowd, some fatally. The few remaining sprinted away from the scene. It all had happened so quickly. She turned away from the carnage and fell back into her seat. After regaining her senses, she reached into the backseat and touched Morgan's arm.

"You okay?"

Shaken, Morgan opened her eyes and released her fingers pressed tightly into her ears.

"You're not hurt?"

Morgan shook her head. "No."

Charlie peered over the back of his seat and stared across the street at the bodies lying on the ground. He released the pistol from his grip and murmured to Andy, "sorry."

"For what?" She hadn't seen his paralysis.

"For—never mind."

"Are they gone?" Morgan asked as she slowly sat up.

Andy nodded. "For now." Once her pounding heart settled, she stepped back outside and examined the damage to their truck. Charlie opened his door to join her, and together they stared at the busted front tire.

"Now what? We don't have a spare."

Andy glanced up at the other cars in the street. "No, but we can take a tire off of one of those. But let's do it quickly before anyone else comes."

After finding the right-sized tire from another truck, they removed it and replaced the one on their own.

"It's rather flat," Charlie noted while turning the crank on the jack.

"We'll pump some air into later."

Once back in the truck and moving again, Morgan asked where they were going. But Andy didn't answer right away. Her attention was fixed on the three people in the street that she had just turned into corpses. She sucked in a sharp breath and pressed down on the gas to escape the scene. *I've killed someone... more than one. I am a killer...*

Morgan repeated her question. "Where are we going?"

"Jesus, Morgan! Let me get us out of here first, okay?"

Morgan fell back into her seat and looked away, tears in her eyes.

The truck fell silent as Andy backtracked across the Potomac. Horrible decision, going north. And now they were running low on gas. And food.

Chapter IV

*B*en Kelly tapped his fingers impatiently against the doorframe of his old pickup truck as he waited for his cousin, Jim, to exit the convenience store—the fifth one they'd stopped at that day. An ancient minivan already sat parked outside the store. If the previous four stores had not been vacant, they would have passed this one entirely, especially with another vehicle parked out front. But they were getting desperate.

Ben checked his watch. Nearly seven o'clock. The sun was beginning to set behind him, and he cursed under his breath. They should've been in Tennessee by now.

The day hadn't gone as planned. After a quick start that morning, the engine of their truck overheated after a rodent found its way under the hood. It took hours to find the pest; hours of precious time they couldn't afford to waste. Worse still, Ben was starving, and not a scrap to eat anywhere.

While stewing in frustration, he heard the front door of the convenience store burst open, followed by the sound of people shouting. Jim was the first to appear, his right hand grasping for the pistol in his holster. Ben stood up, startled by what he saw.

A girl was arguing with Jim. Secured across her torso by a strap over her right shoulder was a military combat rifle. And by the way she handled the weapon, he could tell that she knew how to use it.

Seconds after she appeared, another young woman emerged from the doorway.

"Andy! Wait!" she yelled.

Ben jumped out of his truck and grabbed his own gun before making his way to the scene. "What's going on?"

His cousin turned to him, clearly aggravated. "They're taking all the food!" he yelled and made a gesture toward the two women.

Without a word, Ben turned and gave each of them a long look. The unarmed one was tall and wiry. Rather pretty, she had delicate features and dark, wavy hair, but her face was pale and she had a bruised eye in the latter stages of healing. The first girl was shorter than her friend, trim and athletic, with sharper features. Her long, unruly blond hair hung over her muscular shoulders, but it was her eyes that were most remarkable; green like emeralds and filled with the intensity of a wild animal.

These eyes were now looking at Jim as though she were ready to attack, but instead, she opened her mouth. "We were here first. This food is ours," she declared unapologetically and leaving little room for argument.

"Just because you got here first doesn't mean you can take everything that's in there," Jim countered.

This only angered the girl more, but her friend stopped her before she could protest further. "We can share. There's plenty in there for all of us."

Moments later a boy came out of the store carrying four or five plastic bags full of food. He headed directly to the minivan.

"What, you taking everything?!" Jim scoffed as he watched the boy place the bags inside the van. Meanwhile, Ben drew a step closer to the group. The blond reacted by grabbing the brunette's arm protectively.

Ben examined the three strangers carefully. "What are two girls doing out here alone?"

"They aren't alone!" the boy called out as he slammed shut the rear door to the van.

Ben squinted at the boy's face. The resemblance to the brunette was undeniable. "You two related?"

The boy gave a faint nod. "She's my sister. Who are you?"

"Ben…this is my cousin, Jim." He looked directly at the blond as he spoke. Her unflinching gaze stared back. He tilted his head and said to her, "You guys aren't from around here, are you?"

"What does that mean?"

"Especially *you* two." Ben gestured toward the brother and sister. "Your accent.

It's different."

"Charlie and I are from England," Morgan replied calmly in an attempt to ease the tension. "I'm Morgan. And this is Andy. She's American."

Ben laughed at the word. "American? There's really no America anymore."

"Yeah, we saw the Washington Monument," Andy replied with biting sarcasm. "Now, we'll share the food, but only if you can tell us where or how to find gas around here."

"This is the third vehicle we've driven in today, and it's almost out of petrol... again," Charlie added.

Both Ben and Jim looked surprised. "You were lucky to find *any* car with gas," Jim replied.

"We'll help you find gas, but it won't be anytime soon," said Ben.

"Why's that?" asked Andy.

"Because there aren't any airports nearby."

"Airports?"

"Best secret ever. You'll see."

Andy glanced at her friends with a look that said, *should we trust these guys?*

"We aren't psycho killers or anything," Jim assured. "We're just heading west through Tennessee."

"What's in Tennessee?" asked Charlie.

"We're just driving through. We're not stopping there except to get gas," Ben answered vaguely.

Andy looked again at Charlie and Morgan for their thoughts. Both indicated that they should accept the offer. They had no plan, and their efforts to get out of DC had taken them far off course and onto a lonely stretch of highway in western Virginia.

Andy turned back to the cousins. "Alright, we'll follow you. But in case you're lying, just know that we're not just carrying these guns for the hell of it. We know how to use them."

Ben smiled back. "I have no doubt that you do."

"They're pretty," Jim said to his cousin once back in their truck.

"Who, those girls?"

"No, the trees on the side of road," he retorted. "Yes, of course those girls. The tall one reminds me of Karen."

Ben's hand clenched tightly around the steering wheel at the sound of the name, and Jim quickly changed the subject. "I wonder what their story is. Where do you think they're from?"

"England and America," Ben said in a mocking tone.

"Yeah, but where have they been? Something happened to her…Morgan. That bruise around her eye definitely has a story to it."

Ben nodded. "Somebody must've smacked her pretty hard." After another moment, he said, "Hey, didn't the other one say something about the Washington Monument? And now they're headed south?"

A mixture of concern and bewilderment slowly appeared on Jim's face. "What are you saying? That they could be working for *him*?" He shook his head. "No way."

"But he knows we would never suspect two girls driving in that piece-of-crap minivan. It's the perfect disguise if you think about it. He might be the Devil, but he's also smart."

Jim frowned as he glanced backward. He hoped that Ben was just being paranoid. "I think you're wrong. And you'll just piss them off."

"Probably but better to find out now than later, right?" Ben said rhetorically as he applied pressure to the brakes.

Jim sighed. "I was hoping we might make some friends."

"Okay, I'll try not to piss off your future girlfriend…which one?"

"The brunette," Jim answered without hesitating.

Ben smiled to himself. "Fine with me."

Chapter V

C harlie was asleep in the backseat of the minivan as Andy drove, her eyes staring dully at the taillights of the truck in front of them. She was exhausted. The day had been endless.

She looked over at Morgan sitting beside her and was surprised to find her still awake. "Aren't you tired?" she asked quietly so as not to disturb Charlie.

Morgan rolled the back of her head against her seat. "My body's tired, but I'm not sleepy."

"Really? I'm exhausted."

"Want me to—?"

Morgan didn't finish. Instead she sat up and made a face that Andy could barely make out in the waning daylight.

"What's wrong?"

"Can you stop the car? I feel sick."

Andy immediately applied the brake without noticing that the truck ahead was doing the same. The sudden deceleration awakened Charlie in time for him to see his sister leap out of the van.

"Is she okay?" he asked.

"Yeah, just carsick."

Andy stepped outside as the two boys approached.

"She okay?" Jim asked.

"Just carsick," Andy repeated.

Morgan recovered quickly and apologized to everyone.

"Don't be sorry," Jim assured. "You need water or anything?"

"That would be great, thanks."

As Jim returned to the truck, Ben took advantage of the moment. "So, where are you guys coming from?" he asked, trying to sound casual. "Before Washington, I mean."

"Bermuda," Charlie quickly answered.

Ben couldn't have been more surprised had the answer been the Moon. "Are you joking?"

"Nope," Andy replied as she placed a comforting hand on Morgan's shoulder. "We were there for five years. Ever since the virus."

"What were you doing in Bermuda?"

"Vacation," Andy answered.

Jim returned with a glass bottle filled with water. He handed it to Morgan, who thanked him.

"So you guys sailed here from Bermuda?" Ben continued.

"Bermuda?" Jim repeated, sounding amazed. "Wow, what's it like there?"

"Not much different than anything we've seen here so far," said Andy, purposely vague. "Just add some ocean."

"When did you leave?" Jim asked.

Andy looked at Charlie. "What, about a week ago?"

"Yeah. It was your birthday, remember?"

"Oh, right." Andy shook her head. "The days are blending together. Until today, we've been on a boat most of the time."

"Where are you two coming from?" Morgan interjected, wanting to change the topic from anything involving the last month.

Ben and Jim exchanged looks.

"New York," said Ben flatly.

"New York *City*?" Andy inquired.

Ben cleared his throat. "Yeah."

"I've never been to New York, even before the virus. "What's it like? Any better than DC?"

Ben looked down at his shoes and kicked at a stone. "Not really."

"Just a lot more people," Jim added, rather hastily. "That's actually why we left. Not enough food and too many people. You know how it is."

Andy looked back and forth between the two. "Yeah. We know how that is."

Ben glanced at his watch. "Let's get moving. I hate driving in the dark."

The group separated back into their respective vehicles.

"What d'ya think?" Jim asked after Ben started the engine.

"Not sure, but it's hard to imagine making up something like Bermuda."

"Isn't that in the Caribbean?"

"Can't remember."

"Do you think we can trust them?" Jim pressed.

"Trust them? Not yet, but I believe their story."

"Fair enough."

In the minivan, Andy was behind the wheel again, and after a few minutes, Charlie had fallen back asleep.

"You sure you're okay?" she asked Morgan. "Is it the food? Or the water, maybe?"

"No, it's not any of that," Morgan shook her head. She looked down at her delicate hands. Her face crumpled and tears sprang from her eyes.

Andy now understood. She reached over and squeezed her friend's hand. "It's going to be okay," she whispered. "I'll make sure everything's okay."

Morgan wiped her eyes and nodded. "Just don't say anything to Charlie? I don't want him to know—not yet, anyway."

"Of course," Andy replied, employing her bravest tone despite her own distress. What were the odds? One in a thousand? Ten thousand? A million? Part of her wanted to go back to Bermuda just to find those boys and put a bullet in each of them.

They drove on in silence. Relieved of her secret, Morgan drifted off, leaving Andy alone with her thoughts. The sun disappeared over her left shoulder as the minivan continued along the Interstate. It was uncomfortably hot, and she felt like her skin couldn't breathe. Even with windows rolled down, the rushing wind offered little relief.

The events of the past few days replayed like a movie in her head. The rotting body in the car. The horrific state of the Washington Monument. Being shot at by faceless, nameless strangers, then killing some of them. Ben saying, *There's really no America anymore.* What did that even mean? Did countries no longer exist because those who were once in power were now dead? And did anyone even care about such things anymore, or had daily survival consumed everyone's thoughts that there was no longer room for anything else?

In Bermuda, she and her friends had struggled to survive, but they still managed to fill their days with meaning: reading, learning, and teaching. Without this, they would have been little more than animals, fighting each day just to live to the next, and Andy couldn't help thinking that this was the only future she had to look forward to.

More tired than she could ever remember, she leaned against the open window with her elbow and cradled her head in her left hand. The temperature began to fall as the sun made its western descent, and the air coming through the window now was refreshing. For a few miles, her mind became mercifully blank. With both Charlie and Morgan now sound asleep, a welcome serenity enveloped her for a few peaceful moments.

Then her mind drifted to the two young men inside of the truck she now followed. They seemed nice enough, but there was definitely something mysterious about them, especially Ben with his reticent demeanor. Andy presumed he often avoided personal questions and topics, preferring instead to throw the attention back on someone or something else. His cousin, Jim, seemed less guarded and friendlier.

They didn't look like cousins, or any blood relation for that matter. Both were handsome and about Andy's age. Ben was at least six-one or six-two, and looked strong enough to lift twice her weight with ease. He reminded her of a younger, but rougher version of Clark Kent, with his dark brown hair and memorable blue eyes. A Superman in a worn T-shirt, tattered jeans, and dirt under his nails.

Jim was just a tad shorter than Ben and leaner, though still sturdy. His sandy blond hair was cut short like a soldier's, and his eyes were either green or hazel… Andy couldn't recall. And despite their initial argument over the food, he had a boyish charm that made him instantly likeable.

Her thoughts were interrupted by the minivan's slow but steady decline in speed. After checking the fuel gauge, she flashed her headlights. The truck's brake lights illuminated ahead, and Andy stopped a few yards behind them, seconds before the engine went dead. Neither driver had bothered to pull over to the shoulder—they hadn't passed a single car the entire day.

"Finally out of gas?" Ben called out to Andy after everyone was back outside.

"Yeah."

"Then grab your stuff. But two of you will have to sit in the back."

As she and her friends transported their things out of the minivan, Ben was glad to see that their possessions were few. More stuff meant more weight, which meant lower gas mileage, and three extra bodies was weight enough. Then, knowing his cousin would appreciate it, he suggested that Morgan ride in the front of the truck with Jim. "Tired of listening to him all the time," was his feeble excuse. "My ears need rest."

"Um, okay. Thanks," Morgan muttered. "Charlie, you okay sitting in the back?"

But Charlie was already following Ben into the truck bed. "No worries," he called out.

"The wind will feel good," Andy added, preempting the same question. She climbed in last and quickly positioned herself into a corner at the rear. Once they were underway, she closed her eyes.

Ben found himself glancing over at her in the dark even though he couldn't see her face, or that she had already fallen asleep.

❧❀❧

After what felt like a few hours, Andy woke up. It was still dark, and since she never wore a watch she could only guess what time it was. The truck was driving much slower than it had been, and they were weaving through treacherous terrain with many hairpin turns and altitude fluctuations. She wondered where they were when she saw a passing sign for Route 441 reflecting off the headlights—a route that meant nothing to her.

The air had grown cooler, so she pulled the bottom of her oversized sweatshirt over her knees and grabbed a blanket lying nearby. Apparently, it wasn't the first time someone had slept in the back of this truck. After snuggling herself into a cozy bundle, she looked up at the sky and released an unexpected gasp. Thousands upon thousands of stars shone like tiny pin pricks of light in the navy sky. Within the span of a few minutes, Andy witnessed three shooting stars. It reminded her of Bermuda at night, with the smell of moist forest trees replacing the salty sea air and the rhythm of small waves lapping at the coastline.

"Pretty, isn't it?"

Ben's voice startled her. She could barely discern his silhouette, making his voice seem disembodied. "What?"

"The stars…they're beautiful out here."

"Oh, yeah. They are."

A long pause followed. Andy didn't know if the brief exchange was meant to be the start of a conversation, so she remained silent.

"So what was Bermuda like?"

Okay, a conversation it was. "Bermuda? Bermuda was a little bit of everything, I guess."

"How do you mean?"

"Well, it's tropical in the summer, but the winters can be—"

"—Hang on. I can't hear you."

The truck had begun to pick up speed, and the passing wind made hearing difficult. Ben slid back to the rear of the truck bed until he and Andy were sitting across from each other. Charlie, meanwhile, was still asleep at the front of the bed.

"Sorry, say that again," Ben said after settling in.

"I said it's tropical in the summer, but the winters can be pretty cold." Andy had to almost shout her words to be heard.

"Because it's not in the Caribbean, right?"

"Right. It's much farther north."

Off to her left, the faintest light of dawn could be seen. "How can you drive so long without stopping?"

"This truck has three tanks. We could drive a thousand miles without stopping if we had to."

"Three tanks? Trucks don't have three tanks."

"No, but Jim and I modified this one."

"I bet that comes in handy." Unsure of what else to say, Andy returned her gaze to the stars. The approaching daylight would soon fade their intensity. She tried to close her eyes again but found she was no longer sleepy. "Where exactly are you guys headed?"

"New Mexico."

"What's in New Mexico?"

"Nothing. Just seems like a good place to hide out for a while."

"Hide from whom?"

"No one in particular. Just to get away from all the people."

"Seems like a long way to go just to get away from people."

Ben laughed. "Yeah. Maybe." His voice faded. Then he asked, "What made you leave Bermuda?"

My best friend was beaten and raped…

"It's complicated."

"I'm sure it is." He didn't press further.

"Where are you and your cousin from?"

"Virginia, in the suburbs outside DC. Our parents lived two miles from each other."

"You two don't look related."

Ben laughed again. "We both look like our mothers, and it's our fathers who were brothers."

"How do you know so much about cars?"

"Jim's dad was a car mechanic. We used to hang around his shop on weekends just watching him, and we picked up a lot. After the virus, we had all the time in the world to mess around with cars."

Andy nodded. It was similar for her and learning about medicine. "You like working on cars?"

"I do. And I'm good at it. Cars make sense to me. And what do you do for fun, other than sailing across oceans?"

"I read a lot. Mostly stuff about human anatomy and medicine. My father was a doctor." It was odd to talk about herself with a complete stranger.

"Cool. What kind of doctor?"

"He was a heart surgeon for a long time, but then switched to having his own general practice when I was nine or ten."

"Why did he switch?"

"The hours. I barely saw him when he was a surgeon. With his own practice, he could finally join me and my mom at dinner."

Ben began to ask something else when the truck slowed down and then stopped. Jim and Morgan emerged from the front, both chatting about something that Andy couldn't hear.

"Hey, my butt's getting numb," Jim began, mainly addressing Ben. "Let's switch for a while."

Charlie woke up. "Where are we?"

"Eastern Tennessee," Jim replied.

"Is it cold back there?" Morgan asked Andy, looking content—happy even.

"Not really. There are some blankets," Andy replied, holding hers up to show Morgan. "You guys sleep back here often?"

"When we have to," Ben replied before hopping down to the ground.

"Charlie, do you want to ride in the front?" Morgan asked.

"No, I'll stay here. I'm tired."

Morgan reached over and tousled his hair. "Okay, but don't snore." She climbed into the back, along with Jim.

"You're the one who snores," Charlie accused with a yawn.

Morgan froze with embarrassment until Jim said, "Don't worry. You can't hear snoring over the engine or the wind."

"I don't snore," she insisted.

It suddenly dawned on Andy that she hadn't had anything to drink or gone to the bathroom in at least twelve hours. Thinking about it not only made her thirsty, but aroused the need to find a bush somewhere. "I need to pee," she declared and headed directly toward the forest that lined the highway.

"I do too," Morgan echoed, following her into the misty trees.

Charlie looked at Jim and Ben. "Take the other side then?"

Without a word, boys and girls separated to opposite sides of the road and reconvened at the truck minutes later. After a quick bite and some water, they were ready to move again. Andy joined Ben in the front of the truck as the others piled into the back.

"So how much farther until we run out of gas?" Andy asked Ben when they were underway.

Ben glanced down at the dials in front of him. "Probably another two hundred miles. We'll make it to Nashville and stop at the airport there."

Andy nodded and turned her attention to the passing scenery. As the early morning mist began to fade, the blue-green hues of the mountains became more vivid. "Beautiful," she murmured to herself.

"Ever been around here before?" Ben asked as he maneuvered the truck around several sharp turns.

"No, never. You?"

"Once, when I was about eight or nine. I mostly remember the smell."

"Yeah, it's so fresh. These trees are…potent." Andy turned her gaze from the window and stared sideways at him for a long moment. She opened her mouth to speak, but hesitated and looked away.

"Something wrong?"

"No…just thinking."

"About what?"

"I was just thinking about the last time I took a shower," she lied. "It's been two days since I last rinsed off in the ocean. I'm starting to feel pretty dirty."

"Well, get used to it," said Ben unsympathetically. "Must've been nice living on an island and always having a place to take a bath."

Andy nodded absently. "Just a matter of stepping outside and jumping off the dock."

"Sounds amazing. Were there a lot of survivors?"

"I guess. For its size, I mean. Bermuda is a tiny island, and even though we lived far away from everyone else, things just got too dangerous. That's why we left." Though truthful, Andy would never reveal the real reason for their departure. That was Morgan's secret to keep, not hers.

"Makes sense," Ben replied. "Having your own space, your own corner of the world…it's worth everything. Once it's gone, it's time to move on."

"And that's why you're going to New Mexico? To find your own corner of the world?"

He shrugged. "Maybe."

"So why are you headed west now? Why not sooner?" Despite the dim morning light, Andy could clearly see Ben's body stiffen and his jaw harden, and she almost regretted asking the question.

He reapplied his grip on the steering wheel and cleared his throat. "Things weren't always so bad. Life was pretty quiet for a few years after the outbreak. It didn't get really bad until about…two years ago."

"What changed two years ago?"

He released a hand from the steering wheel and ruffled his hair. It was a nervous gesture that she had noticed once already. "Probably the same thing that happened to you in Bermuda, but over a much bigger area. You know, kids fighting over food and water…gangs spreading and starting wars with each other…stuff like that."

Andy knew Ben was holding back and that she wouldn't get any more out of him, at least not now. But questions continued to enter her mind. "Do you and Jim have friends in New Mexico?"

He shook his head. "No, no friends."

"It's pretty dry there, right? Won't it be hard to find water?"

"There're lots of rivers…big ones, like the Rio Grande. 'Grande' is Spanish for big, you know."

She let out a chuckle. "I know."

"Sorry," he said timidly and cleared his throat again. "Anyway, the winters are warm there, and it's got mountains. I could never live on flat farmland like the middle of the country."

"Yeah, me neither."

Ben took his gaze off the road and turned to Andy. "Well, since you don't seem thrilled by New Mexico, where would you rather live?"

She hadn't really thought about it. Getting to the continent had been her only concern for the last month. "I don't know, but if I could really go anywhere, I guess

I'd pick somewhere by the ocean. I already miss the ocean, and it's only been a few days. But not an island. I don't want to feel that trapped again."

"Maybe a bigger island then…like Hawaii?"

"Hawaii would be big enough, but it's in the middle of the Pacific. I'd need a really big boat or be able to fly there. Hardly options."

"Oh, I don't know. I'll bet there are a few people out there who can fly a plane." Andy looked at Ben with skepticism.

"What, you don't think some rich parents ever gave their twelve-year-old son or daughter flying lessons?" he challenged. "You learned about medicine from your dad. Why wouldn't flying be the same?"

Andy shrugged. He had a point. "I guess so. It just seems very risky."

"And cutting people open isn't risky?"

"I've never cut anyone open," she quickly replied. "I'm nowhere close to being a surgeon. You could barely consider me a nurse."

"Maybe, but I bet you could be a surgeon if you wanted to."

"Sure, if medical schools still existed, but not now…"

"I'm sure you could figure it out."

She scoffed. "Surgery is not like fixing a car. You mess up the slightest thing, and your patient is dead."

Ben nodded slowly but countered saying, "True, but aren't most people who need surgery going to die anyway? You're just giving them a chance, even if it's a very small chance. And after a while, you'd get better at it."

"Yeah, after watching several people die in the process."

"Well, isn't that part of being a doctor? Even the best surgeons lose patients."

"I know, but maybe I'm just tired of death," she replied with a shrug and stared off to her right.

"Or maybe you're just scared."

Andy turned to protest when Ben reached over without warning and opened the glove box, grazing the top of Andy's bare thigh in the process. "Sorry," he mumbled as he fished inside and pulled out a can of peanuts. "Want some?"

She cracked a smile. Of course she wanted some. "Thanks."

"Would you open it?" He asked, holding the can out to her with his right hand, his left hand on the steering wheel.

"Yeah, sure."

The smell of roasted nuts and salt filled Andy's nostrils the moment she peeled back the aluminum seal. She grabbed a large handful before holding the can out for Ben.

"Thanks," he said and helped himself.

The entire can was gone in minutes.

"Is there any water?" she asked.

"There should be some water bottles behind the seat," Ben said after finishing his last mouthful. "Can you grab me one, too?"

The water quenched Andy's dry, salty throat. It was the best thing she'd ever tasted.

Chapter VI

*M*inutes passed into hours as Andy dozed off. As Ben had predicted, the truck made it to Nashville without running out of gas. Just before reaching the city, he took the exit for the city's airport. The decrease in speed was enough to wake Andy.

She rubbed her eyes and looked around. "Where are we going?"

"Getting gas," said Ben. He followed signs for "Airport Services" and continued around the main terminal until reaching a restricted area where only airport vehicles were once permitted. Not surprisingly, the airport was utterly void of any sign of life.

"Airplane fuel?" Andy blurted aloud. "That works in cars too?"

"Some airplane fuel can run a car, but it's such a high octane that it'll ruin the engine," Ben replied as he weaved around airplanes and other various support vehicles. "When gas ran out, people never thought to check out airports, but all these vehicles for moving luggage and stuff around needed gas. Even some of the really small planes use the same gas as cars."

"That's clever."

Ben shrugged off the compliment. "Let's just hope we're lucky and that no one else thought to come here before us."

They did have luck in the form of a full, untouched tanker truck of gasoline, direct from an oil refinery.

"But hasn't this been sitting here for five years," Morgan commented once everyone was out of the truck. "Doesn't petrol get stale or something?"

"Nah, these tanks are vacuum-sealed. Gas only goes bad when it's exposed to the air," Ben replied as Jim headed toward the rear of the enormous tank carrying what appeared to be a small toolbox.

The others watched as Ben and Jim opened the valves at the rear of the tank and somehow managed to get the fuel moving into their own trunk's tanks. Their speed and dexterity was impressive.

"I take it you two have done this before," said Morgan.

"How else do you think we managed to keep driving all these years?" Jim replied, flashing her a warm smile.

As the precious liquid filled the truck's tanks, Ben reached behind the front seats and retrieved three large, cylindrical plastic containers, each empty.

"How much do those hold?" Charlie asked.

"About eight or nine gallons," said Jim, grabbing one of the containers from Ben. He began to fill it up. "They'll give us another four hundred miles."

"We should make it to New Mexico without having to stop again," Ben added.

Andy looked at Morgan and Charlie to gauge their reaction to the plan, as they hadn't discussed it yet. But neither seemed fazed by the notion. There was no better plan at the moment. There was no other plan at all. They were going to New Mexico.

When Jim topped off the last container, he screwed on the cap and put it into the back of the truck.

"That's it," he proclaimed.

"Let's try finding some more containers around here," said Ben. "It'd be stupid to not take more gas if we can."

Together the group found anything that would contain even a few ounces of gas, filled them up, and continued on their way.

They drove. And drove. The landscape changed. The lush foliage of Tennessee thinned out as they moved west beyond the Mississippi River. Long, pale green grass, slave to the will of the winds, dominated the landscape. Crossing streams allowed everyone to enjoy much-needed baths to remove the film of dirt that clung relentlessly to their skin. On the second night, they stopped at an abandoned motel near the Oklahoma-Texas border. The beds were old and creaky, and the air was stale, but everyone was too exhausted to care. Andy was asleep before her head hit the pillow. Shortly after dawn, they were driving again, across the Texas

Panhandle. The green grass turned to yellow, and the trees seemed to disappear completely.

If they ever once passed another person or moving vehicle, they never saw. The highway was lonely and desolate, and the random scatterings of abandoned vehicles only made it appear more so. During the silent stretches of time when not sleeping, her mind drifted to thoughts of how uncertain her future was. And Morgan's.

Though they hadn't talked about what had happened since leaving Bermuda, Andy had detected brief but unmistakable expressions of both fear and shame on her friend's face as her mind struggled to come to terms with the fact that a baby might be growing inside her belly, something that would rely on her to keep living and breathing for its own survival? Or would she only think of it as a parasite; a reminder of the battered and bloody mess she'd been while lying on that filthy bathroom floor?

Ben was driving when they entered New Mexico, and Andy was once again sitting beside him. At one point, she noticed him yawning and offered to drive. Though grateful, he declined.

Reaching down between her feet, she lifted her backpack off the floor and placed it on her lap. She unzipped the small front pocket of the bag and fished inside for the iPod her parents had given her on her thirteenth birthday. It was the last gift she'd received from them. The battery was long dead, but she had a car adapter. It was the only way to recharge it now.

"You mind if I plug this into your cigarette lighter?"

Ben glanced at the iPod and charger in her hand and shook his head lightly. "No, go ahead. It's under the radio."

"Thanks."

The battery symbol on the screen lit up. Smiling, she plugged the earbuds into her ears and skimmed through her old playlists. She picked one, pushed "play," and leaned back in her seat. She closed her eyes.

"What are you listening to?" Ben asked just as the music got underway.

Andy opened her eyes and whirled her finger counterclockwise around the touch wheel to decrease the volume. "Sorry, what?"

"What are you listening to?"

She opened her mouth to answer, then stopped and cocked her head to the side, her eyes narrowing on him. "Promise you won't laugh?"

Ben raised a hand defensively. "Well, I can't promise I won't laugh if you say something like 'elevator music.'"

"No, definitely not," she shook her head. "It's Bach."

Expecting a look of disdain, Andy was surprised by the flicker of interest that crossed Ben's face instead.

"Which one?" he asked.

"Which symphony?"

"No, I mean which Bach? Wasn't there more than one composer named Bach?"

"Uh, yeah," she said with surprise. "This is Johann Sebastian Bach. He was the father. The famous one."

"That's right. But weren't there others? His sons or something?" he replied, scouring the depths of his memory. "Was it fifth grade? No…sixth grade. Mrs.… Mrs.…God, what was her name?" He snapped his fingers in an effort to force it to come to him. "Mrs. Johnson! That's it!" Ben lightly smacked the top of the steering wheel upon remembering. "Mrs. Johnson was my music teacher. God, I haven't thought about her since…well, school. She was this sweet, older lady—at least sixty. But she loved music, especially Bach. She called him 'Herr Johann,' and she would go on and on about the greatness of the 'Bach musical dynasty.' Jim and I used to joke that she was in love with him." He shook his head and smiled at the memory. "We were pretty stupid back then."

"You and Jim were in the same class?"

"No, I was a year ahead, but we had all the same teachers." Ben combed his fingers through his hair once again. "Can I listen for a sec?"

Andy shrugged at the unexpected request. "Uh, sure. Here." She passed the earbuds to him and moved the iPod closer. As he secured the speakers in his ears, she resumed the music. She watched him closely as he listened, but his expression never changed and his eyes remained fixed on the road ahead.

"What's the name of this one?" he asked after more than a minute had passed. "I've heard it before."

"It's one of his cello suites…Suite Number 1 in G major, the *Prelude*," Andy read off the small screen.

Ben nodded slightly, then added after a long pause, presumably once the music ended, "It's just one instrument."

"It's the cello."

"It's beautiful." He passed the earbuds back to Andy. "It's too bad it's so short. Just when you get into it, it ends."

"I know…it's my favorite." Andy was amazed by Ben's interest. "My mom used to play it at concerts. She was a cellist with the Chicago Philharmonic. That's where I'm from."

He let out a whistle. "Wow. She must've been really good."

"She was. Before she died, she was the principal cellist. That's the lead cellist in the entire orchestra." Andy glanced down at the iPod in her lap. "Anyway, a few weeks before my thirteenth birthday, she played this piece during a concert that was being recorded. As a birthday present, she and my dad bought me this iPod with the recording already loaded onto it."

"So what I just listened to is actually your mother playing?" Ben asked with mounting astonishment.

Andy nodded and smiled proudly. "I was in the audience when she played it. She was perfect."

"It sounded perfect. I can't believe that's your mother playing."

"It is." After a pause, "She was killed in a car accident a few months later."

Ben took his eyes off the road and turned to her. "She didn't die from the virus?"

"No. The accident was the autumn before. I was in the car with her."

"I'm sorry." He returned his eyes to the road. "Were you hurt?"

"No. Barely a scratch."

Neither said anything for a moment. Then Ben asked, "Did you ever play?"

"What, the cello?"

"Or any instrument?"

"No. I didn't like sitting inside and practicing. I liked playing sports instead."

"So more of a tomboy then, huh? No surprise there."

"What's that supposed to mean?"

"Nothing. You just look…athletic."

Ben brushed his hand through his hair again. "So Chicago. If that's where you're from, why aren't you going back there? Do you have family or friends there?"

Andy gazed down at her iPod. "No family. None still alive, I mean. And I didn't have a lot of friends in school."

"Not one of the popular kids?"

"Hardly." She looked up at him. "Were you popular in school?"

"I don't know. Maybe. I didn't really think about it."

"That means you were."

He smiled but said nothing and kept his eyes on the road. She looked off to her right.

After a long silence, "You guys should stick with us," he said, then added quickly, "If you want to, I mean."

"But you hardly know us. What if you get sick of us?"

He laughed. "I doubt it. You and your friends seem smart, and you can obviously take care of yourselves."

"And what, everyone else you meet is stupid and lazy?"

He raised an eyebrow, indicating she wasn't far off the mark. "Let me ask you," he began. "Before the virus, when you were in school, did you get good grades?"

"Yeah, I guess so."

"And when you were in Bermuda, did you guys feed yourselves by fishing and growing your own food?"

"Yeah, we fished almost every day, and we had our own garden."

"Okay, and I suppose you all read a lot of books, right?"

"Uh, yeah…hundreds, probably."

"That's makes you the exception. Most survivors can barely read or feed themselves, so they either steal food or rely on others to feed them. They're totally helpless. They're like infants. But you three managed to sail hundreds of miles from Bermuda and survive. Alone." Ben gave Andy a long look. "Yeah, you're *definitely* the exception."

She turned away and looked out the window to her right. "My dad used to say that ignorance was dangerous."

"He was right. But all that means is that you've got the upper hand."

"'Knowledge is Power,' Sir Francis Bacon."

"Okay, now you're just showing off."

Andy laughed. "Sorry, but I have to give credit to Charlie for that one. He likes famous quotes."

"He seems like a smart kid."

"Charlie's a genius. His I.Q. is off the charts. We've tested it."

"Well that's good because we need all the brains we can get."

"Then I guess we'll *have* to stick around then," she teased after feigning a sigh. "Unless a better offer comes along."

"I wouldn't hold my breath." Ben smiled broadly at her.

And at that moment, a sudden and strange warmth erupted somewhere in the lower part of her abdomen. It was like nothing Andy had ever felt before, and she recognized that it had everything to do with the person sitting beside her.

Eastern New Mexico was dry and hot. Andy felt like she was standing in an oven, her skin cooking under the intense sun. She wore a baseball cap and a thin white linen shirt over her T-shirt to keep from getting sunburned, though neither could ward off the heat. Even the warmest days in Bermuda had never been this hot. And then there was quiet, like a void. Gone were the sounds of the ocean and the tangible feeling of moisture on her skin.

Sitting in the back of the truck with Ben and Charlie, she turned to Ben when they slowed enough for him to hear.

"I know this part of the country is a desert, but did you guys ever think how hot the summers would be when you picked this place?"

Charlie agreed. "After all those dreary winters in England, I'm all for warm weather, but this is *hot*."

"But it's quiet," was all Ben said.

The last stretch of their journey ended a hundred miles west of the Texas–New Mexico border in the town of Santa Rosa. It was a small town and from all initial appearances, entirely deserted.

When she was ten, Andy's father bought her a book of photographs of the Grand Canyon. Young Andy had scoured through its pages until the binding nearly broke, and the images of brilliant reddish-orange hues that continually changed with the shifting sun were engraved in her mind. But this eastern portion of New Mexico, with its bland, brownish plains covered with tufts of burro grass, was anything but brilliant despite being in the same part of the country. This plus the heat inspired little confidence in their decision to come to New Mexico. But for the sake of much-needed rest, they stayed in the town of Santa Rosa for more than a week.

They found two modest homes across the street from each other in a quiet neighborhood; enough room for everyone to have their own bedroom. Days were spent either in the shade or at the nearby lakes in the area. Santa Rosa, as they soon discovered, was surrounded by many lakes, an unusual geographic advantage for a town situated in such an arid climate. But other than sunbathing and swimming in the lakes, there wasn't much else to do or see in the town, and food was nowhere to be found.

Walking home together following their third day at the lakes, Andy and Morgan ran into the first strangers in town. While rounding a corner from one street to the next, Andy was stunned to see three people coming towards them. The eldest, a girl well into her teens with long dark hair, stepped protectively in front of the other two, a young boy and girl. "Who are you?" she asked with equal surprise.

Andy and Morgan instinctively held their hands up to show they were no threat.

"We're...we're staying down the street. We're not here to bother anyone. I promise," Andy replied.

The girl pointed to Andy's hip. "Then why do you have a gun?"

"It's just for protection," she insisted.

The girl's eyes darted back and forth between them. "How long are you planning to stay?"

"We don't know yet. What's your name?"

The girl hesitated, her wariness palpable. "Maria. This is my brother and sister, Julio and Carmen."

Andy smiled to ease the tension. "Andy."

"And I'm Morgan."

"And it's just the two of you here?" Maria asked.

"No, there's my brother, Charlie, and two others we met back in Virginia," Morgan answered. "You want to meet them?"

Maria's eyes grew wide. "Virginia? What are you doing here?"

"Long story," Andy muttered before quickly adding, "How long have you been here?"

"Almost five years. Three months after 'El Brote' we came here from Juarez."

"'El Brote'?" Andy attempted to repeat.

"The outbreak," Maria translated. "The virus."

As she and her siblings followed Andy and Morgan to their temporary home, Maria candidly revealed that her father had been a wealthy man with close ties to the Juarez drug cartel when members of a rival cartel murdered him only three months before 'El Brote.' His children quickly became targets themselves.

"What happened after the virus?" Morgan asked Maria as they turned onto their block.

"The children of the rival cartel came after us to keep control over the remaining drugs. They tried to shoot me but the bullet hit the side of Carmen's arm instead. We got away and came here."

Andy looked back at Carmen walking behind her and noted the scar on the outside of the girl's right shoulder. She looked like a miniature version of her older sister.

"How old are they?"

"Carmen is ten and Julio is thirteen."

Andy looked over at Julio. Like Charlie, he bore a strong resemblance to his sisters. "And how old are you?"

"Eighteen," Maria answered. "You?"

"Nineteen."

"You must be one of the oldest then."

"Probably." Andy stole a lengthy glance at Maria. With her dark hair, bright hazel eyes, and slender figure, she decided that Maria was very pretty, and once inside with the others, she keenly observed how Ben in particular reacted to meeting Maria. But his response seemed ordinary, she judged.

"Do you have any food?" Maria asked once all introductions were made.

"Just what we brought with us in our truck," Jim replied.

"You should come by my house. I'll cook everyone dinner," she offered.

An hour later, they all gathered in Maria's dining room and marveled at the food she had prepared. There was chili, cornbread, and a salad with the freshest of vegetables. After everyone sat down, she asked where they were all from.

Charlie explained how he and Morgan were from England and had met Andy in Bermuda.

After a spoonful of chili, Maria turned to Jim and Ben. "What about you two?"

Andy watched the cousins carefully as Jim answered for both of them. Unfortunately, he revealed nothing more than what she already knew: that they had been living in Virginia at the time.

"Virginia's near Washington DC, right?" Maria asked. "I was always terrible at geography."

"Yeah, DC sits at the north of the state," Ben answered.

Maria turned to her brother. "Julio, do you remember those three boys who passed through here about a year ago? They were a little older than you. I think they were from somewhere near DC, right?"

Julio shook his head. "It was Philadelphia."

"That's right, Philadelphia. I think they were on their way to Phoenix to find old friends or something. They didn't say much about where they came from. It seemed like it was something they didn't want to talk about."

"How did you learn English?" Charlie asked.

"My father sent us to a private school that taught in English half of the day," she replied, and Andy noted an edge in her voice.

Sitting at the end of the table, Morgan was the first to excuse herself. She had been quiet all evening and now looked tired and pale. After thanking Maria for the meal, she asked Andy for her pistol before returning to their house a few blocks away.

After she left, Jim turned to Andy with a look of concern. "Is she okay?"

Andy forced a smile. "She's fine, just a little tired."

Andy woke up to the sound of Morgan crying and crept quietly into her room to avoid waking Charlie across the hall. "Morgan?" she whispered softly as she tiptoed toward the bed, moonlight streaming in through the window. With Morgan's back to her, she could see her body shaking. She sat down on the edge of the bed and gently stroked Morgan's hair. It was something her mother used to do when she was upset. Morgan made no effort to sit up or move but continued to cry. It broke her heart to see her friend in such a state.

"Andy...how can I raise a child in this world? A child that I don't even want."

She didn't say anything. She just remained still and let Morgan speak through her sobs. "I'm so tired...so tired of feeling like there's no end to it all. Every day is such a struggle. Food...water... petrol. Even going to the bathroom is an effort. Will things ever get easier?"

"We'll do what we've always done," Andy said. "We'll adapt and we'll get through it together." She knew she was trying to reassure herself as much as Morgan.

"But where are we going to go? We can't stay here. This town is empty and there's no food. No ocean to fish, no garden to grow. It's dry and dead here. And hot. I can't sleep at night. All I do is sweat, and the bigger I get, the more I'll sweat..."

"...Shh...It will be okay. We don't have to stay here. It's just temporary until we come up with something better."

Morgan rubbed her moist eyes and looked up at Andy. "I'm so sorry I'm such a burden. All of this is my fault. If I hadn't...if those boys had never—"

Andy abruptly stopped her. "Don't you *ever* say that. You're not a burden, and none of this is your fault."

"But if it weren't for me, we'd still be happy in Bermuda."

"Morgan, I never wanted to stay in Bermuda forever. I wanted to come home. I'd wanted to return for a while, but I was only going to leave if you and Charlie wanted to. You two are my family, and you always will be. The only good thing that goddamned virus ever did was bring us together."

Morgan's face broke into quiet laughter. "You should curse more. It suits you."

"Maybe I will," she replied, smiling. "But seriously, you'll be okay. And your baby will be okay. I promise."

"But where else can we go?"

"I don't know, but I'll talk to Maria tomorrow. Maybe she has some ideas."

"What about Jim and Ben?"

Andy shrugged. "They'll do whatever's best for them, I guess."

"Will you ask them to come with us?"

"You want me to?"

Morgan hesitated a moment before nodding. "It's nice having other people around to talk to. Not that you and my brother aren't enough, but you know what I mean."

Andy smiled faintly. "Yeah, I do."

"So you'll ask them, then?"

"Sure, but why don't you ask them?"

"I don't want them to think I'm asking for help because I'm pregnant and I need them to take care of me."

"But they don't know you're pregnant. *You* don't even know for sure."

"I'm pretty sure." Morgan reached beneath her bed and retrieved a small plastic stick. A pregnancy test. "I got it from the drugstore yesterday. It's positive."

Andy frowned at the stick. "Ok, I'll ask them. But if they don't come, you'll still have Charlie and me, okay? No matter what."

Morgan grabbed her hand and gave it a squeeze. "I know. Thank God for both of you."

Chapter VII

*A*ndy didn't sleep much that night. Things had been easier in Bermuda. There was never any apprehension about the future. It just came, day by day, and they'd survived—they'd adapted.

But this was different. Morgan was right. There was no ocean to fish and no garden to grow; only dry, desert soil and heat. She wondered if they would've been better off staying back east in some beach town in North Carolina or Virginia. But it was too late to go back. They had been seduced by the offer of help from Jim and Ben when they had never needed help before. Now that they had accepted it, they seemed more off-track than ever.

Worries consumed her all night, and by five in the morning, she'd had enough. She needed to clear her head. In the darkness of her room, she fished around for her clothes and shoes. After tiptoeing out of the house, she wandered toward Maria's home.

Upon reaching their home, she was surprised to see Maria standing at the end of the driveway. More surprising was the presence of a mid-sized trailer truck with its engine running. There were two young men inside and Maria was speaking in Spanish to someone in the passenger's seat. When the truck drove off moments later, she still hadn't noticed Andy.

"Maria?"

She whirled around, startled. "Andy! God, you scared me! What are you doing here?"

"Sorry. I couldn't sleep, so I went for a walk and just kinda ended up here." After an awkward pause, she added, "Mind if I ask what that was about? The truck, I mean."

"I'm just trying to help out some friends from Juarez. Things are still very bad there."

"It seems like things are bad everywhere."

"True. It's either living in the middle of nowhere, like here, or in the middle of chaos with all the other survivors."

"So you chose the middle of nowhere?"

Maria's jaw hardened. "We had no choice. Julio and Carmen were so young when everything happened, and they depended entirely on me. I became their mother. When Carmen was shot, I had to make a choice."

"That's a lot to ask of a thirteen-year-old."

Her eyes narrowed as she gazed off toward the horizon. "They're my brother and sister. I'd do anything for them. Even come to a dead town like this. I don't want to be here, but there were no other options. And I have friends depending on me."

"Will you ever leave here?"

"Someday, if things get better in Juarez. But I've decided that if things aren't better by my twentieth birthday, we'll go somewhere else. That's a year and a half from now. I can make it here until then."

"Where would you go?"

"Colorado. I've heard rumors from people travelling through here that some of those ski towns managed to become pretty organized in the past year or two. I've even heard that they have power and electricity in most of the homes again, and water too. But you also have to be invited by its residents to live in those towns."

"Invited? How?"

Maria shrugged. "I don't know exactly, but like everything these days, if you have certain skills or things that people want, you have a better chance."

Andy wondered how valuable her skills as an amateur doctor would be. "Which ski towns did you hear about?"

Maria frowned. "Why, you all thinking of leaving already? We were hoping you would stay awhile."

"Well, we would stay longer, but Morgan...well, it's complicated."

"She's pregnant, right?"

Andy looked at her with surprise. "Probably. How did you know?"

"Actually, it was just a guess, but last night before she left, I noticed her touching her stomach a lot. I thought maybe she wasn't used to my spicy chili but then thought it could be something else."

"Pretty observant."

"Well, that's what happens when you're the daughter of a man who constantly got death threats. You learn to watch your back and watch others."

Andy wondered about the people in the truck that had just departed. *Were they somehow involved with drugs? Was that a 'thing' that people still wanted? Is that how Maria got access to the kind of food she had served last night?* "Do you miss your father?" she asked, keeping these other questions to herself.

"I miss my mother," Maria replied easily. "And if Julio and Carmen were around, I'd say I miss my father too. But in reality, it's hard to miss someone who was friends with violent drug dealers and killers. My brother and sister were too young to know what he was really like, but I remember. I keep my feelings to myself, though. It's not worth ruining their memories."

"Memories are all we have now," Andy muttered before turning the conversation back to Morgan. "Please don't say anything to the others about her being pregnant. Even Charlie doesn't know. I'm the only one she's told."

"Of course. So when will you all leave?"

"I don't know, but probably in a few days. I'll talk with the others first."

"Well, let me know when you decide." Maria put her hands on her hips and looked off toward the east. The sun was just about to appear. "Another day," she said with a heavy sigh.

Morgan awoke to the now-familiar sensation of nausea and hurried outside to vomit since the bathrooms had no water to flush. When she finished, she saw Andy walking toward the house. "You're awake?"

"Couldn't sleep." Andy noticed Morgan holding her stomach. "You okay?"

"Just morning sickness."

She nodded with a look of sympathy before glancing at the house across the street where Ben and Jim were sleeping. "Any sign of them this morning?"

"No, but I just woke up."

"I ran into Maria while walking. She was already awake." She didn't mention anything about the mysterious truck or Morgan's pregnancy but recalled the rest of their conversation.

"Do you think she's right about those ski towns in Colorado?" Morgan asked.

"Maybe. She said it was all just rumors, but why couldn't it be true? It's not impossible to imagine that some survivors actually managed to get a whole town up and running again."

"It sounds like a bloody miracle to me. But if it's true, then sign me up."

Laughing, Andy turned to head across the street. "I'll get the map from them and figure out the route we'll take north."

"You'll ask them now?"

Andy looked back.

"To come with us, I mean?"

"Might as well."

After crossing the street, she knocked on the door once, twice, then three times. After the third knock, she suddenly realized how early it still was, but it was too late. Ben answered, his eyes half-open and wearing only his jeans.

"Oh, sorry," Andy blurted. She averted her gaze from his bare chest. "Forgot how early it was."

"Didn't sleep?" He rubbed his eyes with one hand and backed away from the door to let her inside. She hesitated a moment before entering.

"Not really. I woke up a while ago and went for a walk."

He walked toward the kitchen and took a seat at the tiny dining table. Andy followed but didn't sit down. Instead, she stood in between the kitchen sink and the refrigerator, neither of which were operational. Stuck to the front of the fridge with magnets were pictures of some family who had once inhabited the house. Children possibly long gone and parents long dead.

"Where did you walk?" Ben asked.

"More like 'wander,' but I ended up at Maria's."

After Andy recounted her discussion with Maria, he said, "So you want to go to Colorado."

It was a statement, not a question, but she responded as though he were asking. "Maybe…yes. It's worth checking. If it doesn't work out, we can always come back here."

Ben sat back in his chair and cracked his knuckles, one at a time. He was thinking. "By 'we,' you mean you three?" He was going to make her ask.

"And you and Jim, if you want to come." There, she thought. Nothing more than a simple offer.

He looked at her for a long moment, which made her uneasy, and she wondered if he knew that he could affect her that way.

"I'll ask Jim when he gets up," was all he said.

Andy merely nodded. There was nothing more to say, so she asked to see the road map.

"Yeah, it's in the truck. I'll grab it."

"No, I can get it…"

But Ben was already back on his feet and walking toward the door. He reappeared a minute later with the map. Instead of handing it to her, he returned to the table and laid the map out flat. He leaned over and began to study it.

"You don't have to do that," she insisted as she moved toward the table. "I can look at it later."

"I'm just curious," he said, then gazed at her with a mixture of suspicion and amusement. "Maybe you don't want to tell me where in Colorado you plan to go."

"I don't know where we're going yet." Her eyes moved from the map to Ben's chest and then quickly she turned toward the kitchen counter. She noticed a blue T-shirt lying in a pile and picked it up and threw it on top of the map.

Ben looked at the shirt for a second and then looked back at Andy. He smiled and picked up the shirt. "This isn't mine. It's Jim's."

"I'm sure it fits."

"Am I making you uncomfortable? Not wearing a shirt?"

Andy's hand clamped around the edge of the countertop. "You look cold," was her feeble reply.

"It's like a hundred degrees out."

"Well, you're making me cold just looking at you." She knew how stupid she sounded, so she reached for the map and snatched it off the table. "I'll bring it back later." She bolted out the front door without looking back.

Not ten seconds after Andy returned Morgan was hammering away with questions. "So what'd Ben say?"

"He said he would talk to Jim after he woke up."

"Did he say if they'd be interested in going?"

"If Jim says yes, then I think they will."

Charlie emerged from his bedroom and entered the living room where they were sitting. His hair was disheveled and his steps were uneven. "Good Lord, what are you two babbling about?" he mumbled before plopping down next to Morgan.

"Sorry," Andy said before filling him in on the morning's events. When she finished, he simply blinked his eyes a few times, then stood up.

"I'm starved," he said stumbling into the kitchen. "I need to elevate my blood sugar levels before I can even think about Colorado."

Andy began to chuckle, which provoked Morgan to laugh as well. "Your brother says the funniest things sometimes."

"I know...so technical."

"What are you two saying about me?" Charlie called back from the kitchen while opening a can of peaches. "I need to spend less time with girls. I'm surrounded by too much estrogen."

When he returned to the worn sofa with his opened can of peaches, Morgan reached inside the can, plucked out a slice of peach, and put it in her mouth. After swallowing, she smiled with satisfaction.

"Get your own food!" he whined, making Andy giggle so hard that her sides hurt.

"See, this is exactly what I'm talking about!" he cried before gobbling up any remaining peaches. He threw the empty can down on the coffee table and headed to the front door. "I'm begging Ben and Jim to come with us to Colorado...for *my* sake!" The front door slammed behind him, its echo resonating throughout the house.

Andy looked over at Morgan. "Well there you go. They'll definitely come with us now."

Morgan looked at her with hopeful eyes.

Andy looked away toward a window next to the front door. The sunlight was intensifying. It was going to be another hot day. "I really don't understand why Ben and Jim chose to come here."

"Me neither. It's hard to believe that just a few weeks ago we were in Bermuda. This place is so different from anything I've ever seen before. It's like being on Mars or something."

"What's even stranger to me is that in the two thousand miles we drove to get here, we never once ran into another person until we met Maria and her brother and sister. Every town we passed was like a ghost town. I know we didn't stop anywhere long enough to see much, but still..." She turned away from the window and sank back into the sofa. "Where could everyone be?"

"Well, they aren't in this town," Morgan replied with a weary sigh.

"Right now, at this moment, I actually miss Bermuda."

"So do I, which scares the hell out of me."

"You know," Andy began slowly. "You should just tell you brother about being pregnant. You might feel better."

"You're what?!" Charlie had walked back in the house.

Morgan stood up with urgency. "I thought you went to talk to the guys."

"I forgot my…wait, Morgan, you're pregnant?"

She looked at Andy then back at Charlie. "Yeah…"

"But…but how?"

Morgan made a face. "You really need me to explain it to you?"

Charlie looked away with embarrassment. "No, of course not. I know how but…was it…" He didn't finish. Morgan's body had gone rigid. "Okay. Then we'll figure it out," he recovered and looked to Andy for help. "Right?"

She managed a smile. "Right."

Chapter VIII

*D*espite all doubts, the group of five left Santa Rosa headed to Colorado. Maria and her siblings stopped by to bid farewell, bringing with them a large box of food, both canned and fresh.

"If it doesn't work out, we might be back," Andy said to Maria before hopping in the truck.

Wearing a sad smile, Maria replied, "For my sake, I hope you do. For your sake, I hope you don't. But you know where I'll be, at least for the next year and a half."

The ski towns of Echo, Arapahoe, Loveland, Keystone, and Copper were all utterly vacant, while Breckenridge and Vail weren't interested in acquiring more residents. "Not enough food," was the reason. And as explained by three male residents who gave Andy and Morgan uncomfortably long stares, Beaver Creek had a shortage of women in town and was only interested in new female residents.

"Thanks, but we'll pass," Andy told them before slamming down the gas pedal until the tires squealed.

"Whoa, don't make me regret letting you drive!" warned Ben from the passenger's seat.

"Can you believe those guys?" she went on.

"Yeah, it's shocking," he said sarcastically.

"What, you don't think that was just a bit…misogynistic?"

"Get used to it," he muttered under his breath.

"What?"

"Nothing. Turn left up here."

"I know," she snapped.

The rest of the ride was silent until they reached Aspen. Upon entering the town from the north, they were stopped by a barricade similar to the one outside Beaver Creek. This one was guarded by four male teens, each armed. It seemed as though everyone was armed these days. Two of the young men approached them.

"Morning," said Jim, who was now behind the wheel. "We're looking for a place to stay for a while." It was direct and to the point. They were all too exhausted for pleasantries.

The guard on Jim's side glanced at his very expensive-looking watch. "It's afternoon, actually. Twelve-fifteen to be exact."

"Alright, good afternoon then," he muttered, unsure of what to say next. He turned to Charlie, who was sitting next to him. Equally confused, Charlie shrugged, so he looked back at the guard who had yet to say anything else. "So, uh, any chance we can go through?"

Instead of responding, the guard reached behind to his back pocket and unclipped a push-to-talk radio. He turned away from Jim and began communicating with someone, taking the conversation out of earshot.

"What the hell is going on?" Andy whispered in the back.

"Don't know," Ben said.

A minute later, the guard returned and clipped the radio back onto his pocket. "You can go through, but you have to leave your weapons here."

"Sorry, not going to happen," Ben called out, preempting any response from Jim or the others. "Our weapons stay with us."

But the guard stood firm. "Those are the rules. Either you leave your weapons here with us, or you turn around and head back to wherever you came from."

The tension in the air lingered until Morgan spoke. "Why don't two or three of us stay here with the weapons and the rest go through and see what the deal is?" Her voice was weak from fatigue but her words were resolute.

"Alright, I'll go," Andy quickly volunteered. She was losing patience with these towns.

"I don't like it," Ben said with a shake of his head.

"Well, what choice do we have?" Morgan snapped back loud enough for the guards to hear. "They don't know who we are or what our intentions are. You can hardly blame them for being careful."

"She's right," Andy said. "I'll be fine."

Biting his lower lip, Ben turned away in defeat. Meanwhile, Jim and Charlie got out of the truck to join the discussion.

"Andy, I'll go with you," Charlie offered.

Morgan opened her mouth to protest the notion of her brother venturing into the unknown before realizing she was about to contradict her own argument.

"Alright. Let's get this over with," Andy said brusquely. "The two of us will go," she called out to the guards and gesturing to herself and Charlie.

The guard standing nearest to the truck radioed ahead to some unseen person, telling them that a male and a female were coming their way, along with a brief description of Andy and Charlie.

"Where exactly are we going and how far is it?" she demanded of the guard.

"Walk along this road for about two miles. You'll see more guards waiting there. They'll show you to where to go."

Andy and Charlie exchanged uneasy glances, and she wondered if they should take the truck and just leave the others with the weapons to save time. But then if they got into some kind of trouble, their friends would be too far away to help. No, best to leave all their resources in one place.

"If we don't come back in two hours, come after us," Andy muttered to Jim, who was holding her rifle. "We'll walk quickly, so it shouldn't take longer than that to find out what the deal is."

"All right, we'll stay in the truck just in case," he replied.

"Don't do anything stupid," Morgan said to both Andy and her brother as they began the two-mile trek.

Andy glanced over her shoulder and gave her friend the most reassuring smile she could manage.

Nataliya Ivanova stood watching through the enormous second floor window of her home as the two strangers approached the front gate. She had already instructed the gate to be opened, and as they passed through and headed up the long driveway, she was able to get a good look at them. The male looked to be a little younger, with the build of someone still in the midst of adolescence. The girl was older. It was difficult to tell yet if the girl was pretty, but from a distance, the possibility was there. Nataliya didn't mind pretty girls, as long as they weren't prettier than her.

Once the two strangers reached the front door, she headed toward the top of the large spiral staircase to greet them. She waited until they were let inside by her guards and were standing in the expansive foyer before she took her first step down the stairs. She liked how people were forced to look up at her as she made her way around the staircase, as though she were on stage and everyone else was the audience.

"Hello," she said, her accent immediately noticeable after one word. "My name is Nataliya. Nataliya Ivanova."

She approached the two strangers and extended her hand. They each shook it as she gave them a quick once-over. Though it pleased her that they both looked dreadfully dirty and tired, she hated to admit that the girl was indeed very pretty. She would clean up well, she thought with dismay.

"Andy."

"Charlie."

Nataliya tilted her head to the side and gave Andy a questioning look. "Andy? That is a boy's, I think?"

"It's short for Andrea," Andy said. "Where's your accent from."

"Russia," Nataliya replied curtly. "So, come in and sit down."

She led them to the living room, which was large and beautifully furnished. Adjacent was a kitchen that even the pickiest gourmet chefs would have been hard-pressed to find fault with. Her father had bought the house when she was nine-years-old while still living in Moscow during a time when foreign entrepreneurs began taking an interest in American real estate. The multi-million dollar home was one of the largest in Aspen, and it remained occupied by Nataliya and her younger brother, Mikhail, after their parents' death.

"This is a beautiful home," Andy commented.

"Thank you," Nataliya replied simply as she gestured for the two guests to take a seat on one of three sofas in the large living room.

"How long have you been living here?"

"Nine years, since we moved from Moscow."

"And it's got air conditioning," Andy commented with interest. "Does everyone in Aspen have electricity, or just certain homes?"

Nataliya interpreted Andy's question as implying that she and her brother had special privileges others didn't have. "All homes that are occupied have electricity. The solar power and hydroelectric plants that were built in Colorado just before the virus are still functioning and give us power, though I don't pretend to understand anything about it," she said with a dismissive wave of her hand. "There are other people who handle that."

Charlie, however, was interested, but Andy cut him off before he had a chance to open his mouth. "So, Nataliya," she began, businesslike. "There are five of us here. The three others are Morgan, who is my age and Charlie's older sister, and Jim and Ben, who are cousins and both about my age as well."

"And you want to come live here in Aspen?"

"Maybe. We'd like to have a look around first, but the fact that you have electricity here is incredible."

"Yes, it is very nice here," she replied haughtily. "But not just anyone can live here, you know? There are rules."

Charlie and Andy exchanged glances. "What rules?" asked Charlie.

"Well, I will explain," Nataliya rose to her feet. She headed toward the kitchen and opened the large refrigerator. "Are you thirsty? Hungry? You both look like you could use some water and a good meal."

"Um, water would be nice," Charlie said, trying not to sound too eager.

"Andy?" Nataliya queried as she grabbed two glasses from one of the cabinet shelves.

"Sure, thank you."

Nataliya poured filtered water into the glasses and returned to the living room. She placed them on two coasters on top of the Brazilian rosewood coffee table and sat back down. Andy and Charlie picked them up immediately, each finishing more than half the glass before stopping to take a breath. Nataliya looked on with amusement. "Maybe I should bring the pitcher over too?"

When neither Andy nor Charlie declined the offer, Nataliya returned to the refrigerator to retrieve the pitcher. "So, the rules," she started. "There are a few, but basically, if you want to live in Aspen, you have to work. Some people take care of the power and water, others take care of the food, and some take care of security—as you can see—but everyone works and we all benefit from it. Money is worthless, so the only things of value are things we all need to live and survive."

"What if you have special skills?" Charlie asked as he poured himself another glass of water.

Nataliya raised a well-groomed eyebrow. "Skills? Like what?"

"Well, Andy's father was a doctor, and she's been learning and practicing medicine for the past five years…"

Nataliya tried not to appear too impressed.

"...and I have an I.Q. of 188."

"And what exactly does that mean?" she asked as though a high I.Q. was of little significance.

"It means that he's smart enough to build a spaceship and send it to Mars if he wanted to," Andy retorted defensively. "Charlie's ridiculously intelligent."

"Well, we do not need to send anything to Mars, but I guess I see your point," Nataliya responded condescendingly, which annoyed Andy. "What about the other three...sorry, I have forgotten their names."

"We haven't known Ben and Jim long, but from what I can tell, they are very good with cars...fixing them, modifying them...that sort of thing," Andy said.

"That could be very useful," Nataliya conceded. "There are not enough mechanics here."

"And Morgan, my sister, is very good with children," Charlie added brightly. "She's also a teacher. Reading, writing, math..."

Nataliya pursued her lips together in a disapproving manner. "We really do not need any more babysitters. We have plenty already." Then, sensing Andy's rising irritation as well as silently admitting that the skills the others had were indeed valuable, she quickly added, "But I suppose we cannot have a bunch of idiot children running around here that cannot read or write, no?"

Andy forced a smile. "So, are you the one who decides if we can live here?"

Nataliya slowly shook her head. "Not entirely. Aspen has a council. There are ten of us on the council and together we vote on who can become a resident. But because I am the leader of the council, I decide whether or not a potential new resident is offered a trial period of one month. After the month, the council votes to determine if they can stay or not."

"So what's your decision about us?" Andy asked directly.

"I'll have to meet your friends first before I make a decision."

"They won't leave our weapons behind," Charlie assured. "So unless you let them through with them, you won't meet them."

Andy reinforced Charlie's words with a nod.

Nataliya thought about it for a quick minute and said, "I'll tell the guards to let them through with their weapons." She grabbed the radio from the kitchen, and after a few transmissions, she returned and sat back down in the living room.

"I'm surprised you're not using mobile phones yet," Charlie observed.

"Not yet, but we are working on it."

"I'm sure Charlie could help with that," Andy said as she cast him an encouraging smile.

Nataliya smiled thinly. "I'm sure."

A few minutes of awkward silence passed while waiting for the others to arrive, during which Charlie asked a disinterested Nataliya about the solar power plant. Andy, however, ignored the conversation as her gaze shifted back and forth from Nataliya to the expansive room around her. She seemed to fit perfectly amidst such luxury. Impeccably clean, her long, golden brown hair had a shine to it that Andy's used to have during the days of hot showers and shampoo. Her complexion was milky and flawless, not dirtied and reddened by the wind and sun like Andy's. She was tall and slender, her build similar to Morgan's, and her clothes were right out of a fashion magazine. Jewelry that appeared to contain fine gemstones dangled from her ears, neck, and wrists. Although Andy didn't understand the need to dress beyond basic functionality, she admitted that Nataliya's efforts toward her physical appearance, combined with her God-given beauty, had a very intimidating effect. Andy glanced down at her hands. They were dirty and callused from the years in Bermuda. Nataliya's were lily-white and adorned with rings. As Andy began to surreptitiously clean the dirt from underneath her fingernails, the front door opened.

A guard entered the house first, followed by their friends. Thankful for the distraction from Charlie's litany of boring questions, Nataliya bolted off the sofa and scurried to the grand foyer. Andy and Charlie followed but without the urgency of their host.

After waving the guard off and introducing herself to the three strangers, Nataliya gave Morgan the same judgmental inspection that she'd given Andy. Immediately disliking Morgan's own beauty, she quickly moved her attention to Jim and Ben. Here, she perked up. "My goodness," she began, placing her hand to her chest in an overly-dramatic fashion. "Andy did not mention that you two were so handsome."

Andy rolled her eyes. "Andy didn't think it was important," she replied sharply in third person.

Nataliya ignored the remark and requested that they all return to the living room.

As everyone followed her, Ben pulled Andy aside. "Who the hell is this person? Where's she from?"

"She's from Russia," Andy whispered. "Apparently, she's the leader of some council that governs Aspen."

He frowned. "So she's like the chief in this town?"

"No clue. But be nice to her. She doesn't like me already."

Once everyone was seated in the living room, Nataliya repeated for the others the general rules of living in Aspen, her role on the council, and the month-long trial period. "There's an empty house down the road from here," she said while keeping her eyes on Ben. "You can all rest and take a shower and then stay the night after dinner here. It's not quite as big as my home, but I think you will find it comfortable. I'll ask the guards outside to take you there."

Everyone seemed happy with this plan and agreed to return at seven o'clock for dinner. Anxious to leave the house and Nataliya's presence, Andy exited the mansion first as Morgan hurried behind her.

"Is it just me," Morgan began when they were out of earshot, "or is Nataliya sort of a bitch?"

Andy released a laugh. "Sort of? I love how she only wanted to talk to Ben and Jim. Especially Ben. She couldn't pull her eyes off him."

"I noticed that too. Let's hope they saw through her act and weren't hypnotized by her perfect hair and sexy accent."

"Your accent is better."

"Thanks," replied Morgan, grateful for the compliment. "Still, she seems to have everyone wrapped around her finger. The guards do anything she asks."

Charlie approached just then, his face clouded over. "I think I annoyed Nataliya. She kept ignoring my questions about the solar power plant."

"I wouldn't take it personally," Morgan replied, giving her brother a sideways hug.

As Ben and Jim caught up to them, Ben drew up beside Andy, asking, "Do you ever wear perfume?"

"God, no. Why?"

"She reeked of it. She kept leaning toward me and I couldn't breathe."

Smiling, Andy looked down at her fingernails and no longer cared about the dirt beneath them.

Chapter IX

$\mathcal{N}$ ataliya's description of the home where Andy and her friends would be staying that evening had been modest. The house, which was just a few hundred yards from Nataliya's, was quite impressive. Though indeed smaller, it was spacious with décor more rustic than Nataliya's elegant yet pretentious style. Everyone had their own bedroom, and only Ben and Jim had to share a bathroom, all of which had running water. It was miraculous.

There was a sense among the group that they would be staying longer than one night. Though agitated by Nataliya's attention to Ben, Andy knew it would likely result in an invitation to stay for at least a month. But when she stepped into the shower—her first in five years—she decided that she could put up with almost anything if she could experience this every day. As the large showerhead above her and jets positioned along the shower walls propelled warm water over her body, she felt as though a layer of something beyond dirt and sweat was sliding off her skin and disappearing down the drain.

As she toweled off, there was a knock at the door. Wrapping the towel around her, she opened the door to find Ben standing there. She instinctively pulled the towel tighter above her chest.

"Sorry, I didn't know you were in the shower." The apology was flat, and Ben seemed to hardly register her lack of clothing.

"No problem. What's up?"

"Jim and I are going to drive around for a bit. You know, check out the town.

If you want to come, we'll wait for you to get dressed."

"Alright. What about Morgan and Charlie?"

"They're both taking a nap." Then, as an afterthought, he added, "Morgan looks exhausted today. Is she okay?"

"Yeah, I think so," she said with a casual shrug in an effort to appear unconcerned. "I mean, I think we're all tired, right?"

"True," he answered slowly, brushing a hand through his hair. "We'll be downstairs when you're ready."

"All right, just give me a few minutes."

After getting dressed, she quietly poked her head into Morgan's room. She was sound asleep, her soft breath in perfect sync with the rise and fall of her chest. She looked so fragile.

She closed the door and descended the stairs, her long, wet hair pulled back into a loose French braid. As she reached the bottom, her stomach growled loudly. She had grown accustomed to ignoring pangs of hunger out of necessity, but since returning to the continent, meals had become much more unpredictable, and her clothes were becoming loose. Though concerning, Andy worried more about Morgan. Her friend was becoming increasingly thin when her body needed to be strong and well-nourished.

"Okay, ready," she announced, entering the room.

"Where did you put your weapons?" Jim asked her.

"In my room, under the bed."

"When we get back, you should put them in my room," Ben said. "I found a good hiding place in the back of the closet."

"Okay."

They set out and locked the front door behind them with the single set of keys they had been given. Ben volunteered to sit in the back of the truck while Jim drove.

"Maybe we can find another car soon," Andy said hopefully while climbing into the passenger's seat.

As they pulled out of the driveway, Jim turned to her and voiced the same concern about Morgan that Ben had earlier. "Is she okay? She looks ill."

"She's just really tired. So am I. We're not used to this…all this moving around, I mean. We never needed to travel around that far in Bermuda. And in less than a month we've traveled thousands of miles. It's been overwhelming." Despite the recurring omission of several key components to the story, Andy voiced the honest truth. She *was* exhausted. Damn exhausted.

"I keep forgetting that."

Though not knowing exactly where they were going, Jim managed to make his way out of the winding neighborhoods to downtown Aspen, where the streets were arranged in a grid pattern. Other vehicles were parked along the sides of the road, but no one seemed to be driving. Instead, people were either walking or riding bikes.

Andy suggested that perhaps they should also park and walk around. "Maybe we can check out some of these stores," she added as they got out of the truck. "See if they're all empty or not."

"Sure, and maybe there's someplace to get food. I'm starving," said Ben.

"Me too," both Andy and Jim said simultaneously.

As they began wandering around, Andy was struck by how clean the streets were. The people looked clean as well, wearing clothes that appeared crisp and new. It was a stark contrast to the raggedy jeans and threadbare T-shirt she was wearing. Her current wardrobe was sparse in quantity and variety, and although nearly everything she owned was at least a couple years old, she'd never noticed it until now. Another detail was the sense of purpose everyone seemed to possess. Nobody was loitering or watching time pass out of boredom. People were bustling about as though they had things to do.

After leaving the truck behind, they approached a grocery store and were shocked to find that people were inside buying food. Instead of money, people used gold tokens similar to those once used at fairs for buying rides on Ferris wheels and playing games like Skee-Ball.

"Too bad I haven't been to a carnival lately," Ben commented as they watched others picking out fruit, vegetables, meat, and milk—all of it was for sale. Andy could hardly believe her eyes.

"Where do they get all this?" she mumbled under her breath.

"From my brother and me."

"Huh?" Andy looked around to find the source of the voice. "Who said that?"

"I did."

Sensing that the voice had originated from somewhere below her waist, Andy looked down to her right. Kneeling on the floor, tying her shoelaces, was a slight girl with bright blue eyes and shoulder-length hair that was as light as Andy's. When she stood up, she stood a few inches shorter and appeared to be in her early teens.

"Hi, I'm Susan." She politely extended her hand to Andy, who shook it.
"Andy."

Susan then shook hands with both Ben and Jim, who introduced themselves in return. "You must be new here, huh? My brother told me that some new people came in this morning."

"Your brother?" Ben asked.

"Yeah, his friend is one of the regular guards working at the north gate on Route 82. Brian and I—that's my brother—we live on a farm right off of 82, about ten miles north of here. We raise everything: horses, bulls, cows, sheep, and chickens. Then we sell what we don't eat here, which is most of it."

"Just the two of you?" Jim said with surprise. "That's a lot of work for just two people."

Susan laughed and shook her head. "It would be, but no. We have help from a few people who live here in town."

"What exactly do you sell?" Ben asked.

"The sheep are for meat only. We keep the cows and bulls alive for milk and breeding. Same with the chickens. We keep them for their eggs until they stop laying them, and then we kill them for meat. Well, I don't kill them. Brian and a couple of the others do all the killing. I'm too scared to do it. I take care of feeding all the animals instead, which is a whole other job. Harvesting hay is a pain, you know?"

Andy nodded as if she did know. Fishing and growing vegetables was much simpler.

"And what do you get in exchange for the food?" asked Jim.

"We get what everyone else gets: electricity, running water, clothes, other food. It works out pretty well for everyone."

Andy smiled at the girl. She had a genuine and friendly demeanor.

"So are you guys going to stay here or what?"

"Well, we aren't sure yet." Andy glanced back and forth between Ben and Jim. "But we'll know more tonight after we have dinner with Nataliya. I guess it's up to her."

Susan made a face. "Yeah, I know."

Her expression and tone gave Andy pause, but before she could press further, a tall and lanky young man with scruffy blond hair approached Susan. She assumed this was her brother, Brian, which was confirmed after Susan introduced him to everyone.

"Nice to meet you guys," Brian said. He then handed some tokens to Andy so they could buy food. "It's not much but it'll tide you over for a few days."

She smiled gratefully, and Ben and Jim both thanked him.

"I hear Nataliya is having you over for dinner. Don't worry about her. She'll let you stay for a month. She just gives the impression that Aspen is super-exclusive or something. The fact is we need all the extra hands we can get." Brian looked at his watch and told his sister it was time to go.

"If you want, I'll come by your house tomorrow afternoon. Help you get settled and tell you all the things Nataliya won't."

"That'd be great," Andy replied.

As Brian was leaving the store, he gave her a long look that escaped her notice.

Morgan was awake and sitting in the living room downstairs when Andy and the cousins returned. It was after five o'clock and the angle of sunlight had shifted considerably throughout the house. "Where did you all go? I was worried when I woke up and you were all gone."

Andy shot both Jim and Ben an irritated look. She had assumed that one of them had mentioned something to either Morgan or Charlie before they left.

"Sorry, we didn't want to wake you," Jim quickly apologized and took a seat next to Morgan on the sofa.

"It's okay, I'm just glad you're back," Morgan replied as she delicately placed one hand on her lower abdomen, the gesture Andy noticed more often since her discussion with Maria. "Charlie's still asleep, I think. So where did you go?"

"Just downtown and wandered around a bit," Andy said. "You won't believe what we found: an actual grocery store that's selling food. Fresh food, like steak, chicken, fruit, vegetables…you name it."

Morgan's eyes grew wide. "Selling food? Are you serious? But…how? And what do people use to buy the food?"

"Tokens. We met a brother and sister who live on a farm not far from here. They explained the token system to us," said Jim.

"Were they nice?" Morgan asked. "Nicer than Nataliya, at least?"

"Much nicer. You'll meet Brian, the brother, tomorrow," said Andy. "He said he'd to come by in the afternoon."

The food purchased at the store with Brian's charitable tokens was sitting in a bag at Ben's feet, and he bent down to pick it up before heading to the kitchen. "Anyone hungry?" he called out. "I could eat a whole cow right now."

The others agreed.

"Morgan, you better wake your brother," Ben said as he grabbed a butcher knife. "Otherwise he'll miss out."

⋯⋯

After an incredible meal of fresh steaks, potatoes, and spinach with carrots, they walked down the road to Nataliya's house for their second dinner.

"You're a good cook," Andy said to Ben as they made their way down the curving road lined with tall pines. They were walking behind the others.

He laughed lightly as he kicked at a stone on the ground. "It's not difficult with a decent kitchen and food that doesn't come from a can."

"Makes all the difference, doesn't it?" She looked up at the sky during its last couple hours of daylight, then took a deep breath in through her nose and let it out while enjoying the crisp scent of the trees. "You know, I could get used to this place. Living like this."

"I know. But I just have a feeling that it's not what it seems."

"Don't say that," she urged, despite the fact that she had similar doubts. "You'll jinx it."

"Sorry, but when something's too good to be true, it usually is."

Charlie reached the front gate first and pushed the button to let them inside. The gate swung open soon after, and then the front door of the house. Making her way up the drive, Andy saw a boy of twelve or thirteen standing in the doorway. She correctly guessed that it was Nataliya's brother, Mikhail.

"Come in," he said with a sullen expression on his face. There were no pleasantries or gestures of politeness. He lacked the thick accent of his sister.

They entered the house tentatively, as Mikhail had already scurried off somewhere inside the house. Nataliya entered the foyer moments later and gestured for everyone to come inside.

"You will have to forgive my brother. Manners are something he lacks."

Andy and Morgan eyed each other after this understatement.

Seven sets of dinnerware and silverware encircled three silver platters of hot food with steam rising upward, and two other plates with food that Andy could not yet identify. In between the platters were two lit candles. If Nataliya's intention was to impress her guests, she had succeeded, though Andy decided that such efforts were aimed at targeting solely Ben's attention.

It became glaringly apparent that their host had not lifted a finger to prepare the meal when two young girls emerged from the direction of the kitchen, one of them approaching Nataliya. "Everything's on the table. Is there anything else you need?"

"No, thank you, Jenny," Nataliya replied politely to the girl but with an air of authority. "Come back around ten or so. You can clean up then."

The two girls nodded and quickly left the house. Meanwhile, Morgan and Andy exchanged glances again as they read each other's minds.

"All right, everyone sit down," Nataliya said. She had changed out of her clothes from the afternoon and had put on a summer dress that enhanced her slender figure. As hostess, she took a seat at the head of the table and gestured for Ben to sit beside her. Andy sat next to him on the other side. The other end of the table was occupied by Mikhail, who skulked into the room a moment later.

As brother and sister, Nataliya and Mikhail looked very much alike. Their facial features, particularly their eyes, carried a strong resemblance. Though Mikhail was dressed far more casually than his sister, his clothes appeared new, like everyone else's in town.

Once everyone helped themselves to the food, Nataliya initiated a conversation. "So, how do you like your home?" After chorus of affirmatives from her guests, she smiled, looking pleased with herself. "Yes, this is one of the nicest and most expensive neighborhoods in Aspen," she continued, as though the monetary value of a home still had meaning. But perhaps here in Aspen, Andy suspected it might.

Nataliya began talking to Ben, asking him if they managed to see any part of the town. He nodded in return and politely described their afternoon outing. Meanwhile, Andy became preoccupied with her potatoes, wondering where the cheese came from. She had no clue how to make cheese, but she knew that squeezing a few udders was merely the first step of many that followed. Later, she began observing the others.

Everyone spoke politely to Nataliya, careful not to offend her, and Nataliya, who controlled the conversation, seemed to enjoy that. Mikhail remained silent, however, his eyes never leaving his plate. Being an amateur student of medicine, Andy began to wonder if he possibly had some kind of developmental disorder, like autism. But after she caught him rolling his eyes and making faces at her friends' remarks throughout the meal, she decided that he was merely a spoiled brat who didn't like strangers in his house. When he finished his plate, he pushed his chair back and left the table without a word. His sister didn't seem to notice or care.

There were only a few comments Nataliya made during dinner that were of any interest to Andy. She learned that nearly eight hundred people currently lived in Aspen, ranging in age from five to nearly twenty. "I am not quite the oldest," Nataliya added. "But close." Andy also learned that Brian was one of the ten members of the town council, and then determined by the sudden change in Nataliya's voice that she wasn't happy about that, which came as no surprise given what he had said about her that afternoon.

After everyone had eaten more than enough, Andy decided it was time to get to the point of the evening when Morgan beat her to it. "So, Nataliya, you said this afternoon that you would let us know this evening if we could stay here or not. What's your answer?"

Andy smiled covertly at her friend's bluntness.

Taken aback, Nataliya blinked once, then twice before responding. "Getting straight to the point, I see." She then took a long sip of water as though purposely trying to create suspense.

"Well, I have to admit, you have skills that we could use here, so for now, I do not see any problem with you staying for a month. After that, the council and I will decide if you can stay permanently. Sound good?"

Everyone nodded in agreement.

"Excellent. I hope you all enjoyed dinner." She pushed herself away from the table and stood up. "Well, I apologize, but I have some things I need to take care of before I go to bed. I believe Brian will be coming over to your house tomorrow to talk to you all about the tasks each of you will be given, along with the rules that we all must live by here, myself included."

Andy had her doubts about that last part.

"I did not want to go over all of that tonight since you all must be tired," she continued as she rushed everyone to the front door and bid them goodnight.

Once they were through the gate and out of earshot, Charlie declared, "That was rather painless."

"Almost painless," his sister responded. "She sure has a way of making everything about her, doesn't she?"

"Honestly, I was hardly listening," Andy said. "I was more curious to know how the cheese got into my potatoes. That and her brother's behavior. What a brat he is!"

"I didn't notice him being bratty," Ben piped in.

"That's because you were too distracted by Nataliya's flirting," she said with an edge.

"Hey, I can't help it if she finds me irresistible."

"Then she's got strange taste," Jim teased, provoking a hard punch on the arm from his cousin.

Annoyed, Andy let out a moan and walked ahead of the others. Morgan caught up to her as the boys held back. "I wonder what important things she has to do at this hour," she said.

"Who knows? Maybe Brian can tell us more tomorrow."

"What's this Brian like?" Morgan asked, lowering her voice.

"He seems nice enough, though we only met for a minute."

"Is he cute?"

Andy shrugged. "Yeah, I guess so. Does it matter?"

"Not really. I was just curious. You think we'll get to stay here for a while?"

"Don't know. I guess we'll see."

"I hope so. I think we could be happy here."

Happy. Happiness had become practically irrelevant. But maybe Morgan was right.

Chapter X

*A*ndy slept better that first night in Aspen than she had in months and attributed it to the cool mountain air, eating well the day before, and not having to drive around to find a new place to live.

After getting out of bed, she headed downstairs to the kitchen, grabbed an apple, and settled into a comfortable lounge chair on the large deck off the living room. She closed her eyes to enjoy the warmth of the rising sun on her cheeks, only to be stirred moments later by the sound of the glass door opening from the inside. It was Ben.

"Morning," he said groggily.

"Morning. Sleep well?"

"Like a rock. You?"

"The same. I think I was asleep the second my head hit the pillow." As he sat beside her, she asked, "Think you and Jim will stick around?"

He combed his fingers through his hair in that now-familiar way and cracked his knuckles. "For now."

"For now? What else are you looking for?"

Ben faced her, his expression stern. "Nothing. I'm just saying that this place will do for now."

⚜

There was a knock on the door. It was Brian. "Wow, nice house you guys got," he said after stepping inside and giving it a once-over. "One of you must've done something right for Nataliya to give you this place."

Andy raised her hands. "Definitely wasn't me."

He immediately understood her full meaning. "No, probably not. She doesn't like most other girls her age, especially those who are pretty."

She wasn't sure whether or not he had just complimented her, but she didn't dwell on it. "Come in," she said, closing the door behind him. "Where's your sister?"

"She's at home. She wanted to come, but she had to take care of the horses."

"How many do you have?"

"Four. They can be a pain to feed and care for, but we need them to haul things into town, especially with gas from the refinery being so hard to get."

Andy opened her mouth wide in disbelief and then asked, "Gas is being *made*?"

"Yeah, but it's a work in progress. It was only six months ago when it started being produced again, but since there's only one refinery in Colorado, we have to bargain with nearby towns to get some. Luckily, most people here in Aspen don't drive much. Everyone just uses their bikes or walks. Whatever gasoline we get is mostly for people who need to drive outside of town, like me and Susan."

Andy led Brian into the living room and gestured for him to take a seat. "Still, I'm surprised gas is being made at all."

"Why? The technology exists. We just had to figure out how to do it ourselves, like everything else."

"I guess." Everyone knew that performing brain surgery or building skyscrapers was possible; the hard part was learning *how* when there was no one left to teach.

Morgan descended the stairs just then and headed toward the living room. She held out her hand to Brian and introduced herself. "So I hear you live on a farm."

"Yes. It was our childhood farm. After our parents died it was all we had left. Susan was so young, so it was up to me to take care of it and figure out how to keep the animals fed and healthy. But eventually we got the hang of it and began exchanging food for things in town." Knowing that any useful commodity produced before the virus would soon run out, he and a few friends decided that if they could learn how to make things and perform the same jobs that adults had, they would survive indefinitely.

"So is that how you became a member of the council? Because you helped start everything?" Morgan asked.

"That plus I was one of the oldest survivors, so others were willing to listen to me, I guess. Age and experience were everything back then."

"Who are the others on the council?" asked Andy.

"Five of them are friends that I went to school with. Two of them work as mechanics and repair things. The other three have farms like me, two for agriculture and one for livestock."

"I assume Nataliya isn't one of those friends. She doesn't seem the mechanic-farm girl type," said Andy with a chuckle.

Brian hesitated before answering, indicating there was a story involved, but just as he was about to answer, the front door opened. Jim, Charlie, and Ben entered.

"Afternoon. Are we interrupting?" asked Jim.

"No, we were just talking about how the council here was formed," Andy said.

"How did Nataliya get to be a part of the council?" Morgan asked.

"Well," Brian began. "I'm sure you all guessed that her family was insanely wealthy. Her father had to have been a billionaire to afford a house like that. I didn't know her or her brother before then, but afterwards, she and her friends took most of the food in the supermarkets and most of the gas that was left at the pumps. Only after food and gas ran out did they finally realize they needed to work with others. Things got better after that, but she and her friends still have a lot of influence."

"Why is that?" asked Andy.

He looked down at his feet and shook his head. "A lot of the younger girls think she's the greatest thing because she still dresses and carries on as if the virus never happened. I guess she reminds them of how everything used to be. And a lot of the boys are afraid to get on her bad side. But in truth, Aspen would be much better off without them."

"She had two girls cooking for her last night," Morgan recalled with a frown.

"Exactly. They think she walks on water around here. I'm just glad Susan isn't like that."

"So you just have to put up with it?" asked Jim.

"Yeah, unfortunately, until more people see things my way. But in the meantime, Nataliya and three of her friends are on the council, and she's technically the leader, but it's really just a title to keep her happy. You'll meet them all soon, but my advice is not to trust any of them."

"What about Mikhail? What's his story?" asked Andy.

"No story," Brian said matter-of-factly. "He's just a pain in the ass. Spoiled and lazy like his sister."

"Do most people here own guns?" Ben asked, abruptly changing the subject.

"I think almost every home here has a gun of some kind. With all the wild animals in these mountains, people need to protect themselves—and of course we use them for hunting."

"Was there ever a concern that people would use them against each other?" Ben continued.

"Not really, most people here knew one another growing up, and after the virus, nobody could stomach the idea of killing more people. I think it's actually safer knowing that everyone has a gun. You're less likely to get into a serious argument."

"So what about us? What should we do for work?" Charlie asked.

"Well, it's sort of up to you really, although I know that we really need more mechanics and people who are handy with equipment, and we need help on the farms. Raising crops and animals is a ton of work."

"Ben and I can help you with the mechanical stuff," Jim offered. "We're good with fixing cars. My father was a mechanic."

"That's perfect. You can start tomorrow if you want."

"I can help with that sort of thing too," Charlie volunteered.

"Um, sure." Brian sounded uncertain, understandable since Charlie, being both younger and smaller, didn't immediately appear to be either particularly handy or strong.

But Morgan quickly stood up for her brother. "Seriously, when we were in Bermuda, he could fix just about anything."

"Okay, sounds good," Brian replied sheepishly.

"I can help on the farms," she suggested. "I can also teach the younger children reading and writing and math. I did that in Bermuda."

"Awesome, you can help my sister if you want. She works too much already. Or you can help my friend Scott on his farm. And I know Diana at the school needs some help a few days a week. There's just too many kids and not enough teachers." He turned to Andy. "What about you?"

She shrugged. "Any need for a doctor? Nataliya said you don't have one here."

"Nataliya doesn't really know who does what jobs around here, but she's right. We need one."

"Well, I know a few things," she replied humbly.

"She's brilliant. She once saved my big toe from having to be cut off from gangrene," Charlie said proudly.

"Well, I'm convinced," Brian said. "You can work at the hospital, which is walking distance from here."

"Great, I'll go there later and check it out."

Brian also explained that no job was considered more important than another, so everyone got paid the same amount for every hour they worked. One token per hour of work, whether you fed horses or taught a five-year-old their ABCs. While it wasn't always fair, it kept people from arguing that their job was more important and they should be paid more.

"Who keeps track of how many hours someone works, or does everyone just trust each other not to lie?" asked Morgan.

"Well, that's the tricky part. For most jobs, it's obvious how many hours you put in because you're working with other people, so you can't really lie. Solo jobs are harder to track, but people around here know each other pretty well and know which people are more willing to lie about their hours than others. Those that lie get called out on it enough, and eventually they stop doing it."

"What about Nataliya?" Andy asked. "If she doesn't lift a finger, as you say, how can she earn any tokens?"

"She claims that her work as council leader is enough," Brian said with disdain. "Believe me, I've tried arguing against it many times. I'm on the council and so are some of my friends, but we still work all day. I've just accepted that it's a battle I'm not going to win."

Chapter XI

Autumn 2022

The summer passed quickly, and though everyone was working long hours at their new "jobs," they actually enjoyed being busy, the work giving them all a sense of purpose. The council voted unanimously that the five newcomers could stay after the first month, and despite Ben's initial unwillingness to commit to staying in Aspen, he never mentioned anything about leaving again.

Despite her curiosity, Andy never asked Ben about his past. At random moments, however, she would sense a melancholic side to him that she attributed to some painful event that happened before they met. Though he laughed and joked along with everyone, there were times when his mind seemed to be miles and years away.

Andy jumped right into her work at Aspen Valley Hospital and usually spent eight or nine hours there every day. The first weeks were dedicated to cleaning up the place. The hospital was still well-stocked with drugs of all kinds that had barely been touched—much to her surprise—and when she asked Brian what happened when people got sick or injured, he said they had simply let nature take its course.

"But what if someone broke a bone or got seriously ill?"

"If it was a broken bone they usually took painkillers and let the bone heal on its own. But no one has gotten really sick yet, and antibiotics always seemed to cure infections."

"So that's it? Just painkillers and antibiotics?"

"Yeah. But we've been lucky, but luck has a habit of running out."

Morgan tried actively to hide her pregnancy. She would do as much physically as everyone else, even though she felt tired and weak. Her belly was starting to show so she hid it with giant shirts and dresses. She was always on her feet and pushing her body to go beyond her capabilities.

One morning, she woke up and felt something moist and sticky by her hip, and when she lifted her hand, her fingers were crimson. It was blood. She felt around her body and noticed that it wasn't coming from a wound or a cut. "Andy!" she yelled for her friend.

In her pajamas, Andy scrambled into Morgan's room and upon seeing the blood she rushed over to her side and began to evaluate the situation. "We have to take you the hospital. I need to do an ultrasound...I haven't done it before, but it's the only way to know if...if it's gone..."

"Don't say that...not yet..."

"Are you in pain?"

Morgan shook her head. "No, not really."

Andy quietly got Morgan out of the house and into the car without anyone noticing. She sped to the hospital as Morgan sat beside her with tears in her eyes.

"Don't think the worst until we know. There's no need to panic."

Morgan nodded and blinked away the tears. When they arrived at the hospital, Andy set up the ultrasound machine and prepared Morgan for the test. Just then, Jim, Charlie, and Ben came running in.

"What's happened?" asked Jim out of breath. "I walked into your room and saw blood."

"Are you injured or sick?" Charlie begged for an explanation.

"Guys, I need to help Morgan right now...we can talk about it after," Andy said, waving them out of the room.

Charlie and Ben retreated from the room to give Andy some space to perform the exam, but Jim stayed put. He took hold of Morgan's hand as Andy gently ran the probe with jelly over her stomach.

"Why are you checking her stomach?" asked Jim.

"Jim, I'm pregnant...or I was," Morgan said as she quietly cried.

"Pregnant? But..."

Then suddenly all three of them heard a faint beating sound. It was a heartbeat.

"Andy, is that..." Morgan began.

"Yes. The baby's alive. You didn't miscarry."

Morgan hugged Jim tightly and began to cry harder into his shoulder, but now she was crying out of relief.

Jim held onto her without saying another word.

"What is it?" Ben asked as Andy stepped out of the exam room.

Unsure how to begin, she said, "Do you remember Morgan having a bruised eye the day we met?"

Ben nodded. "I remember."

"Well, the reason is because she was attacked…raped, actually. That's why we left Bermuda."

"What?"

"And…well, now she's pregnant."

"Oh my God," he said breathlessly. "I mean, I figured there was something you guys were keeping from us, but I never would've guessed this."

"It was awful. I found her after…after it happened."

Ben started to ask something, but Andy held up her hand before he could speak. She couldn't bring herself to talk anymore about that night. "Sorry, but there are images from that day that I will never be able to get out of my head. I'd rather not relive them right now."

"Is she still pregnant?" Charlie asked.

"Yes, the baby's heart is beating. But I need to run more tests to see what caused the bleeding and if the baby is healthy. I think that Morgan overworked herself so for now I've put her on bed rest."

"Can I go in and see her?

"Yes. But give Jim a few more minutes with her. I think he's a bit shocked."

After that terrifying morning in the hospital, Jim would not leave Morgan's side. He made sure she didn't have to lift a finger. Andy made it a priority to learn how to operate the x-ray, the ultrasound, and the MRI properly. She needed to make sure that she could test if Morgan and her child were healthy, and she used the ultrasound machine regularly to check on both her friend and her fetus.

Slowly, Morgan strengthened not just physically but emotionally. She enjoyed helping Susan care for the animals on her farm and found the work therapeutic. Three days a week she taught reading and math to children at Aspen Elementary School. Diana, the young woman who was the head teacher at the school, was a quiet but genial girl, and they got along very well from the beginning. There were half a dozen teachers who taught nearly three hundred children between the ages of five and twelve. After turning thirteen, the children stopped going to school and began working, although Morgan offered to continue teaching some of them more advanced reading and writing classes two evenings a week. Several accepted her offer, and she quickly became a favorite at the school.

Once it became known that there was a "doctor" working at the hospital, people began seeking Andy's assistance for injuries and ailments that they had typically ignored in the past. Using the x-ray, she reset dislocated shoulders and other small bones that had suffered from improper alignment when fractured the first time. In early September, a friend of Brian's had a bullet lodged in his shoulder when it ricocheted off a tree while hunting elk. Not confident enough to use anesthesia properly, Andy gave the boy a few shots of whiskey to dull the pain and successfully removed the bullet from the muscle tissue.

Gradually, her expertise grew, and it pleased her to know that she was learning how to do things that very few others could. At night, she stayed up late reading books and old medical articles on childbirth, and together with Charlie, they planned for every contingency in the event that something went wrong.

To Andy's surprise, she and Ben slowly formed a close friendship, and though she wondered privately about the possibility of it becoming something more, she never acted on it. She was too timid—scared even. She would have moments of extreme self-doubt. Yet their friendship was solid, founded on mutual respect. They shared many interests, including a profound love of history. Both had read several books on various periods of human civilization, from ancient Greece to the end of the twentieth century. They would often debate late into the night on how the course of history would have changed if one small and seemingly minor event had occurred differently or not at all.

Ben seemed to appreciate that Andy was the only girl he'd ever met who could not only use a gun with great skill and accuracy, but could also shoot an animal without flinching. When he mentioned this to her, she explained that it had been difficult to kill her first fish in Bermuda, adding, "I hope you don't think of me as cold-blooded just because I don't mind shooting a deer."

He laughed. "Of course not. No one wants to kill Bambi, but we don't want to starve either."

As for Charlie, when it came to deciding what to do each day he was like a kid in a candy store. He picked tasks as he liked, though everything he did was helpful. Some days he would help Ben and Jim, proving to be a competent mechanic and repairer of various machines. Other days, he helped Susan and Brian on their farm, and Susan quickly developed a crush on him. Though initially wandering into unfamiliar territory, Susan soon got the better of him. After all, she was a fun, vibrant fourteen-year-old who worked hard and enjoyed being outdoors. Andy and her friends were quick to like her; she had spunk and wasn't afraid to speak her mind.

Despite the work involved to keep the town running, there was also time for fun. The habits of a generation born and raised during the age of online social networking, cell phones, and high-definition televisions were replaced by more old-fashioned entertainment. For the first time in years, Andy played games like tag and hide-and-go-seek with many of the younger children. Football, soccer, and baseball games became a regular occurrence after dinner during the longer summer and early autumn evenings. Storytelling around campfires would often follow, or they'd watch old movies shown on a big screen downtown in the park. All of it brought back a piece of childhood, something that had been missing during the years of pain, fear, and uncertainty. Sometimes Andy would think about Maria and her brother and sister, and how they would be much happier in Aspen. She hoped to see them again one day, but doubted she would.

The only consistent source of aggravation that marred an otherwise tranquil life was the very existence of Nataliya and her friends, all of whom seemed to believe they were somehow better than the rest of the town and therefore too good to do any real work.

"Can't we just force them out of town at gunpoint?" Andy once asked Brian, partly joking but mostly serious.

"They have guns too, Andy.'"

"Did you ever think of leaving Aspen and going elsewhere?"

"Sure, but I would feel like I was giving into them if I left. They'd win out of forfeit."

"I understand. I wouldn't give in either."

For the most part, Andy and her friends ignored Nataliya's inner circle and their transgressions. As new residents of Aspen, it wasn't their place to make waves.

Tensions escalated one snowy day in mid-November. As usual, Andy was working at the hospital. That morning, she gave Morgan another sonogram, and following an uneventful afternoon, she headed toward the main entrance of the hospital to end her day. As she passed one of the operating rooms, she heard a commotion from inside. When she entered the room, three boys were in the midst of a struggle in the far corner. One of the boys, Nathan, a rather frail kid of eleven that Morgan taught, was pinned against the wall by Mikhail and his friend Heath. They were threatening Nathan with the defibrillator and were about to shock him when Andy quickly intervened.

"What the hell are you doing? Let go of him!"

Mikhail and Heath immediately looked as if they'd been caught with their pants down around their ankles, though they maintained a firm grip on Nathan.

"Did you hear me? Let go of him!"

"And if we don't, what are you going to do?" Mikhail sputtered as Heath sneered viciously at Andy.

Staying calm, she reached her hand inside the backpack she carried to the hospital every day and fished around until she found her loaded pistol. Using both hands to hold the weapon, she pointed the barrel back and forth between Heath and Mikhail.

"Let him go or you'll both get a bullet to the leg, and I won't pull them out."

After a tense silence, Heath and Mikhail reluctantly released Nathan. Gesturing with her pistol, she ordered the two out of the room. Fuming with anger, Heath and Mikhail skulked to the door.

"You'll regret this, bitch!" Mikhail said with a flourish as he followed Heath outside.

Wordlessly, she followed and watched them exit the hospital with her pistol grip remaining firm. Then she returned to the operating room and tucked the weapon back into her bag.

"Did they hurt you?" she asked Nathan, moving toward him.

He shook his head. There were tears in his eyes. She gently placed her hands on his shoulders. Only after touching him did she become aware that her own hands were shaking.

"What happened, Nathan?"

But he was too upset to answer. A tear that had been hanging on precariously to his left eyelid finally gave up its fight and fell to the floor.

"Nathan, it's okay, you can tell me. I won't let them get away with it. I promise."

Wearily, he lifted his gaze to meet Andy's. She took a step back to give him space. Huddled in the corner, Nathan appeared smaller than usual. "They thought I saw something that I wasn't supposed to, but when I told them I didn't see anything, they didn't believe me."

"What did they think you saw?"

He shrugged weakly. "I don't know. I mean I don't know exactly what I saw."

"But you did see something. What was it?"

He bit his lower lip and his gaze went to the floor.

"Nathan, please. I can't help if you don't tell me."

He wiped his tears and looked up. "It was last night. I was over at a friend's house for dinner with a few others from school. It was Alison's house. Her older sister makes the best hamburgers." This remark brought a brief smile to his face, and Andy smiled in return. "Anyway, after dinner, I went to the store to see if Mark was still there and if he needed any help."

Mark was Nathan's older brother and a friend of Charlie's who ran the grocery store in town. Andy would often see him there cleaning up after closing.

"I didn't see Mark inside the store when I got there, but I saw that the lights had been left on. I figured Mark must have forgotten, so I went inside to turn them off." He paused and wiped at his eyes again. "I heard noises coming from the back of the store, like people talking or something. So I went to the back and saw that the back door was open, and that all the freezers were empty. I figured that the store was getting robbed, so I hid behind one of the shelves near the freezers. I should've just left the store, but I wanted to see who was robbing us. I saw three people standing in front of a truck outside. It was Heath and his brother, Garrett, talking to someone else. I didn't recognize him, which I thought was strange, because I know everyone in town."

Another pause and a trembling breath.

"Then I decided to leave before they saw me, but when I moved, I accidentally knocked over a jar of applesauce. It crashed and broke on the floor. They heard the noise and came running inside the store. I turned off the light switch so they couldn't see and went out the front. When I got outside, I ran as fast as I could all the way home. I didn't think they saw me, but they knew it was either me or Mark. We're the only ones with keys to the store."

"Did you tell Mark?"

"Yeah, when I got home. He went down to the store, but no one was there. The back door was closed and the jar of applesauce had been cleaned up. The freezer was still empty, but its doors were closed."

"And you have no idea who the third person was?"

Nathan shook his head firmly. "Never seen him before."

"But what does Mikhail have to do with this? He wasn't there."

"I don't know, but he's friends with Heath."

Andy glanced briefly at the room. "What were you doing here anyway?"

He lifted his right pant leg and revealed a bloody bandage on his shin. "It happened when I ran from the store. I thought the bleeding would stop but it hasn't. I guess Mikhail and Heath followed me."

Andy bent down to get a better look at the wound. "That's a nasty cut. Let me take a look at it now."

After mending his shin, she escorted Nathan out of the hospital. "Do you want me to walk you home?"

He hesitated before nodding sheepishly. "If you don't mind. I feel like Heath and Mikhail are waiting for me somewhere."

"Okay," she replied tenderly as they set off along the snowy road.

After safely dropping Nathan off and explaining to his brother what had happened, Andy returned home. Mark was visibly shaken by news of the incident, and his expression was an intense mixture of worry and anger.

As she walked home, Andy couldn't shake the image of Nathan being pinned against the wall by Heath and Mikhail, each holding charged defibrillator paddles mere inches from the boy's chest. The last thing she wanted was to disrupt the fragile balance of power that existed in Aspen, even as unfair and absurd as it was. Being banished as winter approached with Morgan more than five months pregnant was not an option. But she didn't want to sit by while kids like Nathan were being bullied.

Distracted by her thoughts, including how to take better security measures at the hospital, she nearly missed seeing Ben on the street outside their home.

"Didn't you hear me calling your name?" But upon seeing her face, he immediately recognized that something was wrong. "What is it?"

"I'll tell everyone inside," she replied after an exhausted sigh. "Right now, I just want to get warm."

As they walked up the driveway, Ben put a reassuring arm around her shoulder. Grateful for the gesture, she allowed herself to lean into him all the way to the front door.

Both Brian and Susan were over for dinner, so everyone heard the story. When Andy finished, everyone looked to Brian, whose expression had grown increasingly tense as he listened.

"And he had no idea who the third person was?" was his first question.

"No. Nathan said he never saw him before."

"Have there been any other robberies or anything like that lately?" Ben asked.

Brian thought for a moment and started to shake his head when Susan stopped him. "Remember back in the spring when Gracie's sister lost her snowmobile?"

Brian scratched his head, slowly recollecting the memory. "You mean Cathy? Yeah, I remember."

"Yeah, she kept saying that she didn't lose it but that someone took it right after the last snow storm. Remember how no one believed her?"

"Yeah, she wanted me to bring it up at the next council meeting, but I didn't think it was anything serious, especially since it happened to Cathy–she's a nice girl but she's pretty spacey and is always losing things."

"Maybe Cathy was telling the truth?" Morgan suggested.

"I know *she* thinks she was telling the truth. Cathy may be a lot of things, but she's not a liar," Brian said.

"Are snowmobiles rare enough in Aspen that people would want to steal them?" Andy asked. "I don't see that many around."

"They used to be everywhere. A lot of homes had them, and of course the ski patrol had a ton for the slopes, but most of them either broke down or disappeared the first winter after the virus. That year was pretty rough, and a lot of kids left to go to other towns and took snowmobiles with them."

"Are you going to say something to Nataliya about her brother?"

He pursed his lips together. "I'm sure she knows whatever Mikhail's up to, so she probably knows about what happened with Nathan. I'll say something to her tomorrow."

"What about Garrett and Heath?" Charlie piped in, angry on Mark's behalf. "They can't get away with this. Someone has to say something to them."

"I'll say something to them, but only if you say so, Brian. This is your town. We're just visitors," Ben said.

The word "visitors" sounded odd to Andy. She didn't think they were temporary residents anymore, not after nearly four months.

Brian obviously didn't think so either. "You're all part of the town now. But let me talk to Garrett and Heath, though I'd be more than happy to have you and Jim back me up."

"Happily," Jim said.

"Nathan's the sweetest boy," said Morgan with a sad frown, and Jim gave her hand a consoling squeeze. "I can't believe they would do that to him."

"I can," Ben countered. "Look how they treat everyone in broad daylight."

No one said anything for a moment, and Andy noticed that Brian had become particularly pensive. "What is it?" she asked him, rousing him from his thoughts.

"Nothing," he began, shaking his head. "But I was just thinking about some things I've noticed recently that seemed odd, but now I think they might actually be related to all of this."

"Like what?"

"Well, at the end of last year we didn't have any gas in town. I mean *no one* was driving *anywhere*. Susan and I came into town only once a week, on horseback, to pick up supplies and check on how things were going. It wasn't until the refinery outside of Denver started producing gas that we were finally able to start using our cars again. But about a month before that, I noticed Garrett driving around in his SUV, and I asked him where he got the gas. He told me he had some stored in his garage at home, but at the council meeting a few days before he was complaining how there was no gas left in town. At the time I just figured he'd traded for some."

"Remember the liquor at Juniper's birthday party last spring?" said Susan, referring to one of Nataliya's friends and another member of the council.

"Oh, yeah, I forgot about that," he replied before explaining to the others. "Nataliya likes to have birthday parties for her friends, big surprise. And she also likes to have tons of liquor at these parties. Bourbon, scotch, vodka…you name it. Except at Juniper's birthday party in April, her supply ran out, and so had everyone else's by then."

"Nataliya was pissed," Susan said with a giggle.

Charlie turned to her and asked, "Why did you go to a party for someone you abhor?"

"Are you kidding? I didn't go, but Brian did," she replied.

"She invites everyone on the council. I only go because it would create more problems if I didn't. Anyway, after Juniper's party, all the liquor in Aspen was supposedly gone."

"But then June comes, right before you all got here," Susan continued, "and it's her sister Sparrow's birthday. I went to that party, but only because my friend Karen really wanted to go."

Out of the corner of her eye, Andy thought she saw Ben flinch after Susan spoke, but she ignored it and continued to listen.

"I kept trying to convince her not to, but she's always trying to make friends with the 'popular' people. So I go to the stupid party, and Sparrow, Juniper, and all their close friends were drinking liquor and getting drunk. But this time they weren't sharing it like they'd always done in the past. Instead they were keeping it for themselves and hiding it from everyone else until they got too drunk to care."

"So where did it come from?" Charlie asked.

"Who knows?" Brian replied flatly. "The simple explanation is that one of Sparrow's friends had some liquor in their house that they'd forgotten about, but I doubt it. They must've gotten a fresh supply from *somewhere* between April and June."

"Is liquor something the town tries to resupply when it runs out?" Andy asked. "I gave your friend some whiskey when I pulled that bullet out of his shoulder, but it was a small bottle that I happened to find in some desk drawer at the hospital."

Brian shook his head. "No, liquor is the least of our priorities. It's not something we ever worried about when we ran out. And I could care less if Nataliya and her friends have a large stash of liquor. I'm just worried about how they got it."

Chapter XII

December 2022

In the six weeks since the incident at the hospital, little had changed. Work continued as usual, though everyone tended to stay indoors more during the cold, snowy days. Ben spent more time gathering and chopping firewood to keep everyone warm than doing any of his normal work. The electricity, though fairly dependable, was still temperamental, and a day without heat was not uncommon.

Brian spoke with Nataliya the day after Andy saved Nathan. Though she defended her brother and denied involvement in robbing the store or any other nefarious behavior, she knew her comfortable living depended on residents like Brian and his friends, so she promised to confront Mikhail about what happened at the store. Wary of her promises, Brian raised the incident at the council meeting two days later where a full-fledged war of words erupted.

"You have no proof!" Garrett barked at Brian. "Nathan will deny anything that Andy told you."

"That's because you've made him too scared to talk!"

The meeting spiraled out of control even further, with old feuds resurfacing until they peaked into threats of violence. The only thing that prevented actual blows was Garrett recognizing that he was outnumbered, both physically and numerically. But before storming out of the meeting, he came within inches of Brian's face and snarled at him, "Get ready to pay for this!"

No one saw much of Brian after that. Susan still came by the house often, but mainly to spend time with Charlie. She told him her brother was making himself scarce until everything blew over. When Charlie asked if anything like this had ever happened before, she shook her head firmly.

Two days before Christmas, Brian finally came over to the house for dinner. It had been two weeks since anyone but Susan had seen him.

"Well, look who's at the door," Jim said as he moved aside to let him in.

"Yeah, I know. Sorry," Brian said.

Everyone couldn't help but notice how tired he looked, as though he hadn't slept in weeks.

"Sorry we're late," he added as he took off his coat. "It took us a while to get all the cows and horses water. Our pipes froze, so I had to take care of that while Susan melted the snow one bucket at a time."

"It's too bad you two can't just move in here with us," Andy said as she entered the living room momentarily from the kitchen. "Or at least move your livestock somewhere closer, like Scott's farm."

"He and I talked about that," said Brian. "Unfortunately, his farm isn't big enough for both his cattle and mine."

"Well, let us know how we can help."

"Thanks, I will."

"How are Daisy and Suzie?" asked Morgan, referring to two of their horses. "I miss seeing them every day." It had been almost a month since Morgan had stopped working on the farm. Nearly seven months pregnant, her daily routine now consisted of a few hours of teaching in the morning, a long nap in the afternoon, and helping with chores in the house. Still, beneath her sweaters and heavier winter clothing, she barely showed. Few people outside her circle of friends even knew she was pregnant.

"They're good, but I think they miss you too," Susan replied as she kicked the snow off the bottom of her boots onto the mat at the front door.

Ben entered the house from the garage where he'd been tinkering with his truck. He headed to the sink to wash his hands, passing Andy who was back in the kitchen cooking dinner on the stove. He gave her a friendly nudge with his elbow. "What's up?" he muttered as he scrubbed the grease off his fingers.

"Susan and Brian are here," she replied without turning away from the stove. "You hungry?"

"Always."

He dried his hands off on a towel and was just about to ask her if she needed any help with getting dinner ready when Brian approached.

"You need any help?" he asked.

"Yeah, thanks. Can you defrost the steak in the microwave and then chop it up into pieces? I'm making fajitas."

"Wow, sounds great," he said while reaching for the frozen steak on a plate next to the microwave.

Looking uncertain, Ben backed out of the kitchen and wordlessly moved into the living room where everyone else was sitting. Moments later, they heard Brian cry out, "Jesus!"

Ben rushed into the kitchen first and saw Andy grab a towel. She pressed it firmly against Brian's hand. He winced in pain as Susan scurried over to him.

"What happened?" she cried, then saw the blood on the knife.

"It was stupid, really," he replied with a strain in his voice as Andy continued to apply pressure to the wound. "My grip just slipped."

"Will he need stitches?" Susan asked worriedly.

"If I can't stop the bleeding."

"I'll take you guys to the hospital," Ben offered.

Andy removed the towel to inspect the cut. "Yeah, we need to go. It's pretty deep."

It usually took Andy fifteen minutes to walk from the house to the hospital. Using Ben's truck, they arrived in two minutes.

"Do you want me to come inside?" he offered as he dropped Andy and Brian off at the main entrance.

"No, we'll be fine," she replied. "It won't take long. You don't have to wait for us."

"You sure?"

"Yeah, we'll be fine," she repeated as she moved away from the truck. "Seriously, it's too cold for you to wait here."

Appearing hurt, Ben mumbled, "Suit yourself," and drove off.

Later, as Andy stitched, Brian commented on her skill. "You're really good at this, you know?"

"What, stitching a finger?"

"Well, just in general. You're a good doctor."

She scoffed at the compliment. "Thanks, but I'd hardly consider stitching up a finger qualifying me as a doctor."

"I wouldn't say that. Whenever I went to the doctor as a kid, all he would ever do is look into my ears and throat and bang my knees with that little hammer. Didn't seem too difficult."

Andy laughed heartily. "There are so many other things I haven't even begun to learn or that I'm too scared to try."

"Like what? Surgery?"

"Sure. I've never cut a person open before. If I ever do, I'll probably end up killing them."

Brian cocked his head to one side and said, "Maybe, but if someone gets sick or injured enough that they need surgery, they'd probably die without it, right? All you'd be doing is giving them a chance to live, no matter how small. And if they die, it's not like anyone can sue you."

Andy laughed again and recalled Ben telling her something similar. "I know. And you're right about all that." Then, sighing, "It's the act of cutting someone open. Not to mention giving anesthesia first. That's an entirely separate specialty."

"See, that's why you're a good doctor—or at least you will be one day. You understand what it takes to do something right."

Andy was done treating him, but they didn't leave the hospital right away, continuing to chat despite that it was almost as cold inside as outside. The heat was turned on only during the day and only in certain rooms to conserve energy.

"You make it sound like I have a rare quality or something."

"You do, Andy." Brian looked down at his bandaged finger, his expression solemn.

"What's wrong?" she asked.

He looked back up. "It just feels like everything my friends and I have worked so hard to build is about to fall apart and there's nothing I can do about it. It makes me so mad that people like Nataliya and Garrett can get away with doing whatever they want and to hell with the consequences."

"I know. It's completely unfair."

"Life isn't fair, though."

She cracked a smile. "You sound like my dad."

"Yeah? Well, he was right."

"I still don't understand. Doesn't everyone see that they do absolutely nothing to help out in this town? This isn't high school, Brian. It's survival. It's about being able to feed yourself, having clean water to drink, and staying warm in the winter. I would gladly make enemies with anyone if it meant that my friends and I could stay alive."

"I know, but I just wish more people felt the way you do, but as long as everyone is getting what they need, people will continue looking the other way. Just human nature, I suppose," he added with a heavy shrug.

"Maybe, but I swear to you, if Nataliya or any of them do anything to hurt me or my friends, I'll fight back. I promise. Going after poor Nathan was bad enough. Going after those I care most about...well..." She raised an eyebrow. "Things would get ugly."

Brian smiled broadly. Then he started to speak, hesitated, but ultimately continued. "So, if one of them tried to hurt me, you'd go after them?"

"Of course," she replied matter-of-factly.

"Your friends are lucky to have you. And I'm glad you consider me one of them, especially since you already had such close friends when you got here."

"I've known Morgan and Charlie more than five years, but I only met Jim and Ben a few weeks before coming here. I consider them all my friends." She looked down at her hands and brushed her palms on her jeans. "You're all so lucky to still have family," she continued. "I don't have anyone but my friends. I'm kinda jealous. And now Jim and Morgan seem to be... together."

Brian examined his bandaged hand and chuckled lightly. "Yeah, and my sister and Charlie hang out all the time, which is a little weird, but she's almost fifteen, so..."

"See, all six of you are connected now, but I'm still just everyone's friend," Andy remarked with regret.

"What about you and Ben?" he asked pointedly.

She blinked, taken aback by the question. "Me and Ben? We're just friends. Why?"

Brian shook his head casually. "Just curious. You two seem...I don't know. Sometimes more than friends."

"Well, we've become good friends, but it's tricky to get beyond a certain point with him. There's a part of him that he keeps hidden from everyone. I don't know why, but unless that changes, I don't think I'll ever be more than just his friend."

"But you've thought about it? Being more than just friends, I mean?"

She looked down at her boots and smiled awkwardly. "Sure, I guess." Then, feeling the need to explain further, she quickly added, "I think most girls do that with guys they know. We put each of them into one of two categories. There are the ones you know you will only ever be friends with because you only feel friendship for them, and then there are the ones that you always consider the possibility of something more happening. At least that's how it is for me. But I haven't known too many boys my age, so I could be wrong." She drew her gaze up from the floor and looked directly at Brian, then shrugged as though to say she had no further explanation to give.

Brian started to ask something when a sudden crash erupted outside the treatment room. Being closest to the door, Andy opened it and peered outside. Glancing left and right, she realized what had caused the noise. An IV stand that had been placed in the hallway to the right of the door had fallen over. Confused as to how it could've fallen over on its own, her eyes darted in all directions, looking to see if someone was nearby and had knocked it over.

"What was it?" Brian called from behind.

"Just an IV stand that fell over. I meant to move it today."

"It just fell over by itself?"

"I know. Weird," she said, and they both shrugged it off before heading back home.

New Year's Day came and went amidst a blizzard that knocked out much of the power throughout Aspen. Brian and Susan were stranded in their home for more than a week. Before, people would have rejoiced at the snowfall and the superb ski conditions it created, but now it was merely a nuisance.

The snow finally ceased during the second week of January, and one day, after the town worked tirelessly to turn the power back on, everyone took advantage of the fresh powder and went sledding on the ski slopes.

After a few hours, Andy began heading over to the hospital. She had a nagging feeling all afternoon that she'd accidentally left the door unlocked to the room where most of the drugs were kept. After finding some had gone missing a few weeks earlier, she'd moved all the drugs to one room and installed a more secure lock on the door, but the lock was useless if she forgot to use it.

Daylight was fading as she walked the now-familiar route to the hospital, and the sun began its descent behind the mountains by the time she arrived. Once inside, she quickly checked the door in question and discovered that she had indeed locked it the day before. Feeling stupid, she unlocked the door and checked supplies inside, just in case. After verifying that nothing was missing, she relocked the door and went home.

❦

As twilight turned to dusk, Morgan began pacing back and forth in front of the fireplace. Andy had still not returned from the hospital.

By now, everyone had returned to the house, and Brian and Susan were about to head home until it became clear that Andy might be in trouble.

Ben and Charlie went to check out the hospital, but they came back less than an hour later without Andy and without any answers.

"Where the hell could she be?" Morgan cried out.

Jim did his best to calm her down. "She probably just wandered down to Main Street and got caught up talking to someone on her way back. Maybe someone got sick or injured and she went to help them."

This explanation seemed to soothe Morgan for a while, and Susan and Brian decided they needed to head back home before it got too late.

"We'll come back in the morning," Brian said before heading outside.

Morgan managed to fall asleep, as did Jim and Charlie. Ben, however, lay awake almost the entire night, save a few restless hours of sleep. At dawn, he rose out of bed and checked Andy's room to see if she had returned in the middle of the night. But her bed was empty. He threw on his clothes and went back to the hospital, hastily trampling through the snow while following a pair of tracks that were likely hers from the evening before. The sun was rising off to his right, and the rays of light hit his cheek with sobering harshness. Once inside the hospital, he searched every room and closet he could open, but found no sign of her and headed back home.

About halfway there, Ben noticed on the side of the road, where the curb rose up several inches beneath the snow, there was a dark piece of fabric that turned out to be a glove: a woman's glove he recognized as Andy's. A few feet away and nearly hidden by the snow was something small and green. Ben reached down into the hole and retrieved the item. It was a small, empty syringe.

Ben shoved the glove and syringe into his coat pocket as he examined the snow around him. There was a cluster of footprints of various sizes that stopped abruptly in the middle of the road where a few sets of tire tracks crisscrossed in both directions. Ben counted three different boot prints, including those he guessed to be Andy's.

Minutes later and out of breath, he was home. He went directly to Jim's room, knocked first, and when there was no answer, he darted down the hall to Morgan's room and just as he was about to knock on the door, Jim opened it.

"Good, you're awake."

"Yeah, we both are," Jim replied, looking back at Morgan, who was lying on her side on the bed and facing Ben. She held her bulging belly with one hand while using her other to push herself into a sitting position. She looked exhausted. Ben wasn't the only one who hadn't slept.

"Did you find her?" she asked, her voice heavy with worry.

Looking grave, he shook his head. "No. I think she's been kidnapped."

Chapter XIII

A monstrous headache greeted Andy when she woke. Her ears began to ring, and she immediately wished for her iPod to listen to her mother's cello music to make it stop. Then she opened her eyes.

She was lying on what felt like a carpet in a darkened room. There was a single window with light streaming in around the edges. When she slowly sat up, she found that her winter coat was gone, as was the sweater she had been wearing beneath it. Only her t-shift remained. Her jeans felt thick and heavy, as did her winter boots. She groped around with her hands until she felt the leg of a chair. Dizzy and disoriented, she pulled herself up. Her legs wobbled, and she fell onto the seat. She closed her eyes until the spinning lessened.

She moved unsteadily toward the windows and pulled aside the thick curtains. Warm air hit her face as she stared straight ahead at a crisp blue sky behind a tall, skinny tree. She blinked once—then twice—with the realization that it wasn't a snow-covered pine tree.

It was a palm tree.

"So you are accusing me of somehow *arranging* for Andy to be kidnapped? Is that what you are telling me?"

Brian, Ben, and Jim had practically stormed into Nataliya's home, all three of them armed and ready for a fight. They stood in the vast living room, the same room where Ben and Jim met her on that first day in Aspen nearly six months earlier.

Nataliya lounged casually on her plush sofa in an attempt to appear unaffected by either their forced presence or their accusations.

"Cut the crap, Nataliya. Tell us where she is!" Brian demanded.

"Get out of my house right now, or I will call the guards and force you out!" she yelled.

"I've already called them." The voice came from behind. It was Mikhail, descending the staircase with a self-satisfied sneer on his face. "They should be here any minute."

Ben lifted his rifle and aimed it directly at Nataliya. "The safety's off. Now tell us where Andy is."

Mikhail flew down the rest of the steps, but Brian held him back at gunpoint with his own rifle.

Seeing the object of her desire aim the barrel of a gun at her face rattled Nataliya, but she remained defiant. "I am not telling you anything. There is nothing to tell."

Ben moved the barrel a few inches to the right and pulled the trigger. The deafening shot landed squarely in the headrest of the sofa mere inches from Nataliya's head. She let out a piercing scream and retreated to the furthest corner of the sofa.

"I've got twenty-nine more," he said in a remarkably calm voice as he followed her movements. "And unless you tell me where Andy is, I swear the next one will draw blood."

Then, lowering his head, he lunged forward and shoved the end of the gun barrel into her chest.

"Are you crazy?" she cried out, her eyes wide with a mixture of fear and anger as she pressed her back hard into the sofa.

His eyes narrowed. He moved the pressure of the barrel from her chest to underneath her chin, pinning her in place. "At this moment…yeah, I probably am a little crazy, and I don't want to have to put a hole in that pretty face of yours, but I will. *Now answer me!*"

But Nataliya could say nothing. Any anger she'd felt had disappeared, and now her face reflected only fear. As tears pooled in her eyes, she slowly shook her head as if pleading with Ben to believe her. But he wanted answers, and someone in that room had them. His hand began to tremble on the trigger, until Mikhail suddenly burst out in a panic, "She doesn't know where Andy is!"

All eyes turned to him as Brian edged closer, nudging him with his own rifle. "But *you* do, don't you?"

Mikhail's cockiness had entirely vanished, and all that remained was a scared boy whose shoulders began to quiver.

"Tell us, Mikhail," Jim demanded evenly. "Tell us, and no one will get hurt."

"Traded?" Morgan shrieked. "She's been traded? What does that mean? Traded for what?"

"A kilo of cocaine," Ben replied bitterly.

"Cocaine!" she cried. "My best friend was taken for some…white powder? Petrol, maybe, or food. I could wrap my head around that, but bloody drugs? Are you kidding me?"

"She was taken west to Grand Junction," Ben continued wearily. "From there, she was sent somewhere else. She could be anywhere by now."

"Sent by whom?"

"People who trade and bargain for things," Jim answered. "This particular group operates out of Grand Junction, but they're just one link in a whole chain of people who do this. Apparently, Andy's medical skills were considered valuable enough to be worth a kilo of cocaine."

"So they don't just trade *stuff*, they trade people too? Who *does* that?" Morgan demanded from no one in particular.

"Can we find the people who took Andy?" Susan asked. "Did Mikhail tell you who they were?"

"We just know their names, but I'm going to Grand Junction tonight to find them," Ben declared. "I'll need gas, as much as you can give me," he asked Brian.

Brian hesitated, but eventually nodded.

Morgan, meanwhile, began to shake her head. "I can't stay here," she announced plainly. "I can't live down the street from people who traded Andy's life for some bloody drugs!"

"None of us should stay here. We made serious enemies today," said Ben. "If we don't leave soon, someone's going to get killed."

Jim looked up at his cousin. "You want me go with you to Grand Junction?"

"No, I'll go alone," Ben replied firmly.

A mixture of relief and doubt appeared on Jim's face, and before he could change his mind, Ben offered him and Morgan a suggestion. "You two should head back to New Mexico and meet up with Maria. She should still be there."

"Yeah, okay," she uttered faintly while straining to hold back tears.

Jim squeezed Morgan's hand. "What about you two?"

Brian and his sister exchanged glances. It was a question that they never thought they would have to answer, but the consequences of the day's events had changed everything. The fragile stability of their lives had been shattered.

"We'll stay here through the winter," Brian replied as he improvised a plan. "When spring arrives, we'll meet you. We can give our livestock to Scott."

"What about you?" Susan asked Charlie apprehensively.

Charlie eyed his sister's belly. Had Morgan not been pregnant, he may have answered differently, but instead he said, "I'll go with Morgan and Jim."

She smiled weakly. She understood. The situation had placed obligation over desire.

Andy stared out through the window. Beyond the palm tree was the ocean. Which ocean, however, she couldn't guess. The sound of the waves crashing below was faint but distinct. The salty air was a reminder of Bermuda.

The light from the window revealed that she was in a room with only the chair and a small table. Part of the room was a small bathroom, which she made use of. When she tried to flush the toilet, nothing happened so she put the lid down. She moved to the door and tried the handle, but it was locked from the outside. She then shook the handle in desperation and pounded on the door with her fist. She even tried kicking, but it refused to budge.

"Hey! Hey, open the door!" she cried out and pounded again.

A moment later, the door opened suddenly. With her arm in mid-swing, Andy stepped back, startled. A young man her own age stood before her. In his hands he carried a tray with food. She eyed the tray. She was starving.

"Where am I? Who are you?"

"Jeremy," the young man answered as he walked past her and into the room. He placed the tray on the table, then looked back. "You need to eat."

She hesitated. She wanted every bite of the food on the tray, but she wanted answers more. "Where am I?"

"Malibu," Jeremy answered. "Now eat."

"California?"

"Where else?"

She thought about bolting out the door but saw that Jeremy had a gun tucked into the waist of his jeans. So she obeyed his instructions and sat in the chair. As she began devouring a plate of fruit, Jeremy leaned against the wall and watched. When she finished, she gulped down an entire glass of water. After catching her breath, she asked, "Why am I here?"

He blinked, then said calmly, "You'll see."

She scoffed and glanced at the open door.

"Don't even think about it," he warned.

"Don't even think about what?"

But he said nothing. He was watching her intently.

Andy started to speak but stopped. Her eyelids were becoming very heavy. She looked at the empty glass, then back at Jeremy. "What did you give—?"

Before she could finish, she blacked out, her head landing on the tray.

Driving west on Interstate 70, Ben hoped to reach Grand Junction before nightfall. As the miles passed and the windshield wipers shoved wind-driven snow away, he forced his eyes to blink and regain focus on the road. The conditions were unforgiving. Ice coated the Interstate like a skating rink, and with no one to salt or plow the roads, the only hope was that the weather would give him a break, but his speedometer never went above 40 mph. He banged his hand against the steering wheel in frustration, and then scolded himself for getting so upset. Andy could be anywhere by now. Or she could be dead. "No," he said aloud. "She's not dead. No way." He turned up the volume on the CD player to drown out his thoughts and pressed down harder on the gas.

The snow eventually stopped, but nightfall had come. Grand Junction was dark and cold, and he had no idea where to begin. Mikhail had confessed a couple of names but nothing else. And without a soul in sight to ask, there was nothing to do but wait until morning. Even if he wanted to start knocking on people's doors, his body was too exhausted to try. He parked in a vacant strip mall and leaned his seat all the way back. After zipping up his coat, he closed his eyes. Within minutes, he was asleep.

Waking up at dawn, Ben immediately began his search for Jake Andrews and Kyle Hartzell. At the cashier's station of an abandoned Chinese restaurant in the strip mall, he found a phonebook for Grand Junction, as well as a detailed road map of the city and flipped through it, searching first under "Andrews." He found almost one hundred people listed with that last name. There was no way to know which home was Jake's since his name would not be in the phonebook–only his parents' names would be listed. So he then tried "Hartzell" and saw only three names. With any luck, Kyle might still be living at home.

After eating some food he'd brought from Aspen, Ben used the map to maneuver his way to the neighborhood where the first "Hartzell" in the phone book lived. This first address was empty, as was the second. Discouraged, he went to the third address and knocked on the door. This time, someone answered.

"Who are you?"

Ben looked down at the young girl. "Uh, does someone named Kyle live here?" he asked.

"Kyle's my brother."

"Can I talk to him?"

The girl turned back and called out her brother's name. Soon after, a young man appeared at the door. He looked to be a couple years younger than Ben and had a disheveled appearance. Under different circumstances, he was someone Ben probably would've avoided.

"What do you want?" he demanded in a hostile tone.

"Kyle? I need to talk to you," Ben said equally as aggressive. "You have a friend named Mikhail in Aspen, I think."

"So what do you want?"

"I want to know where you took a girl named Andy three days ago."

Kyle glanced at the rifle Ben was carrying and then wearily eyed his size and stature. "Come in," he said, backing away from the door. "You're letting in all the cold air."

Ben obeyed and entered the modest home. He followed Kyle into the kitchen. The sister remained in a small living room by the front door but was still in view of the kitchen. She picked up a doll and began playing with it but she kept her eyes on them.

"So how do you know Mikhail?" Ben began.

"Through my business," Kyle responded curtly.

"And what business is that?"

"I buy and trade things. That's how I keep my sister and I fed."

"By *things* do you also mean *people*?"

"Maybe."

"Well maybe you can tell me where you took Andy. Or where you sent her,"

Ben retorted with growing impatience.

"If I start telling the friends of the people that I trade where they are, that wouldn't be good for business, would it?" He spoke without remorse, leading Ben to believe that he'd done this before.

"So you won't tell me?"

Kyle stared at him with glassy eyes. "No," he grunted and walked into the living room. He took a seat across from his sister and lit up a joint. After exhaling a lengthy drag, he said to Ben, "I'll give you some pot if you get outta here."

Ben didn't respond. Instead he walked into the living room and briefly considered grabbing the sister and using her as leverage. But doing such a thing would make him no different than Kyle—or Mikhail. So he did the only thing left to do—he bargained.

"I'll tell you where you can find a ton of gas if you tell me where Andy is."

"How much gas?" Kyle replied, his interest piqued.

"More than you'll need for years."

There were boxes and brown paper bags everywhere in the living room, all taped and sealed to keep the contents inside well hidden. Things Kyle was probably trading, Ben assumed. He pointed to a particular stack of boxes. "There are some maps on top of that stack. Show me where this gas is, and I'll tell you where the girl is."

Ben retrieved a map of Colorado and spread it out on the cluttered coffee table in the center of the room. "If I show you," he began, "how will I know that you're telling me the truth about where she is?"

Kyle shrugged nonchalantly and exhaled more smoke. "You'll just have to trust me."

"I don't trust most people, especially…human traffickers."

"Take it or leave it, man."

Again, they seemed to be at an impasse. Kyle leaned back into the sofa, took another drag from his joint, and blew the smoke upwards. Ben looked over at the young girl with sympathy.

"Salt Lake City," he said, relenting.

"Where exactly?"

Kyle flipped over the map, which displayed neighboring Utah. Within the small inset at the bottom was a detailed map of Salt Lake City. He pointed to an intersection of two major roads south of the airport.

"I took her there, but she probably won't be there now. Merchandise moves fast."

Ben cringed at the word but said nothing. He turned the map back over to the Colorado side and kept his end of the bargain.

"Here, there's a small airport just south of this town. Glenwood Springs Municipal Airport. You'll find the gas there." He quickly left the house, taking the map without bothering to ask. After starting the engine, he caught sight of Kyle's sister running toward the truck. He rolled down the window. "What is it?"

"My brother lied," she said, catching her breath. "He didn't take her to Salt Lake City. He took her here." She held out a piece of paper.

Ben took it and read an address scribbled in black ink. "Los Angeles?" he muttered aloud before trying to calculate whether he had enough gas to get there.

"I'm sorry my brother lied to you. He lies to everyone."

He pulled his eyes off the paper and looked down at the girl. She was tiny for her age, though most children these days were malnourished. Her hair was parted into two long, stringy ponytails, and her round face was highlighted by bright green eyes. He looked at her with a mixture of gratitude and sadness. Gratitude for the enormous favor she'd just done him. Sadness that her brother was the kind of person he was.

"Thank you for telling me the truth…what's your name?"

"Amy. Was she your girlfriend? The girl my brother took?"

The question caught Ben off-guard. He blinked at first, and then slowly shook his head. "No, she's just a friend. A very good friend."

"I hope you find her."

"Me too."

Just as he was about to pull away, he looked back at the girl, hesitated, then put the truck into park. "You know, Amy, you don't have to stay here. I know a place where you can go and be with good people. Nice people who will help you."

She gave him a doubtful look. "I can't leave my brother, even if he is a liar and everything else. He's still my brother and he takes care of me."

"I understand," said Ben. "Take care, Amy."

As he drove off, he watched with sadness as the girl ran back to her house.

Chapter XIV

*A*fter being mostly unconscious for four days, Andy was fed a large meal. Jeremy again watched her eat. When she asked again what she was doing there, he kept silent. She picked up the glass of water, inspected it, and placed it back on the tray.

"It's just water. I promise," he said with a smirk. Then he retrieved a small handgun from inside the back pocket of his jeans and placed it on the small table next to the tray. It was the same type of pistol she'd left behind in Aspen. "It's not loaded, but you'll need it for tonight."

"What for?"

"You'll find out soon." He turned and left the room without another word.

A few minutes later, the door opened. It was him again, but this time two other men were with him. "It's time. Take your gun," he said.

"Time for what?"

He didn't answer and turned and walked away as the other two waited for her to exit the room. She eyed them as she passed but neither seemed to give her any notice. They walked behind her as she followed Jeremy through a short hallway and down a flight of stairs. They were in a vacant house. When Jeremy reached the front door, he opened it and said, "Get in the car."

Andy peered outside and saw a black Mercedes sitting in the driveway. "Where am I going?"

His face remained stoic. His eyes looked over at the two men, who grabbed her from behind and pulled her outside toward the car. They forced her into the backseat and then drove off.

Shaken, Andy stared numbly through her window as the Mercedes headed east from Malibu on the Santa Monica Freeway. The sun was descending over the horizon behind her in the rear window. At one point, she considered escaping by trying to convince herself that it wouldn't hurt to jump out of a moving vehicle going 70 mph.

"Where are we going? Please tell me!" she begged the men in the front, but neither threw her even a glance.

The Mercedes exited the freeway and headed south on I-110 for a brief moment before approaching the University of Southern California. After passing the campus on the right, they took another turn south. People were crowded everywhere on both sides of the road, and they all appeared to be moving toward the stadium.

Andy looked down at the pistol resting on the seat beside her. She picked it up and discreetly checked the chamber to see if indeed it was empty. It was. She tossed it back and watched helplessly as they got closer to the stadium. The car maneuvered its way around the south side before pulling into a gate. Throngs of people from every direction were moving toward the front entrance as though they were being drawn inside by some unseen force. Then suddenly, the Mercedes disappeared into a dark tunnel under the stadium. Moments later, it stopped.

"Get out," the driver ordered as the other man stepped outside and opened her door.

Her heart pounding, Andy sprang out of the car. Had the two men not been armed, she would've made a run for it, but as she stepped further into the underbelly of the stadium with a useless gun, she felt her chances of escape evaporating.

They reached the locker room formerly used by the opposing teams and went inside. With the exception of a single light bulb in the ceiling, the room was dark. There were seven other people; five were handcuffed and sitting on benches near the lockers and two standing over them with rifles keeping guard.

"Sit down," one of the armed men ordered, and she grudgingly obeyed. She took a seat at the end of a bench beside a frail boy who could not have been more than eleven or twelve.

The guard approached her with a pair of handcuffs, and before she could resist, he slapped them around her wrists. She looked up at him with defiance, but like the others, his face was expressionless.

"What time is it?" the other guard asked the one who had brought Andy from the car.

"Almost seven-thirty."

"Let's go grab a drink. We've got time."

The three men left the locker room and locked the door behind them, leaving Andy alone with the five other captives. She turned to the frail boy sitting next to her. "What's going on? What are we doing here?"

The boy's eyes remained fixed on the floor. His face was deathly pale and his forehead was sweating. She turned to the other four and saw the same catatonic expressions on their faces.

"Why am I here?" she asked the boy again, this time more softly.

"Shut up!" he snapped back violently.

Startled, she slowly inched away from him. Confused and scared, she looked at the others, imploring them with her eyes to explain. When no one even looked her way, she got up and moved to stand firmly in front of them. "Somebody better tell me what's going on, now!"

"Or what, you'll kill us? We're all dead already, you included. So please leave us alone."

She stared dumbfounded at the boy who had just spoken. He was less frail than the first, but still young. She eyed him with disbelief and slowly crouched down until her gaze met his.

"Please," she begged. "Until a few days ago, I'd never been to Los Angeles in my entire life. I don't know this city or anyone here. I was kidnapped from my home in Colorado and then I woke up and I was here, and I have no idea why. Can you please, *please* tell me what's going on?"

The boy stared back at her. Dark circles hung beneath his lifeless eyes. He blinked once, then twice before finally answering. "It's a game, and we're the losers."

"I don't understand…"

"It's called *One Shot* because we each get a bullet. Just one." Each of them would be taken up to the field where thousands of spectators would be waiting. One of several "referees" would load their pistol with a single bullet, and then they would be ordered to stand on the ten-yard line on the east end of the field while still handcuffed. Sixty yards down the field stood their opponent, but instead of a pistol with only one bullet, the opponent wore body armor and was given a fully-automatic rifle and multiple magazines of thirty rounds each. The goal of *One Shot* was brutally simple: who could kill the other first in two minutes. Both the competitor and the opponent were allowed to move around the field, but neither could cross the fifty-yard line at midfield. If the competitor survives these two minutes, they would play two more rounds, and if they survived the third round, they would be freed.

"How long has this been going on?"

"Every Saturday for more than a year."

"Has anyone ever survived the game?"

The boy gave her a look that required no further answer. But he said it anyway. "No. Never."

"Never?"

He said nothing more.

"And people come to watch other people die?"

He responded with the faintest shrug.

"But I don't understand. Who controls the game?"

But before she got an answer, the locker room door opened again and two guards returned. One pointed to the boy sitting on the bench that she had first spoken to.

"You're up."

He could hardly stand, and his knees buckled when he did. When he left the room, he didn't look back, and no one else seemed to react to the sound of the door locking shut after he left.

Minutes later, the noise of the crowd began to swell from above. It was interrupted by scattered rounds of gunfire, then silence. And then the crowd erupted. Andy looked at the four others in the room, but no one reacted to the noise. Instead, one sat praying, his eyes squeezed tight and his lips barely moving. Another rocked back and forth with his knees hugged to his chest. The boy who explained the game was now completely still, like a statue. He seemed to be the one most at peace with his fate.

Soon after, the door opened again, and the two guards returned. They gestured to the praying boy. "You're next."

The cycle repeated itself. Another competitor disappeared, followed shortly after by a wave of noise from the crowd, then gunshots, and then a burst of cheers. It was after this second cycle when Andy finally grasped the hopelessness of the situation, and she joined the remaining three boys in silent agony. She would die amidst the cheers of thousands of strangers who knew nothing about her, not even her name.

The third competitor was soon taken away, followed by the fourth. Only two people remained, Andy and the one who had spoken to her. As the noise from the crowd began to grow above them once again, her eyes frantically searched the room for something, anything, that could help her flee. She stood up and looked inside each of the lockers.

"You won't find anything."

"When they come back, we should try to make a run for it."

He shook his head. "They'll find us."

"Don't you want to live?"

His eyes met hers. His expression was resolute. "No, I'm ready to die. There's nothing worth living for anymore."

"You don't mean that. There's always something worth living for."

"Like what?"

"Like family. And friends."

"I don't have any. They're all dead or gone."

"You can make new friends."

"Not here."

"Then leave. Leave Los Angeles."

He shook his head firmly. "No, it's too late. It's time to go."

The locker room door abruptly opened and the guards entered to retrieve yet another victim. One of them looked at the boy and said, "I hope you last longer than the others. The crowd isn't too happy with the performances tonight."

The boy slowly rose from the bench and walked toward the door with more dignity than the previous four combined. Before disappearing through the doorway, he looked back at Andy one last time. "I'll see you soon."

The door slammed shut, leaving her alone with the echo of those words.

Ben pushed his way through the crowd to get as close to the field as he could. He'd missed witnessing the first competitor getting slaughtered, though he had heard the roars from the crowd several blocks away.

Every spectator entered the stadium through a single gate on the western side of the Coliseum, and everyone was checked for weapons by one of dozens of heavily armed men and women. Though the evening was unseasonably warm, even by Los Angeles standards, Ben wore a baggy sweatshirt over his T-shirt. He needed someplace to conceal his rifle, which he had separated into its two main components. One half was jammed into his right sleeve and other in his left. Stuffed into each sock was a thirty-round magazine. When he passed through the gate, one of the entry guards asked him to lift up his sweatshirt, which he did without hesitation. Satisfied and anxious to let the remaining stragglers through, the guard quickly waved him off without a second look. Once beyond the entrance, he scrambled to a secluded corner beneath the stadium in the perimeter outside the numbered gates and quickly reassembled his weapon. He removed his sweatshirt and inserted one magazine before concealing the weapon by wrapping the sweatshirt around it.

Inside, the entire eastern half of the stadium was empty, the reason for this became clear when Ben saw the fifth competitor take his position on the field as two minutes on the scoreboard began its countdown: the opponent rained bullets eastward as the competitor ran frantically back and forth. Many of the bullets became lodged into the steps behind the end zone below the long-extinguished Olympic Torch. The single nine-millimeter round in the competitor's Glock posed little threat to the spectators, for rarely did the competitor get a chance to fire before being gunned down.

Standing now on the southwest side of the stadium, thirteen rows up from the fifteen-yard line, Ben had a good vantage point of the field and the opponent. He arrived in time to see the fifth competitor become yet another victim as several bullets entered the boy's torso. Flinching, he turned to a bystander as the body was dragged off the field. "How many so far?"

"Five," the bystander replied as the noise of the crowd began to die down.

"All boys?"

"Yeah, but I heard there's supposed to be a girl tonight. I think she's the last one, so she's probably next."

Suddenly, the crowd began to make noise as the next and final competitor stepped onto the field. Though she was more than a hundred yards away, Ben could tell instantly by her stature and gait that it was Andy.

Chapter XV

*A*fter passing through the end of the dark and dingy tunnel, Andy emerged onto the field and was greeted by the jeering crowd. In the distance, the latest victim of "One Shot" was being dragged off by two of the referees. As she crossed the field, she passed her opponent who was waiting for her to get into position. Tall and broad-shouldered, he gave her a cold look of indifference before reloading his weapon.

Her heart was pounding so fast that she could feel the blood pulse through her head, her neck, and even the arteries in her wrists. The noise of the crowd behind her was thunderous. Her eardrums were not accustomed to the onslaught, and a sudden flash of her discussion with Morgan months earlier in New Mexico resurfaced.

Where could everyone be?

Everyone was in Los Angeles, where more than fifty thousand people had flocked to the Coliseum and were now cheering in anticipation of her death.

Daylight was long gone, but the lights of the stadium kept the field well lit. As she approached midfield, Andy swore she heard someone calling out her name. Her eyes darted all around, but there were too many people. Or her nerves had tricked her hearing. In her right hand still handcuffed to her left, she held the pistol. A referee approached her and snatched it out of her hands. As he placed one round in the chamber, her eyes narrowed on him with a mixture of contempt and disbelief.

room where Ben and Jim met her on that first day in Aspen nearly six months earlier.

Nataliya lounged casually on her plush sofa in an attempt to appear unaffected by either their forced presence or their accusations.

"Cut the crap, Nataliya. Tell us where she is!" Brian demanded.

"Get out of my house right now, or I will call the guards and force you out!" she yelled.

"I've already called them." The voice came from behind. It was Mikhail, descending the staircase with a self-satisfied sneer on his face. "They should be here any minute."

Ben lifted his rifle and aimed it directly at Nataliya. "The safety's off. Now tell us where Andy is."

Mikhail flew down the rest of the steps, but Brian held him back at gunpoint with his own rifle.

Seeing the object of her desire aim the barrel of a gun at her face rattled Nataliya, but she remained defiant. "I am not telling you anything. There is nothing to tell."

Ben moved the barrel a few inches to the right and pulled the trigger. The deafening shot landed squarely in the headrest of the sofa mere inches from Nataliya's head. She let out a piercing scream and retreated to the furthest corner of the sofa.

"I've got twenty-nine more," he said in a remarkably calm voice as he followed her movements. "And unless you tell me where Andy is, I swear the next one will draw blood."

Then, lowering his head, he lunged forward and shoved the end of the gun barrel into her chest.

"Are you crazy?" she cried out, her eyes wide with a mixture of fear and anger as she pressed her back hard into the sofa.

His eyes narrowed. He moved the pressure of the barrel from her chest to underneath her chin, pinning her in place. "At this moment…yeah, I probably am a little crazy, and I don't want to have to put a hole in that pretty face of yours, but I will. *Now answer me!*"

But Nataliya could say nothing. Any anger she'd felt had disappeared, and now her face reflected only fear. As tears pooled in her eyes, she slowly shook her head as if pleading with Ben to believe her. But he wanted answers, and someone in that room had them. His hand began to tremble on the trigger, until Mikhail suddenly burst out in a panic, "She doesn't know where Andy is!"

All eyes turned to him as Brian edged closer, nudging him with his own rifle. "But *you* do, don't you?"

Mikhail's cockiness had entirely vanished, and all that remained was a scared boy whose shoulders began to quiver.

"Tell us, Mikhail," Jim demanded evenly. "Tell us, and no one will get hurt."

"Traded?" Morgan shrieked. "She's been traded? What does that mean? Traded for what?"

"A kilo of cocaine," Ben replied bitterly.

"Cocaine!" she cried. "My best friend was taken for some…white powder? Petrol, maybe, or food. I could wrap my head around that, but bloody drugs? Are you kidding me?"

"She was taken west to Grand Junction," Ben continued wearily. "From there, she was sent somewhere else. She could be anywhere by now."

"Sent by whom?"

"People who trade and bargain for things," Jim answered. "This particular group operates out of Grand Junction, but they're just one link in a whole chain of people who do this. Apparently, Andy's medical skills were considered valuable enough to be worth a kilo of cocaine."

"So they don't just trade *stuff*, they trade people too? Who *does* that?" Morgan demanded from no one in particular.

"Can we find the people who took Andy?" Susan asked. "Did Mikhail tell you who they were?"

"We just know their names, but I'm going to Grand Junction tonight to find them," Ben declared. I'll need gas, as much as you can give me," he asked Brian.

Brian hesitated, but eventually nodded.

Morgan, meanwhile, began to shake her head. "I can't stay here," she announced plainly. "I can't live down the street from people who traded Andy's life for some bloody drugs!"

"None of us should stay here. We made serious enemies today," said Ben. "If we don't leave soon, someone's going to get killed."

Jim looked up at his cousin. "You want me go with you to Grand Junction?"

"No, I'll go alone," Ben replied firmly.

A mixture of relief and doubt appeared on Jim's face, and before he could change his mind, Ben offered him and Morgan a suggestion. "You two should

"You like watching people die? Haven't you seen enough death?"

The referee smirked as he handed her back her pistol and quickly returned to the sidelines.

Alone amongst thousands, Andy looked up at the scoreboard. It still read "00:58" from the end of the previous round. She moved slowly past midfield, her heart pumping two hundred beats a minute.

This is how I die...

Her palms were sweating profusely, and she switched the pistol from her right hand to her left to dry her trigger hand on the jeans she'd been wearing for four days.

I will die in these clothes...these dirty jeans, this filthy shirt...my hands bound together like an animal...

As her palm pressed firmly against the right front pocket, she felt something small and hard by the outer seam. As she continued her death march to the ten-yard line, she reached inside and retrieved a small object. When she looked to see what it was, she stopped. It was a single bullet. She had shoved it into her pocket during her last hunting trip in Colorado, where it had remained hidden.

The tiny object created such an intense spark of hope as an idea formed in her mind. Careful not to be seen by one of the referees, she stuck the bullet inside her mouth underneath her tongue. Then she marched, more quickly now, to her position on the ten-yard line.

Before turning to face her opponent and the surrounding crowd, she closed her eyes and took a deep breath. When she opened her eyes and saw the scoreboard, it read "02:00."

As Andy crossed the fifty-yard line, the noise of the crowd swelled. Ben cried out her name three times before giving up. His view of the field was blocked as people's arms started flailing about. Frantic, he shoved his way between the spectators to get closer to the field, but the first four rows were packed so tightly that it was impossible to go any further.

With time running out, Ben made a split-second decision and scrambled toward the aisle and up the staircase to a less crowded row. He shot a quick look at the press box above him and saw that there were people inside. Probably the unseen controllers of the game. While crossing from Section 9 to 8, he saw Andy approach the ten-yard line. There wasn't enough time. He weaved through the crowd to Section 7, cursing at people who refused to move.

The scoreboard flickered "02:00."

He escaped to the outer edge of the crowd at midfield. As he turned and bounded down the stairs dividing Section 7 in half, he heard the first shot of gunfire, then many more in rapid succession. A riotous roar exploded from the crowd. Panicking, he looked up and saw Andy lying on the ground, unmoving.

Collapsing to the ground as his rifle fell beside him, Ben's shoulders slumped and began to quiver.

When the first shot went off, Andy bolted to the right, immediately aimed at the opponent, and released her single round. She continued to sprint as a burst of fire flew at her. A bullet grazed her back, but adrenaline masked any pain. She fell to the ground, rolled over once in the overgrown grass, and came to a stop on her right side.

As the crowd roared, she maneuvered the bullet inside her mouth and spat it out. With the pistol still in her right hand, she retrieved the bullet with her left. She discreetly exposed the gun's chamber and inserted the bullet.

She sensed someone approaching but forced her eyes to stare straight ahead into a dead-man's gaze. Out of the corner of her eye, she saw feet approaching. It had to be the opponent, the large, husky young man. He was within yards of her now.

Not yet...

Two more steps...

Wait...wait...

Then like a jack-in-the-box, she sprung upright and faced her opponent squarely and so quickly that he didn't react. Her arms were already outstretched with the front sight of the pistol aimed directly at his forehead. She pulled the trigger.

The sound of the bullet shattered the drone of the crowd.

The opponent flew violently backward and fell to the ground with an audible thud. The shot had struck right between the eyes.

A strange silence fell over the stadium. Even she sat frozen for a long moment, her arms still holding the pistol in the same position she'd fired it. A voice inside her head urged her to move. She scrambled to her feet, awkwardly tucked the pistol into the side of her jeans, and grabbed the rifle lying next to the dead man.

Suddenly, gunfire erupted off to her left, disrupting her tunnel vision. Her head spun wildly around.

"Andy!"

The sound of her name was jarring until she realized it was Ben heading toward her after he mortally wounded two referees to reach her. He grabbed her left arm and pulled her toward the end zone behind her, but the sight of him paralyzed her.

"Ben! What...?" she stammered.

But there was no time. He yanked at her arm again more forcefully. "Run, Andy! Run!"

Regaining her senses, her feet began to move, and she followed closely behind him as he ran under the goal post and up the steps leading to the center arch beneath the Olympic Rings.

The remaining referees ran after them as the unruly crowd began spilling over the sides of the barrier and onto the field. They scrambled up the steps as the referees began firing after them with their own weapons, each widely missing his mark. At the top of the steps, Ben continued to sprint beyond the outer gate with Andy only mere strides behind. He looked back once to check that she was keeping up with him.

At the top of the steps was a locked gate with a single padlock. Ben took aim and fired at it twice, but it remained intact. "Dammit!" he growled before firing once more. The lock broke and he shoved the gate open.

Andy looked back and saw the shadows of people reaching the top of the steps. "Go!" she yelled. More shots were fired as they ran through a cluster of trees off to their left, concealing them briefly in the darkness.

They sprinted nearly a mile, weaving through the streets of the campus until they reached Ben's truck. Minutes later, they were heading north on I-110 and exiting onto the San Bernardino Freeway. Finally safe, the city passed by them in the dark. Neither spoke for many miles. They turned north onto I-15 and left the City of Angels behind.

"Are you hurt?" Ben asked.

"No...no, I'm fine," said Andy.

Her voice was flat and barely above a whisper. She was staring down at her hands as an uncontrollable barrage of visions began to fill her head, and when she closed her eyes, she saw herself pulling the trigger, her opponent flying backward. She heard the boy's voice saying to her, *I'll see you soon.*

"I thought you got shot."

At the sound of Ben's voice, Andy opened her eyes and stared straight ahead as the truck's high beams illuminated the darkness of the highway just before it enveloped them.

"No. Faked it."

But as she said this, Ben turned to her and saw in the dim light a bloodstain on her back near her shoulder. "Are you sure?"

He glanced once at the road before taking a closer look. A nearly four-inch square section of her T-shirt was soaked with blood. He reached for it with his right hand, but she jerked away the moment he touched her.

"Sorry, sorry," he repeated, pulling his hand away.

Shaking now, she looked over her left shoulder. She couldn't see anything, so she reached behind with both hands, as they were still cuffed, and winced as her finger hit the wound.

"Let me stop so I can get a better look," he said as he began to slow down.

"No, keep going. It's nothing."

But he was already applying the brakes. He didn't bother pulling onto the shoulder. No one else was on the road.

"I said it's nothing," she insisted.

"You don't know that, you can't see it."

Andy sighed with annoyance but kept quiet as Ben put the truck into park and turned on the overhead light. Then he carefully pulled downward at the collar of her T-shirt, but this only caused further pain.

"Here, lift up your shirt in the back."

She gave him a look.

"C'mon, I just want to make sure there's not a bullet lodged in your shoulder."

Agitated, she pulled her T-shirt completely over her head so that she was wearing only her bra. She groaned.

"You didn't have to pull it over your head."

"Just look at it already!"

With one hand, Ben brushed her long hair away from the wound and gently felt around her shoulder with the other. Andy tensed beneath his hands from the pain, but she remained still and didn't make a sound.

"It's just a graze. A deep graze, but that's all. You'll have a scar."

She heard the relief in his voice, but he still insisted on treating the wound right then. She made no objection and even began to relax as he used the contents of the first aid kit he kept behind the seat to clean out the gash and cover it with gauze.

"That'll do for now. We'll change it when we get to Santa Rosa."

"Santa Rosa?" Andy repeated as she put her shirt back on.

Ben got the truck moving again before answering. "We left Aspen after you got taken. No one could stay once we found out that Mikhail and Garrett had traded you for drugs."

"Drugs? They traded me for drugs?"

He nodded and then turned to his left and muttered, "Everyone wants drugs."

"So Morgan and Charlie are in New Mexico?"

"By now, yeah. Jim, too. They're meeting up with Maria."

"What about Brian and Susan?"

"They're staying in Aspen through the winter. They'll join us in the spring."

"What about their farm? They'll just leave it behind?"

"Yes. They'll leave it behind."

"Poor Brian. That farm means so much to him," she murmured.

With this remark, Ben slammed on the brakes until the truck came to an abrupt stop once again on the dark, lonely stretch of I-15. Andy let out a yelp as her body flew forward, straining the seat belt across her chest.

"Poor Brian? Poor *Brian*? Are you *kidding* me?"

"What the hell...?" she snapped back as she steadied herself.

He turned off the engine before squaring his body to hers. He grabbed the shoulder of her seat, leaned forward, and stared into her eyes. "Andy, I just spent the last two days and nights running after you. Do you have any idea how difficult it was to find you? Do you know what kind of people I had to beg information from?"

"So what? You want a gold star or something? I just spent the last *four* days in a tiny room while being drugged just so that I could end up shot to death like a wild animal in front of thousands of crazy people!" Her voice had become hysterical, but she didn't stop. "And now you expect me to *thank* you? For what? For saving me? Well, guess what, Ben! *I* saved me...*I* did! *I* shot that guy right between the eyes! *I* killed him!"

As she spat out these last words, she pointed to her chest with both of her constrained hands for emphasis. Then she threw herself back against her seat, forgetting her shoulder wound, and yelped in pain. Ben started to reach out to her, but she turned away and curled into a ball.

"Just drive, Ben," she mumbled dully as she shut her eyes, spilling tears down her cheeks. "Just drive."

But he made no move to obey. Instead, he remained quite still and gazed at her and then out the windshield for a long moment. "When I saw you fall to the ground on the field, I thought that was it. I thought you were dead, and it…" He didn't finish.

Andy remained still and made no sound of acknowledgment. Ben looked and saw the rise and fall of her ribcage. She was already asleep. She hadn't heard him.

He released a sigh and put the truck back into drive.

When Andy awoke, she noticed the truck wasn't moving. After blinking her eyes open, she glanced at the clock on the dashboard. It read 4:07. She rolled over and saw that Ben had pulled to the side of the road to take a nap. His seat was reclined as far as it would go, and he was lying on his back with his arms crossed over his chest. His face was turned slightly toward her.

A wave of guilt struck her as she lamented her earlier words to him. He was the last person who deserved her anger. He had traveled alone across hundreds of miles. And had found her. She should have thanked and hugged him a thousand times for dragging her off the field and getting her out of the city alive. Instead, she had scorned him for not reaching her sooner.

Tenderly, she reached toward him until the rattle of her handcuffs made her withdraw. She turned away and opened the door to step outside. Her legs ached and her hunger and thirst were overwhelming. She glanced back and forth along the dark, abandoned highway before shutting the door. The sound woke Ben, and by the time she walked around the front of the truck and opened the driver's door, he was already rubbing his eyes.

"I'll drive if you want to sleep," she offered.

He looked up at her and bobbed his head drowsily.

He stepped outside and started to move by her when she grabbed his arm. "Wait." She threw her encumbered arms over his head. "Thank you," she whispered into his ear and hugged him tightly. "Thank you for finding me."

He gently pulled her head toward him and kissed the top of her head.

"I almost died," she said into his chest.

"I know."

Abruptly, she pulled away and slipped into the driver's seat. "Let's get moving," she said crisply in an effort to push back more tears. "Is there any food and water?"

"Uh, yeah. There's a bag behind the seat." He walked to the other side of the truck and climbed in. "You must be starving."

"More than I can ever remember."

They drove in silence as Ben fell back asleep. Andy was wide-awake. It was as though all her senses had been suddenly heightened. The wound in her shoulder throbbed, but strangely, it didn't bother her. It reminded her that she was still alive.

The first mile marker she noticed read "157," and shortly after that, she saw signs for Grand Canyon National Park. She glanced at Ben and checked the gas gauge. He and Jim had recalibrated it to reflect the two additional tanks that had been added. The needle currently stood at just over half a tank, which really meant that more than a tank and a half of gas remained, not including the full containers in the truck bed. She knew it would be a frivolous waste of a rare commodity, but the image of the boy leaving the locker room and his haunting last words echoed again in her mind.

Screw it.

When the truck reached the exit for Route 64 heading north, she took it.

Andy heard the sound of tiny rocks shifting as Ben's footsteps approached.

"Is that what I think it is?" he said as he drew up beside her.

"It's amazing, isn't it?" she whispered, her eyes fixed on the majestic view. "My mom always talked about bringing me here."

Ben watched Andy as she spoke. The gentle morning wind played with her hair, the red-orange light reflecting off her glowing cheeks.

"After she died, my dad asked me if I wanted to come here that summer… the summer of the virus, but I didn't want to go without her. So we went to Bermuda instead." She looked down at her foot and kicked at a rock, let out a tiny laugh, and said, "My mother travelled all over the world for her concerts, but the one place she really wanted to come was here, and now I understand why." Then looking over at Ben for the first time, "Have you ever been here before?"

He shook his head. "No. Just pictures."

"Not the same."

"Not even close."

They stared at a view that once drew millions.

"Wish I still had my old phone to take a picture," said Ben. "Even if a picture isn't the same."

"I never had a phone. My parents said an iPod was enough."

"You didn't feel left out?"

"What, texting?" She shook her head. "I didn't have many friends to text anyway."

Ben turned away from the view and looked behind him. Andy had driven off the visitor's parking lot and onto the sidewalks that lead directly to the lookout named Mather Point. "Are the keys in the truck?"

"Yeah. I left them in the ignition."

"Is there some kind of welcome center or something like that?"

"Yeah, it's right back there." She gestured toward the direction with her head.

"I'll be right back."

When Ben returned, Andy was sitting on the large slab of stone at the observation point, her gaze fixed on the view. "I hit the jackpot," he said as he approached carrying a plastic bag.

"Yeah? What'd you find?"

"Trail mix and dried fruit in the gift shop. There were bottles of water too, but all plastic."

Over the years, the chemicals in the plastic broke down and contaminated the water, making it undrinkable. Glass-bottled water was like gold, and finding any left was rare. Trail mix and dried fruit, however, never really went bad, despite what the expiration date read. The taste would be stale, but it kept a person alive.

Ben dropped the bag of food on the ground as Andy slid off the slab and met him at the rail that ran around the perimeter of the observation point. It was no longer stable.

"Just don't lean on it," he warned.

They stood watching the sunrise as the light danced off the vastness of the landscape.

"How did you know where to find me?"

He smiled sheepishly, and Andy was once again struck by how handsome he was.

"I didn't. It was total dumb luck. The address in Los Angeles I was given turned out to be a dead end. But then some random people told me about the stadium, so I took a stab in the dark and went there. If it hadn't been for them, I would've missed you."

"But you didn't. You found me and got me out of there."

"I might've gotten you out of there, but you shot the guy on the field. How did you do it? I thought you only got one bullet."

"There was a bullet in my pocket from one of our hunting trips. I found it when I got to the field."

He turned away and shook his head. "Unbelievable. But why didn't you just shoot him with the first bullet?"

"Because I wanted him to think that I didn't have anything left to kill him." Then, after a pause, "I also suspected that the first bullet was a blank."

"You think so?"

"Yeah, why not? Whoever controls that game doesn't actually want anyone to win, so why risk using a real bullet when no one can tell the difference from a blank."

"You can tell from the recoil. Did it feel different?"

"Honestly, it's all a blur to me. My heart was racing so fast…I barely remember anything."

"Well, it was a hell of a shot you made. I couldn't believe it when I saw you sit up and fire it off."

"Me neither." She looked down at her feet and kicked at another stone. "I'll still never get used to the idea that I've killed people."

"You'd be dead if you hadn't shot that guy."

"I know. I'm not sorry about it, but it's still weird knowing that I'm actually capable of doing it."

"You ever kill anyone before? Besides that one time in DC?"

"No, never. I don't think it's something I ever *want* to get used to."

"You shouldn't ever want to get used it, but you may have to do it again someday."

Andy nodded vaguely but said nothing further about it. She didn't want to talk about death or killing anymore. "You know, if it hadn't actually happened to me, I would've never believed it."

"Believed what?"

"Everything that's happened these past few days. And now standing at the edge of the Grand Canyon, miles away from anyone. It's just so unreal." She turned to Ben with a frown. "I don't know what to expect anymore. I mean, there was never any explanation for why I ended up at the stadium. It seemed like something that happened all the time…kids being forced onto the field like that for some sick entertainment."

"That's anarchy," he remarked solemnly. "The strong prey on the weak."

"So nowhere is safe?"

"Nowhere I've been."

She looked back at the view. "You don't think things will ever change, do you?"

He cast her a sideways glance. "No, I don't. Nothing I've seen so far makes me believe anything will be like it was again."

There was not a hint of doubt in his voice, but she still challenged him. "I think deep down, most people want to be safe and have some kind of order in their lives. Look at all the people in Aspen who wanted it, and except for Nataliya and her friends screwing it up, it worked."

"Just because somewhere seems nice and organized doesn't mean it is. Nataliya and her friends were the ones running Aspen despite how many others were really trying to make it work. We're all fighting our own DNA. We're programmed to be selfish and look after ourselves and do whatever it takes to survive, no matter what."

"I disagree," she replied, crossing her arms across her chest. "If human beings weren't meant to live together peacefully, we would've been extinct long ago."

"I'm not saying it's impossible for people to live in peace again, but I don't think it'll happen in our lifetime. We're back in the Dark Ages. The first Dark Age lasted, what, a thousand years?"

Andy pursed her lips together disapprovingly. "Well, if you keep thinking that way, you'll become a victim of your own expectations."

Tired of arguing, Ben motioned toward the truck. "Let's get going," he said. "Everyone's worried about you."

"Yeah, okay." She took one last look at the Canyon before turning away with a touch of sadness. "Too bad we can't just stay here," she said wistfully as they drove off.

Ben glanced down at her hands and gave her wrist a gentle squeeze. "We'll get those things off you as soon as we get back."

Andy grimaced at the handcuffs on her wrists.

Chapter XVI

Spring 2023

*I*n Santa Rosa, the comforts of life in Aspen were grudgingly forgotten. Gone were the large heated homes, the hot showers, and the grocery store with its fresh food. The people they had grown to care for were missed as well, and Andy regretted that she never had the chance to say goodbye. But no one was more missed than Brian and Susan. Their arrival was anxiously awaited.

Everyone busied themselves with work similar to what they had done in Aspen, though performing each task now seemed more arduous. Without the camaraderie that came with building and maintaining a community, work had become tedious and more exhausting.

During the last week in February, Andy sensed Morgan becoming increasingly nervous as the birth of her child loomed. According to their calculations, her due date was around the first of March.

Morgan had accepted the idea of delivering an infant with all the uncertainties of this new world, but as the event approached, she began to panic. "How will I feed it? There's barely enough food for us."

"All you need to know is that this baby will have not just you, but all of us. We'll all love this child like it's our own," Andy assured her.

In the early morning hours on the second of March, Morgan delivered a healthy baby girl after ten hours of grueling labor. The infant was named Kathryn. Everyone called her "Katie."

Katie had delicate features, wide brown eyes, and the finest of brown hair on her fragile head. Though no one ever said as much, it was a relief that she resembled Morgan so much and that there was no visible sign of the father's degenerate genes.

Andy was relieved beyond words that her friend had safely reached the end of the nine-month ordeal that had begun so violently the summer before. The birth had been difficult, but Morgan had pulled through unscathed. Now everyone enjoyed seeing a new life grow and change right before their eyes.

May 2023

One night in late spring, there was a sharp knock at the front door. Andy was the first to hear it, so she quickly rose out of bed before a second knock could wake Katie. As she made her way through the house with her flashlight, she heard the soft pitter-patter of rain hitting the roof. She grabbed her pistol from a drawer in the kitchen and checked that it was loaded. As she leaned in toward the door to look through the peephole, there was another loud knock that made her jump back several feet.

"Jesus!" she hissed in the dark before leaning in once more to take a good look. In the moonlight, she could make out two figures wearing raincoats with hoods over their heads. As one turned sideways, she recognized Susan's profile.

"Susan!" she gasped and fumbled with the lock before finally getting the door open.

"Well, it's about time!" Brian exclaimed as he stepped inside. Andy quickly put her index finger to her lips to silence him. She was smiling, however, and when it registered who had greeted him, his eyes grew wide.

"Oh my God…Andy? You're…you're here? How…?"

"Shh." She gestured for him to come inside and placed her gun on the kitchen table.

Susan followed her brother and expressed the same shock. "We thought we'd never see you again," she said too loudly.

Once again, Andy put her finger to her lips. "I know. But right now we have to be quiet."

"Oh, sorry," Susan whispered. "Is everyone asleep?"

"Morgan and Jim are…and Katie, the baby."

"Oh!" Susan cupped her hands over her mouth. "Morgan had a girl? What's she like?"

"She's adorable. Now keep your coats on. Let's go across the street and we'll talk. I'm sure Charlie will want to see you anyway. He and Ben are staying over there."

Susan smiled in the darkness, flashing her teeth, and in seconds she was back outside. Brian, however, still couldn't believe Andy was there. "What happened to you?"

She didn't answer and instead gestured once more toward the door, but he shook his head. "I'm exhausted. You go across the street with Susan. I think I'll just fall asleep right here on this couch."

Without waiting for permission, Brian moved into the living room and removed his coat before plopping down on the couch. He kicked off his wet shoes and laid his head on a pillow.

Andy tiptoed upstairs to retrieve a spare blanket and found him already asleep by the time she returned. She gently placed the blanket over him before putting on her coat. Susan was waiting outside.

"Your brother looks exhausted."

"He's just been fighting a cold."

"He's already asleep on the couch."

"I'm not surprised. He drove the whole way here, and it rained almost the whole time."

The rain was steady so they dashed across the street. Andy knocked on the front door. When Charlie opened it, a wide grin spread across his face.

"Took you long enough!" was all he said before launching through the doorway to give Susan a long embrace.

❦

The next morning began with introductions. Maria and her siblings finally met the friends they had been hearing about for more than four months, and Katie was introduced to Brian and Susan.

"Oh my God, she's so cute!" Susan squealed as Katie clenched onto her pinky with her tiny hand as Morgan beamed.

"What are things in Aspen like?" Andy asked Brian.

"It got much worse after you all left. We stopped having council meetings, and every day more people were talking about their stuff getting stolen. Everyone kept coming by to ask us where you'd all gone. I swear, in all the years living on that farm, we never had so many people dropping by to visit. I think they wanted to know if you'd found somewhere better to live."

"Then the day before we left, Garrett and Heath showed up and threatened to shoot our cattle if we tried to take them with us," Susan added while bouncing Katie in her arms. "We lied and said we weren't leaving but they didn't buy it. Then Mikhail showed up and said he'd kill us if we didn't give them our cattle right then."

"The whole world has officially gone mad," said Morgan.

"What's worse is that they'll end up killing those animals because they have no clue how to take care of them," Brian lamented.

"If things were so bad, why did you wait so long to come?" Charlie asked.

"Because winter lasted forever this year and the snow didn't melt off the roads until last week," Susan replied.

"Well, at least you made it. That's all that matters."

Later, Maria invited everyone to her home for dinner, and as before, the meal was fresh and home-cooked. How she accomplished this remained a mystery, but no one bothered to question it when their stomachs rumbled with hunger.

A week after her twentieth birthday, Andy took a break one evening from reading a medical book that Charlie had rescued from Aspen and went across the street to talk to Ben. He was tinkering around with Maria's truck, which had been giving her problems for a while. "How's it going?" she asked.

Ben looked up from under the hood. His hands were covered in grease, and he was sweating. The truck's stereo was on, playing rock music from the CD player. She recognized the song but the name of the band had slipped her mind.

"I should be done soon. Her timing belt needed to be replaced."

"Is that difficult to do?"

He shook his head. "The first few times, maybe, but now it's like changing a light bulb."

"I'll take your word for it. What band is this?"

He took a swig of water from a thermos and wiped his mouth with the back of his hand. "Def Leppard. My dad listened to them a lot growing up."

"So did mine, I think."

The sun was beginning to set, and they watched it descend behind the row of homes on their street. Ben started to say something when he saw his own truck make a turn onto their street and head toward them. "Good, they're back. I'm starving," he said as he wiped his hands off with an old rag and shut the hood of Maria's car.

Charlie, Brian, and Jim had gone hunting. As the truck approached, two extra people could be seen riding in the back.

"I thought this town was empty," Andy said as the vehicle drew near. Ben's eyes followed hers.

The truck pulled up to the curb beside the house and Jim hopped out of the back before it completely stopped. Carrying a hunting rifle, he marched directly toward Ben. "Don't worry, I checked them for weapons," he muttered under his breath.

Andy heard the words and her eyes darted to the two strangers. They were older boys, each carrying a large backpack as they stepped out of the truck. Along with their scruffy appearance, they wore expressions of fatigue and hunger.

"Thanks, you have no idea how grateful we are," one of them said to Andy after she returned from the house with two large glasses of water. They emptied the glasses within seconds.

Their names were Kevin and Matt. Their car had run out of gas fifteen miles east of Santa Rosa, and they'd been wandering west on I-40 when Jim and the others came across them on their way home.

"Wait, Ben? Ben and Jim?" Matt pointed back and forth between the two cousins after introductions.

"Yeah?" Ben replied wearily after a moment's hesitation.

"Your last names aren't 'Kelly,' are they?"

Ben and Jim exchanged the quickest of looks before Jim took one step back and raised his rifle until the barrel was pointed directly at Matt. "Who are you?" he demanded as both of the boys' hands shot up in the air.

"Whoa, whoa! We're not looking for you two, believe me," Kevin pleaded.

"Yeah, the reward's not *that* good. Besides, we're unarmed. If we were hunting you, we'd have guns."

"So if you're not looking for us, what are you doing here?" Ben challenged.

"We're just trying to get to Phoenix," Kevin replied. "We both had family there and wanted to know if they're still there."

"Where were you before? New York? Philly?"

"New York. Brooklyn."

"Why aren't you two armed?" Jim asked as he lowered the barrel of his rifle slightly.

"We were, but our guns were stolen from us when we were sleeping one night in a campground in Missouri, along with all our food."

Suddenly, Morgan could be heard shouting, "Grub's up!" from across the street, alerting everyone that dinner was ready. Holding a squirming Katie, she emerged from the house and began heading toward them until she saw Jim holding a gun in front of two people she'd never seen before. She stopped dead in her tracks and twisted her torso to shield her child.

"It's okay!" Jim called out to her.

"Who's that?" Matt asked with curiosity. "And what's with the baby?"

"Just neighbors," Jim quickly responded.

"So why did you guys leave New York now?" Ben asked, putting the questions back on the two strangers.

Kevin looked away as he brushed his fingers through his hair. "Yeah, well, it's gotten worse...much worse."

"You probably won't believe this, but Sean's still got the virus, and he's still using it," Matt said.

More confused than ever, Andy watched as Ben and Jim give each other stunned looks.

Shutting his eyes and shaking his head as if he couldn't believe what he had just heard, Ben finally blurted out, "What are you talking about? How...?"

"Sorry, man...what you and Jim did at the laboratory last year was legendary, but you didn't destroy it all," Matt replied apologetically.

"It's true," Kevin went on. "Everyone thought there might finally be a chance to finish Sean forever, but six months after you guys disappeared, people started dying again, but this time in larger numbers." He then made a sweeping motion with his arm. "Whole towns and suburbs have been wiped out. Whoever Sean's found to make more of the virus is very good, and very quick."

"There must've been some sample he had stashed somewhere," Matt further explained.

Ben turned away as though he couldn't take hearing anything more. Even Jim had to grit his teeth to stay composed, and he gestured absently toward the house across the street. "C'mon inside. You must be hungry."

Anxious, Andy and Morgan looked at each other and then back at Ben and Jim with questioning gazes. Morgan's eyes narrowed on Jim while Andy crossed her arms over her chest. "You two better start explaining things."

Jim looked at Ben, who started to shake his head. "We will," he replied, ignoring his cousin. Then he and Morgan disappeared inside with Katie.

Andy cast Ben a long and discerning stare before wordlessly following the others inside.

Standing alone, Ben stared down at his dirty hands. He shut his eyes and pinched the bridge of his nose. "Impossible," he breathed.

Chapter XVII

*M*att and Kevin had finished their meal and soon after fell asleep on the living room floor in the house across the street. Everyone was still gathered at the dinner table.

Andy began the inquisition. "Sounds like you two were pretty famous back east." She glared pointedly at Ben.

"What all do you know about the virus?" Jim began.

"Nothing really. All we heard in Bermuda was something about a government project."

"Something top secret," Charlie added. "The news stopped once everyone started dying."

"We heard pretty much the same thing," Maria answered.

"Us too," said Brian.

"So the part about the virus being some top secret government project was correct," Jim confirmed. "What most people didn't know was that the virus was designed to be a humane biological weapon."

"How could a biological weapon be humane?" Morgan asked dubiously. "Was it supposed to kill people quicker or without pain or something?"

Jim shook his head. "Not that kind of humane. From what Ben and I were told, the virus was designed to distinguish the difference between an adult male and everyone else based upon the level of testosterone and other hormones that are naturally in the body. Those with high enough levels of testosterone who came in contact with the virus would be killed; those who didn't would survive."

"Why would the government create a virus like that?" asked Morgan.

But Maria had figured out the reason before Jim could answer. "So they could go after men like my father without worrying about killing women and children in the process. My father always knew that the DEA and the Mexican government would never go into his home if they thought his family was inside. That's why he did all his business inside our house."

Julio frowned as his sister spoke but said nothing.

"That's right," Jim continued. "Terrorists in the Middle East used the same tactics. The virus was supposed to be a way to get around that problem."

"So how did it end up killing everyone over a certain age, both men and women?" asked Andy.

"Because it wasn't finished being tested. One day, a scientist left the testing facility not knowing he was infected," Jim explained. "And the rest is history."

"Where was the virus developed?" Charlie asked.

"Fort Detrick. It's in Maryland, about fifty miles or so outside of DC."

"Fort Detrick?" Andy repeated with surprise. "I've read about that place in some of my medical books. I thought that lab was shut down decades ago."

"Apparently not."

"How did you learn all this if it wasn't on the news?" Charlie asked.

"We knew the son of the scientist who accidentally released the virus."

"Is that this Sean person you were talking about?"

Jim glanced at his cousin. "This is really more Ben's story to tell, so I'll let him tell it."

Ben was still staring at the lit candles in front of him. He swallowed hard. No one spoke once he began to explain.

The virus was the best thing that could've happened to Sean Taylor. Freed from the laws that society once lived by—laws that were not his own—he could finally fulfill his potential.

He had started at the bottom with everyone else, but as his fellow survivors wallowed in self-pity in their empty homes, he had acted quickly and strategically during those first weeks and months following the outbreak. And he never shed a tear for his parents, and there was no older sibling to mourn during those lonely hours between dusk and dawn.

Sean's father had once stood in the same room where he now sat, and for nearly an hour, he had been lounging in the plush swivel chair with his feet propped up on the Resolute desk. Sunlight waned through the three windows behind him, the only indication that it was getting late.

This was his first trip to DC since the virus. The condition of the city was shocking. Just getting downtown had been nearly impossible. The roads were still clogged with cars, but everywhere had been abandoned. He had not seen a single soul the entire day.

Taking his feet off the desk, Sean spun around in the chair and stared upward, alternately fixing his gaze on and off the Seal of the President of the United States plastered on the ceiling. He smiled.

Later, he departed the White House by descending the steps on the south side of the building and frowned at the rainbow of spray paint on the white columns. The weeks of anarchy immediately following the virus had taken its toll on several monuments throughout the city, and the White House was no exception. He walked across the South Lawn toward the car waiting to take him back to New York.

"His name is Sean Taylor and he controls almost everything in New York, Philadelphia, some parts of Boston, and everywhere in between. He's a narcissist, he's manipulative, and...*evil*. I've never met anyone else like him in my entire life.

"In the early days after the outbreak, when everyone else was too scared to think, he was already plotting. His father was some general in the Army, so he knew to do things like stockpile weapons and food before anyone else could. And he had a way of getting people to do these things for him. If you thought Nataliya was bad, she's got nothing on Sean. He made people believe that he cared about helping them and about getting the city working again. And early on, he did work hard, which only convinced everyone that he was someone they could trust.

"You probably remember those early days how age was everything, and the older you were, the more the younger survivors listened to you. Sean knew this, and he soon had a large following of survivors in New York. Then he picked his favorites to become his 'Directors.' Directors controlled specific things like food supplies or water treatment or getting power back to the city. There were nine of them in New York, and each was pretty powerful on his own.

"But Sean also knew he needed some of the smartest survivors to get things working again, so he went through hundreds and hundreds of school records at the best schools all over New York and had people find these super-smart kids—ones who skipped a few grades and even some who were in college—and convinced them to work for him. Kids like you, Charlie."

Charlie cracked a rueful smile as Ben continued.

"The power grid was the first priority, and within a year, most of the city's power was back on. And it was Sean who made that happen. After that, everyone wanted to work for him. Then he developed a kind of class system for everyone living in New York. The first class is the Directors, with Sean at the top. The next class is the army, or the *Infantry*, as we all called it. Sean started recruiting male survivors twelve years or older. Three thousand were chosen from more than ten thousand volunteers, and they became the Infantry, which has its own ranks like any army, and a Director leads it. Officially, the Infantry is like the police; they're meant to keep order, but they really spend most of their time spying for Sean and stealing from the rest of the people. People ended up dead when they refused to give up their possessions, but now no one bothers to put up a fight.

"*Fixers* are the third class. All those smart kids that Sean recruited early on were the first Fixers. Then other survivors with useful skills were recruited; mechanics like me and Jim, farmers like you two…" Ben nodded toward Brian and Susan. "…even kids whose parents had taught them to fly airplanes. Anyone with a rare but valuable skill was recruited to be a Fixer, and it was the job of the Infantry to find these people…and they searched everywhere for them."

"Why did he call them Fixers?" asked Andy.

"Sean didn't want them to get an inflated sense of self-importance by calling them 'experts' or 'specialists.' But he never would have gotten where he is today without them. I mean, how many kids do you know who can fly a plane? I didn't know anyone like that growing up, but Sean managed to find them, and now there're a couple thousand of them."

Looking tired, Ben combed his fingers through his thick, dark hair. "One thing Sean insisted on was that every Fixer had to be a male." He glanced at Andy as an expression of disgust appeared on her face.

"No one in the Infantry and no Fixer has ever been a girl. For whatever reason, Sean thinks girls are worthless except for sex, so about three years after the virus, when the testosterone really started to kick in, he made up the fourth class. He thought it would be amusing to find the prettiest girls in New York and keep them around for him and the Directors. He called them *Helens* because they were all beautiful like Helen of Troy.

"Most of the girls he found resisted at first, but once he starting giving them certain privileges, they changed their minds. They live in nice apartments, wear new clothes, and always have enough food to eat. Some Helens are addicted to the attention they get. Some do it just to stay alive and live better. And since healthy girls are more fun to have around than sickly ones, Sean doesn't mind giving them these things as long as they do what he wants. And they make his Directors happy, which makes *them* more loyal.

"Everyone else in the city is a *Dreg*. They're the biggest group, but they've got no power. Life for them is based entirely on a system of reward and punishment. If you do something to piss off the Directors, the Infantry, or even some of the Fixers, the water and power in your house gets shut off and your food rations are cut, or you're sent to one of the prisons Sean reopened. But if you do something to help him, like ratting out a neighbor for lying about the number of people living in their house in order to get bigger food rations, then you get rewarded. It all brings out the worst in everyone. No one knows who they can trust, and as long as everyone remains suspicious of one another, there's no chance of anyone banding together to revolt."

With his forehead glistening with sweat, Ben took another sip of water. It was as though he'd suddenly aged ten years in the last few hours. After a final sip, he said, "Everyone just walks around the city like zombies, too scared to wake up." Then he put down his water and abruptly stood up. "I'm going for a walk. Jim, you can tell them the rest."

Without another word, he picked up his rifle and left the house, confusing everyone by this sudden halt to the story. When Andy started to rise from her chair to go after him, Jim motioned for her to leave him alone.

"You have to understand," he began, "Ben was a Director and one of the few people Sean really trusted. He blames himself every day because he turned a blind eye to Sean's behavior for so long. But he had a good reason. See, Ben had a younger sister. Her name was Karen."

⁕

The roads on the Capitol Beltway and I-95 heading north were riddled with potholes, and with every jarring hit to the car's suspension, Sean's patience dwindled.

The driver, a Dreg with connections, had forgotten to bring extra containers of gas for the drive back to New York, and with two hundred miles to go, only a quarter tank was left.

Sitting alone in the backseat, Sean leaned forward until his face was within inches of the driver's right ear. "I'll give you ten minutes to find more gas after we run out. If you don't find any by then, I'll leave you on the side of the road." He leaned back in his seat and rolled down the window. The summertime humidity was oppressive, but turning on the air would only burn more precious fuel.

The driver said nothing as fear in the form of beads of sweat rolled down his forehead and into his eyes, causing him to swerve the car slightly and strike yet another pothole.

"Go ahead. Hit another one," Sean barked as the Infantry officer sitting beside the driver grasped the handle of his holstered pistol.

The driver quickly steadied himself. However, an hour later the gas tank ran dry and the car died between Wilmington and Philadelphia.

"Really?! How stupid are you?!" Sean mocked the driver. "You didn't even *try* getting off the highway and checking a gas station. Get out of my car!"

Stepping outside, the driver began to beg for mercy and apologized incoherently before urinating in his pants, but Sean gave him no notice and went to the trunk. He grabbed a long-range push-to-talk radio and transmitted a few instructions to someone at the other end. Then he grabbed a small bag containing food and water from the back seat before signaling to the officer.

The officer removed the gun from his holster and fired once at the blubbering driver. The bullet struck his abdomen, guaranteeing a slow and painful death. He slumped to the ground, writhing in pain. Sean and the officer continued walking along the highway for a few miles until another car arrived.

"Karen survived the outbreak like the rest of us. She and Ben were very close. The three of us were close, which was lucky for me since I was an only child. Ben's always been more like a brother than a cousin, and Karen was no different.

"Unfortunately, she was also a diabetic who needed daily shots of insulin, but with the supply shrinking, it became a big problem for her. We stocked up as much as we could, but there was only so much we could find, and it wasn't as if Karen was the only survivor with diabetes."

"We left Virginia a few months after the outbreak to find more insulin and stayed in Philadelphia for about six months. By then, Sean was close to turning power back on in New York, which we often heard rumors about, so we decided to go there next.

"We found a decent apartment in Queens, and few weeks later, Ben was approached by someone about fixing cars. We repaired a few of the abandoned cars in our new neighborhood, and soon we were both given positions as Fixers. It was nothing different than what we did in Aspen—but being a Fixer meant that you got better housing, more food, and medicine. So Karen never ran out of insulin.

"By the time we finally met Sean, we'd already been living in New York for more than a year. I remember the day because it was Karen's fifteenth birthday. We'd moved into Manhattan by then and were living right off Fifth Avenue in this huge apartment probably worth millions back in the day. We had some friends over and there was even a birthday cake. And suddenly Sean showed up with some of his friends. He seemed normal enough, but you could tell right away that he was intelligent. We didn't know why he came but later found out he wanted to meet Karen. She was a very pretty girl, and he'd heard about her from his friends. Ben and I were protective of her because of her diabetes, but also because boys were always chasing her, even before the outbreak.

"But Karen was always shy around strangers, so when she met Sean, she didn't say much to him. Then a few days later, he asked Ben to become the Director of Transportation, which Ben accepted only because it would help Karen get her insulin. He had a few hundred people assigned to him, including me and a few other Fixers, but the majority were Dregs. They worked hard and learned quickly... we were all learning. Ben and I might be good with cars, but we didn't know anything about fixing an entire subway system, which became his responsibility. But we did it. It took us months, but we finally got it working, which made Sean very happy. After that, he began to confide in Ben more and told him about plans to expand to Philadelphia and Boston. But Ben never trusted Sean, especially when he began selecting girls to become Helens. Some of the other Directors told Sean to choose Karen, but he refused, and at the time I wanted to believe he did it out of respect for Ben. She had just turned sixteen and had boys chasing after her left and right, but the only one she showed any interest in was this kid named Tim.

"Tim lived in our neighborhood in Queens when we first came to New York, and he and Karen clicked from day one. They spent a lot of time together, even after we moved into Manhattan. He would bike over the Queensboro Bridge every day to visit us, and after a while, he stayed with us in our apartment. He didn't have any surviving family, so we looked out for him. Ben and I showed him how to fix cars, and he actually became pretty good at it."

The memory formed a faint smile on Jim's face that quickly dissolved.

"Over time, Sean became more and more obsessed with Karen. But he wasn't in love with her. He just wanted to *own* her, and her having so many admirers only made his obsession stronger. Ben and I became afraid that he would hurt her, but we couldn't confront him about it. She needed her insulin. So we kept quiet, made sure Karen was never alone, and decided to find enough insulin on our own so we could leave New York. So we told Sean we were going to check out the subway in Boston, which he obviously thought was a great idea, and while we were gone, Karen stayed with Tim back in Queens.

"We actually worked on the subway to avoid suspicion and even got part of it working again, but most days, one of us would disappear for hours at a time and search any hospitals, doctors' offices, and pharmaceutical companies within a hundred miles of Boston. It took almost two months, but we finally gathered enough insulin to last Karen five years, which we hoped would buy her enough time until someone figured out how to make it again."

"But doesn't insulin have an expiration date?" Andy asked suddenly.

"Yeah, it does, but Karen had been using expired insulin for years without any issues. It just becomes less effective as it gets older, which just meant that she had to monitor her insulin levels more carefully as time went on.

"When Ben and I returned to New York, we planned to leave that same night and go west somewhere to start over."

Jim let out a labored sigh that seemed to resonate throughout the room.

"But when we got back, we couldn't find Karen or Tim anywhere. It was like they had vanished. We asked everyone, but nobody knew anything until finally someone told us that Tim had been shot."

A collective groan erupted among the group, but Jim pressed on.

"The Infantry had tracked down where Tim lived, and they came and took Karen after killing him in his own home. It was a week after Ben and I went to Boston. Sean kept Karen locked in his apartment in Manhattan and drugged her with heroin until her body became addicted to it. By the time Ben and I reached his apartment to confront him, it was too late. The combination of the heroin and her diabetes had been too much for her to take, and she died less than a day before we showed up."

A gasp escaped from Morgan and Susan at the same moment. Jim responded with a firm nod as though confirming this horrible news. A single tear formed in the corner of Andy's eye, and she quickly wiped away.

"I was devastated, but Ben went into a rage when he saw Karen's body. He would've killed Sean with his bare hands had others not shown up to defend that sick bastard. We were lucky to escape and take her body with us. We drove all the way to Washington DC and buried Karen in the National Cemetery in Arlington. Ben wanted her somewhere important. Someplace she deserved." Jim briefly covered his face with his hands. "It was awful. For a few weeks afterward, we stayed in the same neighborhood in Virginia where we grew up. And then Ben started drinking. He couldn't stop blaming himself for his sister's death. I tried to tell him it wasn't his fault, but he wouldn't listen, and for a while I thought he'd never get over it.

"One day, I managed to keep him sober long enough to go hunting in the woods near our neighborhood. On the walk home, we ran into some guys driving through the area, which was strange because outside of New York and Philadelphia, most people got around by walking or biking or riding horses. There just wasn't any gas. So we assumed they were from up north, and after we started talking to them, we realized they were Fixers. Sean had sent them to look through the Pentagon and a few other government buildings.

"We invited them to our house for dinner, and eventually one of them started spilling secrets about Fort Detrick and the virus. He said his father had been one of the scientists who'd developed the virus and described how it was accidentally released before all the testing was done. Then he said there were still samples of the virus at the Fort, which was now deadly to all survivors beyond a certain age… including most of us in this room."

A shudder shot down Andy's spine as Morgan curled up into a ball on the couch and hugged her knees tightly to her chest.

"Soon, Sean began sending even more Fixers to the Fort to study the virus."

"But wouldn't he be worried about it killing him too?" Brian asked.

Jim shrugged. "The virus is such a horrible memory for everyone that people fear it more than guns. You can survive a bullet, but no one survives the virus…no one our age. Sean probably figured the risk was worth it."

Jim stopped to take a sip of water from Ben's abandoned glass. As he leaned forward, Morgan placed a comforting hand on his shoulder.

"It was Ben's idea to blow up the lab at Fort Detrick, and in the beginning it was his way of getting revenge for Karen's death, but later we knew that we *had* to destroy the virus. If we didn't, then Sean would have it, and if he couldn't control it, it could end up spreading all over again. So we went to West Virginia, found some explosives at some coal mines, and then staked out the lab to figure out when it was usually empty.

"One night last summer, we snuck into the lab, poured gasoline everywhere, and lit the whole place on fire. Then we set off the explosives to make sure everything was completely destroyed." Jim made a circular motion with his hands. "It was a gigantic fireball that could be seen for miles. Afterwards, we headed south, and that's when we met you three on the highway."

Jim finally stopped. No one spoke. It took the piercing sound of a gunshot from outside to startle everyone from their thoughts. Within seconds, everyone was out of the house.

Beneath the moonlight in the middle of the street, Ben was wrestling Kevin on the ground. Both were straining to gain control of Ben's rifle. At the same time, Matt was kicking Ben in the ribs.

Jim and Brian ran into the scuffle. After more kicks and punches, Jim and Charlie wrangled Matt away from Ben, and Brian yanked the rifle out of Kevin's grasp.

"They lied," said Ben, breathless as he peeled himself off the pavement. "They're working for Sean. I heard them talking." He grabbed his rifle from Brian and turned it on Kevin and Matt. He was prepared to fire.

Neither denied the accusation and instead were strangely silent. Their looks of defiance were unmistakable, even in near-darkness.

"Let's give them a ride to the desert," Jim declared after a tense moment. "We'll drop 'em somewhere west of here…far off the Interstate. They can walk back to New York for all I care."

"That's better than they deserve," Ben snapped bitterly.

"Yeah, it is, but we're not like them, Ben. And we're not like Sean."

He lowered his rifle before releasing a long sigh. "No, we're not."

Chapter XVIII

*A*ndy woke just as the sun emerged above the horizon. Her sleep had been restless; dreams of people she didn't know chasing her through dense forests that transformed into the busy streets of a large metropolitan city. She always managed to escape her pursuers just in time.

She tiptoed through the house as everyone slept and stepped outside. As she crossed the vacant road, she saw the outline of someone sitting on the front steps of the house across the street. Startled, she took a few stumbling steps backward as the figure stood up.

"Andy, it's me." It was Ben's voice. When Andy's eyes finally adjusted to the dawning light, she approached and took a seat beside him as he sat back down.

"Sorry, I didn't mean to scare you."

"When did you guys get back?"

"A few hours ago."

"Did they tell you anything, like how many others are after you?"

"No, they didn't say a word. We left 'em on the side of a road about ten miles west of Route 84. They'll have to walk for miles before they get to another town."

"Do you think they'll try to come back here? Should we leave?"

He bobbed his head once. "We'll have to. I don't think they'll ever come back here, but if they somehow make it back to New York, they'll tell Sean where we are." The idea of leaving Santa Rosa wasn't especially upsetting, for she held no great attachment to the place. "When should we leave?" she asked as she glanced back at her house.

"As soon as possible. Though I don't know how we'll be able to go anywhere at all. We're almost out of gas, and I don't know what the alternative is."

"We'll figure it out." There was so much more Andy wanted to say but she had no idea where to begin. Instead she asked, "Did you sleep at all?"

"A couple of hours."

"It's impressive what you and Jim did. Destroying that lab. Destroying the virus. That took guts."

Ben shrugged off the compliment and looked down at his hands. "We just did what needed to be done." He dropped his head down in frustration. "It wasn't enough, though."

"Did the Fixers ever tell you why the virus was so deadly?"

"They said it was designed to be a 'rapid killing agent,' which meant that from the moment one person is infected, either by injection or through the air, that person can then infect someone else within a minute or two."

"So, if I was injected right now with the virus, and then a minute later you came and sat next to me like you are now, I'd infect you immediately?"

"Right. But people were also supposed to die within minutes and not walk around for days infecting innocent people, which we all know isn't the way it worked out."

"And you think he still has the virus?"

Ben cracked his knuckles before answering. "He must've stashed some vials somewhere away from the lab. And now he's probably got some Fixer in another lab working to replicate it."

"But those guys—Matt and Kevin—couldn't they have been lying to you about the whole thing? Maybe it was just a trick to get you and Jim to go back to New York."

"Maybe," he conceded. "Anything's possible."

The daylight had intensified to the point where Andy could finally make out Ben's face. He looked exhausted, almost ill.

"What does he look like?" she asked suddenly.

"Sean?"

"Yeah." It was the first time either of them had uttered the name.

"I guess he's about my height and build. Brownish-blond hair. What I remember most about him are his eyes. They're *piercing* blue. And when he looks at you, it's like a laser going through your skull to read your thoughts." He turned to face the sunrise. His gaze was distant, as though he were looking at something miles away. "Karen used to say that whenever Sean looked at her, it was as if he was telepathically injecting fear into her body." Then, with a faint smile, he shook his head slowly and said, "She was good with words."

The remark made Andy's heart swell, and without even thinking, she placed her hand on top of Ben's and gave it a firm squeeze. "I'm sorry about your sister."

Wordlessly, his gaze shifted down to her hand on top of his. He turned his hand over until their palms touched, and stared down at their contact before sliding his hand away. He slowly rose to his feet. "I'm tired as hell. Going back to bed."

Andy stood up and met Ben's eye level by climbing one step higher. Without thinking, she reached out and placed her hands on his shoulders. She stood up on her toes and kissed him on the forehead. When she pulled back, she met his confused gaze before turning away. She stepped down and headed back across the street.

"Get some rest," she called back to him. "Sounds like we've got some planning to do."

"It would be nice to stay somewhere longer than a few months," Morgan said to Andy later that morning while feeding Katie.

"You want to stay here longer?"

"I don't know…not really. I miss trees and green grass. I don't think I'm meant to live in the desert."

"Me neither, but at least we're all together this time."

"Thank God. This time I won't have to wonder if I have to give birth without you because you've gone and gotten yourself kidnapped."

Andy laughed. "No chance of that happening again. I think I've actually grown eyes in the back of my head." Then she rose from the sofa and moved over to the window facing the street. "I still can't believe everything Jim told us yesterday."

"It explains a lot."

"Like what?"

"Like why Ben's so quiet sometimes. And why he was so determined to be the one to find you after you were kidnapped."

"What do you mean?"

Ignoring the question, Morgan shifted Katie's weight in her arms and rolled her eyes. "God, she's getting heavy." Her daughter began to coo adorably. Morgan stood up and began circling around the room, gently bouncing her up and down. "But at least now she can hold her head up."

Andy approached and offered Katie her pinky finger. The infant happily gripped it with her whole hand and squealed, making them laugh. When her smile faded, Andy's face turned serious. "Why did Ben insist on going after me?"

"Because he's in love with you," Morgan replied quickly as though she were finally ready to rid her mind of the secret.

But Andy shook her head in denial, and laughed at her friend's ridiculous suggestion. "No...no, he's not. Why would...?"

"Why would he love you? Bloody hell, Andy...you're beautiful, smart, compassionate..."

"Has he said anything?"

"He doesn't need to. But it's pretty obvious from how he acts around you and looks at you. Even Charlie sees it, and my brother isn't exactly perceptive when it comes to this sort of thing. I mean, Susan had to practically snog him before he got the hint."

Andy gently retrieved her pinky from Katie and took a step backwards. Stubbornly, she placed her hands on her hips. "I think you're just imagining it. He would've said something by now."

"No, he wouldn't. Look at how long he kept everything about his sister a secret. He's not going to say anything."

"Well, *I'm* not going to say anything."

"Why? You don't feel that way about him?"

Andy quickly turned away and headed back to the window. "It doesn't matter how I feel because I think you're wrong. He's just a friend and he won't ever be anything more."

With a heavy sigh, Morgan gave up the argument. "Whatever you say."

"All of you are still coming over for dinner, right?" Maria asked Andy as she finished dicing an avocado.

"Yeah, I think so. Ben and Brian are hunting, but they should be back in time."

"I can't believe those guys were really looking for Ben and Jim...and so far away. Makes me worried how many more are out there looking for them."

"I know. Now we have to leave again."

Maria paused for a moment, then asked, "When will that be?"

"Not sure, but probably not for a few days. The biggest problem is that we're out of gas."

Maria began cutting a second avocado in half and scooping out the soft insides of the fruit. "How much do you need?"

Andy rapped her fingers on the counter. "As much as we can get, fifty gallons, maybe? It depends if we take one car or two."

"I'll see what I can do."

During all the months spent in Santa Rosa, the mystery of how Maria managed to acquire such valuable commodities had remained a secret, but no one ever pressed her about the issue.

"Are you still sticking with your eighteen-month timeline?" Andy asked, avoiding details.

Maria frowned. She was now smashing the avocado into a pulp. "I don't know. Things aren't going too well back home, and I'm starting to lose hope."

"So why don't you come with us?"

"And go where? You don't even know where you're going."

"I know, but we could use you, and I know that no matter where we go, we'll need all the help we can get."

"Sounds like you're going into battle or something."

Andy smiled as she stared absently at the surface of the kitchen table. "You know, I keep wondering what we're doing here every day. I mean, we get up every morning, we find food to eat, we take baths in the lake, we find wood to burn, and then we go to bed. Then we do it all again the next morning. And that's it."

"So? You want something more meaningful in your life?" Maria asked with a hint of admonishment. "You're also forgetting that you're safe with your friends, and you're helping Morgan raise her child. Isn't that enough?"

"Honestly, it's not. Not for me. Not when I know how things could be."

"Like in Aspen?"

"Like the world. There's all this knowledge of science and technology out there to be learned and be used again. But we're not."

"I see your point, but it was science that created the virus in the first place."

"I know, but it was a mistake. Humans make mistakes."

"A pretty big mistake."

"I know." Andy rubbed her temples. "I guess I'm just...restless."

Maria put down her knife and looked at Andy, her eyes narrowing. "What are you really saying?"

"I'm saying that I need to do...*something*. Something important. Like..." The words came out at once. "Like destroying whatever's left of the virus. Finishing what Ben and Jim tried to do."

Maria absorbed the words. "That would mean going to New York."

"If that's where the virus is, then that's where we need to go."

"What if those two guys were lying? They lied about who they were, so they could've been lying about everything else."

"But what if they were telling the truth? Should we just ignore the possibility? We all know how deadly the virus is, and if there's any truth to their story, then all of us are in danger."

"It seems like a long way to go just to prove those two liars weren't lying about everything. Plus after what we heard last night, New York sounds like the last place I would want to be."

"Well, victories aren't won in paradise."

"Very poetic," quipped Maria.

Neither spoke for a moment as Maria folded a diced tomato into the avocado mixture. Then she said, "I doubt you'll convince Ben or Jim to go back to New York."

"It *would* be the last place that anyone would look for them."

"Maybe." A smiled formed on Maria's face, and then she looked at Andy with a curious expression. "Maybe this will work." Moving away from the counter, she opened a cabinet drawer on the other side of the kitchen and retrieved a bottle of wine. She handed it to Andy, who took it tentatively.

"What's this for?"

"Nothing. Just something I thought you might enjoy...when you talk to Ben about your plan, you should share this with him. He might be more willing to listen."

"Are you trying to get us drunk or something?"

Maria laughed. "It'll take more than that to get you both drunk, though I'm sure Ben would *love* to get you drunk."

Andy rolled her eyes. "God, not you too. You're all imagining something that's not there."

Trying hard not to smile, Maria held her hands up as though denying an ulterior motive. "Well, as my *abuelita* used to say, 'a little alcohol makes everything easier.'"

⊸◦❦◦⊷

"You're insane. I'm not going back."

Ben and Andy were sitting alone on the curb in front of Maria's house. Her first attempt was unsuccessful, even after begging him to listen to his conscience.

"My conscience is clear. Jim and I did our best to destroy the virus. If Sean still has it, which we don't even know for sure, then there's really nothing we can do. Someone else can try to stop him, but I'm done with it all."

"You don't really mean that, do you?" she implored. "Ben, I saw you last night. I've never seen you so upset when you found out it hadn't been destroyed."

"That was before I overheard those guys talking about taking Jim and me back to New York. As far as I'm concerned, everything else they told us was a lie." His eyes narrowed. "Why are you so eager to go?"

"I don't know...I can't explain it," she said and abruptly rose off the curb. "Wait here, I need to get something."

Minutes later, Andy emerged from her house with the bottle of wine in her hand and a rusty corkscrew in her back pocket. Even in the waning daylight, Ben could clearly see what she was carrying.

"I wouldn't have taken you for a drinker," he teased.

"Time to find out what the big deal is."

"You've never drank before?"

Andy smiled sheepishly. "Not really. Just at a couple of weddings when I was a kid. Some champagne...that sort of thing. Come on, let's go for a walk."

Ben hesitated before rising to his feet. "Where're we going?"

"Nowhere in particular."

He extended his hand for the bottle and took a glance at the label. "Cabernet Sauvignon. California. 2014." He handed the bottle back to her as they walked down the street. "I'm sure it'll be good."

"Have you ever had a drink...oh!" She stopped dead in her tracks and palmed her mouth with her hand.

"What?"

Frozen with shame and embarrassment, she shook her head and muttered, "I totally forgot..."

"Forgot what?"

"Uh, yesterday, Jim told us that after...after Karen died, you...Ben, I'm sorry. I wasn't thinking..."

He put up a hand to stop her. "It's okay. It was a long time ago."

"I'll go put it back."

"No, don't. It's fine. I'm not in danger of becoming an alcoholic, if that's what you're worried about. Even if I was, it's not like I can just go to the local liquor store."

"I wasn't worried about that, but…are you sure?"

"Yes, I'm sure. I admit it was bad after Karen died, but it's been almost two years."

Still uncertain, Andy shrugged tentatively.

They reached a small park near their neighborhood. There was a playground in the center, and they sat next to each other on the swings.

Andy opened the wine and threw the cork aside. "Sorry, I didn't bring glasses," she said.

"No worries, I don't mind swapping spit with you."

"Very funny."

She took a healthy swig from the bottle and handed it to him. "You were right," she said after swallowing. "It's not bad. Not that I could tell if it was."

Ben took a long sip from the bottle. After finishing, he wiped his mouth with the back of his hand and nodded in agreement. "Pretty good."

They drank half the bottle before any meaningful conversation began. Andy's thin frame, meager diet, and inexperience with alcohol made her especially susceptible to its consequences. But she found it easier to speak more freely despite her tongue growing heavy. When she handed the bottle back, she dabbed her lips with her fingertips and said, "Did you ever think that maybe you're meant to go back to New York and finish your fight with Sean? Like it's your destiny or something?"

He looked at her as though she had lost her mind. "Man, you're a lightweight."

"I'm being serious. Don't you ever wonder why we survived when others just a few months older didn't?"

With a somewhat strained laugh, he took another large gulp from the bottle and shook his head. "That's just how things turned out. I never thought more about it."

"But what about Sean? How does someone like that get to be so powerful so quickly? And how does he stay in power? Doesn't anyone try to challenge him?"

"You know European history," he began, passing the bottle back to her. "So take Henry VIII. Just a whiny, spoiled jerk who used his power to get whatever he wanted, right?"

"Right."

"But he was also ruthless."

"Uh yeah…beheading two of his wives…going to war against France whenever he felt like it…beheading more people…fathering Bloody Mary…" Andy could feel herself rambling, but Ben didn't seem to notice.

"See? He was still a problem even after he was dead."

"What's your point?"

"My point is that even though he did all these things that had to have pissed off the English people, he still managed to hold onto the throne for…how long?"

She looked up at the darkening sky as she reached deep into her memory. "Almost thirty-seven years…no, thirty-eight."

"So for almost four decades, this guy managed to stay King of England despite all his bad behavior. People were afraid to stand up to him, no matter how much they disagreed with him. Because if they did, they'd lose their head, right?"

"Right."

"Okay, now take Sean. He's probably more intelligent and maybe less, uh, emotional than Henry VIII, and he's smart enough to know that if you provide food and water to people and get rid of millions of rotting corpses, they're more likely to ignore all the bad things you do. Then he's got this way of making you want to please him."

Watching Ben as he spoke, Andy thought she saw a look of shame cross his face.

"And he was so good at justifying his behavior," he added after a pause.

"Like how?"

"Like when he would punish people and take away their rations for a week, he would say he just wanted people to understand that getting life back to normal meant taking orders without question. That people needed him to tell them what to do or there would always be chaos."

"What did the other Directors think?"

"They were all too scared to do anything. Not that I was any better. Three years went by before I woke up and saw Sean for who he really is."

"But you were young. Just a kid." Andy could feel her words beginning to slur. "What about Jim? What did he think?"

"He didn't deal with Sean as much, but he didn't like him from the beginning."

They were quiet for a bit as the bottle of wine quickly emptied. Ben offered the last sip to Andy. Her body felt warm all over and her vision was a bit unsteady, made worse by the increasing darkness. When she leaned over to stand the empty bottle on the ground, she nearly fell out of her swing and started to giggle.

"Wow, you're drunk!" and he began to laugh as well.

"I am *not*," she replied a bit too loudly as she steadied herself in the seat. "Just a little tipsy."

"Whatever you say."

"Oh, shut up. I'm sure you'd love to take advantage of me!"

"Why would I do that? I'd never take advantage of a friend."

"A friend?" she repeated, blinking. "Is that all I am to you?"

"Uh, yeah. What else would you be?" He gazed off into the distance, his mind probably far away.

Feeling suddenly rejected, Andy looked down and kicked at the rocks at her feet. "So what are his weaknesses?"

"What?"

"I said, what are his weaknesses? Sean's. His vulnerabilities," she slurred the last word.

"Why?"

"Just answer me. How could he be beaten?"

Staring down at the ground in front of him, Ben became pensive and inhaled a deep breath. "Well, he's too confident. Thinks he's invincible. He's very careful of who he trusts, but once someone's in his inner circle, he'll trust them with everything." He paused. "But maybe not after what I did."

"What else?"

"He underestimates women. He thinks you're all less intelligent than he is. He has surrounded himself with girls who don't question him." Ben glanced sideways at Andy. "He wouldn't know how to handle someone like you."

She released a derisive laugh, and as its sound faded, an idea slowly formed in her mind. "Maybe that's it. Maybe that's the key."

"What are you talking about?"

She ran her fingers through her hair in the same manner he often did. "I'm not sure of what I'm talking about right now. Must be the wine."

"It's not just the wine. You're really serious about going to New York, aren't you?"

"Did I say that?" she replied, feigning comprehension.

"C'mon, Andy, I know you. You get an idea into your head and you turn into a bulldog."

"I do *not*."

"You just proved my point. You're the most stubborn person I know."

"Oh, like you're any better," she snapped as she attempted to shove him by swinging sideways, but with her diminished reflexes, she missed her mark and hit him on the side of his ribcage instead.

"Whoa, what are you doing?" he teased as he deftly grabbed her hand, proving that despite the wine, *his* reflexes were fine. He didn't let go of her hand right away.

"See, I told you it was the wine," she managed to say between giggles. "Give me my hand."

"Not until you tell me why you want to go to New York." His grip tightened. "Tell me," he repeated, his voice lowering to a more serious and somewhat desperate tone.

Her giggles stopped. She looked at him in the last remnants of daylight. "Stop it," she declared with drunken wistfulness. He let go of her hand. Frustrated by both her lack of mental clarity and the sudden stirrings of emotions, she stood up.

"Wait, where are you going?" he called out to her in the dark.

"To bed," she said as she stepped forward. But then she stopped and muttered, "No, not bed...I don't know." She put her hands up to her forehead. Feeling dizzy, she took a stumbling step backward.

Ben quickly stood up and placed his hands on her shoulders to give her balance. "Slow down...slow down."

"I'm fine. It's just the wine."

"Let's head back home," he said.

Without further argument, she began to walk cautiously forward. They made it halfway home when she abruptly stopped.

"What is it?" Ben asked her.

Andy's eyes first fell to the ground before she lifted her gaze to the vanishing horizon. "It's not that I *want* to go to New York, but I just have this nagging feeling that I'm *supposed* to go. Does that make sense?" But before he could answer, she said, "I'm sorry. I don't know what I mean anymore."

He grasped her shoulder. "If you want to go to New York, I can't stop you. If there was anyone who could beat Sean, it's probably you." He released her and looked away. "You're...you're an extraordinary person."

She stepped closer toward him. "Then come with me," she urged him, nearly whispering. "I need you there."

Staring at the ground, he shook his head "I can't."

"You can. And you'll see how *extraordinary* I can be."

Chapter XIX

*M*aria, we need drugs. As much as you can get your hands on." She glanced up from her plate of food and looked at Andy. "Which ones, specifically?" She knew what Andy was asking, but she wanted her to be clear.

"Heroin, marijuana, cocaine…if you can get it," Ben rattled off the items as though he were delivering a grocery list.

A week earlier, Maria had travelled to Albuquerque and back to meet up with friends from Juarez. She went alone, leaving Julio and Carmen behind, and when she returned, she made the decision to leave Santa Rosa.

In an attempt to undo some of the sins of her father, she had been secretly working to free survivors forced into slave labor to continue the production of heroin and marijuana throughout northern and western Mexico. The children of her father's enemies, those from the rival drug cartel, had been kidnapping survivors in Juarez and other cities and enslaving them to cultivate cannabis and poppy plants. The luckier ones avoided this backbreaking work and instead were used to transport cocaine still being produced in Colombia to Mexico.

"The outbreak hardly affected the drug trade between my country and yours," she explained. "After the first six months, everything was back to how it was, except easier without borders to worry about."

Drugs had become the new form of currency in the post-virus world. With cocaine, heroin, marijuana, and all their dangerous combinations, survivors could temporarily escape their miserable existence. Maria understood this grim reality and that drug production would never stop, so she and a small group of trusted friends still living in Juarez decided to exploit the drug transport system as a way to rescue the slave laborers from their plight. Like before, every gram of every drug was still tracked, but when it came to keeping track of their laborers, the cartel was sloppy. If someone went missing, they could easily find another as a replacement.

Because of her forced exile to Santa Rosa, Maria had only been able to minimally assist her friends, who had carefully maneuvered their way into the roles of the drivers of the trucks that transported the drugs north to America. They would falsify the numbers detailing the amount of drugs they were carrying and keep the difference for themselves, which they would then use to trade for other necessities, like food and gas. And within the cargo they would hide a person or two, whatever they thought they could get away with, and head to Santa Rosa. Once there, Maria would house and feed them until they regained their strength before sending them on their way, sometimes alone and sometimes with another shipment of drugs heading deeper into the States.

"That's what you saw me doing that morning last year when that truck was driving away from my house," she recalled for Andy. "Those were my friends in the truck, and we had just put two young girls inside. It took nearly a week for the wounds on their backs to heal enough so they could stop sleeping on their stomachs."

Nearly half of the drug shipments that came from Mexico passed through Santa Rosa on I-40, and many of these shipments were bound for New York. Maria further revealed that she had heard rumors about what was going on there, but hadn't pieced the puzzle together until Ben and Jim had told their story. "Unfortunately, the cartel in Juarez has only gotten stronger in the last year. Their numbers have increased and lately they've been keeping better track of their laborers, which has made our work much more difficult."

But what ultimately made her decide that it was time to leave was learning during her trip to Albuquerque that the cartel had stopped keeping handwritten records detailing each shipment and had started using computerized ones. This now made it impossible for her and her friends to continue falsifying the shipment records. "In a way, it's probably for the best. We were fighting a losing battle, and the fact that we were still helping the cartel transport the drugs was only keeping them in control. And every time we saved one, another person was taken to replace them."

Her decision made, Maria vowed she would never have anything to do with drugs again. But sitting now at her kitchen table, she considered Andy and Ben's request carefully.

"I have to know exactly what you need the drugs for. If you really need them to help take down this Sean person, then I'll make an exception."

"We need them to bribe people in Sean's network. People that might know where he's keeping the virus. And to buy some supplies that we'll need once we get to New York."

"And that's it?"

"That's it," Andy assured.

"Well," she began, "since this is the last time, you might as well take advantage of all my connections. I'll get you more than just drugs. I'll get you to New York by the end of next week."

"We can keep trying to convince ourselves that Sean will simply disappear and never send people to find us again," Jim said to Ben, "or we can figure out a way to finally destroy him. But we'd be fooling ourselves if we think he's a problem that'll just go away. This is our fight, so let's finally finish it. For Karen, if not for us." He rarely mentioned Karen by name, but he knew when he could use her memory to make a point.

Ben thought about the decision to go to New York long and hard, but ultimately he had no choice. He had to destroy the virus forever.

Concerned about Katie and Morgan living in the dangerous city, Jim suggested staying in Princeton. "It's only fifty miles from the city, and it'll probably be empty with all the students and professors being dead."

"And the university library has got a ton of books that would be great for gathering information," said Charlie with a blush of excitement.

Brian remained strangely quiet about going to New York. He didn't seem to have an opinion one way or another on the matter, which struck Andy as odd. He had been pretty quiet in general since coming to Santa Rosa, and she wondered if he regretted leaving Aspen.

The night before they were planning to leave, he came to talk to her. She was organizing her medical books when he knocked on her bedroom door. "Come in," she called out.

Brian entered and closed the door behind him.

"What's up?" Andy asked distractedly.

He leaned against her desk. "I, uh, I was wondering if you could look after Susan for me when you all get to New York."

She stopped her sorting and looked up at him with confusion. "What are you talking about? You're not coming with us?"

"No, at least not right now."

"I don't understand…"

"I need to go back to Aspen for a bit. There's some stuff I need to take care of first."

"Umm, okay," she muttered slowly. "Does Susan know you're not coming?"

"Yeah, I already told her."

"And she's okay with it?"

"She's fine. I know Charlie will take care of her, but I'd feel better if you looked out for her, too."

"Well, of course, but I have to admit that I still don't understand why you need to go back to Aspen, especially after what happened to me there."

"It won't be forever, I promise. But I left some really good friends behind."

"Okay…is it because you're worried about going to New York?"

"No, I'm not worried, and that's actually why I need to go back to Aspen."

"I still don't understand."

He took a deep breath. "I know. I'm not explaining myself well. See, I really believe in what you're all about to do because in a small way, I was trying to do the same thing in Aspen. And now I feel like I've abandoned my friends, so I'm going back to convince them to come with me."

"Oh…"

"I don't know exactly what you'll all be up against in New York, but you'll probably need more help."

Taking a step toward her, Brian gently tapped Andy on the side of her arm. "I miss my friends, Andy, and if I'm going to do this thing with you all…take on this Sean character and destroy the virus, then I need to give them a chance to start their lives over again too. Or at least offer them the choice." His eyes narrowed. "Does that make sense?"

Andy's mouth curled upward into a smile, and she nodded. "Makes perfect sense, but what you should've said is that you *are* coming to New York, but you need to make a detour first."

He let out a laugh. "I guess that would have been a better way of saying it."

"So when will you leave?"

"Tomorrow, when you all leave. Maria said she'd get me enough gas to get back to Aspen and then all the way to New York."

"So you've already told Maria that you're not coming with us?"

"And Ben and Jim. I figured that since New York is really their territory and their past, I needed to tell them first."

"So Maria knows. And if Susan knows, then Charlie knows. And if Jim knows, then Morgan knows."

Brian looked guilty. "Um, yeah."

"So basically, everyone already knows you aren't coming with us. I'm the last person you've told?"

"Well, I didn't want you to try to talk me out of it."

"I wouldn't have tried to stop you if you had explained all of this to me."

But he raised an eyebrow skeptically. "Really? I would've tried to stop you if the situation were reversed."

"You would?"

"Of course." He paused, then said, "I like you, Andy. A lot."

"Oh."

Brian smiled broadly at her and she was suddenly struck by how handsome he was. She'd hadn't noticed before.

"Just think about that…while I'm gone." Without waiting for an answer, he turned and left the room.

"I will," she whispered to herself.

Around eight o'clock in the morning, a large tanker truck pulled up to an intersection half a block away from the two houses. Behind it was parked a truck with a small trailer attached.

Charlie and Susan were first to spot the trucks. Maria was outside with Julio and Carmen.

"Don't tell me that that's what I think it is," Charlie said as he pointed at the tanker with astonishment.

Maria laughed. "And it's completely full, too."

"God, how many gallons is that?" Susan asked, equally in awe.

"Gallons? I don't know, but I think around thirty thousand liters."

"How in the world did your friends get so much gas?" asked Susan.

"They stole it in the middle of the night. It came all the way from Venezuela."

"They stole it?" Susan and Charlie repeated at the same time.

"Won't they get caught?" Charlie added. "Or killed?"

"No. My friends aren't going back to Juarez. They're going to Miami after they drop us off in New York. They've got friends and relatives there."

She glanced back at her three friends who were gathered at the front of the tanker and talking to Julio and Carmen. "We all decided together that it was time to leave. The danger just isn't worth it anymore. They are going to take care of Julio while we are in New York."

"Why isn't Carmen going with them?" asked Susan.

"She wants to stay with me. Plus, Julio has good friends going to Miami that he misses, and he's getting too old for me to tell him what to do."

"Whoa, is that thing full?" Brian asked as he and the others approached.

"Just about," Maria confirmed, smiling with satisfaction.

"What's in the other truck?" asked Andy. Maria frowned and gestured for her and Ben to follow and headed toward the smaller trailer. She opened the back of the trailer with Ben's help, and Andy saw something she'd never seen before: kilograms upon kilograms of illicit drugs. More precisely, three hundred kilos of high-grade cocaine, heroin, and marijuana, all wrapped and vacuum-sealed.

Frozen with his arm still in the air from lifting the trailer door, Ben was stunned. "Holy…"

"That's…that's a *lot*," Andy said with her eyes wide open.

"Well, you said to get as much as I could get," Maria said as she climbed into the trailer and made a sweeping gesture with her arms. "This should be enough to get some people talking, I would think."

Still in disbelief, Ben stepped up to join Maria inside the trailer before gingerly placing his hand on top of the stack of wrapped heroin. He seemed afraid to touch it.

"Sad that this is what it takes to do something good," Maria said as she turned and hopped out of the trailer. "It's time to find another way." She walked past Andy and headed back to the rest of the group, leaving them alone.

Ben looked down at Andy, then back at his hand still touching the stack of heroin. "This is what killed my sister." His voice wavered slightly.

"You sure you want to do it this way?" she asked cautiously.

"No, I'm not sure, but I don't know of another way right now." He stepped out of the trailer.

"Okay, then we won't worry about it until we need to." She stepped up and closed the trailer door. "Let's just get to New York first."

Brian put his things in Jim and Ben's truck, which they were lending to him.

"Just make sure you bring it back in one piece," Ben joked after handing over the keys.

"I will, I promise," he said and then hugged Susan goodbye.

She forced a smile and said, "Don't stay there long. And watch out for yourself."

"Yes ma'am," he replied in jest in an effort to maintain his composure. "You be careful."

She gave her brother one more hug. "I love you."

"I love you, too." He then said goodbye to everyone else before getting inside the truck.

Andy was the last to speak to him. "I'll take good care of her," she promised.

"Thank you. I'll worry a lot less knowing that."

She gave him a hug, which wasn't unexpected since both Morgan and Maria had also hugged him farewell. But when she pulled away, he sneaked a quick kiss to her cheek before slipping into the driver's seat. "Be careful," he muttered to her as he started the engine.

Andy stood still and touched the spot on her face where his lips had been. She didn't notice Morgan come up beside her until Katie made a few noises in her mother's arms.

"I know Ben likes Brian well enough, but I'm sure he's glad he won't have any competition for a while."

Andy didn't respond.

Chapter XX

*M*an, I'm beat." Andy rubbed her eyes one at a time since she was driving. The clock on the dashboard read 11:57. "It's midnight already? Where did the time go today?"

"Want me to drive?" Morgan asked even though Katie had just fallen asleep in her arms.

"No, let's not wake her. I'll be fine," she replied with a yawn.

"How much farther is it?"

"Not far. We should be crossing the Delaware River in a few minutes."

Morgan nodded, although she had no idea where the Delaware River was in relation to Princeton. She'd been too busy dealing with Katie the entire trip to have a chance to look at a map.

Between driving in a slow-moving caravan, tackling the spotty road conditions stretching between New Mexico and eastern Pennsylvania, and stopping multiple times to check the safety of bridges to ensure they could support the immense weight of the tanker, the journey had been exhaustingly long. What normally would have been a three-day trip had taken them six, and once they arrived, they'd still have to find a decent place to live.

Andy glanced back at Jim in the rearview mirror. He was asleep in the backseat. "I'm glad someone's getting some rest," she said quietly to Morgan.

Morgan craned her neck to look. She smiled down at Jim but said nothing, and returned her focus on Katie and the road ahead.

They were in the last vehicle. In front of them was the other pickup truck, which Ben was driving along with Charlie and Susan. Maria, Julio, and Carmen had remained with their Juarez friends in the tanker and trailer.

Andy mused how the drive west the year before had seemed far less arduous, and she could only attribute this sentiment to the excitement she felt last year of heading somewhere new and mysterious with the two young men they had met along the way. But now they were like soldiers going to war, and all the inevitable difficulties they would face seemed more real as the battlefield approached.

After crossing the Delaware River, they passed through Trenton and continued on with surprising ease until Princeton appeared in the distance. They got off the highway just south of the university, and the four vehicles pulled over to the side of the road. Everyone stepped outside and regrouped near the front of the tanker.

"Now what?" Susan asked once they were all gathered.

With a flashlight in hand, Ben placed a map of New Jersey on the ground and positioned the light on the center. Everyone huddled together to get a better look.

"We need to hide all this gas somewhere," he began, taking charge. "It's too big to take into the neighborhoods without risking others seeing it. The less people who know we're here, the better."

Andy pointed to something on the map. "What about one of these parks? Or this golf course?"

Ben stroked his chin with his free hand. Out of everyone, he seemed to be the most alert. "Yeah, that could work. It's not exactly hidden, but it's better than putting it in some parking lot. We'll find a warehouse or somewhere else later, but for tonight, let's just get it off the road."

He looked at Maria and each of her friends. "You guys okay with that? I mean, it's your gas."

"No, it's *our* gas," she corrected. "My friends will only take what they need to get to Miami."

"Okay, then we'll put the tanker here," he pointed to a spot on the map, "the Princeton Country Club. It's just down the road."

That next morning, Maria said a tearful goodbye to her friends and Julio. After their departure, she spent the rest of the day comforting Carmen, who was particularly upset to see her brother leave.

"I hope I did the right thing by letting him go," Maria confided in Morgan.

"It's impossible to know what the right decision is anymore, but you're doing what you think is best," Morgan consoled. "And you wanted to protect him from any possibility of being exposed to the virus now that he's of age."

Biting her lip, Maria still wasn't certain, but there was little anyone could say to ease her mind. Everyone was uncertain if the journey was all for a foolish pursuit. Only the fear of a potential repeat of the outbreak kept them motivated.

That night, after a long day of settling in, Ben announced that he was heading into the city. He didn't expect anyone to go with him, as everyone was still worn out, but after gaining a second wind, Andy felt the desire to see the New York she'd been visualizing for days.

"Take your pistol and wear something to conceal it," he instructed her. "We might be walking once we reach Manhattan."

Despite the summer heat, she brought a lightweight sweatshirt with her, which she tied around her waist to conceal her Glock. They also brought some bottles of water, dried fruit and beef jerky, two bikes, and two sleeping bags, just in case. Ben also took a kilo of cocaine with him, which he divided into ten smaller bags of a hundred grams each. He weighed each carefully with a food scale he had picked up at a Wal-Mart in Oklahoma for this very purpose. The rest of the drugs had been hidden in the garage of one of their new homes.

Ben drove, since he knew the way. Little was said during the drive. Many hours of comfortable silence had already passed between them within the confines of a car. The darkness gradually lessened as street lamps and lights within homes became visible from the highway. It seemed contradictory that the person responsible for restoring this light could be so dark and twisted.

"Where are we going exactly?" she asked as they passed Newark Airport.

"Jersey City. We'll have to park there since we can't drive through the Holland Tunnel."

"Why not?"

"Because only the Directors and certain people in the Infantry are allowed to drive cars in Manhattan. Not even Fixers can drive in the city. Jim spent every day working on cars, but he wasn't allowed to drive them except to make sure they worked. The only way he and Karen could get around the city without walking or biking or taking the subway was if I drove them."

"You're kidding."

"No, I'm serious. It's meant to control the population, like a lot of other things—but it wasn't always that way."

They crossed Newark Bay and into the peninsula of Bayonne just south of

Jersey City.

"So what happened?"

"It started because of the Holland Tunnel."

"Sorry?"

"Well when the tunnel was built about a hundred years ago, a ventilation system was installed to remove the carbon monoxide emissions created by all the cars passing through. Without it, drivers would asphyxiate before they could get through the tunnel, especially if they were stuck in traffic. When the virus was released and people died while passing through the tunnel, it became clogged with thousands of vehicles and dead people. You can imagine the smell in the summer heat. But without power, the ventilation system wasn't on, and it ending up taking weeks to clear both directions of the tunnel. So until power returned to the city, no one dared to drive through the tunnel even after it was cleared, and by the time Sean got the power back up, everyone was used to crossing the tunnel on foot or on bikes. And with gasoline running out and with the subway working again, he decided to outlaw driving in Manhattan entirely."

"So we'll have to bike through the Holland Tunnel?"

"Yep."

"And you just thought to mention this to me now?"

"Well, I was afraid that if I told you we would have to bike under a river to get to the city, you wouldn't come," he said with an unapologetic smile.

She merely smirked and shook her head. "So once we get into Manhattan, where are we going?"

"To see an old friend. Hopefully he's still living in the same place."

"You trust him?"

"I trust him more than most people."

"You don't sound certain."

"Well, he hates Sean almost as much as I do, so I'm willing to take the risk."

They pulled off I-78 before reaching the tunnel and searched for a place to park. Lights were on throughout the neighborhood and people were scattered everywhere, some huddled in clusters on street corners and others wandering about. Ben parked on a quieter street in the area. After turning off the ignition, he reached behind his seat and grabbed the backpack containing food and supplies, as well as his loaded pistol and a baseball cap. He put the cap on and pulled the brim down low over his eyes. In the dark, he was practically unrecognizable. Though he did not have the same level of concern about Andy being recognized, he also made her wear a baseball cap. Better to obscure her appearance now and avoid being identified later, he had told her.

Andy holstered her pistol to her right hip with a belt. The air had cooled a bit so she put her sweatshirt on, which easily concealed the weapon.

Miraculously, there was light inside the two-lane tunnel, though only every third or fourth light was actually turned on. It made for a long, dim ride through the one-and-a-half miles of tunnel that stretched under the Hudson. The air became increasingly stale as they reached the halfway point, and Andy could only imagine the smell created by hundreds of decaying bodies trapped inside. A few people passed by in the opposite direction, some on foot and some on bikes. Ben stuck to the outside of the right lane and kept his gaze downward to avoid even a microsecond of eye contact. Andy stayed behind him until they emerged on the other side several minutes later.

"What day is it?" he called out to her as she pulled up beside him.

"Uh, Tuesday, I think."

"You aren't sure?"

"No, I'm not sure. The Date and Time app on my iPhone stopped working six years ago. Sorry."

"Very funny."

"Why does it matter what day of the week it is?"

"Because on Mondays, Wednesdays, and Fridays there are random checkpoints throughout Manhattan to check everyone's ID going through."

"IDs? But we don't have any IDs," she said panicked.

"I know. That's what we're taking care of tonight. But we need to get to Chinatown."

"Is that far?"

"No, but there's usually a minefield of checkpoints between here and there. So to be safe we'll head south and circle along the edge of the island. You up for that?"

"How far are we talking?"

"A few miles."

"Fine. I'll follow you."

They rode south along the Hudson side of Manhattan, skirting beside the water on West Street until it ended at Battery Park. The Statue of Liberty was visible in the distance. Shrouded in the darkness, the Lady's silhouette could be seen in the moonlight passing through the clouds high above. Whatever array of lights that once illuminated the statue had not been turned back on.

They pedaled on, farther east, stair-stepping through the crowded Financial District that was now bustling with a very different kind of commerce: drugs and prostitution. As Ben made a sudden right turn onto Wall Street, Andy nearly fell off her bike while distracted by the half-naked girls wandering about and looking to trade their skin for either food or drugs. She caught her balance in time to avoid a large pothole.

After travelling north a few blocks, they turned west and headed back inland. Upon reaching Chinatown, the swell of people roaming the pavement forced them to dismount. Ben ducked into an alley to hide their bikes.

"You really know your way around this town," Andy commented as she wrapped a chain around her front wheel and the frame.

"Yeah, I surprised myself," he replied as he strapped his bike to hers with a second chain.

She followed him back onto the street. The crowds of people were loud and a dizzying mélange of music blared from the storefront windows of defunct Asian food markets and noodle houses.

As they maneuvered through the crowd, Ben drew close to Andy. "Don't tell anyone your name. You'll understand why soon," he said loud enough for her to hear above all the noise.

She nodded once.

"Just pick another name for now," he went on. "It doesn't matter what, but nothing that sounds like Andy or Andrea. And a last name too, okay?"

"Got it."

Half a block later, they made their way to the nondescript front door of a narrow residential building. The door was sandwiched between what used to be two restaurants on the bottom floor within the same building. Ben opened the door without any resistance. After passing through a tiny entryway, they climbed four flights of stairs and headed down the narrowest of hallways. The air was nearly as stifling as inside the Holland Tunnel. They passed three apartments on each side, and then Ben paused at the fourth. He stepped off to the side to avoid standing directly in front of the door and gestured for Andy to move off to the other side. When he retrieved his pistol from his backpack, she placed her right hand on the grip of her own.

Ben gave Andy a quick glance and then knocked on the door. Half a minute passed without any sign of life on the other side, so he knocked again, louder. This time they could hear the sound of footsteps approaching. Following the rattle of at least three different locks being undone, the door partially opened, concealing Ben on the other side.

"Who the fuck are you?"

Andy blinked back at the person standing in front of her. "Excuse me?" she blurted.

He was about Ben's age and height but had a slighter build. His head was shaved and his face was fairly ordinary, neither overwhelmingly attractive nor unattractive. The most remarkable thing about his appearance was three uniform scars running diagonally across the side of his neck as though someone had tried slitting his throat with a wide-tined fork.

"Excuse you? You're the one standing outside my door." His voice was gruff and the accent was unmistakably Boston.

"Still haven't learned any manners, have you, Danny?" Ben stepped into view and gave the stranger a friendly smirk.

Danny blinked as recognition sank in. "Holy shit...Ben Kelly! What are you doing here?"

"Keep your voice down!" he hissed back. "You know how thin these walls are!"

Danny recoiled after realizing his error. "Man, sorry, but you scared the hell out of me." He opened the door wider. "Quick, come in."

Andy followed Danny inside. Ben shut and locked the door behind them. After passing through a short and narrow hallway, they entered the space that comprised the majority of the tiny apartment. Everything from the paint on the walls to the carpet beneath their feet was in desperate need of a renovation that would never come. Sitting on the couch in the living room were two young men deeply engrossed in a video game.

"Where's Jim?" Danny asked.

"He's around."

"Dez...Liam...turn that off. You'll never guess who's here," Danny called out over the flash and bang of guns firing.

The two men ignored him until one of them finally defeated the other. He pumped his fist in the air repeatedly as the other flung his hand controls halfway across the room in frustration.

"You guys piss me off," Danny declared as he bent down to pick the hand control off the floor before turning off the television. "It's a miracle that I haven't reported you two to the Infantry yet for driving me insane!"

"Dude, I just beat Li in *Halo* for the first time ever! You know how long I've been trying to beat him?"

"Dez, I don't give a shit. We got visitors."

Danny's friends turned around and finally realized that two other people were in the apartment.

"Ben?" Dez asked doubtingly.

"No way!" Liam yelled.

Dez scurried around the couch to get a closer look. Liam, blinked in disbelief but moved in closer as well.

"Oh my God, it is you!" Dez cried. "What the hell are you doing here?"

Smiling, Ben stepped forward and gave Dez a firm one-armed hug. "Good to see you, Dez." He then gave Liam a friendly nod of recognition. "What's up, Li? You keeping these guys out of trouble?"

The young man cracked a smile. "Barely," he said as he moved toward Ben with his hand extended. He shook it warmly.

"And who is this fine-looking creature? Where have you been hiding?" Dez said to Andy.

"I'm Katrina," Andy said and she shook his hand.

Puffing his chest out, Dez shook her hand and took yet another step closer. "I'm Dez. It's short for Desmond, and I'll be hurt if you don't remember it." Then while still holding her hand, he gave Ben a look, "What's a beautiful girl like her doing with *you*?"

"All right, take it easy, Romeo. It's too soon to be giving me grief already."

Though Andy had to practically pull her hand free from Dez' grasp, she laughed at his bold yet harmless flirting. "I won't forget your name, Desmond," she replied pointedly. Then, turning to the other, she said, "You're Liam?"

Liam's face brightened. "Yes, but you can just call me Li."

"Nice to meet you."

"You know," Dez said to Ben, "she could be a Helen."

Ben cast him a sharp look. "Don't even start."

"Is that really a reference to Helen of Troy?" Andy asked.

"That's the rumor, but I kinda think it's an ex-girlfriend of his," said Danny.

"Or his mom," Dez countered. "That's another rumor."

"Man, that's messed up," said Danny. "Isn't there, like, a name for that?"

"Oedipus complex," Liam piped in.

"No, that's not it."

"Yes, it is," Liam insisted. "Go check the *Wikipedia* files."

At the mention of *Wikipedia*, Andy's interest piqued, but before she could say anything, Ben cut in. "As interesting as this is, can we get down to business?"

"Yes...*thank* you, Ben," Dez said with exaggerated intonation. "Let's talk about why you and this beautiful girl are here." He gave Andy a wink.

"We need IDs," said Ben bluntly.

"That's it?" Danny replied as though he were expecting more.

"Yeah, that's it. We need nine of them. If you give me something to write with, I'll give you all the information you'll need...names, ages, and physical descriptions. Of course, my name will be different."

"All right, no problem," said Danny. "I'll need two days. Can you come back then?"

"Depends on when the Infantry does their checkpoints. Is it still Monday, Wednesday, and Friday?"

"Yeah, that hasn't changed."

"And today's Tuesday?"

"Yep."

Ben glanced at Andy, who returned a satisfied smile.

"Then I'll be back in two days around the same time. That okay?"

"Yep," Danny said as he grabbed a scrap of paper and a pen from somewhere in the kitchen and handed them to Ben, who took a seat at the small dining room table and began to scribble feverishly. Andy inched closer to him, attempting to read his writing over his shoulder.

A minute or so later, he put the pen down and looked back at her. "Here," he said, handing her the pen. "I forget how old Julia and Michelle are. Can you look this over to make sure I didn't make any other mistakes?"

She stared at him awkwardly for a second until realizing what he was really asking for. "Sure," she said as casually as possible before trading places with him at the table.

On the paper, Ben had written nine fictitious names for their friends, along with their age and a brief physical description that consisted of sex, height, and hair and eye color. The list was nearly complete except for Katrina's last name. She quickly added one before handing the complete list back to Ben.

"Looks fine," she said. "Julia's eleven, not ten, so I changed that."

It seemed that Carmen was going to be Julia from now on, at least if she ever came into the city.

"Here you go." Ben gave the paper to Danny.

He looked over the list as everyone else waited. "There are three males on this list, all age twenty and about the same height with brown hair and brown eyes. I assume you're one of them?"

"Yeah."

He squinted as he took a hard look at Ben's face. "But your eyes aren't brown."

Ben raised an eyebrow. "Don't worry about that."

"But which one of these three names are you gonna be?"

"Don't worry about that either," was Ben's definitive response, ending any further discussion about his "name" or the list of names in general.

Danny shrugged and let it go.

Ben glanced at his watch before removing the ten bags of cocaine from his backpack. He placed them on the kitchen table in a neat row.

"Shit, that's a lot of coke. Where did you get this stuff?" Danny asked.

"They're each 100 grams. You'll get another kilo on Thursday when I pick up the IDs."

"Fair enough."

Ben threw his backpack over his shoulder, signaling that it was time to leave. First, however, he nodded toward the cocaine on the table. "Promise me you'll use that stuff to buy food and not to string out prostitutes."

Danny crossed his arms over his chest. "Jesus, Ben, who do you think I am? You know I ain't like Sean or his guys."

Realizing he'd gone too far, Ben held up his hands remorsefully. "Yeah, sorry. I know that."

Satisfied by this apology, Danny relaxed his stance and mumbled, "It's okay."

Ben turned toward the door to leave, but Dez caught him first. "Whoa, hold up. You're not leaving here without telling us where you've been all this time, or why you're back."

"Not tonight," he said. "See you Thursday."

He exited the apartment with Andy following closely behind. They went back to the alley to retrieve their bikes. They paused a few minutes for some food and water.

"So who were those guys?"

"Just some hackers who helped Jim and me last year. Sean keeps records about everyone and everything in this city on a server uptown. These guys have access to the server, so they can add or change pretty much anything on record, including names of people living in the city."

"So they're Fixers?"

"Just Danny. Li and Dez could both be Fixers if they wanted to, but they'd rather fly under the radar. They just work with Danny on the side for jobs like this one. It's risky, especially for Danny. If Sean found out what he was doing, he'd kill him. So Danny's pretty picky about what jobs they take. They can't mess with the data too much, but this one's easy to hide. Adding a couple of names to a list of about a million won't be noticed."

Andy nodded and ate another dried apricot. "So everyone registered has an ID? Like a driver's license?"

"Yeah, except it's a bracelet with a barcode on it. And if you want to live anywhere in or near the city and have access to food, water, and electricity, you have to register yourself and wear the bracelet."

"That doesn't seem so bad. The government used to have birth records on all of us, so how is this any different?"

"It's not, really, and I never had an issue with Sean making everyone register themselves. It's everything else that he does that I have a problem with. Once you're in the system, then you have to work. Food and clean water and power don't just magically appear—I get that. The problem is that Sean uses the Dregs like slave labor."

"Slave labor," Andy repeated. She frowned and thought of Maria.

"They're treated like dogs by the Directors and the Infantry, and everyone over the age of seven has to work."

"So why do people stay here…people like Danny? He seems smart. Why don't they try to go out and survive on their own like we've done?"

"Some do. A few stay because they doubt anything outside New York would be any better, but most stay because they're scared and helpless. Most people aren't like us; you know that. And when you're so hungry that you feel like you're digesting your own stomach, you'll do whatever it takes if someone is giving you food, even if it's someone like Sean."

Ben took a bite of beef jerky and offered the remainder to Andy. Starved, she finished the rest of it. Together, they chewed away in silence. He edged closer to the end of the alley and glanced around. The streets were as bustling as earlier.

"You don't trust these guys?" she asked suddenly after she finished eating.

"What do you mean?"

"Well, you told me not to tell them my real name, and then you didn't tell them which name on that list was supposed to be yours. I assume that means you don't trust them."

"It's not that I don't trust them. It's just safer for everyone if they know as little as possible about who we are and what we're doing here. Sean has tortured people for information, and he's got spies all over this city just waiting to find people like us. The fact that I'm already at the top of his list of enemies means that I have to be ten times more careful. And so do the people who are close to me."

"People like me."

"Exactly. Believe me, you don't want Sean knowing your real name."

"All right, so besides getting through checkpoints, what else do we need IDs for if we don't need food or water or power?"

"To get into nightclubs."

"Nightclubs?"

"Uh-huh. Sean kept a few of them open, and now they're wild and crazier than ever. They're every teenage boy's dream."

"Sounds terrific," she said sarcastically.

"Well, it's also our ticket to getting the information we need about the virus. The Directors and the Infantry love the nightclubs, and if anyone knows whether Sean's hidden the virus somewhere, it's them."

Ben finished his water and put the empty bottle back in his bag. Andy was still thinking about the nightclubs as she unlocked their bikes.

"So did you randomly pick 'Katrina' or did you know someone with that name?" he asked.

"It was my mother's name. Katrina Wilson. That was her maiden name."

"Really? How did I not know that already?" He sounded almost disappointed, as if this were something that he should have known about by now.

"Well, I don't know *your* mother's name. What was it?"

"Ingrid. Ingrid Andersen."

"Andersen…that Danish? My dad's family was Danish."

He nodded. "Her family was from Denmark. She was the first one born in the States."

"And Irish on your father's side?"

"Yep. You can't get more Irish than 'Kelly.' I think that's the only reason Danny even bothers to help me," he said with a grin.

Chuckling, she moved closer to him in order to put the bike locks back inside his bag. She looked up at him and smiled faintly. "I like that name. Ingrid, I mean."

"Yeah, my mom was cool." He returned the smile. "You would've liked her."

Even in the darkness of the alley, Andy could still make out his translucent blue eyes. "How did you know everyone's eye color?" she said, suddenly frowning. "I've known Morgan and Charlie for six years, and I couldn't tell you what color their eyes are."

Ben shrugged. "I knew we were going to need IDs so I made a mental note of everyone's eye color and approximate height over the past few days."

"But your ID will say that you have brown eyes, not blue."

"Well, that's what colored contacts are for. I can't go through checkpoints looking like Ben Kelly. Any guy who's about my age with my description always gets a second look."

"You have colored contacts?"

"Yeah, some disposable ones I've got stashed away, just in case."

She shook her head and turned away. "That's too bad. Your eyes are gorgeous. Be a shame to cover them up."

Ben was momentarily thrown by this comment. Andy had never acknowledged his looks, not to him at least.

Chapter XXI

*G*reen Haven Correctional Facility was one of the larger prisons in New York. But despite sitting some seventy-five miles north of Manhattan, Sean hadn't chosen the prison because it was close to the city, but because it sat in a quiet, rural area of the state. It provided the space and secrecy he needed.

There were eight cellblocks in the prison, lettered A through H. A through D were closed cells, while blocks E through H were open cells facing each other in an aviary-like configuration. Each block had two hundred and fifty-two individual cells, of which all were vacant except for the few that were used by the Fixers to sleep in after a long day of work. Cellblock D, however, had undergone extensive renovations.

It was early afternoon by the time Sean reached the prison. He made the drive alone, only informing his closest advisor, Luke, where he was going. He walked by several guards at the entrance, each greeting him a little too eagerly, and headed directly to Cellblock F. When he reached the only occupied cell, he peered inside.

"Wake up," he barked between the bars to the girl crumpled on the tiny bed in the corner.

The sound of Sean's voice startled her, and she quickly stirred from her slumber. Wordlessly, she got up and walked to the bars. Having barely eaten for nearly a week, it was a struggle for her to stand, and the fatigue showed on her face. Though more pale than normal with a hint of circles under her eyes, Lily Haines was still a sight to behold. Her stunning beauty had suffered no ill-effects from the difficulties of a post-viral world. She was thin, as most women now were, but Lily still had all the curves that could excite every male from pre-pubescent boys to full-grown men. And yet Sean's first remark to her was, "You look like crap."

Lily hugged her arms tightly around her chest to guard against the drafty air. Her long dark hair draped over her folded arms, and her hazel eyes averted Sean's own piercing blue stare. She remained silent not out of fear but out of defiance.

"Fun being in here, isn't it?" Sean went on, finally taking his eyes off Lily to look around at the vast and empty space that surrounded them. "All alone and without any Directors to sleep with."

"I only did it because you've been ignoring me for weeks now. How else was I supposed to get your attention?" She stepped within inches of the bars. Anger colored her cheeks as her almond-shaped eyes narrowed on Sean. "I'm sick of you screwing the other girls and then getting jealous if I even *talk* to another guy. It's not fair!"

"Life's not fair. Get used to it," Sean responded coolly as he stood perfectly erect. "And just for that, I'm leaving you here another day. Someone will drive your skanky-ass back tomorrow."

Looking as though she was either about to cry or scream, Lily did neither and instead hardened her jaw. Defeated, she turned away and retreated back to her tiny bed. Sean smugly watched her lie back down before leaving. There was one more thing to do.

∽≈✦≈∼

"I don't know how you do it, man," Dez said to Ben on Thursday not a minute after he entered the tiny apartment in Chinatown with Andy, Morgan, and Maria. "Where do you find these gorgeous women, and can you tell me so I can go there too?"

The three women laughed lightly. Andy had warned them about Dez' flirtatiousness.

"It won't do you any good if I told you. All the pretty ones left with me," Ben quipped.

"Well, it sure seems that way." Dez ogled each of the girls shamelessly.

"Yo, Dez, leave 'em alone," Danny called out from the kitchen. "They didn't come here to be harassed."

"I'm not harassing you, am I?" he asked the girls while wearing a mischievous grin.

"Dez, get outta here," Danny ordered. "We got work to do."

With his hands held up in a mocking surrender, Dez inched toward the door. "Fine, Mister Grouchy Pants. I was going to the food bank anyway." Turning back to the girls, he bowed dramatically before grabbing each girl's hand to kiss. "Good night, ladies," he said with exaggerated gallantry before leaving the apartment.

Danny came into the living room where everyone else was seated. "My apologies. There's just no explaining him."

"Don't apologize. He's funny," said Morgan smiling.

"I'm glad *you* think so," Danny replied.

"What did he mean about a 'food bank'?" Maria asked.

"It's exactly what it sounds like…just a place for people to buy food. I think there's, like, fifteen in Manhattan and about another thirty in the other boroughs. Of course, the lines are a nightmare. Today I waited two goddamned hours, and by the time I got to the front of the line, the only things left to buy were apples and eggs. I eat so many eggs that I feel like I'm gonna sprout feathers or something."

"What do you buy the food with?" Andy asked as she silently wished they had brought along some extra food for him and his friends.

"Credit. It's like money. Each person has to work to get credit, and every job has a certain value. Most Fixers, like me, get a thousand credits a month, which is a lot. I usually have extra at the end of each month. Other jobs, like working in the water treatment plants, get less…maybe three or four hundred credits a month."

"The dirtier the job, the worse the pay?" Morgan commented aloud. "Well that's nothing new."

"And let me guess, Sean decided what each job was worth?" asked Andy, her voice tinged with disdain.

"He and the Directors," Danny replied, nodding toward Ben.

"Wait, *you* decided what each job was worth?" asked Andy, turning toward him, but he quickly shook his head.

"Not exactly. I had this whole idea where each job would be paid based on whatever the average was for the same type of work before the outbreak. I thought it was fair and made the most sense, but no one listened to me. In the end, Sean decided on his own what everyone would be paid."

"So why does Sean even bother hearing the Directors' opinions if he doesn't listen to them?" Maria asked.

"He wants them to feel like they're important because he trusts them to manage everything that keeps people fed and the lights on. Like my ol' man used to say, 'happy employees are loyal employees,'" Danny said with his colorful accent. "No offense, Ben, but you know that's true."

Ben waved away the comment without issue.

"So, about this credit that everyone gets," Morgan continued. "People get credit every month?"

"Uh-huh, it's electronically linked to your ID," Ben said. "So when you go to anywhere that requires credit like food banks and nightclubs, you scan your ID and the 'cost' gets deducted from your credit. And then Sean can monitor everywhere you've been and everything you've bought."

"Yeah, like 'Big Brother,'" Danny added as he suddenly pushed himself out of his grungy armchair. "Speaking of IDs, I've got all of yours ready. Hang on a sec."

He disappeared into what was likely a bedroom and returned moments later with a handful of metal bands in one hand, a small electronic-looking box in the other, and a laptop tucked beneath his arm. He sat back down and placed the bands and small box on the rickety coffee table in front of him before firing up the laptop. "So today I was told that Sean wants to add fingerprints to everyone's ID file."

Ben frowned at this bit of news. "Why?"

"Dunno. That jerk Doug told me, so you can guess how that went."

"Oh, man, I forgot how stupid that guy is."

"Well, he hasn't gotten any smarter since you've been gone. I think I'm just getting better at dealing with his total failure to communicate the simplest instructions."

"Who's Doug?" asked Maria.

"He's the Director of Census and Labor, which just means he's supposed to make sure everyone is registered with an ID and is assigned a job. But he's a total idiot who only got the job because Sean wanted to sleep with his sister." Danny then paused to rub his eyes with one hand. "Most people just ignore him, but he's a daily headache for me."

"So why the fingerprints?" Ben asked. "Has there been a spike in people forging or stealing other people's IDs or something?"

Danny shook his head. "No more than usual. Maybe Sean wants to get rid of the ID bands completely so that people just use their fingerprints, which, I gotta admit, would make sense. There's more than a million people registered in the five boroughs, and with people losing their IDs all the time, it's a major pain for people to prove who they are. Fingerprints would solve everything."

"So you need to scan our prints," Andy said. "But won't that completely defeat the purpose of you having an alias?" she asked Ben.

"It shouldn't," he replied, sounding certain. "It's not as if Sean's got a copy of my prints. And anyway," he went on as he combed his hand through his hair, "Jim and I burned and deleted all our medical and school records in Virginia last year, which were the only thing that had my fingerprints. We destroyed Karen's records too. If Sean ever searches for our old records, he'll find nothing. It's like we never existed."

Andy raised her eyebrows as she listened to Ben. She had no idea the measures he and Jim had taken to erase their pasts.

"As long as they're not asking for a photo ID, I'm not worried," he concluded.

"That ain't gonna happen soon," Danny assured. "With the data rates we gotta work with right now, photo files are too big to transfer from the main server to all the food banks and checkpoints. It would take five friggin' minutes just to check one person's identity. No one's got that kinda patience."

Not a moment later, the lights throughout the entire apartment began to flicker—once, twice, and after the third time, they went out completely, and the apartment became pitch-black.

"Terrific," Danny muttered as the others reached into their pockets and backpacks to retrieve flashlights. Maria found hers first and illuminated the room. By the time the others found theirs, the lights flickered back on.

"Does that happen a lot?" Morgan asked.

"All the time," Danny replied with a sigh as he plugged his laptop into the wall. "And always when I'm about to do something with my computer."

Everyone waited as Danny hooked up the fingerprint scanner to the computer. Once everything was ready, he looked up.

"So I told Doug that I'd only scan prints for new people who were registering for IDs, but knowing Sean, he'll demand that everyone else start scanning their fingerprints at checkpoints to get them on record, so better to get yours on record now by me than some Infantry punk."

"Do you need all ten prints for each person?" Ben asked.

"No, I just need one fingerprint per file. But I can add up to five prints per person."

"Good. I want you to add one of my prints to three separate names. Can you do that?"

Danny blinked a few times before his face broke out into a smile, making him look almost handsome. "What are you up to, Ben?"

"Only good things, I promise."

"All right…whatever you want. If anyone ever finds the glitch, which I doubt, I'll just say I accidentally copied the same print to three different names."

"Also, I'll need to add another print, maybe two, to each of the three names, but it will be someone else's prints."

Danny looked up and gave Ben the same smile before breaking out into a chuckle. He held up his hands. "Like I said, whatever you want."

The girls exchanged glances as each silently attempted to decipher Ben's plan. When Andy figured it out, she wordlessly expressed to the others that Ben, Jim, and Brian would be sharing multiple aliases.

Ben scanned the print of his right index finger first, which Danny copied to the files of the three aliases that he would be using: John Simmons, Michael Wilkins, and Matthew Thompson, all age twenty with brown hair and eyes and a height of six-foot-one. There was no meaning behind the three names; Ben had simply found them in a phonebook a few days earlier. Danny handed him the ID bracelets for all three.

Morgan went next. She scanned two of her fingerprints, which Danny quickly added to the file of her new name, Sarah O'Brian. "A good Irish name," he said with approval as she bit her lip.

Andy followed Morgan and applied her right thumbprint to Katrina Wilson's file before being handed her ID. It was similar to a medical ID bracelet except that there was a small black-and-white barcode where the person's medical condition would normally be inscribed.

"And last but not least, Isabel…" Danny said, looking at Maria, smiling awkwardly at her.

"Torres," Maria responded, giving her fake last name.

"Right," Danny muttered as he fumbled through the remaining ID bracelets to find her name. "Here we go."

She sat beside him as the others had done to scan her prints, but he appeared to be slightly flustered by her presence and made more than a few keystroke errors when updating her file. As she stood to return to her seat on the adjacent sofa, his gaze lingered on her for more than a few seconds, but he quickly caught himself. Only Ben seemed to notice as he suppressed a smile.

Danny then held up the remaining IDs. "I've still got three more…Henry, Kathy, and Julia."

"Here, give 'em to me," Ben said, holding out his hand. "They can get their prints scanned at the checkpoints."

"Whatever you want."

"Jim will come by in two days to scan his thumbprint, and he'll bring these." Ben held up the bracelets for the three male aliases: John, Michael, and Matthew.

"And you want me to add his thumbprint to all three?" Danny asked.

"That's right."

"No problem. Just tell him to come by before ten."

Narrowing his eyes on Danny, Ben gave him a knowing look. "What, you hitting the clubs or something?"

Danny looked sideways at Maria for a spilt-second as he placed his laptop on the coffee table before answering. "Well, what the hell else is there to do in this town for fun?" he said unapologetically as he leaned back in his chair and cupped his hands behind his shaved head. "I gotta blow off steam somehow. I can't keep watching Li and Dez play video games every day. I'll go insane!"

"Does everyone still go to *Papillon*?"

"Yeah, I hear it's packed almost every night."

"What's *Papillon*?" Andy asked.

"It's a nightclub in the Meatpacking District," he murmured, still looking pensive. "You know if Luke still goes?" he asked Danny.

"Probably. Sean's there at least three nights a week, so Luke's gotta be there too."

Ben stood up and announced that it was time to go. "Thanks, man."

"Hey, easy day, brother," said Danny. "Part of me wants to know what you're up to, but the rest of me doesn't wanna know a thing."

From his backpack, Ben pulled out the second kilo of cocaine that he'd promised. However, Danny waved it away. "Nah, man. What you gave me last time was enough. Just tell Jim to bring me some food when he comes if you got any to spare. Something other than eggs or apples." Then he whispered out of earshot of the girls, "Hey, I know I give Dez shit for almost every word that comes outta his mouth, but I admit he's right about those girls. They're gorgeous, particularly that Isabel. Instead of a kilo of coke, I'll take one night with her."

"I'll be sure to pass that along," Ben replied sarcastically.

"Seriously, what did you do? Go to L.A. and find all the leftover models and movie stars or something?"

"I met them all just like I met you—by accident."

As Ben chucked, Danny shooed away the gibe with a wave of his hand.

"Whatever, you lucky bastard. Maybe if I looked like you, girls like that would also fall right into my lap too."

Sean looked at his watch with impatience. More than five minutes had passed since one of the guards went to find him a hazmat suit. After another five minutes, the guard finally arrived. He was wearing a cumbersome blue hazmat suit and carrying another.

"Jesus Christ! How long does it take to find a suit? Aren't they supposed to be kept in this room and not beyond this door?"

From within the confines of the suit, the guard nodded up and down meekly, and a muffled "sorry" was heard from beneath his helmet.

Sean snatched the suit out of the guard's hands and hastily put it on. "Let's go!" he barked once all the seals and zippers were closed. The guard wordlessly obeyed, and after passing through two hermetically sealed safe rooms, they stopped at the prep room to recheck their suits. Satisfied that everything was in order, Sean gave a nod to keep going. Once inside the next room, he turned on the safelight and carefully opened the medical freezer.

Inside were seven small glass vials sitting on a metal tray. Sean carefully picked one up with his gloved hand and examined it. The contents of the vial looked like water and appeared to be equally as harmless.

In the six years since it had been unleashed on the world, the virus had never been called anything else. It didn't need a unique name, for it had entirely redefined the meaning of the word. The explosion at Fort Detrick had destroyed most of the vials and all the research documents, but these had miraculously survived.

Sean placed the vial back in the freezer and closed the door before turning to the guard. "When was he infected?"

"Uh, eight days ago."

"Then let's get moving."

The guard opened the cipher door to what was referred to as the "vacuum room" before approaching the final safe room. Beyond that was their destination.

"The Pit" was nothing but an empty room, cold and sterile. The windows had been sealed off and covered to suppress the faintest beam of light from the outside world. A single florescent light bulb high above in the ceiling gave the room meager illumination.

The guard remained by the door while Sean approached the only prisoner in the room, a boy who had been caught stealing food from one of the food banks.

Though only a few millimeters of protective material guarded him from infection, Sean stepped forward to get closer to the boy.

Wearing only the thinnest of hospital gowns, he was experiencing nearly all of the major symptoms: large, puss-filled boils on his arms and legs, uncontrollable shivering despite suffering from a fever, and profuse sweating. Death would come within hours, but not without severe pain. Soon his lungs would fill with blood. In the end, the virus simply asphyxiated its victims to death.

In his agony, the boy barely registered Sean's presence. The intense shivering and pain numbed all senses to anything outside of his own skin. He knew his end was near and it couldn't come fast enough. Suddenly, a gloved hand grabbed his arm, and seconds later a needle was inserted into a vein in his forearm and a liquid was injected into his body.

"How long will it take to know if it works?"

"Hard to tell," the Fixer answered Sean through his helmet. "But if he's still in the same shape by morning, we'll know it failed."

Sean stared down at the trembling boy and wondered how excruciating the ordeal truly was. "When you find out, send someone to let me know," he commanded before turning to leave.

Chapter **XXII**

01 August 2023

*T*his time turn your back to me." Bent over at the waist with her hands on her knees, Andy looked up at Ben like she wanted to give him a hard kick to the groin, but a real one this time. She was breathing heavily, as was he.

"C'mon, I'm not doing this to be a pain in the butt. I want to make sure you can defend yourself," he insisted between breaths and beckoned her with his hands. "Let's go."

After slowly standing upright, Andy raised her hand. "Give me a minute."

"No. Go now. If you can do it when you're tired, you'll be able to do it anytime."

Knowing he was right, she took another deep breath. "All right," she said hoarsely, and turned her back to him.

They were in the backyard. The cool weather enjoyed during those first days of their arrival had transformed into the persistent mugginess of summer, and despite it being nearly eight o'clock in the evening, their faces were red and glistening with sweat.

Andy prepared herself with another deep breath as the faint sound of Ben's shoes walking on grass drew closer. A tense pause followed, then he grabbed her from behind, his arms bear-hugging around her chest and arms. The sweet scent of his sweat just barely hit her nose as she reacted swiftly to the attack by stepping one foot out to the side and squatting down to lower her center of gravity. Still moving fluidly, she jutted her elbows out to the sides, which loosened his grip just enough for her to break free.

"Good," he said approvingly. "Let's do it again."

Andy didn't complain this time, and they repeated the drill three more times before Ben decided she was ready for the next scenario.

"Now this time, raise your arms up, and my arms will go underneath them."

As with the other scenarios, he would slowly walk her through the sequence of movements until she understood exactly what to do to defeat her attacker. With her back to him once again, she raised her arms, which allowed him to wrap his arms around her even tighter than before.

Ben caught a hint of the fragrance of her hair. "God, you smell…"

"What, I smell?" Horrified, Andy broke away, startling him, and she quickly sniffed underneath her arms.

"No, no…you don't smell bad," he said, laughing. "I meant to say that you smell nice."

"Oh…" She self-consciously brushed loose strands of hair away from her face. "It's this new shampoo that Maria and Carmen made. It's got lavender and some other sweet things in it. Chamomile, I think," she added hastily. "I don't really know."

"Well, whatever it is, it smells amazing." And without warning, he stepped forward and leaned in to smell the top of Andy's scalp again, catching her off-guard, and she instinctively backed away. "Relax. I just wanted to smell you again," he said before shutting his eyes tight and looking embarrassed. "Sorry, that sounded weird."

"Just a little."

"Want to try again?" he asked.

"Okay, but after this one, I'm done for the day."

"Fair enough."

Andy turned around once more as Ben stepped forward to wrap his arms around her.

"Now do the same thing. Step out to the side and squat down."

She followed the instructions.

"Good. Since I have a tighter grip on you, you'll have to use your arms and feet to disable me. So look back and use your elbows to strike me in the face."

"Oh, that sounds fun." She looked back and smiled.

"Funny," he smirked before continuing with the lesson. "You can stomp on the feet to further injure the person, but I would go for the face first, either with your elbow or the back of your forearm. Almost anytime you strike someone anywhere on the front or sides of their head, their instinct will be to close their eyes. If you're lucky, they'll grab their head. Either way, that's your window of escape."

Andy returned her gaze straight ahead as he released his arms and stepped back. "Ready?"

"Ready."

After she lifted her arms, Ben stepped forward and grabbed her again. With impressive speed, Andy deftly maneuvered out of his grip, turned herself around, and threw the base of her right palm up within an inch of his nose. He blinked and took a step backward. "Nice work."

They repeated this scenario a few more times and then ended the training for the day.

"We'll do it again tomorrow."

Andy nodded and unwrapped the rubber band that held her ponytail in place. She rubbed her scalp, which released the aroma of the homemade shampoo. It *did* smell good. "How big is he?" she asked.

"Who, Luke?"

"Yeah."

"I guess he's about my height and build."

Andy studied Ben. He was a good eight or nine inches taller than she and easily seventy to eighty pounds heavier. "Is he as strong as you?" she asked, her eyes looking anxious.

He didn't answer right away. Instead, he tilted his head to the side and then looked away. This made her uneasy.

"I won't lie to you. Luke's pretty strong." Sensing her apprehension, he quickly added, "Just remember that he'll likely be drunk or high or both. That will take away some of his advantage."

She looked down at her feet and muttered, "Right."

"You'll be fine. You'll be the last thing he expects."

Looking up, Andy set her gaze to the rear of the house. Through the window that looked into the living room, she could see Susan and Charlie playing a game of cards with Maria and Carmen. Probably poker. Meanwhile, Morgan was reading a book at the kitchen table while feeding Katie. Candles flickered throughout both rooms, as there was no electricity. Princeton sat outside of the zone where power had been restored, and they were too far north from Philadelphia to receive it from that end.

"How did you learn all this self-defense stuff?" she asked

"You'll laugh when I tell you."

"Why?"

Ben stepped over to a wooden bench that separated a small rock garden from the lawn that covered the majority of the backyard and sat down. Andy edged over to him but remained standing.

"From watching *YouTube* videos that I got from Danny."

"*YouTube?*"

"Yeah. Danny has access to every video file that people uploaded on *YouTube* up to the days just before the outbreak. He's also got access to all the files from *Wikipedia* too."

"What?"

"Yeah, but get this. Within a year after the outbreak, Sean sent people to the headquarters of both of those companies to bring *all* of their servers back to New York. He didn't want anyone else to get their hands on all that information."

"Oh my God," Andy breathed.

"That's the kind of person we're dealing with. While we were all scared and starving, Sean was busy transporting thousands of terabytes of data across the country. Do you know where *YouTube* and *Wikipedia* had their headquarters?"

"No idea."

"California and Florida. Both thousands of miles from here."

Andy rubbed her eyes as her anxiety returned. "And Danny has access to those files?"

"Yeah. Part of his job is to go through all the video files and delete all the crap that has no real value, at least to Sean. You know…videos that parents used to upload of their kids doing funny or cute things…useless stuff like that. But of course Danny keeps copies of the really funny things and then gives them to Liam and Dez to sell."

"People buy old videos from *YouTube?*"

"Sure," Ben replied with a shrug. "It reminds them of the old days, I guess."

It had never occurred to Andy that such things would now be so important. She took a seat on the bench and hugged her knees to her chest. Her shoulder touched Ben, and she made no move to distance herself. "He's devious."

Frowning, he turned to her. "Who? Danny?"

"No, Sean."

"That's just one of about a hundred words you could use to describe him."

She rested her head on his shoulder. He wrapped his right arm around her and pulled her an inch closer. Andy closed her eyes, and settled into him. Just a friendly hug.

"Ben?"

"Yeah?"

"Please don't tell me 'I told you so,' but I'm beginning to think that this might not be such a good idea."

"What, the nightclub?"

"Yeah."

He swallowed hard. "Andy, you already know what I think of this whole plan, but I've been trying for weeks now to think of some other way to do it. So has Jim, but the fact is that neither he nor I can be involved. If Sean gets even the slightest idea that we've returned, he'll either add so much security to wherever he's hiding the virus or he'll move it and we'll never find it again. And since Luke is probably the only person who knows if Sean actually has the virus and where he's hiding it, the only options are to either kidnap him and force the truth out of him with torture, or..."

"Or do what we're doing instead."

"Yeah." Ben gently tussled Andy's hair. "I just...I feel like I'm throwing you to the wolves. I feel like a coward."

She abruptly sat up and turned toward him, her eyes burning bright. "Hey, we've been through this already. I insisted on doing this. You just have to accept that this is *one* thing that you can't do." Her voice rose in both intensity and volume. "I admit I'm scared, but if we're going to succeed, we'll have to do some dangerous things. You know that better than anyone. You've already sacrificed enough. Let some other people handle the burden for a while."

Ben managed to smile.

"I don't want you to worry about me," she continued. "Maria will be with me the whole time, and between the two of us, we'll get it done, especially after all these self-defense lessons you've been giving us. So stop worrying so much. You've prepared me well, Yoda." She gave Ben a gentle punch into his arm.

"Yes ma'am," he said with a smile.

She smiled back at him and their eyes met for a moment too long. Feeling the tension, Andy released her knees from her chest and planted her feet on the ground. "I need to wash up," she said.

"Ahem, yeah, me too."

Ben followed her inside. He went upstairs to clean up while she went to talk to Morgan in the kitchen. "What are you reading?" she asked.

"Calculus," Morgan replied, looking up from her book. "Charlie found it at the library on campus. He said it would be a good one to start with."

"Calculus? I didn't know you liked math that much."

Morgan grimaced. "It's not that I like it, but I often thought that I should learn some more advanced math so that I could teach it."

Andy's thoughts turned to her medical books sitting in a box in her bedroom, and she felt a pang of regret for neglecting her own studies of late. "Sounds like a good idea." She glanced down at her friend's wristwatch. "When did Jim leave?"

"About an hour ago, right after you and Ben went outside," Morgan replied without lifting her eyes from her book.

Andy offered her pinky finger to Katie who was lying in a vibrating chair positioned on the kitchen table. The baby latched onto her finger with her entire hand but without her usual vice-like grip. Her eyelids were beginning to look heavy.

"She's getting close. Want me to put her to bed?"

Morgan released the pen she'd been using to take notes and looked up at her daughter. "Nah, I got her."

While Morgan put Katie to bed, Andy wandered into the living room.

"Not again!" Charlie lamented as Susan raked in the pot of chips to her corner of the table while imitating an evil laugh.

"Ha! That's right, sucker!" she cackled. "You can't beat me!"

Both Maria and Carmen threw their losing hands of cards onto the table. Andy assessed the damage Susan had caused to everyone's stack of chips. Hers was easily triple the size of the others.

"Wait, didn't Susan win last night too?" Andy teased Charlie. He and Susan had had a longstanding poker rivalry since their days in Aspen.

"Why, Andy, I do believe that you are correct," replied Susan, her voice dripping with sarcasm.

Charlie made a face.

"Hey, you got a sec?" Andy asked him, her tone now serious.

"Yes, I have more than a second," he replied, relieved to have an excuse to leave the table. He followed Andy into the kitchen.

"What do you know about truth serum?" she asked him as he took a seat at the kitchen table.

"Truth serum?" he repeated with surprise. "Not much, I'm afraid."

"Do you know if it's actually real or if it's just something that Hollywood made up?"

"Oh no, it's real. It's called *sodium amytal*. But other than that, I don't know how it works or how reliable it is. *Rohypnol* might be better, but it causes memory loss." After a pause, he added, "Why do you ask?"

Andy sat back in her chair and let out a weary sigh. "I'm trying to think of all possible ways to get the location of the virus out of Luke, assuming he even knows where it is."

"Sounds like you've got some doubts."

"Well, yeah. I can't help but feel like we're all taking a giant stab in the dark here."

"Who's taking a stab in the dark?" Susan entered the kitchen.

"Oh…no one," Andy quickly muttered to contain the conversation. The last thing she wanted was for everyone to think she doubted her own scheme. After all, she had insisted on being the one to go to *Papillon*, an idea that Ben still hated despite his efforts to appear perfectly at ease with it, and despite all of their preparations.

"Did I hear you say something about truth serum?"

Andy closed her eyes, feeling foolish for even considering the notion. "It was just something that popped into my head earlier today. I'm sure it won't even work."

"I'll look into it. You never know, right?" said Charlie.

"I guess," Andy muttered before mustering a smile of gratitude. "Thanks, Charlie."

"No worries. Want to come with me to the library tomorrow?" he asked Susan.

Her face quickly fell. "Oh, I would, but I'm going with Morgan and Maria tomorrow to find clothes, remember?"

"Oh, right. I forgot," he said, frowning. "Oh well, then. It'll be boring anyway."

"What are you talking about? I love going to the library with you," she replied as she reached over and stroked his hair. "I always feel smarter when I leave," she added. He reached up and playfully grabbed her wrist.

Though smiling at the pair, Andy couldn't help but feel a twinge of envy.

⁂

"How'd it go?" Ben asked Jim.

Sitting closest to Ben, Andy thought she caught the faintest hint of aftershave.

"It went fine. Danny came through, as usual," Jim said. He then pulled out two ID bracelets from his backpack and handed one to Andy and the other to Maria. "You're both registered as Helens now. Nothing else has changed except your classifications."

"What's today? Sunday?" Andy wondered aloud.

"Yeah, and I think if we're going to do this, it should be this week," Ben said with an edge to his voice. "The sooner, the better."

"I agree," echoed Jim. He looked back and forth between the two girls. "Are you two ready?"

They exchanged a quick glance before nodding in unison. Inside, however, Andy's heart began to pound.

"We're going to go look for clothes tomorrow," Maria said. "After that, we'll be ready."

"Good. Wednesday is the best night to go," Jim said. "Danny said that's the night Dregs are allowed into the club, which means that the guards will be distracted with the crowd."

"Which means less focus on everyone else, right? Including the Helens?" Andy asked.

"Hopefully. You and Maria should have no problem getting in without a second look. Once inside, you're in the clear." Though Jim made that task sound easy, everyone knew differently. While both he and Ben were forced to remain on the sidelines, Andy and Maria would be placing themselves in the crosshairs.

"You were gone for more than three weeks. What happened?" Sean was careful with his tone as he addressed Chad so that his words sounded authoritative but not accusatory. He wanted people to think he trusted them but make no mistake that he was still the one in control.

Chad, however, recognized the distinction. "The Fixers took longer to investigate the Metro than expected," he replied calmly. "You were right about them…smart but totally helpless."

They were sitting in Sean's office in his Fifth Avenue apartment. Both had just returned to New York: Sean from Philadelphia, and Chad, an Infantry officer rising quickly through the ranks, from Washington DC. Sean had selected him specifically for the assignment.

"I know, but they have their uses, clearly," Sean countered. "What about the people? Did you even see anyone?"

"No. The infrastructure is in ruins. Most of the city's power lines are above ground, not like here where everything is underground. All the storms these last few years have done major damage. We're talking miles and miles of lines that need to be fixed. It'll take months and probably a few hundred people."

Sean frowned at the news, though he wasn't surprised. "It was the same in Philly, but I got that fixed." Turning to his computer, he opened a few files that detailed every young man enlisted in the Infantry along with their age, rank, current location, and current duty. Over two thousand were located among the city's five boroughs, while the remaining thousand were either in Philadelphia or shuffling back and forth. "I can give you fifty officers, and maybe a hundred and fifty workers," he assessed after staring at the screen for more than a minute.

"I'd be better off with three hundred," Chad countered.

But Sean remained firm. "For long distance jobs, I never want Dregs to outnumber the Infantry by more than three to one. Otherwise, I risk a revolt. That's how I cleaned up Philly, and DC will be no different."

Chad shrugged. "I'll take what I can get."

"You'll manage," Sean said coolly as he turned away from his computer. "It'll take a few days to move some people around, but you should be back in DC within a week."

After discussing a few other mundane matters, Chad left and headed back to his own sparsely furnished apartment in Chelsea. He walked the mile home, preferring to use his feet rather than a bike. He lived alone, his older brother Thomas having succumbed to the virus.

Upon entering his apartment, he removed his knife from his back pocket and placed it on the kitchen table. He washed his face in the bathroom with cold water. After a quick dinner of apples, milk, hard-boiled eggs, and bacon, he sat in the living room and spent the next half hour sharpening his knife.

Originally from a small farming town in western Iowa, Chad had traveled east to New York three years earlier. Shortly after his arrival, he joined the Infantry and soon caught the attention of Luke, the leader of the Infantry and the second most powerful person in New York. Luke had assigned Chad the task of hunting those involved in a growing underground movement plotting to overthrow Sean and the rest of the Directors. Effective at flushing out this enemy, Chad didn't shy away from violence the way the others did.

The knife, which he preferred to use in lieu of a gun, had been a gift from his father. Two days after receiving the knife, his father was killed in a car accident on a lonely country road. The death was a serious blow to young Chad. His protector was gone, and his mother favored his brother. For years he endured her endless criticisms and lamentations over why he wasn't more like Thomas. Unable to take anymore, he staged a robbery one night and stabbed his mother in the chest with his beloved knife while she slept. Thomas died a month later without ever suspecting his brother.

All of that was long in the past, as were his days in the Infantry. He was approaching the inner circle now.

"Where did you get your dress?"

The girl, probably no older than fourteen and little more than skin and bone, looked at Maria like she had two heads. "Where do you think? From a store."

"Uh, okay. Which store?"

"I don't remember," the girl scoffed. "I've had it for years."

"Well, can you tell us where we can get more clothes like it?"

The girl bit hungrily on her ragged fingernails as she contemplated the question. "What's in it for me?" she finally replied.

"What do you want?" Maria asked.

"Whataya got?"

Maria offered food. The girl mulled over the offer, but asked if there was anything else to bargain with, implying drugs. Maria tried to persuade her otherwise. "No offense, but you look like you need some food."

"Don't tell me what I need!"

Maria shrugged and turned around. "Forget it. We'll ask someone else," she said and began to walk away.

"Wait!" the girl called out. "Give me something to eat, and then I'll tell you."

Maria turned around and gave her a long stare. She was a pitiful sight, like so many other young girls they'd seen wandering the streets of Manhattan. With bloodshot eyes, stringy hair, and a red, runny nose from obvious cocaine abuse, she was the picture of misery.

"Please," she begged. The attitude was gone. Only desperation remained.

"You went all the way to the city just to find some clothes? Aren't there malls in New Jersey?" Andy asked Morgan, who had several garments draped over her arms.

"You and Maria have to fit in with the other Helens, so we had to go to the city to see for ourselves what they wear. And besides, you didn't even want to come."

"Because I hate wearing dresses, and looking for them is even worse."

Morgan placed the dresses on Andy's bed and held up each one.

Andy made a face. They were little more than lingerie. "Seriously? Those aren't dresses!" she cried after Morgan held up a blue piece of fabric that was sheer everywhere except where her bra and underwear would be.

"Well, you *are* pretending to be a prostitute. You have to fit the part."

"Where did you find these?"

"You don't want to know." Morgan plucked a black dress out of the pile and analyzed it. "This one is not as…"

"Slutty?" Andy offered.

"Try it on."

With a sigh, she stood up and slid her jeans off. She stepped into the dress and pulled it up to her waist before removing her T-shirt. The top portion of the dress was a corset design but without lacing. As she adjusted the thin straps, the wire boning hugged her ribs and back, giving her more cleavage than she thought possible.

"Wow. Look at that!" she exclaimed. "It's like magic."

The dress was sexy indeed and, by contemporary standards, not "slutty." Hollywood starlets would have worn something similar on the red carpet.

"I've got shoes to go with it too," Morgan added before disappearing from the room momentarily. When she returned, she was carrying a pair of four-inch black heels.

Andy eyed them suspiciously but tried them on nonetheless. She attempted a few steps but wobbled like a newborn fawn. "I'm practically walking on my toes."

"You'll get used to them, but you need to break them in."

Andy hated the shoes, but there was no escaping them. She would have to get used to not just walking in them but running as well.

"You should show Ben, you know, get a bloke's opinion," Morgan suggested as she fought to keep a straight face and contain the edge in her voice.

"Uh, yeah…maybe," Andy said as she looked at herself in the mirror. "These are *not* comfortable."

"They're heels, Andy. They're not supposed to be comfortable."

Andy left the room and walked over to Ben. She knocked on his door tentatively.

"Yeah?" he called from inside.

She opened the door slowly. He was sitting on his bed reading a magazine.

"Will this work?" she asked meekly while remaining in the doorway. Her hand gripped the doorframe while the other rested flat against her stomach self-consciously. She looked terrified, like a deer waiting to become a wolf's prey.

Ben's eyes widened as he looked up from his magazine. He tossed it aside. "Um, yeah, that'll work. Just don't look so scared."

She released her hands to her sides and adjusted her posture in an attempt to appear more confident. "Better?"

Without responding, Ben sat up and got off his bed. "Come here," he said to her.

Slowly, she stepped inside the room a few feet, from the doorframe.

"No, come *here*," he insisted, gesturing for her to stand right in front of him.

Looking confused, she slowly moved forward until they were face to face. She could almost look directly into his eyes with the heels on.

"So pretend I'm Luke and you finally got me alone. What would you do first?"

"What do you mean?"

"How would you get me to tell you where the virus is?"

"I'll pull my gun on him...you, I mean."

Ben inched closer. "What if I've got my hands all over you? How would you get a hold of your gun from inside your thigh *and* give yourself enough space to get a clear shot, or at least make me believe you've got a clear shot?"

"I don't know...I'll seduce you...him," she quickly corrected.

He raised his eyebrows and smiled. "Seduce him? How exactly?"

Andy's face grew red. "I'll...I'll kiss him," she said, trying to sound certain.

"You sure that'll work?"

She lifted her chin defiantly, her eyes flashing. "You don't think I can seduce someone?"

He shrugged. "How would I know? I've never seen you try to seduce someone. You've never tried to seduce me."

She froze. "No...of course not," she stammered. "What does that have to do with anything?"

"Well, I just want to make sure that you've thought this whole thing through. You have to pretend to be a Helen, and Helens..."

"Have you asked Maria if she knows how to seduce someone?" she interrupted him.

"No."

Andy crossed her arms. "No? But you asked me."

"No, I didn't. *You* asked *me* if I thought you could."

"Now you're twisting my words," she said with a huff. "What you really mean is that you think Maria can seduce someone but I can't."

"I'm not worried about Maria. I'm worried about you."

"You don't care what happens to Maria?"

"Of course I do. Now *you're* twisting *my* words."

"Then what did you mean when you said that you're worried about me but not Maria?"

Ben let out a sigh and ran his fingers through his hair. "Because I know the type of girls Luke goes after, and you fit the type perfectly," he said looking into her eyes.

Andy's infuriation quickly turned to trepidation. Then trepidation shifted to determination. She released her arms and let them hang at her sides. Her eyes narrowed.

"Andy, all I'm saying is…"

But she stopped him. Not with words, but with her mouth. In a single, fluid motion, she closed the gap between them, placed her hands on his shoulders, rose up on the toes of her shoes, and tilted her head to kiss him. She didn't hold back. After a few gentle caresses with her lips against his, she gradually opened her mouth. Ben reciprocated and wrapped his arms around Andy's waist, his fingers pressing into her hips. She slid one hand up his neck until her fingertips dug into his hair, and what started as her proving a point turned into a lengthy embrace that only ended when she finally pulled away. She placed her fingers to her mouth and looked down at her feet. Ben's fingers remained loosely on her body. Still averting his eyes, she gathered enough poise to ask him plainly, "How was that?"

He had to take a deep breath before answering, "Uh, yeah…just do that."

"Okay," was all she could manage to say before backing out of the room. For the rest of the evening, she kept touching her lips as though expecting the same feeling to return.

Chapter XXIII

*T*he beat of the music was hypnotic, the melody sensual. It struck the bones and reverberated through the body, eliciting the desire to move without a care or worry. It was the kind of music that made people rip each other's clothes off.

With their heads and shoulders flung back and their eyes closed, the bodies pressed tightly together, swaying in a blissful trance. A temporary spell was created by both the music and atmosphere, and from the chemicals flowing through their bloodstreams. As she watched from the periphery of the main dance floor, Andy studied her fellow survivors en masse.

Since learning of Sean's existence, Andy had been unable to entirely grasp how in six years' time, a single teenager could rise up to manipulate the lives of a million people as he had done. But watching them now, how they quelled their pain with dance, music, and drugs, the puzzle came together. He didn't care what people did with their lives as long as they respected the society he had carefully designed. And since sex was abundant, and drugs were readily available, the people had enough diversions to numb them from the realities of their existence—and everyone seemed resigned to it. It was simply easier to give up fighting and give in to hedonistic apathy, particularly when a place like *Papillon* existed.

"Excuse me." A young woman brushed up against Andy as she dragged another girl onto the dance floor where they quickly meshed into the sea of people.

Stirred from her thoughts, Andy regained her focus on the job at hand. As she scanned the area for Luke, she briefly locked eyes with Maria, who was several feet away in a seductive red dress and looking equally as stunning. Maria subtly shook her head, indicating that she had not spotted him yet. Though both Ben and Jim had described his appearance, Andy and Maria were told that the best way to identify him was based on location. He was second only to Sean in rank, and therefore would often sit in a secluded area of the club with a few guards nearby to protect him and the Helens who kept him company.

As her eyes and ears grew accustomed to the sights and sounds of the club, Andy strolled about the place with an air of belonging. The shoes that had troubled her only days earlier were now the pedestals from which she would mount her offensive. Her dress hugged the natural curves of her torso, and her hair and makeup had been carefully arranged and applied hours earlier by Morgan and Susan. Assembled flawlessly for the role of a Helen, she now had to act as one: to laugh and flirt and preen for attention while revealing as much skin as possible. Such behavior wasn't natural to her, but for the sake of the unwitting survivors now surrounding her, she would forget who she was for the night.

A few blocks away along Greenwich Street, Ben and Jim were waiting. Susan and Charlie were positioned at the New Jersey end of the Holland Tunnel in two separate vehicles. Nearly an hour had passed since Andy and Maria had filed inside *Papillon*, and there was no way of knowing how long they would be gone. Under the shadows across the street from the club, Ben and Jim had watched the girls enter the club, before they disappeared into the crowd. As he and Jim retreated to their designated rendezvous point, Ben muttered a prayer under his breath.

"She'll be all right," his cousin reassured him.

"Who?" he muttered as he checked his watch, pretending not to be worried.

Jim scoffed. "Are you kidding?"

"I'm worried about both of them."

In the darkness, Jim shook his head. "Sure, whatever."

Ben ignored Jim and rubbed his eyes, nearly rubbing loose his colored contacts. "Danny was certain that Sean wouldn't be there tonight?"

"That's what he said."

"Let's hope so."

"What's your name?"

Andy could smell the alcohol on Luke's breath, she was that close to him. After spotting her from across the room, he had pulled her aside from the rest of his group and immediately started to caress her shoulder and run his fingers through her hair.

"Katrina."

"And why have I never seen you here before, Katrina?"

Andy smiled coyly, thinking it the best reaction. "I just came to New York a few weeks ago."

He smiled back, his eyes staring intently into hers. It made her uncomfortable and she dropped her gaze for a moment.

He lifted her chin with his fingers. "You have a beautiful face, Katrina. Don't hide it."

Andy said nothing as she forced her eyes to stare back into his once more. They were large and hazel. Despite her towering heels, Luke still stood nearly half a foot taller and was physically very fit. It was obvious he believed that no girl could resist him, and though Andy did find him attractive, she was in the habit of comparing every man to Ben, and to her there was no comparison.

"You thirsty?"

She wasn't thirsty, and she definitely did not want to be drinking alcohol, but she couldn't refuse the offer. "Sure, but tell me who you are first," she replied, playing dumb.

"I'm Luke. I'm the Director of the Infantry."

Look impressed. Sound dumb. Be dumb. "Wow. That sounds *really* important."

Luke smiled, obviously pleased with himself. "It is. What I do is very important."

"Really? Why are you here then, and not out there…'directing'?" Though not a stupid question, Andy's tone made her sound like she had left half her brain outside the club.

"Because everybody needs a break from time to time. Even me."

Then Luke slid his arm around her back, sending a shiver up her spine, and guided her toward the bar. Along the way, she caught sight of Maria, who didn't see her as she walked by. Since they were pretending not to know each other, Andy couldn't call out to her.

"What's your poison?"

"What?"

"What do you want to drink?" Luke restated, clearly amused by the naïveté of his latest plaything.

"Um, whatever you're having," she quickly answered.

"Perfect. Whiskey and water it is."

Whiskey? Jesus...

Luke was served immediately. He passed Andy her drink and escorted her to the private area where his friends were sitting. Introductions were not made—he was not planning on staying on the main floor long. He had his own private room in the rear of the club, which he intended to use shortly.

Currently, his group of friends consisted of three men and four women, each woman dressed similar to Andy. They were all very beautiful, and if she hadn't been preoccupied with the task at hand, she might've felt more self-conscious. Three of the girls were engrossed in heavy flirting with the three young men. Probably other Directors, Andy assumed. The fourth girl, the most beautiful, sat alone and appeared rather bored.

Andy placed her drink on the edge of the coffee table that sat in the middle of the cluster of large sofas and chairs. Several other half-consumed drinks and small piles of white powder that could only be cocaine were scattered across the table.

"Come, sit over here," Luke instructed, indicating a spot beside him on one of the sofas.

But Andy decided to speed up the entire process by sitting on his lap instead. "I hope you don't mind," she whispered in his ear after carefully positioning herself across his thighs. "But this seems more comfortable, don't you think?" She pulled away just enough to stare back into his eyes while lightly biting her bottom lip. Morgan had told her that guys liked this and to do it whenever possible. It seemed to work.

Visibly pleased by the progress he was making, a smile slowly spread across Luke's face. "I agree," he whispered back before kissing her neck. Just as he was about to pull her face toward his, the girl sitting alone reached over and gave Luke a hard slap to his arm with the back of her hand, causing him to abruptly turn her way.

"Who's that?" she demanded with a quick nod at Andy.

"Why do you care?" he snapped before turning his attention back to Andy.

The girl made a face. "Excuse *me*," she said in an exaggerated tone before adding, "I just wanna know who I'm sharing my coke with."

"Hey, this is *my* coke!" Luke yelled.

But the girl flipped her hair angrily. "Whatever," she sputtered. "It's all Sean's anyway, so what difference does it make who he gives it to?"

Andy wanted to tell the girl that she wasn't interested in the cocaine but figured it was better not to say anything that may risk damaging her persona.

"Just ignore her," Luke muttered in Andy's ear as he ran his hand up her back before cupping the side of her right breast. "Lily's still getting over her little stint in prison."

"Prison?" Andy asked a bit too loudly.

"Fuck you, Luke!" Lily shouted as she stormed away from the group. Before disappearing into the crowd on the dance floor, she turned back and yelled to Andy, "Good luck with *that* one, honey. He can't keep it up longer than five seconds!"

Luke's face turned bright red, and he shoved Andy off his lap to go after Lily. He started charging toward the dance floor when his friend reached out and grabbed his arm to stop him.

"Dude, she's not worth it. Let it go."

His nostrils flaring in anger and hands gripping tightly into fists, Luke appeared incapable of calming down, but after several deep but labored breaths, he returned to his seat and beckoned Andy to return. She forced herself to obey.

God, get me out of here, she thought.

"I'm *so* glad I'm not her," declared one of the other girls. "It's gotta suck being Sean's personal slave."

The others seemed to agree and continued to gossip about Lily and Sean. Looking sullen, Luke remained silent. His desire for Andy was obviously gone, and she began to panic. Turning to the table, she grabbed her drink and took a sip before handing it to him. He stared at her and then at the drink before finally grasping it. He took a long, slow sip.

"Forget about what she said," Andy said in as seductive a voice as she could muster and leaned in closer. She lightly grazed her fingertips down his chest until she could feel his stomach muscles tighten. "She's probably just jealous cuz she can't have you…and I can." Sensing a reversal in his mood, she took the glass out of his hand, took another sip, and placed it back on the table. She leaned in even further until her lips brushed his ear and whispered, "Let's go somewhere private." Then, surprising even herself, she kissed his ear and his neck.

⚜

"Luke prefers blonds, at least he does tonight." Maria reported the news after rounding the corner into the alley where Ben and Jim were waiting.

"What happened?" Ben demanded.

"Exactly what we wanted. She got him alone."

"Great, so you just left her there?"

"That was the plan, Ben," Jim gently reminded his cousin.

Pushing his hands through his hair, Ben let out a heavy sigh. "I know, I'm sorry. I just really hate this whole thing. I hate not being able to do anything."

"She looked like she had the situation under control," Maria firmly assured him. She slipped off her heels and stepped into a pair of sneakers that she had retrieved from her backpack.

"I saw her carrying their drinks," she added as she began to tie her sneakers. "He should be talking soon."

Standing behind Luke as he unlocked the door to his private room, Andy adroitly retrieved a tiny plastic bag from underneath the lacey top of her sheer thigh-high stocking with one hand while carefully balancing their drinks in the other. Inside was a small, white pill. As Luke opened the door, she quickly shifted his drink back into her right hand and hid the bag between the bottom of his glass and her palm.

"Here we are," he said proudly as they entered the room. As he closed the door behind them, Andy quickly assessed the room.

The space was modest, about the size of a bedroom, which was what it had been converted to at present. There was a bed in one corner and a plush sofa in the other. Several half-empty bottles of various liquors sat on a small table in the corner adjacent to the door. She made her way over to the table and placed the two glasses down as Luke moved behind her and placed his hands on her waist. She could smell his aftershave, which instantly reminded her of Ben.

"You still thirsty?" he said in a low voice into the back of her head before he kissed it.

Her heart pounding, she clenched her hand around the tiny plastic bag. "Yeah," she breathed and Luke began to kiss her neck. "You have any Coke?"

"Uh-huh," he mumbled and worked his way down her neck.

She wondered if she was going to have to do more than she wanted to get the information about the virus. Or if she was going to have to fight him.

But suddenly, Luke realized something and stood up straight. "Dammit, I left my stash out there with those guys. I'll be right back," he said before leaving her alone in the room.

Releasing a heavy breath, she realized that Luke thought she was asking for cocaine, not Coca-Cola. The Rohypnol that she was holding in her hand dissolve much quicker in a carbonated beverage, as she and Charlie had discovered the day before. They considered grinding the pill first and then placing the powder in the bag, but the powder clung to the sides of everything, making it nearly impossible to slip into a drink with speed. The only solution was to grind the pill right before putting it into the drink and then let it dissolve.

Now that she had a few moments alone, she quickly searched the room for an appropriate tool. Unfortunately, nothing like a pen or a stick could be found. Panicking yet again, an idea struck just when she needed it.

Removing her shoe and quickly wiping off any dirt and dust from the base of the pencil-thin heel, she took the pill out of the plastic bag, dropping the bag to the floor, and pressed down several times on the pill to break it into tiny pieces. "That'll have to do," she said to herself as she quickly transported the powder from the table to Luke's glass. Then she wiped the heel clean with the hem of her dress and threw her shoe back on just as the door reopened.

"Here we go." Luke smiled at Andy and held up a small bag of white powder that he'd left on the table.

Thinking fast, she covered her mouth with her fingertips and started to giggle. "I'm such an idiot! When I said *coke*, I meant soda. But at least your stash is safe." Before Luke could say anything, she grabbed the drinks and handed his to him. "Cheers!" she squealed with delight and took a sip.

He frowned, apparently disappointed that "Katrina" wasn't interested in the cocaine. "Uh, okay," he finally muttered and threw the drugs on the table. "You know it's my birthday?" he added suddenly.

"Oh, really? Well, Happy Birthday!" Andy held up her glass then eyed Luke impatiently as she took another tiny sip. *C'mon, drink...drink!* "This is good," she lied. "What kind of whiskey is it?"

"Jack Daniels," he replied before finally taking a large sip, which he quickly followed with another.

Andy smiled wryly back at him.

"Maria, you should head back. There's no point in you waiting around here... if things go bad..." Jim didn't see a need to finish his thought.

Gone were her dress and high heels. Maria had deftly changed into jeans and a T-shirt while the two young men respectfully looked the other way.

"I left thirty minutes ago. Hopefully she's slipped him the pill by now."

"And it takes, what, twenty minutes before the effects begin?" Ben called out from a few yards away as he kept watch on the people rushing back and forth along Greenwich Street.

"At least twenty minutes, according to what Charlie found during his research."

"That's too long," he mumbled out of earshot of the others.

"You sure you two don't need me to stay?" Maria asked Jim.

"No, seriously, we're fine," he insisted. "You've done more than enough already."

"All right, I'm off then."

"Be safe," he called out as Maria walked her bike toward the end of the alley.

Ben stopped her as she passed him. "Thanks, Maria," he said solemnly. "It took guts going in there."

She merely nodded, and after mounting her bike, she said, "She'll be fine. Don't worry."

He managed a smile. "See you soon."

Maria pedaled onto the Street and turned south. The entrance to the Holland Tunnel was a mile away.

❧❦❧

After intermittingly sipping his drink and kissing Andy, Luke finally finished off the last of his whiskey without any suspicion of what was in his glass.

Meanwhile, Andy took any opportunity she could when he wasn't looking to spill her own drink on the dark-colored carpet. The last thing she needed was several ounces of Jack Daniels coursing through her veins. Suddenly, she spotted the tiny plastic bag that used to hold the pill lying on the floor. She started to panic. Everything could be ruined by this small mistake. She watched Luke fumble with his empty glass as he tried to place it on the table, and quickly she grabbed his drink to help him while kicking the bag under the table.

It was time to switch gears. She placed her nearly empty glass beside his and drew close to him. She ran the back of her hands against his bare, and rather muscular, arms and began to lightly feather his skin with her fingernails.

"So, you're the leader of the Infantry?" she murmured softly.

"That's right." His eyelids were growing heavy.

"So you must be good friends with Sean then, huh?"

"Uh-huh."

Luke impatiently grabbed Andy's shoulders to pull her in even closer, and his fingers ran over her scar, her souvenir from Los Angeles. He peered awkwardly over her shoulder to get a better look.

"Hey, what's that?" he said with labored speech.

Andy glanced behind her shoulder and smiled proudly. "Oh, that? I dodged a bullet in Los Angeles."

His eyes widened, and he stumbled back half a step. "You…you've been to L.A.?" he stammered in disbelief.

"Yep. It was pretty chaotic. Not like here. Of course, L.A. doesn't have a great leader like Sean."

"Yeah…Sean…he's the best!" he blurted in a manner that only an intoxicated person would.

"He is," she pretended to agree. "But I'm sure it helps to have the virus on hand to keep people in line, huh?"

Luke frowned and his eyes narrowed as a window of lucidity emerged. "How… how the hell do you know about that?"

Sitting in near darkness in his office, Danny ran his fingers over the width of the three parallel scars on his neck, an unconscious tick often performed during the hours in front of his screen.

A sharp knock on his door startled him, and he quickly removed his earbuds.

"You Danny?" a shadowy silhouette of a person standing at the doorway inquired.

"Uh, yeah?"

"You like working in the dark?"

"It's easier on the eyes," he replied nervously.

The person flicked on the light switch, allowing Danny to see his visitor clearly.

"Oh, sorry, Sean, I didn't…"

"Never mind," Sean interrupted by holding up a hand. He entered the office and took a seat on the edge of Danny's desk. "So, I've been told that you're updating the database to include fingerprints of everyone registered in the city."

"That's right," he replied carefully.

"How's that coming along?"

"Uh, okay, I guess. More than half of everyone registered has already added their prints to the database."

Sean eyed Danny with his icy blue eyes. "Excellent. Good work. It's people like you that keep this city running smoothly. I'll be sure to mention that to Doug the next time I see him."

Danny smiled uneasily. "Uh, thanks."

Sean got off the desk and headed toward the door. "You should go to *Papillon* tonight," he advised. "You know, relax a bit. Maybe get yourself laid."

"Uh, okay, maybe."

"Yeah, I know…the Dregs are there tonight, but it's better than sitting here alone in the dark, right?"

Without another word, Sean departed down the hall, leaving Danny alone again. He looked up at the florescent lights and groaned as he stood up to turn off the lights himself. "Asshole," he muttered and returned to his desk in the dark.

"It doesn't matter how I know. Just tell me where Sean is hiding it."

By now, Andy had backed a few feet away from Luke and was standing in front of the door. As he blinked back in disbelief at the sudden change of events, she reached underneath her dress in between her legs and retrieved the tiny Ruger LCP that she'd carefully holstered to her inner left thigh, a temporary gift from Ben. She pointed the barrel at Luke's chest. He instinctively took a step back and lifted his arms.

"Who…who are you?" he sputtered.

"Where's the virus?" she demanded. "Tell me or I'll shoot."

Luke gasped out a laugh. "You won' shoot me. You're jus'a H-Helen!"

"Hey, I've shot people dead before, including the person who gave me that scar." She nodded toward her shoulder but kept her aim steady.

He stumbled backward again. The Rohypnol was starting to take full effect. "You…can' sh-shoo' me. They…they'll 'ear it."

"Not with all that music. It's nice and loud out there. Now tell me where the virus is!"

Luke took one more step backward. His foot hit the base of the sofa, and he fell onto it.

"Tell me!" Andy let off a round. The bullet landed expertly in the sofa cushion, an inch from his groin.

The sight of the bullet hole so close to his manhood nearly stunned him into sobriety. "You almost shot me!" he shouted with remarkable clarity.

"Tell me, or the next time I'll hit you so that you never have children." Andy stepped forward and aimed the barrel once again at Luke's groin.

Looking dazed, his eyes slowly refocused on the gun. "Did he send you?" he asked like a scared child.

She frowned. "Who?"

"Ben. Kelly." Luke uttered the name in two separate breaths.

Andy's stomach fell to her knees. Somehow, though, she managed to keep her voice steady. "Who's Ben? Who are you talking about? Tell me where the virus is!"

It was convincing enough, and when she pressed her lips together and looked as though she were about to let the gun off again, he finally cracked. "It's the prison! Green Haven…Green Haven! Don't …please!" Instinctively, he brought his knees to his chest to shield himself and then began to sob.

Only then did Andy lower her gun. She almost took pity on him. "Green Haven Prison," she muttered under her breath so that she'd remember. Then, while keeping her aim on Luke, she stepped over to the table and poured another couple of ounces of Jack Daniels in his glass. She handed it to him and ordered him to drink. He obeyed and emptied the glass in seconds.

"Thank you very much for your cooperation, Luke," Andy said calmly as she gathered up his glass as well as hers. Then, she grabbed the keys to the office from inside his left jean pocket. He didn't bother to resist. The threat of bodily harm had passed, and the combination of whiskey and Rohypnol had sedated him to the point where sleep would soon take over.

Holstering the Ruger back onto her thigh, she hurriedly left the room and locked the door behind her while carrying the two glasses. She didn't want to leave behind anything with her fingerprints in Luke's "office" now that they were registered to her ID.

She left the keys dangling in the lock to make it appear as though Luke had inadvertently left them there and returned to the main floor of the club. Passing through crowds of people busy forgetting their problems, she dispersed the glasses onto two different tables sitting far apart. Finally, she left the club looking as polished as when she'd entered it. She kept her head down and stayed to the outer edge of the sidewalk. She didn't look at anyone as dozens of people passed her on the street, including Sean Taylor.

Ben rubbed his eyes, then blinked several times. But neither his eyes nor his contacts were deceiving him. Who could mistake the arrogant gait or the cold stare, even from yards away? And as usual, walking with two guards behind him. Hastily ducking into the shadows, Ben retreated back to where Jim was standing.

"I just saw Sean!" he whispered sharply.

"Are you serious??"

"Positive."

But before a real panic could settle, the sound of Andy's voice suddenly echoed off the walls of the alley. "I got it!" she cried.

She moved impressively fast in her heels, and Ben released a huge sigh of relief.

"Good because Sean just passed you."

"You're kidding?" Her neck craned back toward the street.

"No, and it's lucky he didn't notice you dressed like…like that."

"Well, I won't be for long." She grabbed her backpack from the ground and quickly changed out of her dress and heels as Maria had done.

"So where is it? Where's the virus?" Jim asked with more impatience than usual.

"Green Haven Prison," she said proudly while kneeling down to tie her sneakers. "Any idea where that is?"

"Nope."

"None."

"Well, I know Luke wasn't making it up. He was very forthcoming after I nearly shot him in the balls."

"Wow," Jim murmured, sounding impressed and even intimidated.

Ben turned away and looked straight up at the narrow sliver of sky between the walls. He could actually see a few stars. "Then it's really true," he whispered.

After gathering all their belongings, they mounted their bikes and pedaled out of the alley.

Sean spotted Lily sulking in the corner of the club, but he ignored her for the time being and headed to where the Directors were sitting. He wasn't planning on staying long. Opening the club to everyone on Wednesdays was a necessary concession he knew he had to give, but the sight of all the sloppy Dregs dancing and spending all their credit getting wasted wasn't something he enjoyed witnessing.

"Where's Luke?" he shouted at one of the Directors over the noise of the pulsating music.

"Who knows. He left with some blond like an hour ago."

Sean frowned and walked away. He made his way to the back of the club.

The first room he came to was Luke's, and upon seeing the keys in the door, he frowned again before opening the door and switching on the lights. Luke was lying in the fetal position on the sofa and snoring loudly.

"Perfect," Sean grumbled. Using the bottom of his foot, he tried shoving Luke to wake up, but it was no use. His Director of the Infantry, the leader of thousands of young men, was comatose.

Disgusted, Sean left the room and slammed the door behind him. He needed Luke to redirect some troops for Chad, but now it would have to wait until morning.

Storming back to the main floor, he found Lily and told her that it was time to go.

"No way!" she yelled, yanking her arms away and nearly falling out of her seat. "I wanna stay."

She was either drunk or high or both, and Sean had run out of patience. He grabbed her arm again but she wrestled free and staggered off into the mob on the dance floor. He didn't go after her. She would come crawling back to him in the morning anyway, like she had done so many times before. She was entirely dependent on him, and they both knew it.

Sean found another Helen and departed the club with her in tow.

"So it worked?"

Andy grinned back at Charlie as she climbed in the car. "It worked. Well, that and a bullet."

"You shot him?!"

"Nearly. He needed a little…encouragement."

"Brilliant. So where is it?"

She repeated the name of the prison.

"Where's that?"

"No clue."

Once Jim put his bike in the back of the truck and got in, Charlie threw the vehicle into drive and sped off, Susan and Maria following them.

The hangover was unimaginably awful, far worse than any Luke had experienced, and there had been many. As he sat up, his temples pounded and nausea took hold. When he tried to stand to make a run for the bathroom, his knees buckled underneath him. He slumped back down on the sofa and vomited on the floor between his feet. Doubled over in agony, he didn't notice the door opening.

"Man, seriously?" Covering his nose, Sean looked down at Luke and the puddle of vomit, and stood as far away as possible. "What the hell did you take last night?"

Luke groaned and slowly sat up. He wiped his mouth with the back of his hand.

"You look worse than shit," Sean spat out, even more disgusted than he'd been hours earlier. "Seriously, you're a Director! If you can't handle your booze or coke or whatever else you've been chugging, then I'm done with you."

Half-listening, Luke struggled to voice a defense. "Man, I think someone slipped me something."

"Who?"

"I don't know. I don't remember anything."

"Jesse said you were with a blond last night. You remember that?"

Eyes shut, Luke rubbed his head. "There were lots of blonds," he muttered dully.

"This is the last time," Sean warned menacingly. "You know too much, Luke. You can't be acting like everyone else, and you absolutely can*not* blackout. You understand?"

He didn't dare open his eyes as he nodded. This small action alone hurt his head.

"Learn to pace yourself," Sean ordered as he stepped to the door. "Now get cleaned up. We got work to do."

Chapter XXIV

October 2023

A small forest butted up against the northwest corner of the prison, and the autumn foliage provided plenty of cover to conduct a safe stakeout. Everything was almost ready. The final step was preparing the escape route.

The previous two months had passed in a flurry of unending preparations. Learning where Sean was hiding the virus turned out to be the easy part. Infiltrating the prison would be much harder.

"I count three guards in the towers again," Jim whispered to Ben while staring through his binoculars.

"The same guys?"

"Yeah, and they all look bored to death."

It was their seventh consecutive day surveilling the prison compound, not including the five nights spent staring through the same pair of night vision binoculars they'd used the year before at Fort Detrick. But watching the building was just one part of the plan.

It had taken three days back in August just to find out where the prison was located after learning the name. Without the Internet, such information was now elusive, and Ben had almost made a trip to see Danny to access his *Wikipedia* files when Charlie found a reference to the prison in an old newspaper article at the university library. Then the real work began.

"Bored is good," Ben replied absently as he scanned the area with his naked eyes.

"It's too bad they're all using night vision goggles. Otherwise we could go in at night," said Jim.

"Yeah, well, nothing's perfect. If it was, one of us would know how to fly a plane." Ben was referring to the small airport just west of the small forest. "A plane would've been a perfect getaway."

Grabbing their belongings, they left their observation point and began the grueling task of clearing a path almost a quarter-mile in length through the forest using machetes found at a specialty knife store near Princeton. Sweat soaked despite the grey, fifty-degree weather, the two young men reached the western edge of the woods an hour later. An overgrown field separated the woods from the small airport. Tired and cold, they hopped into their truck parked on the runway and headed back to Princeton over a hundred miles away.

"I wish Brian would come back," Jim said once they were safely away from the prison. "It's too bad we can't just put a sign on our door telling him where we are. Then we could finally relocate up here and stop making this trip every day."

"Yeah, true," Ben muttered. He leaned his head sideways on the headrest. He stared out his window until the vibration of the tires against the road lulled his eyes closed.

Jim smiled to himself. "Well, it's almost over."

Still awake, Ben let out a grunt and mumbled, "God, I hope so."

Luke had experienced drunken blackouts before—two in the last month, in fact, both of which he'd managed to conceal from Sean, who had been in Philadelphia. Yet that night in early August—his birthday—had been nagging him relentlessly for weeks now. He remembered the blond...Kathy? Kendra? Something like that. But he couldn't remember her face, but she must've been beautiful. He only talked to the beautiful ones.

He was in his room at *Papillon* as he thought through the events of that day. He went over to the table to pour himself a drink, but then he noticed something lying on the floor. "What...why's there a plastic bag here?" he said to himself.

Then suddenly a thought popped into his head. *The virus...the virus...*

He looked over to the sofa that had a bullet hole in it, but until now he had no memory of how it got there. "She drugged me," he said out loud. All at once, snippets of the words that had passed between them surfaced from some dark corner of his mind. He began to sweat. His body shook with fear, like a violent shiver that he couldn't control. Days of agonizing over his recollected memories made him physically ill. The only thing that terrified Luke more than the virus itself was if Sean ever found out he had revealed its location.

I have tell him...I have to tell him...he's going kill me, he thought as he walked from *Papillon* to his apartment. *He'll understand...I was drugged...it wasn't my fault...she nearly shot me...*

Luke dragged himself into the bathroom to throw water on his face. After shutting off the faucet, he stared at the tap. It was early, only nine o'clock, but he was exhausted. There was no way he'd be going out anywhere tonight.

He needed to sleep. Tomorrow he would tell Sean. Or maybe the next day. Nothing strange had happened at the prison in over two months. Another day wouldn't make any difference.

The weeks of planning were complete.

Maria and Carmen made a hearty meal for Andy and the boys before their departure. It was a cold and grey afternoon, no more than a few degrees above freezing, and they would need their strength. There was tension in the air as everyone ate, more so than the night Andy and Maria had gone to *Papillon*.

Andy said goodbye to Morgan and the other girls, and gave Katie a kiss on her plump cheek. Then she climbed into the passenger's seat of the car and immediately cupped her hands to her mouth. Her fingers were like ice.

"Here, I'll get the engine running," said Ben as he climbed into the driver's seat.

"Thanks," she muttered over a shiver.

It felt like winter, and Andy hated winter. Without heat and only a meager amount of body fat to protect her, the months of short days and long nights had become an eternal effort to stay warm. Even in Bermuda the winters had been windy and damp.

"Once this is over, how about we go somewhere warm?"

Ben smiled at the idea. "Where're you thinking?"

"Maybe Florida. Or the Caribbean?"

"You miss island living?"

"On days like today..." Andy's voice faded. The mindless chatter was meant to keep their minds off of what they were about to do.

They were sitting in the driveway as the engine of the beat-up sedan warmed up. Jim and Charlie emerged from the house. They would follow Ben to Green Haven in a second vehicle.

Sean's jaw dropped. "*Please* tell me you're joking!"

As if his body was no longer his to control, Luke's weight shifted back and forth from one foot to the other. Standing just a few feet from the window on the eighty-first floor of the Empire State Building only further toyed with his equilibrium. "Sean, I wish I were, but it all just hit me…just last night," he lied. It had been five days. "I'm positive that she drugged me. I've never felt so sick in my life. You saw me that morning. You saw how messed up I was. Have you ever seen me that bad before?"

Sean raised a skeptical eyebrow but admitted that Luke had a point. "Maybe. But right now I need to know more about this girl. Who was she?"

Regaining his balance, Luke looked squarely out the window and shook his head slowly. "I don't remember much about her. All I know is that she was blond and wearing a black dress and her name was something like Kathy or Kaitlin or something that began with a K."

"Or a C?" Sean added with exasperation.

"Maybe…she didn't exactly spell her name for me, you know."

"Great."

In a sudden motion, Sean pushed his chair away from his desk and shot to his feet. "Let's go," he ordered and was out the door before Luke could turn away from the window.

In the elevator, they descended more than sixty flights before getting off at the fifteenth floor. Sean advanced toward a specific office as a bewildered Luke followed. Without bothering to knock, Sean barged into the office and turned on the light, nearly scaring Danny to death. "Good you're here."

"Uh, yeah…yeah," Danny replied.

With Luke standing beside him, Sean placed one hand on Danny's chair and leaned in toward the computer screen. "Danny, I want you to look up the ID records of every Helen that went to *Papillon* on August…" He looked up at Luke.

"Fourth. August fourth," Luke supplied humbly.

Danny blinked as the instructions sank in. "Uh, okay." A few minutes and many keystrokes later, he brought up a list of seventeen names before pushing his chair out of the way so that Sean could get a closer look.

"Good thing it was a Wednesday. Otherwise the list would be longer," Sean said with a smirk.

"Heh, yeah," Luke echoed in an effort to sound agreeable. "The Helens hate hanging around the Dregs almost as much as we do, huh?"

Sean didn't reply. His eyes rapidly scanned over the list of names. All, except two, he recognized. "You know who these two are?" he said to Luke as he pointed to the third name from the bottom and then the very last name. "Isabel Torres and Katrina Wilson?"

When Danny heard the two names, his heart beat faster. Inching farther away from the screen, he pretended to be looking at some papers.

"Katrina...that's the one, the blond," said Luke. "But I never met her before that night."

Sean turned to Danny and unleashed more orders. "I want to know how many times these two names have been scanned going into *Papillon* in the past three months. Can you do that?"

"Sure," Danny mumbled as he rolled his chair back to his keyboard and typed away until he found the results. "Uh, looks like they were both only there that one night."

Sean frowned as he stared at the screen, thinking. "Tell me when these two names were registered."

"Okay." Danny performed a few quick commands and silently thanked God that he had entered separate dates for all the names that Ben had requested. "Okay, Isabel was registered on May thirteenth and Katrina on June first."

Sean looked away from the screen and turned to the window, briefly noting how unspectacular the view was on this floor. A minute later, he had a plan. "Follow me," he barked at Luke without another word to Danny.

Once the two had left his office, Danny got up to switch off the light. "You're welcome, asshole." For a long while afterward, he stared out his window and wondered what Sean knew and whether or not he should do anything about it.

"God, I miss my truck." Ben was staring at the fuel gauge. They were still eighty miles from the prison, and though they had filled the tank and threw a couple of full jerry cans in the trunk, he was still uneasy.

"We'll be fine," Andy reassured him, reading his mind.

"Yeah..."

"Hey, relax." She gave him a lighthearted shove and a smirk to go with it. Except for the faintest of smiles, he barely reacted.

"I'll relax tomorrow. I'd open a hundred bottles of champagne if we had any."

"Well, I'm sure between the two of us, we can find something to celebrate with."

This time, a genuine laugh escaped Ben's mouth, and he took his eyes off the road to give Andy a proper smile. "Oh, really? And what exactly did you have in mind, aside from champagne?"

She looked down at her hands, hands that were now warm, and averted a coy smile from his view. "Maybe dance."

"Dance?"

"Yeah, why not? People dance when they're happy, don't they?"

After a semi-shrug, he replied, "Yeah, sure."

"So we'll dance. You and me. But I get to pick the song."

Ben looked hard at Andy. "That's all? Just one song?"

She returned her gaze to her hands. She studied the crescents of her fingernails. "Well, one song to start with. Then…"

Gripping tightly on the steering wheel, Ben's hands began to sweat. He looked over at Andy. "It's a deal. Just wear that dress."

She looked up. "What, the one I wore to *Papillon*?"

"Yeah. You looked…you look good in that."

"I think I have it somewhere." She smiled.

⚜

Back on the eighty-first floor, Sean rattled off orders to Luke.

"I want you to send five…no, ten…of your best guys up to Green Haven. I want them to ask the guards stationed there if they've seen anything unusual since early August. And I mean *anything*. Even if it's some cow that got tipped over on a field a mile away, I want to know about it. Then have two of them come back and report what they find by…" Sean looked at his watch. "Seven o'clock. Got it?"

"Got it," Luke said confidently before heading toward the door.

"And, Luke," Sean called out, stopping him. "Don't think I won't forget that you're the reason we're in this mess right now."

Like a scolded child, Luke swallowed hard. He merely nodded and silently left the room.

"Idiot," Sean muttered as the door closed. He picked up the phone that sat on his desk and dialed a number. "Yeah, it's me…I want all video from the night of the fourth of August sent to my apartment within the hour." Without waiting for acknowledgement from the other end, he hung up and left his office.

Fifteen minutes later, he was back at his apartment after walking alone, something he normally wouldn't do in broad daylight, but it gave him a chance to think without his bodyguards hovering around him. He locked his front door and went directly to his den. In the corner behind a desk stood an antique armoire with a safe inside. He opened the doors of the armoire and hastily spun off the combination. The safe clicked open, and he grabbed a large stack of stuffed folders from inside and placed them on his desk.

There was a file for every Director and nearly every Helen and Fixer: school files, medical records, juvenile detention records, and even notes from old therapy sessions with over-priced psychiatrists. Most of the files were kept in a standard filing cabinet on the other side of the desk, but Sean stored the most important ones inside the safe.

Organized alphabetically by last name, Luke's file was on top, labeled "Luke Andrews" on the protruding tab. The contents of his file were underwhelming: a poor math student but decent in history and writing, several disciplinary infractions from grade school teachers but nothing out of the ordinary, and a mild case of childhood asthma that apparently had vanished over the years. The rest of the details were mundane. Handsome, popular, but nonetheless impressionable. Rich parents and an older sister who died with them. Large house in Westchester. The typical profile of an upper-class, white male survivor.

Sean sorted through several others, including Lily's with scribbled notes dictated by her shrink detailing her history of sexual abuse by her stepfather, and Chad's folder with graphic crime scene photos of his mother's murder. Thousands of hours and miles travelled had been spent gathering the total sum of these files.

At the bottom of the pile and out of alphabetical order was Ben Kelly's file. It was empty except for one small piece of paper. Sean had personally found it on the floor of the guidance counselor's office at Ben's elementary school in Virginia. The rest of the file was gone, as was his cousin's, but Sean guessed that the single paper had accidentally been dropped when he and Jim attempted to erase all evidence of their past after fleeing New York the year before. Though cunning of Ben to destroy his files, it was bad luck for him that such a critical piece of information was left behind.

Sean held the paper up to the light and studied the ten individual fingerprints taken when Ben was ten-years old, as indicated by the date stamped on the top corner. The private Catholic school he and Jim had attended recorded students' fingerprints in the event that a student was kidnapped or went missing. It was ironic that something once meant to protect Ben might now help to catch him ten years later.

There was a heavy knock at the front door. "You're late," Sean barked at the kid delivering a single envelope and slammed the door shut before the boy could squeak out an apology. He marched directly to his living room and turned on his large flat screen television. He removed the first of three disks from the envelope and inserted it into the DVD player beneath the screen.

Every single night at *Papillon* was captured on camera, though only rarely did Sean have time to watch any of the recordings. Still, he ordered the recordings to continue. Following more than half an hour of both real-time and scanned footage from six different cameras positioned throughout the club, he found what he was looking for.

The camera angle was not optimal, but it was still clear enough to see what went on. Looking at the blond, it was easy to understand how Luke had fallen prey. She was wearing an enticing black dress that left just a little to the imagination and high heels that showcased her slender yet muscular legs. Her wavy hair extended to the middle of her back, and every minute or so it would glide back and forth over her shoulders as she moved. *Where had she concealed the gun Luke spoke of? Likely inside her thigh*, he thought.

Sean watched and re-watched the film several times. He had never seen the girl before. He would have remembered. There was something different about her, and although he couldn't hear a word that either she or Luke said, he could just barely identify the subtleties of the act she had put on for Luke: a slightly forced smile here, a tentative caress there. But would he have noticed had he not been looking for some clue, or if it had been him instead of Luke? *Probably not*, he admitted to himself.

Sean watched the video nine or ten times. The girl never looked directly at the camera, since there was no way that she would know where it was hidden. Still, her face was clearly visible from several angles. He paused the video on the clearest shot and leaned in closer to the screen. His cold, blue eyes soaked in the image, memorizing every pixel. "Pretty little thing, aren't you?" he said aloud.

By the time they reached Stormville, the small town that surrounded the prison, it was pouring rain.

"Man, this sucks," said Ben as he increased the speed of the windshield wipers.

"Just think of it as a strategic advantage. The guards will be cold, wet, and tired. They'll be slow to react," Andy offered, trying to sound positive.

"So will Jim and I. You and Charlie will be nice and warm inside the cars."

"Not the entire time."

"Oh, sorry...for like, five minutes you'll be outside." Though he was teasing her, there was an edge to his voice.

A few miles from the prison, he steered the car into a vacant gas station and waited. A half-minute later, Jim and Charlie pulled up beside them in the other vehicle. Charlie rolled down the passenger's window.

"Smashing weather."

"Terrific," Ben called back. "Let's check the radios."

Andy fished in her backpack until she found the walkie-talkie that Charlie had encrypted weeks before.

Ben glanced at his watch. It was time. The sky was dark but not too dark. Any later and they would risk trying to slip past the guards using night vision goggles. He looked over at Andy. "You ready?"

She pursed her lips together and nodded.

Ben smiled thinly before turning to the others. "Jim?"

"Yeah, I'm coming."

Both he and Charlie stepped out of their car. Jim slipped into the backseat behind Andy while Charlie got behind the wheel of the other vehicle.

"I'll radio you just before I fire it off," Charlie called out to Ben.

"Okay."

"Good luck." Charlie drove off in one direction while Ben, Jim, and Andy went another.

Once they got to the airport, Ben parked inside one of the hangars. Andy got out of the car first and opened the back of the truck. She retrieved three dark raincoats and two loaded rifles, followed by Jim and Ben who took out their large rucksacks. They slung the rucksacks over their coats, and Andy handed each of them a weapon.

"Here we go," Jim said, trying to sound upbeat.

Together, they marched about half a mile from the hangar to the forest, crossing the runway along the way. As they descended underneath the canopy, Andy remarked favorably about the path they had cleared days earlier. "Where's the rock?" she asked.

"Just up there," Ben said pointing straight ahead.

Andy followed as he stepped off the main path to a narrower path on the left, around the rock. She looked down at it and saw the "X" marked with red duct tape. "Just don't miss it," she said.

"We won't," Jim promised.

They arrived at the opposite edge of the forest and knelt down behind some trees. All three withdrew their binoculars from their bags and scanned the area.

"Still three," Ben muttered, referring to the guards, each in his own tower along the perimeter wall. "Damn, I was hoping they all wouldn't be there."

"And I bet they're all miserable," Andy grumbled. "I don't know why they put up with it."

"Three words," he whispered. "Food, drugs, sex."

Andy smirked. "I get the food, but drugs and sex? Come on…how much of that do people really need?"

"Well, you're not an eighteen-year-old boy."

"No, thankfully," she said as Jim chuckled quietly at the exchange, welcoming the break in the tension.

Andy put down her binoculars and picked up the radio. She ensured the volume was on the lowest setting.

Meanwhile, Ben and Jim grabbed opposite ends of a large ladder they had hidden near the path during their last visit and awaited word from Charlie.

Moments later, a crackle was heard coming from the other end of the radio. "I'm here," Charlie's voice called out. "You all ready?"

Andy looked at the others; both nodded in reply. "Ready," she whispered back.

A loud bang was heard in the distance seconds later, followed by the bright, red glow of a flare soaring vertically against dark, grey skies.

Through her binoculars, Andy watched as two guards scurried down from their towers and disappeared from view behind the prison wall. "There's still one left," she radioed Charlie. "Do it again."

"Roger…"

Half a minute later, another shot erupted in the distance, followed by another flare. Through the lenses, she saw the remaining guard look around as though wondering what to do.

"Once more?" Charlie asked.

Andy and Ben looked at each other. She said, "Once more."

A third flare went off, and the remaining guard finally descended the tower.

"All gone," Andy said into the radio.

"Let's go," said Ben.

They scrambled to the perimeter wall of the prison between the third and fourth observation tower. When they reached the wall, Ben raised the ladder and skillfully adjusted its height until it reached the top while Andy pulled out a rope from Jim's rucksack. It was thick with knots tied every two feet and had a large metal hook on the end. Then she grabbed a wire cutter and passed it to Ben. He climbed the ladder to the top. Keeping his head low, he cut away at the spiraling loops of barbed wire and created a space large enough to pass unhindered. Once finished, he descended the ladder.

At the same time, Jim made two trips back to the edge of the forest to retrieve two hidden fifty-pound weights. Using smaller pieces of rope, he and Andy tied both weights to the first rung of the ladder to weigh it down. When they finished, he and Ben grabbed their rucksacks and weapons. Jim went up the ladder and hooked the longer rope to the top rung and dropped it over the other side of the wall. Then he climbed over and landed safely inside the prison compound.

Before following his cousin, Ben gave Andy one last look as she handed him the radio. Without thinking, he hugged her fiercely and said, "I'll see you soon."

"Don't do anything stupid," she told him.

"I won't." Then he climbed the ladder and gave her a smile before disappearing over the wall.

Alone, Andy ran back to the airport beneath the fading daylight. She approached the rock with the red X and swerved around it to the right off the main path. Fifty or so meters later, she emerged from the forest and picked up speed. By the time she reached the hangar, she was out of breath. Charlie arrived moments later.

"So you can scan them in and compare them to every print on file?" Sean held out the paper containing the ten fingerprints to Danny. He had ripped off the top of the paper where Ben's name had been labeled, however.

"Yeah, no problem." Danny took the paper from Sean. "Give me a few minutes," he added as he fired up the scanner.

"Be quick."

Danny ignored the remark and did his best to appear bored. Sean stood impatiently as Danny scanned the paper into softcopy. He then separated each individual print and stored them as "Unknown 1" through "Unknown 10" before instructing the software to compare each unknown print to the more than one million prints on file, beginning with the left pinky and ending with the right. If the prints belonged to either Ben or Jim, this would allow him as much time to stall as possible. Since neither had scanned a print from their left hand, Danny started with those.

"Anything yet?" Sean demanded.

"Not yet. It might take ten minutes. Each print takes about a minute." Danny leaned back in his chair and squeezed a rubber stress ball with one hand, deciding his disinterested demeanor would likely anger Sean but also deflect any suspicion.

"Can't you make it work faster?"

Danny looked up. "It's a computer. It only listens to ones and zeros."

Seemingly humbled by this remark, Sean backed away toward the window with his arms crossed. It was getting dark outside.

The first three prints came up negative, so Danny entered commands to crosscheck the left index finger followed by the left thumb. After both came up negative, he started on the right hand. Jim had registered his right middle finger while Ben had registered his right index. If Danny's suspicions were correct, Ben's finger would pop up first.

"Six down, four to go," he muttered as he reached for the mouse.

Sean huffed in agitation and turned back to the window when a distinctive beep emitted from the computer speakers, followed by a second and then a third. He whirled around on his heels. "What was that?"

Danny closed his eyes tightly. He was afraid to look at the screen. Meanwhile, Sean sprang toward the computer screen and read off the first name. "John Simmons..." And the second. "Michael Wilkins..." And finally the third. "Matthew Thompson. Wait, three names for one set of prints...what the...?"

As Sean stared at the screen, Danny finally opened his eyes and improvised an explanation. "It's probably just a glitch. I mean, I'm sure the guards at the checkpoints messed up..."

"Son of a bitch." Sean had figured it out.

Stepping away from the desk to allow Danny room to work, he spouted off additional commands. "I want to see every single checkpoint entry for those two girls...Katrina Wilson and Isabel Torres...along with these three names. I want to see them all side by side."

Danny grudgingly obeyed and soon brought up five columns in a single Excel spreadsheet, one for each name. The lists were all short, no more than three time, date, and checkpoint location entries each.

"Move over," Sean ordered as he practically pushed Danny out of his chair. He sat down and rolled the chair as close to the screen as possible.

Danny inched away. He desperately wanted to hit Sean upside the head to knock him unconscious and then chain him to the desk so that he could run off to warn his friends, but the guards were waiting just outside the door.

Oblivious to Danny's futile scheming, Sean studied the screen. His eyes moved rapidly back and forth as they glazed over the spreadsheet. Whoever Katrina was, she had passed through a checkpoint three times, each time within a minute of at least one of the other four names: John Simmons twice and Michael Wilkins, Matthew Thompson, and Isabel Torres on her third and final entry on the fourth of August. All entries had occurred at the same checkpoint, the one near the Holland Tunnel. Sean slammed his hands on the desk. "No. Way." He sprang to his feet. He ran toward the door and disappeared within seconds.

Alone, Danny quickly shut down his computer and left his office. Once outside, he rode back to Chinatown in the rain on his bike. By the time he reached his apartment, he was soaking wet. He moved through his place like a tornado as he packed his backpack for the long, wet bike ride to New Jersey. Before leaving, he left a note for Dez and Li explaining that he would be gone for a least a day but didn't say where he was going.

Chapter XXV

*A*fter the tiresomely long ride up the elevator to the seventy-ninth floor, Sean barged through the door of Luke's office without knocking. Finding the office empty, he reached into his back pocket and grabbed his cell phone. He speed-dialed Luke's phone, but the call refused to go through. Even when hovering against the window, the cell service was non-existent. "What the hell am I paying them for?" he shouted, referring to the nearly one hundred Fixers employed to maintain wireless service throughout Manhattan.

He went to check his office two floors above. There he found Luke sitting at his desk talking on the phone.

Upon seeing Sean, Luke pulled the receiver away from his mouth. "Sorry... my phone isn't working." He returned to his call as Sean impatiently waited for him to finish.

"Well?" Sean said the instant Luke hung up.

"They'll be there in fifteen minutes."

Sean frowned. "Fifteen minutes? I told you two hours ago to send them. It's only an hour's drive from here."

Luke was quick to defend himself. "It's longer than that, and you know it also takes at least an hour just to get out the door. They had to gear up and figure out where they're going first. They've never been to the prison before and most of our maps don't even have the prison marked on them."

"Paper maps," Sean muttered under his breath, then said, "You don't need to remind me of that. I'm fully aware of the limitations of *your* men."

"They'll be there and back before seven, which is what you asked, Sean," Luke replied quickly. "I'm sorry, but I can't give you anything more than that."

Sean didn't respond. Instead, he took a seat on the leather couch adjacent to his desk. Luke stood up to give back the chair, but Sean waved him back down.

"So guess who your Katrina has been coming in and out of the city with since August?"

"Who?"

"Ben Kelly."

Luke blinked.

"You don't look surprised."

Luke played it off with a shrug. "Who else would be so interested in the virus?"

"Your lack of concern is disturbing considering you were the one who told her…about Green Haven. And now I find out that she's working with Ben."

"But nothing's happened at the prison since she found out."

"You mean since you told her."

Luke groaned. "Yes, since I screwed up and told her. But honestly, Sean, you've got the place covered."

"Hardly." A dozen guards for a huge prison compound was grossly inadequate, but he couldn't spare any more men, especially for a job that was so boring. The ones assigned there hated it enough already, so much so that he'd had to double their salary.

"How'd you connect the girl to Ben anyway?" Luke asked.

"I had that guy Danny compare every one of her checkpoint entries with Ben's. All the timestamps matched."

"Ben's registered?"

"No, you idiot, he's using an alias…three, actually."

"And how'd you figure that out?"

"I have his fingerprints. He recently registered one of his prints to all three names. How he managed to do that, I'd like to know. Might be time to talk to the guys working the checkpoints."

Luke was still confused by the prints. "How'd you get his fingerprints?"

"Off a glass he drank from once," Sean lied. "A Fixer pulled them off for me."

Luke's eyes grew wide. "Seriously? Sounds like something out of the movies."

Sean sneered at the comparison. The secret files he kept in his apartment were truly secret. Only those who had travelled all over the East Coast and farther to gather the files were aware of their existence. And those few people weren't the same as those who knew about the dozen hidden cameras capturing video every night at *Papillon*. And still those individuals knew nothing about the virus at Green Haven. Only he knew everything.

He shooed Luke out of his chair. "Tell me the minute you hear anything. Now get outta here."

"God, this place is enormous," Ben said as he and Jim scurried from one building to the next.

Starting on the opposite side of the prison from where they had entered, they'd already scoured through the entire E through H cellblocks and found nothing but empty prison cells. The entire prison complex itself was a large series of buildings, outer walkways that connected the buildings, and expansive courtyards where inmates once exercised and took in fresh air. There was no way of knowing exactly where the virus was being kept.

Once back inside a building that appeared to contain the old dining hall, Jim laid out a copy of the schematic of the compound, courtesy of Susan and Maria after hours of combing through hundreds of public records at the county courthouse and administration buildings. He pointed to the buildings labeled as cellblocks A through D. "Let's go here next," he said to Ben.

So far, every building and cellblock they'd wandered through had been cold and dark, with stale air and an eerie sensation of abandonment. When they arrived at cellblock A, however, they no longer needed their flashlights. The vast space was illuminated.

They walked slower now, convinced that they were getting close. They turned the bend from cellblock A to B and heard a faint echo of voices that grew louder with every step. Simultaneously, they flipped off the safety switches on their rifles.

"Who are you?"

Startled, both Ben and Jim whirled around on their heels. Their ears had been so focused on the voices coming from ahead that they had not heard the footsteps approaching from behind.

The boy was probably in his early teens, and with his small body encased in a hazmat suit. His head, however, was exposed. Eyes wide, he appeared equally as startled.

"Who are *you*?" Ben countered in a voice more threatening than intended.

"Sean sent us to check on things," Jim quickly added. "He wanted to make sure everything was moving forward as planned." He recited lines from the script prepared for this type of situation.

The boy frowned. "Does this have anything to do with the noises outside?"

Ben feigned confusion. "Noises?"

"Yeah. The guards here just got a call on their radio that they heard some loud noises outside the perimeter. Most of them just left to check out what's going on."

Ben looked at Jim and casually shrugged. "We didn't hear anything, but we just got here. How many guards are usually inside?"

"Seven, but only two are left. They're in the waiting room in case the noises have anything to do with us."

"Sounds good." Ben had no idea what or where the "waiting room" was, but now the biggest concern were the two guards around the corner.

"So are you supposed to be replacing some of the other guards?" the boy asked, his face looking almost hopeful.

"Uh, we're not sure yet," Jim answered slowly.

"Well no one is allowed through the front gate except me, the two other Fixers, and the seven guards. And Sean and Luke, of course. Not even the guards at the front gate are allowed through."

"Because of the virus?" Jim offered, continuing to play along.

"That and the vaccine."

Ben and Jim looked at each other. *Vaccine?*

"Right, yes," Ben hastily answered. "That's actually why we're here. Sean wants an update on the progress."

The boy hesitated for a moment but didn't ask any more questions. "Then I guess you should follow me. You'll both need a suit." He led the way through Cellblock C. Some of the cells had personal belongings in them and rumpled sheets on the beds. When they approached cellblock D, they came to a door with a cipher lock. He discreetly entered the combination and opened the door. "This is the waiting room."

Ben and Jim stood back and gripped their weapons tighter. When they peered inside, however, the room was empty.

"Huh, I guess the guards are further in," said the boy with bewilderment. "You'll have to wait here. I'll go get your suits." He then moved to yet another door on the opposite side of the room and entered the combination on the cipher lock. When he disappeared behind the second door, Ben and Jim turned to each other.

"Sean's developing a vaccine." Jim said first.

"I guess so," replied Ben as he dropped his rucksack to the ground. "But it doesn't change anything. If he creates a vaccine, that'll just give him even more control over what he can do with the virus."

Jim didn't disagree, and they both checked their weapons to ensure they were properly loaded.

The boy soon returned with two hazmat suits in his arms. They were big and bulky and nearly weighed him down. "Here," he said breathlessly as he handed them over. He showed them how to put the suits on properly before stepping back to the door. "Leave your bags and weapons here. They'll be safe."

"No thanks, we'll carry them," Jim said casually.

But the boy hesitated. "Uh…you can't…"

"We're carrying them," Ben insisted sharply, and the boy's face grew scared. Defeated, he silently turned to the door and entered the combination.

They walked through three additional empty rooms with more locked doors. There was still no sign of the two guards or anyone else.

"Here we check our suits one more time," the boy said timidly.

The instructions regarding the suit were taken seriously, and after double-checking every seal, zipper, and flap, they finally entered the room that they'd come to destroy. The dim light, the super-cold medical freezer, and distinctive laboratory equipment were a figurative "X marks the spot." And yet the boy headed straight through this room to yet another locked door on the opposite end.

"Wait, where are you going?" Jim called to him through his helmet.

"To the Pit. You said you needed to see our progress on the vaccine, right?"

"Uh, right. How much farther is it?"

"Just two more rooms."

They entered an impressive-looking vacuum room before reaching the Pit.

When the door opened, there was a distinctive sucking noise originating from the entire sealed perimeter. Though all the previous doors were airtight, this one seemed exceptionally adhesive. There were five people inside: the two guards and the other two Fixers, all in hazmat suits. The fifth was a young girl lying on the floor in obvious distress. Wearing nothing but a thin hospital gown, her bare legs and arms were likely freezing cold. Standing beside her was a shorter person in a suit holding what appeared to be a syringe.

Ben hesitated to enter the room without knowing the identity of everyone, particularly the guards, but stopping now would only look suspicious. The thick door closed behind them with another whooshing sound.

"Who are *they*?" one of the four protected people demanded. Despite the masking effect of the hazmat suit, his demeanor reflected that of an Infantry guard and not a Fixer.

"Sean sent them to check on our progress."

"Why did you let them in here with guns? You know they aren't allowed beyond the waiting room."

"They insisted on bringing them," the boy answered, sounding even more fearful than when Ben had snapped at him.

"So you just decided to let them in?" the guard roared back. He then pointed a gloved finger at the two intruders. "Get out of here and take your guns with you!"

After exchanging one last pivotal look, Ben and Jim knew they had been patient long enough. Raising their weapons in unison, they lunged forward into the room, Ben aiming at the outspoken guard while Jim fanned the others. Everyone except the girl stood frozen in place.

"All right, here's what's about to happen," Ben's voice boomed through his suit. With his aim still on the guard, he turned to the Fixer holding the syringe. "You…you're going to put down the needle and then all of you will follow my friend here to the…waiting room."

The guard took a hostile step forward, but Ben quickly subdued him with a threatening forward thrust of his rifle. "There won't be any more discussion!" he snapped, forcing the guard to retreat backward.

Jim then took a step forward and nodded toward the unfortunate girl. "Has she been infected yet?"

Through the confines of his helmet, the Fixer holding the syringe shook his head. "No," he said, and in reference to what he was holding, he explained, "This isn't the virus. It's the vaccine."

"Well, she's not getting that either," Ben ordered. "Now move! Everyone!"

With a wave of the gun, he motioned to the door as the Fixers plodded awkwardly in their suits toward it. The guards, however, still refused to move.

"Who the hell are you?" the aggressive one demanded.

"It's not important who we are," he answered with restraint. "Now move!"

The other guard finally backed away toward the door, but the first one remained defiant. He looked down at Ben's rifle and scoffed.

"You sure you can pull the trigger…wearing thick gloves and all?"

Ben looked down at his weapon. "You know, you're right."

And with a rapid motion, he flipped the gun around with the barrel pointed over his shoulder and slammed the stock into the guard's head. The flexible plastic of the helmet did little to cushion the blow, and the guard flew backward and fell to the ground. Dazed but not unconscious, the guard didn't get up as everyone else looked on.

Jim poked the other guard in the shoulder with his gun. "Get him out of here. Drag him if you have to."

Angry but obedient, the guard approached his fallen comrade and helped him to his feet. The downed guard's head bobbed about inside the suit. The whack to his head seemed to have induced some sort of memory recall, for when his eyes fixed upon Ben one more time, he mumbled, "I know you…you're Ben Kelly…"

"That's right. Be sure to give Sean my regards."

With Jim following close behind, the Fixers and guards left the room. The girl, meanwhile, had remained motionless on the floor during the entire episode.

Ben walked over to her now and picked up the syringe. He lowered his weapon and extended his free hand. "Come on, sweetheart. Let's get out of here."

Despite her frail appearance, the girl stood up with ease. "Thank you," she uttered softly.

With her dark hair and blue eyes, she had a strong resemblance to Karen, and he smiled warmly at her. They left the room.

"Take her with the rest of them," Ben instructed his cousin when they reached the room where the virus was kept.

Jim directed everyone else to the waiting room as Ben pulled aside the boy who originally led them in. "What's the combination to all these doors? Is it the same?"

Eyes wide, the boy nodded. "It's three then five, then one and two together."

"And they're all the same?"

The boy nodded again, and Ben gestured for Jim to keep moving with the others. Once alone with just the boy, he shut the door behind them and tested the combination to make sure it worked. The door opened, and Ben motioned for him to leave.

"I heard the guard say your name. I know who you are. You're here to destroy the virus," the boy said.

Ben gazed back. "I am," he said.

"But why do you want to destroy everything when we're so close to creating a vaccine?"

Taking a step forward, he gently placed his gloved hand on the boy's shoulder. "Listen…Sean Taylor is using you and everyone else in here for his own twisted plan. He doesn't care about any of you, only what you can do for him. Having the virus *and* the vaccine just makes him stronger, but if the virus no longer exists, then there's no need for a vaccine and everyone will be safer." Then, with a gesture toward the door, he said, "You should run. Run far away from here and use that smart brain of yours for something better than this."

Absorbing this earnest advice, the boy stared back at Ben a few seconds longer. Then he disappeared through the door.

Finally alone inside the room containing the deadliest substance ever known to man, Ben moved with cautious speed. After a rapid scan of the space and everything inside, he placed his rifle on the floor and quickly retrieved several items from his rucksack: half a gallon of gasoline, two bottles of nail polish remover, a bundle of balsa wood, strips of wool fabric, a rubber band, a hammer, and a cigarette lighter.

There were other things inside the rucksack, including C-4 and blasting caps, but these would not be needed. At Fort Detrick, they destroyed the entire building because they didn't know exactly where the virus was hidden. But here, Ben was mere feet from the infernal matter.

He moved over to the medical freezer and carefully opened the door. Inside were two shelves, and on each was a metal tray with several glass vials of what could only be the virus and the still-untested vaccine. He removed the trays with care and placed them on a nearby table, then removed the shelves before unplugging the freezer and sliding it to the middle of the room. He flipped the freezer over so that the door faced the ceiling. With the freezer door hanging open, he placed the glass vials inside, one at a time.

There were three tables in the room, each with various stacks of paper and notebooks, along with a laptop: all containing notes and documentation compiled by the Fixers during their months of research. Moving faster now, Ben gathered the notebooks and every single sheet of paper and placed them all inside the freezer. Lastly, he removed the hard-drive from the laptop and threw it on the floor before striking it multiple times with the hammer. The warped drive was tossed into the freezer as well. After one final check of the room, he poured the gasoline and the two bottles of nail polish remover inside the freezer.

He opened the door to the room and placed his rucksack and rifle inside, using the latter to prop the door open. Then with the bundle of balsa wood, he wrapped the wool fabric around one end and secured it in place with the rubber band. Lighting the end to create a torch, he backed toward the door and threw the torch into the freezer.

Flames erupted to the ceiling. Ben dashed through the door and slammed it shut. Peering through the small glass window, he watched as the fire raged. The heat alone would kill the virus. Satisfied, he grabbed his rucksack and gun and rushed through the series of empty rooms until he reached the waiting room.

Jim was there with just the guards, their feet bound and their hands tied behind their backs. No longer wearing a hazmat suit, he was now holding a radio that had belonged to one of the guards. A near-continuous stream of chatter could be heard from the speaker.

Ben hurriedly removed his helmet. "It's done."

"Good, because we need to go. There's a bunch of guards that just showed up at the security gate."

Ben groaned as he yanked off the rest of his suit, and then he looked at the guards. "Where are the others?" he asked Jim.

"I let them leave. But not these two."

Ben nodded and then they both left the room. They backtracked through the cellblocks. When they emerged outside, they discovered that the temperature had dropped substantially and that the earlier rain had returned in the form of sleet. It stung their cheeks and obscured their vision.

"This way!" Jim cried out once he found his bearings.

Only the faintest amount of daylight remained to permit them to find their way back to the prison wall. Ditching both rucksacks and with his weapon dangling from his back, Jim climbed the rope first. Halfway up the wall, however, a moving flash of light caught the corner of his right eye.

"There they are!" someone shouted. When Ben turned to look, he saw three people with flashlights approaching fast.

"Hurry!" Jim called down from the top of the rope.

With the pursuers not more than ten yards from the bottom of the rope, Ben scrambled to the top of the wall as a searchlight from the closest tower was directed onto him. Straddling it, he grabbed the hook at the end of the rope and dropped it to the ground just as the first pursuer grabbed at it. Then he flew down the ladder.

Waiting at the bottom, Jim had been listening to the chatter about their location over their stolen radio. "Everyone knows we're outside the perimeter."

"Fine, let them chase us."

They ran to the forest and found their path. Using a pencil-thin but powerful flashlight, Jim led the way. As the rock with the X drew closer, they heard voices as flashes of light danced behind them. Jim swerved around the right side of the rock as Ben followed with lightning-quick footing. Seconds later, a loud cry was heard. Ben's closest pursuer had just fallen through the hidden, six-foot-deep hole he and Jim had meticulously dug into the path where the X-labeled rock sat. If lucky, another one would fall in after.

As they cleared the forest and raced to the airport, Ben deftly retrieved his radio from his belt. "Get the cars started...we're being followed!" he shouted into the speaker between breaths.

"Got it!" Charlie responded over the radio.

They ran through the field and across the runway. Ben chanced a look over his shoulder and saw more shadowy figures chasing them, the beams of their flashlights bouncing in the dark. More than halfway to the hangar, he stopped as Jim continued running. Ben lifted his rifle and squeezed off two rounds to scare their pursuers off. But the pursuers maintained their speed like determined predators hunting their prey.

Ben turned back and closed the distance between himself and Jim. As they approached the hangar, he saw Charlie pull his car outside. Jim reached the passenger's door and hopped inside.

Seeing them hesitate, Ben yelled, "Go!" and waved them off. They sped toward the airport exit.

Andy pulled up in the second car. "Get in!" she cried and leaned over to open his door. Ben hurtled himself inside, and the moment he was seated, she pressed hard on the gas. The forward acceleration slammed his door shut.

"What happened?" she asked breathlessly as she rounded the corner and followed the hazy taillights of Charlie's car in front of them.

"We destroyed it but couldn't get out without being seen." Ben looked back through the rear window but his pursuers were no longer in sight.

"But it's gone?"

"Yep, burned to Hell. Forever."

Andy gripped the wheel hard and roared the engine. The road had become slippery with sleet, and she nearly skidded off it.

"Careful!" Ben reprimanded.

"I'm trying!"

She regained control and saw Charlie make a sharp left out of the airport. She prepared to follow him when a second car suddenly went flying by from the right just as she approached the turn. The car was trailing Charlie and was immediately followed by a second vehicle. Upon seeing her headlights, however, the second one screeched to a stop, swerving in the process, and began to turn around.

"No!" Andy cried as she yanked the wheel to the left and T-boned the rear of the vehicle before it could complete its turn. She kept driving as the other car spun around on the slick road.

"I'm going after them." She pushed hard on the accelerator. The car chasing Charlie was in sight.

"Get up close to it and I'll try hitting the tires," Ben instructed as he slid half his body out the window and steadied his rifle.

Andy sped up while, but when she came within a few car lengths of the pursuing vehicle, it skid ninety degrees and blocked the road.

"Go right!" yelled Ben as he pointed to a quickly approaching intersection.

Andy yanked hard on the wheel to turn north along the country road. The vehicle that had been chasing Charlie soon began chasing them and was quickly followed by another car, presumably the one she had T-boned.

"Does Charlie have the other radio?" Ben asked in desperation.

Andy glanced at the cup holders between their seats, in which sat her radio. "No, I have it."

"And I have the other one."

"Aw, crap!"

Ben leaned out the window again and aimed back at the vehicles chasing them.

"Slow down!" he yelled to Andy.

She eased off the accelerator to close the gap. Ben fired several shots. The front vehicle swerved but maintained course. He fired again, this time releasing every round he had left, but the vehicle still advanced.

Andy, meanwhile, reached into her backpack with one hand and found another magazine. "Here!"

He released his empty magazine and grabbed the full one. He skillfully replaced it and took aim again. "Slow down and move left!"

Andy applied the brakes and veered over.

When he fired again, he hit vital components, including the front left tire. The car swerved out of control and was soon struck by the second vehicle behind it. Ben dropped back into his seat and caught his breath. "Nice driving."

"Nice shooting."

They continued heading down a road they didn't recognize.

"Where are we?" she asked.

"No idea." Ben pulled out the map and turned on the overhead light.

The sudden glare prevented Andy from seeing a deer crossing the road until it was almost too late. She swerved and missed the creature but soon went into a tailspin. Her attempt to recover was futile. The car careened off the side of the road into a shallow ditch. "No, no!" she cried and put the car into reverse, but it wouldn't budge.

"Wait, I'll get out." Ben rounded the front of the vehicle. As Andy slowly applied the gas, he pushed as hard as he could, but after five attempts, the car was nowhere closer to breaking free of the muddy trenches that had formed around its tires. The rain had washed away any friction between them and the ground. Accepting defeat, Ben returned to the passenger's side and began grabbing his things.

"We're just going to leave it?" Andy asked incredulously.

"We've got no choice. Whoever's chasing us will be here soon."

She yanked off her seatbelt and grabbed her backpack and raincoat from the backseat. Throwing on the coat, she followed Ben to the other side of the road. "Where are we going?"

"This is a residential area. We'll find somewhere to camp out for a while, but first we need to get off the road."

Andy glanced around. He was right. On the road, they were vulnerable and needed to put distance between themselves and their car. After a quick look at the map, the only plausible direction was to head east.

Ben led Andy off the road and through a thick cluster of trees. When they emerged on the other end, they found themselves in a small neighborhood. But they didn't stop. Still too close to the road, they continued to run in the cold and sleet, hoping to disappear into the night.

Chapter XXVI

*E*xcept for a scant handful of towers, the cellular network beyond the five boroughs had not been restored. To compensate, Sean had built a network of repeaters to extend the range of push-to-talk radios far outside of the city's limits. While nowhere near as capable or complex as a cellular network, these repeaters allowed the Infantry to communicate as far north as Poughkeepsie, as far west as the Pennsylvania-New Jersey border, and as far south as Philadelphia, where the cellular network picked up again. The prison sat at the northern edge of this communication zone.

After getting word about the gunshots and flares, Sean ordered Luke to go to the prison immediately. But by the time Luke arrived, the trespassers had already escaped, and he then had the unfortunate job of breaking the news to Sean; not only had they escaped, but they had destroyed every last trace of the virus.

"So what are you doing to find them?" were Sean's first bitter words to Luke over the radio.

"We think there were three or four of them. They left in two separate vehicles." He paused briefly before adding, "We think one of them was a girl."

"So what happened to the two cars?"

"We chased both of them and they got separated. One of them got away, but we found the other stuck in a ditch on a nearby road. But it was empty."

"Empty? So they got out on foot?"

"Looks like it. I've got everyone driving around looking for them. They can't be too far, especially in this weather."

"I hope you're right. I'm coming up there now to sort out this mess. Scan all the frequencies on this band and check for any transmissions that aren't ours. They're probably using radios to communicate. Out!"

For nearly an hour, they walked north through the dark, passing trees, roads, more trees, and houses tucked away in quiet neighborhoods. They continued on in the cold and rain; the need to increase their distance from Green Haven propelled them ahead.

The sleet pelted Andy's cheeks, turning them red and raw. Both she and Ben were completely soaked through to their jeans, and their shoes weren't fairing much better. Their upper bodies were still dry, but they had grossly underestimated the temperatures. It felt more like January than October, and they hadn't anticipated being outside this long. Andy began to shiver uncontrollably, the chill penetrating to her bones. As much as she wanted to keep going, she feared hypothermia would consume her body if they didn't stop for shelter soon.

Ben was visibly cold as well, and without a word, he took hold of her icy hand and led her down yet another residential street. They had no idea where they were, and the map inside his rucksack was not detailed enough to show anything more than major roads and highways.

The fallen autumn leaves coated much of the sidewalks, and Andy slipped on them more than once before regaining her footing. Ben continued to hold her hand until they reached a two-story house at the end of a cul-de-sac. There were other houses on either side, but this one had a front porch with a stack of firewood sitting out of the rain. Hopefully, it was dry enough to ignite.

No lights were on, as expected, and the lock to the front door easily gave way with a strong push. Inside was pitch black and the air was stale, but it was dry and warmer than outside, which was all that mattered at the moment. Ben panned the entryway with his flashlight and led Andy down a hallway into the living room that had a large fireplace. A pile of wood, considerably smaller than the one underneath the front porch, sat beside it. He touched the top piece of wood. Though covered in dust and cobwebs, it was thankfully dry.

Soon, Ben was busy feeding a growing fire while Andy removed her wet jacket, shoes, and socks. Using her flashlight, she went upstairs and found a few blankets in a linen closet. Still shivering violently, she proceeded to remove her soaked jeans and sweater before wrapping herself in one of the blankets. With her wet clothes in one hand and extra blankets firmly grasped in the other, she returned downstairs to the living room and placed her clothes in front of the fire to dry.

Ben looked up from the fire to her. They hadn't said a word since entering the house. "Here, sit down," he said as he stepped away from the growing fire that soon became a roaring inferno.

Andy kneeled down in front and drew her knees into her chest beneath the blanket. Despite removing her wet clothes and the warmth of the fire, she continued to shiver violently. "God! I c-ca-can-t-t-t...ge-ge-t-t...wah-warm," she stammered through chattering teeth.

Though chilled himself, Ben wasn't shivering nearly as much. He quickly shed his own clothes down to his boxers. After placing his wet clothing beside hers, he picked up one of the other blankets and sat down between her and a large ottoman. Drawing up to her side, he wrapped the blanket around them both. "Body heat," he muttered as he pulled her head into his bare chest. It felt like ice against his skin.

"F-fun-ny..."

"What is?"

"Th-this. L-like a b-bad roh-mance nov-v-vel."

He let out a small laugh. "Andrea Christensen reading trashy romance novels? I'm shocked."

"R-ran outta real b-books in Ber-muda." She tried to smile but her lips kept quivering.

"Sounds like it..." Leaning against the ottoman, he rubbed his hands through her wet hair to warm her head. "Not to sound like a complete pervert, but if you let go of your blanket so that more of our skin touches, you'll get warmer faster."

She released her blanket immediately and wrapped it around them both, creating an additional layer of insulation. She then pressed herself against every possible inch of his skin as he wrapped his arms around her. In time, the fire and the heat from his body thawed the icy chill running through her until the shivering ceased. As she grew warmer, she didn't pull away but instead leaned in closer as her body finally began to relax. With her left ear pressed firmly against his chest she stared at the fire. She could hear the steady beat of his heart. Her eyelids began to flutter as the rhythm lulled her into a welcome sleep.

⁂

Sitting in the dark, Sean stared down at the pistol in his lap. Green Haven was just a few miles away. For six years, he had managed to get where he was without killing a single person with his bare hands. Many people had died under his orders, but he had never actually killed anyone, himself. He'd never pulled the trigger or put a needle into someone's arm. Or plunged a knife into a person's chest as Chad had done to his mother. Sean admired the boldness of the act. The police report from the small Iowa town made no conclusive accusation that young Chad had killed his mother, but a quick skim over the file said it all: he had snuffed the life out of someone he was supposed to love. And he had done it with a knife—an intimate act that also required great physical strength. Sean couldn't help but feel a bit jealous.

He gazed out the car window into the darkness. The rain increased until the windshield wipers struggled to keep up with the pace of the downpour. He exited the SUV the moment it pulled into the prison entrance. He spotted Luke and made a beeline toward him as he stuffed his gun into the back of his jeans underneath his raincoat.

"Well?"

Luke swallowed.

"You haven't found them yet?" Controlling his anger, Sean threw the hood of his coat over his head. "Show me the map."

Luke led him to the rear of his SUV. The back door was open and sheltered them from the rain. Spread out in the back was a detailed map of the prison and the surrounding neighborhoods.

"Where was the abandoned car found?" Sean asked.

"Here." Luke pointed at a side road that ran perpendicular to the main road from the prison, Route 216, the same road that served as the entrance to the airport.

"And where were the cars first spotted?"

"Here, at the airport. It's probably where they staged everything. I've got everyone searching five miles around the abandoned car, but so far, nothing."

Sean squinted at the map and shook his head. "They won't be down here," he said, pointing to areas south and west of the airport. "The second car was abandoned north of this road…216. They were heading north when their car was abandoned, right?"

"Right," Luke confirmed.

"Then they probably kept going in that direction to put distance between themselves and the prison. They'll be up here somewhere." Sean traced a circle with his finger around a large area north of the prison containing many residential neighborhoods. "Move everyone searching south of Route 216 up to these neighborhoods. And tell everyone that the person who finds them will get an entire night with Lily."

◦◦◦

Alone in the living room, Morgan kept the fire going. There was no point trying to sleep. Not even the soft sounds of Katie's rhythmic breathing in the crib beside her could quiet her mind. It was after midnight, and the other girls were all asleep. The house was drafty, and the wind outside seeped through the cracks in the doors and windows. Upstairs, Maria shared a bed with her sister to keep warm while Susan huddled under a pile of blankets in a spare bedroom.

Morgan placed another log on the fire. As it began to burn, there was a knock on the front door. She peered through the peephole, but could barely make out the shadowy figure standing in the darkness. She reached for the flashlight on the small entry table and unlocked and opened the door without removing the chain lock. "Danny?"

"Yeah, hi…Sarah, right?"

She nearly forgot her own fake name. "Uh, right." She noticed that he was soaking wet and immediately took pity on him. "Come in." She ushered him inside. "Sit by the fireplace."

"Thanks," he uttered through chattering teeth. "Sorry to come by so late, but I need to talk to Ben and Jim."

"Oh, they're not here." She shut the door and locked it again. "How did you know where to find us?"

"Ben gave me the address on his last visit to the city a few weeks ago. He wanted me to update Jim's and his ID to indicate that they were members of the Infantry."

He stripped off his dripping raincoat and took a seat on the floor by the fire, and rubbed his arms to get warm.

"You'll never get warm if you stay in those wet clothes," said Morgan.

"My shirt is dry. Just my jeans and shoes are wet. I rode my bike from the city."

She looked at Danny as though he were insane. "What's so important that you had to come fifty miles in the rain?"

Danny looked up at her gravely. "It's Sean. He found out that Ben's been back to the city."

Her eyes grew wide. "What…how…?"

"I knew something was up when he found out your friends were at *Papillon* on the same night back in August, but I didn't know exactly what. When he came around a second time to scan a set of fingerprints that turned out to be Ben's, I didn't have time to stop him from figuring out that Ben had returned."

"But how he get a copy of Ben's fingerprints?"

"No idea. But he was *furious* when he found out Ben had sneaked back into the city."

She didn't know exactly how much Jim and Ben trusted Danny, but the fact that they had reveal to him their location seemed like it was time to tell the truth. She took a seat beside him. "Danny, I'll be honest with you. My name isn't Sarah. It's Morgan. Ben and Jim didn't want Sean or anyone else knowing our real names."

The deception didn't seem to bother him at all. If anything, he seemed to approve of it. "I figured as much."

"Well, I'm sorry you came all this way, but after tonight, it won't matter anymore what Sean knows."

"Well, whatever Sean and Luke were worried about, it seemed pretty serious."

It was the first time Danny had said anything about Luke, and at the mention of his name, Morgan froze. "Luke?"

"Yeah. He was there when Sean started asking about your friends. Isabel and Katrina."

"It's Maria and Andy, actually..." she murmured. She shut her eyes tightly and rubbed her temples. "Bloody hell. This is bad."

"What's wrong?" Danny asked, confused.

Morgan started to explain when another knock on the front door echoed through the house, this time louder and more urgent. When she opened the door with the chain lock still attached, she saw Jim and Charlie standing in the rain on the other side.

"Thank God!" she cried out as she released the chain and opened the door. She hugged Jim tightly before he entered.

Charlie walked into the living room where he spotted Danny. "Who are you?" The two had never met before.

"I'm Danny," he replied, standing up.

"Oh, the hacker?"

Danny held out his hand to Charlie, who shook it. "That's me."

"What took you so long? Where are Andy and Ben?" Morgan asked Jim.

"What, they're not here?" he responded with concern, causing Morgan's face to fall.

"They didn't come back with you?"

"We got separated leaving the airport," said Charlie.

"I'm sure they're fine. They're probably either looking for us or are on their way back," Jim replied with genuine assurance.

"I'm sure," Morgan repeated softly. She leaned into Jim's chest. "Did you destroy it?"

"Yes. It's gone."

Andy awoke sometime in the middle of the night. Her eyes opened as slowly as they had closed, and she became acutely aware of her body and its position against Ben's. In their mutual sleep, her cheek had landed firmly against the center of his chest and her torso, wrapped snuggly under the thin blanket, was cradled within his. With her body temperature restored, the necessity of remaining pressed together had disappeared, but she made no effort to release herself from the grasp of the strong arms still draped around her.

The fire had dwindled, but the area of the room near the fireplace was still warm. As she moved to relieve the crick in her neck, Ben stirred in his sleep but did not wake. She checked the time on his watch lying among their pile of clothes. They had been asleep for five hours, which gave her confidence that they were safe from discovery. After placing a few more pieces of wood on the fire, she returned to her position beside him. The rise and fall of his chest was hypnotic and prevented her from looking at anything but him.

From the day they first met, Andy could never deny her attraction to Ben. His dark blue eyes like the sea before a storm, his jaw set with determination. But over the many months, she had grown accustomed to his appearance and had simply put that particular aspect of him in a figurative box and shoved it aside. After all, his looks had nothing to do with their relationship. They were close friends, confidants in many respects, and always would be.

And yet, as she stared down at him, at long last she allowed herself to admit that she wanted him as something more. She had denied her desires by hiding them deep within a secret compartment in her mind and heart. But this effort had worn her out. He was absolutely everything she could ever want in a man, but what was she to him? She was a tomboy, wild and rough around the edges and not remotely sexy. Perhaps pretty, but she knew her place in the world of superficial appearance. Morgan was a graceful and elegant beauty. Susan, now nearly sixteen, grew more beautiful every day, her smile and demeanor ever intoxicating to Charlie. Maria, meanwhile, was exotic…sultry.

But Andy? Strong. Intelligent. Daring. Yes, all of those applied. They were qualities she was proud to possess. Stunning? Sexy? Gorgeous? No, these weren't words she'd ever use to describe herself.

Still, it wasn't entirely implausible that what Morgan said was true and that Ben could actually love her. Who else would have traveled alone hundreds of miles in the cold winter and hot desert to find her, and then enter a stadium filled with half-crazed, bloodthirsty spectators and dozens of armed men with only a single rifle for protection? Only someone who was more terrified of her death than his own.

As though under a spell, her hand slowly reached out toward his abdomen, his perfect set of muscles never failing to distract her. And now her hand was seemingly acting on its own as her fingertips delicately brushed his skin. They outlined each muscle and ran up and down the length of his stomach, slowly and lightly like feathers. Then, her hand became her own again, and she jerked it back, suddenly aware of what she was doing.

Suddenly, his hand grabbed her wrist. He was awake. Their eyes locked. Without a word, he sat up and let go of her wrist, only to reach around her with both arms and pull her closer to him. Instinctively, Andy looked away. She always looked away. But he stopped her by putting both hands on her face by her ears, urging her to look at him. "Please…don't…" he whispered.

With those two words, Andy realized that he had felt her fear, not just at that moment but at every moment—every aversion of her eyes from his, every inch of space that she had placed between them, every excuse that she had made to avoid her feelings. He recognized her hesitation once again, right there on a cold floor inside a strange, dark house, and he was refusing to let it happen any longer. He was tired of it, and so was she.

Before she could think or feel another thought, he pulled her face toward him until their lips were a mere inch apart. Her breath caught in her throat in the same moment as he swallowed hard. Then he leaned in the rest of the way.

And when she kissed him back, it was not for practice or to secretly play out a fantasy. This was actually happening. This was real.

Time seemed to both speed up and stand still as months of unspoken longing melted away. They kissed without restraint. The sensation of Ben's mouth and tongue against hers was electrifying, and when Andy began running her hands through his hair, then down his shoulder and back, she knew she couldn't stop at this alone.

He moved his hand down from her waist until his palm slid under her rear beneath the blanket. A soft sigh escaped her mouth. With his other hand, he lifted her up and sat her down on top of his thighs, and she wrapped her legs around him. As he started to gently tug at the sides of her underwear, she suddenly pulled back. She looked anxious and uncertain.

"Ben, I've never…never done this."

He blinked. "It's okay. We don't have to."

"But I want to…with you."

"Are you sure?"

She looked into his eyes. They reassured her. "Yes."

Carefully and gently he ran a hand down the length of her stomach and she drew in a sharp breath between her teeth. He then ran his fingers up and down her back, feeling her relax. He kissed her again and whispered, "You okay?"

Biting her lower lip, she nodded, and he kissed away the single tear that had fallen down her cheek. Then he leaned back against the ottoman and hugged her to his chest.

Andy could feel his heart drumming. She looked up at him to let him know she was ready.

Then slowly, he lifted her up off his thighs and gently lowered her back down onto the floor.

Chapter XXVII

When Andy awoke, concern that they had stayed too long in the house immediately gripped her. She checked her watch and was stunned to find that it was after seven. "Crap!" she hissed and quickly stood up. The room was cold once again, but her clothes and shoes were mercifully dry. Once her shoes were laced, she knelt down beside Ben who was still fast asleep on the floor. "Wake up," she murmured gently into his ear. He stirred mildly, so she shook his shoulder. "Sweetie, wake up."

His eyes blinked open, and when he saw her face, he smiled. "Did you just call me *sweetie?*"

"I did. Now get up. It's after seven."

He sat up, but instead of reaching for his clothes, he grabbed Andy's waist and pulled her down to the floor. Squealing, she landed right beside him and laughed. He leaned in and kissed her mouth.

She kissed him back with equal eagerness as the tingling sensation returned in her stomach, but she forced herself to pull back. "Stop that! We have to go!"

Reluctantly and with a groan, he released her and threw on his clothes. "You're spoiling all the fun." He pulled his fleece sweatshirt over his head before reaching for his raincoat.

"I just want us to get away from here," she replied. Wearing a knowing smile, she whispered, "We'll have more fun when we get home. You know, to celebrate."

Smiling in turn, he replied, "Promise?"

"I promise." And she kissed him again before adding as a final joke, "Was I better than champagne?"

"No comparison," was his candid reply, and then his face grew serious. "I never thanked you for doing this," he added.

"Doing what?"

"All of this. For dragging me back here and helping Jim and I finish what we started."

She grabbed at the neckline of his sweater affectionately. "I did it because I knew that deep down, you wanted to come back."

After one final kiss, they quickly gathered their things and went out the door. But when Ben stepped outside, he stopped cold.

Standing in the cul-de-sac surrounded by half a dozen guards stood Sean. Upon seeing Ben, a repulsive, self-satisfied smile spread across his face. "Well, well…isn't this cozy? We've been waiting forever for you two to wake up."

Acting on instinct, Ben placed himself in front of Andy, grabbed his rifle leaning against the wall by the door, and pointed it at Sean.

"I wouldn't do that if I were you."

But Ben steadied his aim and shut his left eye as his right focused in on the front sight. "Why not? Your head is right in my line of fire."

"Because your rifle has no firing pin." Sean pulled out a thin metal object from inside his pocket. It was a few inches in length and resembled a long nail.

"You're bluffing," Ben hollered back, though his voice wavered.

Wearing a smug grin, Sean outstretched his arms as if daring Ben to fire. "Go ahead…pull the trigger."

Without hesitation, Ben flexed his right index finger a second after Sean uttered his last word. Horribly, nothing happened, so he tried again and again until the hideous sound of Sean's laugh forced him to stop.

Both terrified and enraged, Andy fished inside her backpack for her pistol, but her hand found nothing.

"Looking for this?" Sean suddenly revealed her gun and held it up as the guards began to laugh.

"You two really should've locked the doors last night. But I guess you were too busy screwing each other to think about it."

In a split-second motion, Ben whirled around toward Andy. "The back door. Go!"

Her feet propelled her back into the house. There was a door in the kitchen that led to a rear patio. She burst through it and launched over the short fence that wrapped around the patio as Ben ran after her.

Beyond the small backyard of the house lay a cluster of trees. She ran toward them, but just as she was about to disappear into them, two armed guards suddenly appeared from behind the trees and quickly subdued her. She stopped dead in her tracks as Ben nearly ran into her from behind. Within moments, they were surrounded.

Looking up at Ben, Andy saw only terror in his face. Even so, his eyes were scanning the area in a desperate search for another way to escape. But the horrific reality was that any attempt to flee at this point would only result in one or both of them getting shot.

Walking slowly, Sean came around the side of the house to the backyard. He calmly pulled an apple out of his coat pocket and began biting away at it as though he were simply out for a stroll on a crisp, autumn day. "You know, you two make a really cute couple," he said between bites. He entered the circle created by his guards as they maintained their aim on both their targets. Taking another bite, Sean looked back and forth between Andy and Ben, his icy blue eyes dancing with delight. After swallowing, he said, "It's too bad that you won't be able to see what might've become of this beautiful relationship." And with that, he flung the remainder of the apple to the ground, a cue for the guards to grab Andy and pull her away.

She struggled in their grasp, and Ben cried out her name in desperation as the remaining guards maintained their circle around him. One thrust the barrel of his gun into Ben's chest.

"Get off of me! Let...me...GO!" Andy screamed as they dragged her to the front of the house. She kicked and squirmed violently, but the guards' grips were too strong. Sean followed them, marching behind her as he stared into her face and frowned with keen interest.

The guards finally released her when they reached the front curb, flinging her crumpled body to the ground. When she tried to stand up, they rapidly restrained her. An SUV pulled up to the curb, and Luke stepped out of the passenger's seat.

He looked down at Andy and sneered. "Hello, Katrina. Nice to see you again."

"Actually, it's Andy," Sean corrected as he joined his comrade. "At least that's what our good friend Ben called her a moment ago."

Luke seemed to consider the name and nodded in approval. "Andy, huh? Well, nice to see you again anyway, though you look like shit compared to the last time I saw you."

Seething, she stared up at Luke with overt hatred in her eyes but remained silent.

Sean gestured for Luke to follow him to the back of the house. "Watch her," he ordered the guards before he and Luke walked away.

After rounding the house once more, Sean approached the circle of guards who were still restraining Ben. He waved them back to give him more room and turned to Luke. He leaned in close and said in a low voice, "Tell the two guards you trust the most to stay behind and send the rest to the front of the house."

Ben's eyes flashed wildly between Sean, Luke, and each of the guards, desperate to figure out what was going on.

Luke eyed the guards and pointed at two of them. "You two...stay here. The rest of you go back to the front."

The guards obeyed, and as they broke off, Ben took advantage of the moment to break free and run. He managed to get beyond Luke and the guards. Only Sean reacted quickly and retrieved Andy's gun from his coat pocket. With impressive skill, he aimed it at Ben and fired.

The sound of the gun shattered in the air, and the bullet lodged itself into the back of Ben's right shoulder as its momentum hurtled him to the ground. The echo of the shot resonated off the house and trees, and Andy released an ear-piercing scream from the front of the house.

In shock, Ben rolled over and opened his eyes. He saw Sean and Luke standing over him but their faces were out of focus. When at last the pain emerged, Ben grabbed his shoulder and groaned in agony. He couldn't hear what either Sean or Luke were saying, but soon after the throbbing began and the warm gush of blood flowed from his shoulder, he vaguely heard the thunderous crack of two more shots being fired. Neither of them were aimed anywhere near him.

More of Andy's screams could be heard in the distance; louder and more heart wrenching than the first. Ben heard her cries, and they only added to his pain. The gunshot wound was unlike anything he'd ever felt, and his mind raced from thought to incongruous thought. *Should it burn this much?* was his last before the butt of a rifle slammed into his forehead. His vision faded to black.

"You two," Sean said sharply to the two guards. "Ben Kelly is dead...got it? If I hear anything otherwise, you are both dead."

The guards nodded fearfully.

"Good. Now stand over there for a few minutes while Luke and I talk."

The guards did as they were told.

"Take her back to the city. Put her in that closet across the hall from my office and make sure it's locked and guarded. I'll be there after I deal with him."

"What will you do?" Luke asked.

He pursed his lips together, still staring at his unconscious enemy. "I'm working on that."

At that moment, Andy appeared around the corner of the house. Somehow, she had broken free from the guards who were now trailing after her. One of them raised his gun to shoot her.

"No!" Sean yelled out and waved his arms, stopping the guard just in time.

Andy collapsed to the ground when she saw Ben's lifeless body, and she began to sob uncontrollably as the guards dragged her away once more.

Smirking, Sean turned back to Luke. "At least now she'll believe that her beloved Ben is dead."

Staring out the living room window, Morgan held Katie in her arms as she fed her a bottle of formula. With the exception of Katie and Carmen, everyone had suffered a restless night, but she hadn't slept at all.

Neither Andy nor Ben had returned, and by morning, it was evident that something had happened to them.

"I'll feed her," Jim said as he came up behind Morgan. "You should try to get some sleep."

"No, that's okay. I can't sleep."

"We'll find them."

She turned around and gave him a sharp look. "How do you know that?"

"Because I know Ben and you know Andy. They're fighters."

"I won't just sit and wait for them. We've got to do something."

"We'll go back to the prison today and see if we can find out what happened."

She looked hard into his weary eyes. "When you say 'we'll go back,' you mean you and Charlie, right?"

"Uh, yeah."

"Oh and us girls get to stay back and do nothing, is that it?"

He sighed. "No, that's not what I meant…"

"Good," she cut him off. "We all need to go back to the prison and search the area, and if we have to, we'll go to the city and stay until we figure out what happened and find them. No matter how long it takes."

She was being brave, and Jim recognized her need to take charge. Rising to his feet, he leaned over and kissed her. "We'll find them, don't worry," he whispered.

Her eyes welled up, and as she looked away, a large tear rolled down her cheek. It fell and hit Katie's bottle. "What if he has them? What if he…"

"If Sean has them, he won't kill them. He'll play with them and torment them, but he won't kill them."

Morgan looked into Jim's eyes. "I'm not sure if that's better. We better work fast."

Her surroundings were pitch-black and the floor she lay upon was cold. Dazed at first, Andy suddenly remembered everything and she began to weep.

All she wanted was to help others. She couldn't believe that she was a captive once again, all because she had tried to prevent Sean from having control over the virus.

She wept for Ben, the only man she had ever loved, who was now dead because of her. *I shouldn't have pushed him to do this. He didn't need to come back.* She choked when she said his name aloud, and a great pain struck her like a knife stabbing her through the heart. *One night…that's all I got with him was one night. Why did I wait so long?* She thought over and over again.

She didn't care where she was or how long she was going to be there. All she wanted was to die. Death was the only sure way to erase all the pain and memories that would only haunt her forever. She cried until anguish fatigued her to the point of unconsciousness, and she remained motionless on the cold, hard floor for several hours. The only mercy granted to her was a dreamless sleep, one without nightmares or images of Ben.

On the eightieth floor of the Empire State Building, Sean opened the door to a closet guarded by two Infantry officers. Light from the hallway illuminated the dark space. It was small, identical to the closet he had placed Andy in. The space was empty, only measuring six square feet and had once been used as a supply room to store cleaning materials. It was too small for his six-foot-two captive to lie down completely. Sean hadn't planned for that to be the case, but the discomfort the size made was a welcome revelation.

Conscious once again but now encumbered with a terrible headache on top of his gunshot wound, Ben sat with his back against the corner farthest from the door. Sean had earlier instructed a Fixer to check the wound and remove any fragments of the bullet. It had been a clean shot, tearing mostly through muscle and the outer surface of the humerus bone, causing excruciating pain as blood seeped through his bandage. No sedative or painkiller had been given to him all day, and the unrelenting suffering was wearing him down.

Sean stepped inside and closed the door behind him. The darkness returned momentarily until he illuminated a hand-held electric lamp. Though the overhead light worked in the room, he wanted to maintain the illusion of darkness.

Ben's eyes blinked at the sudden sensation of light as he recognized Sean's face.

"Where is she?" was the first thing he said in almost a growl through gritted teeth. Though the room was cold, his forehead glistened with sweat and his right leg shook from pain.

"Oh, she's a lot closer than you think." The smile on Sean's face was sickening. "She's just upstairs. In fact…" Sean looked up and pointed his index finger to the ceiling. "…she's right above you. Just a few feet of rebar and concrete between you and her." He looked back at Ben writhing in agony on the floor. "Unfortunately for you, she thinks you're dead."

Ben's eyes grew wide. "No…she won't believe that!" he gasped, every word a struggle.

"Well, she seemed pretty convinced when I told her. She yelled at first but then turned into a weepy mess. And I'm sure you painted such a nice picture about me to her. You know, how evil I am and how many people I've killed. It would've been harder to convince her that I *hadn't* killed you."

"You *are* evil, you miserable piece of shit!" Ben spat out this last word with what remained of his strength. He let out a grunt in response to the pain and nearly passed out while Sean looked on with satisfaction. "Why don't you just kill me then?" he asked when his breath returned.

"Because that would be too easy for you and less fun for me. See, you destroyed my plans with your little stunt at the prison yesterday, so now I'm going to destroy your life. I think it's a fair exchange."

Ben could only listen now. His will to argue was gone. All he wanted was to black out.

"But before anything else happens," Sean went on, "I'll give you something for the pain because you really look like you need it."

He opened the door and the same Fixer who had cleaned Ben's shoulder entered. Without any instruction, he walked directly to Ben with a syringe in one hand and a flashlight in the other. Sean watched with delight as the Fixer leaned over and grabbed Ben's injured arm. Ben let out a howl, but the Fixer ignored him and injected the needle into the first vein he could find. After releasing the contents of the syringe, he departed the room, leaving Sean and Ben alone once again.

"Did you know that heroin is synthesized from morphine?" Sean remarked flatly. "I understand that the two have similar psychological effects on users. Lots of soldiers became addicted to morphine after they came home from all the wars during the last century." He spoke like a professor giving a lecture. "But several of the Helens tell me heroin is the best high they've ever had. Of course, I can't afford to risk using it personally. Addiction doesn't really suit someone in my position, so you'll have to confirm that for me."

But Ben had barely heard anything. The drug was already numbing the pain in his shoulder, and his mind began to feel a strange sense of calm.

"It's the most difficult drug for me to get my hands on," Sean rambled on. "You should consider yourself lucky that I'm about to invest my limited supply on you." He then took a few steps toward his captive. "But this time, I'll be more careful. You won't overdose like…Kar—like your sister."

Even in his deteriorated state, Ben heard Sean's voice waver, and his anger briefly returned. "You killed her…" he murmured.

"It was an accident. I never meant for…" Sean stopped and cleared his throat. "I loved her."

"You've never loved anybody. You're not capable of it!"

In a surge of rage, Sean took another step forward and delivered a sharp kick to Ben's stomach. Ben let out a sharp cough and rolled over to his side.

Sean knelt down and leaned over until his face was within inches of Ben's ear. "I loved Karen. Just like you love Andy. So I'm going to take her away from you. Slowly, one day at a time. One injection at a time. Soon, you'll love the drug more than you love her. And then one day, you'll forget about her completely. You won't even remember her name." The sound of vengeance in Sean's voice had a deafening effect. He stood up and left the room.

After enjoying his dinner, Sean decided it was time to pay Andy a visit. He had lied to Ben about already speaking with her, for they had yet to exchange a single word. He had checked on her once while she slept in her own tiny room hours earlier, and for some reason, he didn't want to wake her.

The guards opened the door to the closet, and Sean stepped inside. Unlike with Ben, he turned on the light. Andy was still asleep, but the flicker from the bulb disturbed her senses enough to wake her. She looked about until she spotted Sean. Then her face fell and she looked away.

"Oh come on…is that any way to treat your host? And here I was so anxious to meet the person who started all this mess."

But she didn't move. Sean closed the door and stepped around her to face her. He sat down on the floor to meet her eyes, but she recoiled and turned away.

"So that's how it's going to be then, huh? I won't hurt you. I just want to know who you are and how you got mixed up with someone like Ben Kelly."

At the mention of Ben's name, her shoulders trembled. Sean crawled around her crumpled body and faced her once again. This time, she didn't move away.

"Man, he really did a number on you, didn't he?" He leaned back against the wall and crossed his arms over his chest. "I have to admit, I don't get the attraction. I mean, I guess he's good-looking…or *was*, I should say, but I never really saw him with a lot of girls before he took off last year."

He scratched his head as though he were trying to recall something. Andy kept her head down, her hair covering her face.

"There was one girl…I think her name was Jenny…I saw her with him quite a bit, but she was just a Dreg. She was pretty, but nothing compared to one of my Helens. I never understood why Ben wasted his time with her, and I doubt the two of them ever had as much fun as you two did last night."

He waited for a reaction but he would not be satisfied. He reached out and curled a thick strand of Andy's hair around his finger and brushed it aside to see her face. She jerked away.

"Calm down, princess…I'm just trying to see what Ben found so alluring. And Luke, too. That little act you performed back at the club was quite entertaining. I might've fallen for it too." He leaned forward and tried to force eye contact. "Come on, Andy. Say something…I'm asking you nicely."

"There's nothing to say," she mumbled hoarsely.

"Oh, she speaks!"

"Just leave me alone."

But Sean was blithe in his response. "Perhaps you're not aware that torture is not off the table when it comes to getting what I want."

Andy finally looked up at him with hollow eyes. "You said you wouldn't hurt me, but go ahead…torture me all you want. There's nothing more you can do to me. But I'll take my life and what I've done with it to the grave." Then she turned away.

"That's fine. You can remain silent for as long as you want, but until you tell me something about yourself, you'll stay in this room in the dark without food, water, or a bathroom."

At the mention of the bathroom, Andy became painfully aware of the pressure on her bladder. She had managed to ignore the sensation for hours, but now that it had been brought to her attention, she could no longer deny the urge. Lying on her side, she crossed her top leg over her bottom one in an effort to stifle the discomfort.

The gesture made Sean laugh. "See, you won't last another hour, so why don't you stop being so stubborn and answer my question."

Accepting defeat, she pushed with her arms to sit upright. She brushed her hair away from her face and stared defiantly at him. "If I answer a question, you have to answer one of mine."

Sean pondered the proposition for a moment before casually shrugging. "Sure, why not. I'll start. When and where did you meet Ben?"

"That's two questions, not one."

"I'm changing the rules."

She narrowed her eyes but didn't argue. "Over a year ago on a highway in southern Virginia. Now my question: who the hell do you think you are trying to control the virus? Who made you God over all of us?"

Sean held up his hands and snickered. "Whoa, slow down. That wasn't a question…that was an accusation."

She remained stone-faced. "Answer it however you want, but that's my question."

He leaned back against the wall and kept an intent gaze on his beautiful captive.

Looking back at him, Andy suddenly recalled Ben's initial description of Sean. *What I remember most about him are his eyes. They're piercing blue…* The description was dead-on. His eyes were a beautiful, crystalline blue, but there was not even the slightest degree of warmth in them. Instead, they penetrated whatever they looked at. With his stare unwavering, Andy ultimately flinched and looked away.

He didn't seem to notice, for her question had fully occupied him. He took a deep breath and released it before finally speaking. "I don't think I'm God, if that's what you're implying. I'm simply trying to save people from themselves."

Andy let out an audible gasp. "How? By killing anyone who gets in your way?"

"No, that's not it at all. I don't care what anyone does with their lives. They can eat and drink what they want and screw whomever they want and stay out late and go to the clubs as much as they want and do whatever drugs they want. People in this city have the freedom to do all the things that they couldn't do six years ago."

"You actually believe that? You distribute drugs in this city like it's candy… young girls of twelve and thirteen are out there prostituting themselves and are choosing cocaine over food…!"

"Twelve and thirteen is not young anymore, not when you and I are two of the oldest people on the planet. And why not let people do what they want? The world is a mess. At least I'm giving everyone some order and opportunity." He leaned in even closer as his voice raised in volume. He wanted Andy to understand. "You're not from around here, are you?"

She didn't respond, and he didn't wait for an answer.

"Then you can't imagine what this city was like right after the outbreak. Things were brutal and chaotic and people were killing each other in the streets over a single can of food. I brought back stability for a million people! Who else can say the same? People want a leader to take charge, someone to do the worrying for them. There's only a tiny fraction of people who are smart enough and determined enough to do what I have done in the past six years. Most people are simply content to follow and watch the world go by. They're like cattle waiting to be herded. Can't you understand that?"

Andy didn't want to listen to the ramblings of a madman who believed without a doubt that his actions were entirely justified. She raised her eyes once more to meet his, and she spoke slowly and deliberately: "You believe that people are easy to manipulate. You think everyone can be controlled, that they can be bought with drugs and sex and status, but people aren't like that. People want to be loved and to have the freedom to do what they want with their lives. They don't want what *you* think they want. They've been driven to act recklessly because you offer them no alternative. You encourage their self-destructive behavior to keep them from waking up and realizing just how unbelievably *revolting* you are."

Her face crumpled and she turned away as the tears began to flow once again. She slumped back down to the floor and pressed her ear to the cold tiles, completely unaware that Ben was lying just a few yards below her.

"You killed someone I love today," she murmured softly into the air just loud enough for Sean to hear. "You shot him in cold-blood because he was trying to destroy something that should've never existed. You think Ben did it to get revenge on you for killing his sister? No. He did it because he knew that no one should have control over something so deadly." And with that, she closed her eyes.

Even if Sean asked her one more question, she would remain silent. She knew that any further argument with this narcissist and self-proclaimed savior of civilization was futile, as were any additional threats of torture. Sean had killed her love and friend, and sitting a moment longer in the same room with him was more unbearable than any physical torture.

"Go," she whispered. "Just leave me alone. Or just kill me and get it over with."

He wasn't used to being told what to do, but he'd never dealt with anyone like Andy before. He recognized that, and it both intrigued and scared him. Accepting defeat over this round of interrogation, he stood up and left the closet.

Chapter XXVIII

26 November 2023

*A*ndy was no longer in the Empire State Building. Infuriated by her unwavering two weeks of silence in the closet, mere yards from his office, Sean grudgingly transferred her to a lonely cell in an isolated part of Sing Sing Correctional Facility located thirty miles north of the city along the Hudson. It was the only facility that he actually used as a prison. He came to visit her once a week to try to force her to speak, but each time she stubbornly remained mute with an occasional glare as her only form of communication.

After finishing a particularly disgusting meal of cold soup that tasted more like bleach than chicken broth, two guards approached Andy in her cell and informed her that there was someone coming to see her. She was so tired of having to listen to the things Sean had to say. His visits had become relentless and after thirty-nine days of captivity, she was at the brink of talking.

She heard footsteps approaching, and a moment later came the now horribly familiar clanging sound against the bars of her cell. It was one of the guards taunting her with a baton, the same ones former prison guards had used for decades.

"Remember…just two minutes," he said to the visitor before retreating.

Andy looked and saw a fairly small person moving toward the bars wearing a baseball cap and a large winter coat. She immediately got up from her stiff bed. *It's not Sean,* she thought. When the dim light hit the person's face, she recognized it immediately.

It was Susan.

Her eyes grew wide and she started to say something, but Susan stopped her by putting her index finger to her lips. She covertly reached inside her coat and pulled out what appeared to be a large padded envelope and tossed it between the bars. It flew past Andy and landed squarely in the center of her tiny bed.

"Open it after I leave," Susan instructed in a whisper. "There's a letter inside. Read it and memorize it. Then get rid of it. There's duct tape inside. Use it to hide everything else underneath your bed."

"How did you get in here?"

"Drugs. Works every time. Danny's been a huge help, too."

Andy cast her eyes down at her feet. "Ben's dead."

"We know."

"Sean shot him."

"I know. I'm so sorry."

Andy couldn't hold back the tears, but as soon as they fell she brushed them away and quickly composed herself. "How are Morgan and Charlie? And Katie?"

"Good, but they miss you. We all do."

Andy suddenly thought of Brian. "Did your brother come back?"

"He did a couple of weeks ago with Scott. You remember him?"

Andy smiled weakly and responded with the slightest of nods. "I want to get out of here." Her voice shook as tears appeared once again.

Susan reached through the bars and squeezed Andy's arm. "You will. Read the letter. I need to go." Without another word, she left. She didn't look back as her footsteps faded away.

Andy waited nearly an hour before she opened the package. It had been meticulously packed, each object carefully arranged to fit snugly within the envelope. She removed the contents and placed them on the bed: a wristwatch, a key, a small flashlight, a collapsible baton, a small spool of duct tape, the four separate components of a pistol like the one Sean had taken from her, a loaded magazine, a pair of thick rubber gloves, a construction worker's mask, and a small bottle filled with a clear liquid. The last item was a small envelope with a letter and a hand-drawn map enclosed. She opened the letter and recognized Morgan's handwriting immediately:

Andy,

Today is the 26th of November. In twelve days, on the 8th of

December, there will be a power outage in the entire prison at exactly six o'clock in the evening. The 8th is the day of the next guard turnover. The old guards will be replaced by brand new ones who have never worked at your prison before, making it easier for you to escape...

Andy reread the word a few times...*escape...escape...*
Her heart beat faster as she continued reading.

The watch has been synchronized with ours and shows the proper date and military time. The small bottle contains an acid mixture that Charlie concocted. Starting today, spray the lock to your cell every day, twice a day. Wear the gloves and the mask while doing this, as the acid is highly corrosive. Make sure it doesn't contact your skin, and try to spray the lock when you think you won't be visited by guards or anyone else for at least an hour afterward since the smell can be potent. By the time you're ready to escape, the acid should corrode the lock enough to kick the door loose. Use the gun if you need to finish the job and to protect yourself against the guards. Same with the collapsible baton.

The key is for the car that we have staged for you about a mile away from the prison. On the map, you'll find where we've parked it. It's a red SUV without plates and has a full tank of gas. Jim checked everything to make sure it's running smoothly. There will be warm clothes and food inside. In the glove compartment is a map and directions to get to where we are now living. We are no longer in Princeton.

On the other side of this map is a sketch of Sing Sing prison where you're being kept. Study it and memorize the places we've marked where you'll have the best chances of escape if you can't get to the main entrance. We've done everything we can, but this prison is more heavily guarded than Green Haven. Even with the blackout, it will be difficult...but not impossible.

We all love you and miss you terribly. Good luck.

Filled with a wholly unexpected sense of hope, Andy read the letter several more times. She assembled the pistol and loaded the magazine before taping it securely under her bed. Then she donned the gloves and mask and carefully applied the acid to the lock on the door to her cell. The smell from the chemical reaction was intense, but she knew she was safe from detection this late in the day.

She studied both sides of the map before folding it within the letter and slid both papers beneath her pathetic little pillow. Then she taped the mask, gloves, key, flashlight, baton, and the bottle of acid underneath her bed. Finally, she put on the watch and concealed it beneath the cuff of her sweatshirt, the same sweatshirt she'd been wearing since that day at Green Haven. Forty days of sweat and body dander had made it stiff and malodourous.

The wound hadn't healed properly. The risk of infection had been averted, but his range of motion was significantly reduced. Ben could barely lift his arm horizontally without feeling a sharp twinge of pain.

He was still inside the closet on the eighteenth floor of the Empire State Building. By now his eyes were accustomed to the darkness, but the rest of his body was aching and restless. Today he was shaking more than usual and the urge to vomit was acute. It was always like this after the high wore off, but just when the symptoms became almost unbearable, the door would open and the needle would enter his vein. Then the euphoria would come and everything would be perfect for a few hours. He would lie on the floor, though sometimes it felt like he was lying on the ceiling looking down or lying on the wall hanging sideways.

Today when the needle stuck him in the left forearm, he thought of Andy and looked up at the ceiling just before the Fixer closed the door and the light disappeared. He wondered if she was still above him or if she had been moved somewhere else entirely. During the brief moments of sobriety before the withdrawal symptoms paralyzed him, his memory would taunt him with images of their one night together by the fireplace. He would remember the feel of her skin beneath his fingers, the smell of her wet hair, and the sound of her voice. He wouldn't cry, but his eyes would well up as the mental ache over the loss of her existence in his life overpowered him. But then physical pain would set in and the craving for the heroin would begin again.

Day fifty-one

She checked her watch when she woke up that morning. She'd worn it every day since Susan's visit. Time was of little consequence in prison but today it was imperative.

Around four in the afternoon, the guards delivered what she hoped would be her last meal in the cursed place: salty vegetable soup and soggy canned pears. Andy grudgingly ate everything on her plate. She would need her strength.

After pushing her empty tray between the bars and into the barren hallway, she set the alarm on her watch for five-thirty before lying down for a brief nap. An hour later, she awoke with a jolt. It was time to get ready. She tucked the car key and the baton into her pockets and double-checked the pistol. Then she read over the map of the prison one more time and stuffed it into her pocket along with Morgan's letter. With the gun in her right hand and the flashlight in her left, she sat on the edge of the bed—and waited.

The cellblock was quiet. Even the usual hushed noises of guards and prisoners seemed to have faded into silence. Or maybe it was just the ringing in her ears.

At exactly one minute after six o'clock, darkness enveloped the entire prison. Seconds later, shouts of chaos and confusion filled the air.

Andy stood up and approached her prison bars. She gave the door a heavy shake and the latch loosened a bit but not enough. She turned on the flashlight and pointed the beam toward the bed to suppress its intensity from view by the guards before giving the door a hard kick with the bottom of her shoe. The corroded latch gave way and the door swung open. She stepped into the hallway and ran.

Scurrying like a cat, she followed her bouncing beam of light as she passed several prisoners in their cells. Wild yells and whistles erupted as she flew by, but the sounds barely registered to her senses. She took a right turn and then a left and ran into two guards coming from the opposite direction. She raised the beam of the flashlight to their eyes, temporarily blinding them, and then gave the one to her right a sharp elbow to the ear, disabling him. Then she struck the guard on her left with a sideways kick to his knee in the same manner as she had opened her cell door. His leg buckled, and he collapsed to the ground, howling in pain.

In the dark, the prison was an impossible maze to navigate, but she had memorized and envisioned every turn. When she surprised two more guards, she quickly immobilized them with the help of the baton, all the while maintaining her focus on the prison map in her mind.

When she reached the prison's main entry, the chaos stemming from the loss of power enabled her to blend in with the commotion of disoriented guards bumping into one another, and without any further obstacles, she squeezed beyond the last door and emerged into the night.

The cold air hit her lungs and invigorated her body. The Hudson River was a mere hundred yards west, and the moisture in the air was instantly perceptible. It was the first fresh breath she had inhaled in weeks. The sky was crisp and clear, and the light from the waxing moon was enough to illuminate her path to the car.

Her brain extinguished the interior prison map and shifted attention to the exterior map. She raced through the narrow parking lot to the footbridge that crossed over the train tracks running north and south outside the prison compound. Once on the other side of the footbridge, she headed south along the tracks for almost a mile. The buildings and trees on her right faded away until there was just a thin strip of dirt between the tracks and the river.

Though weak from nearly two months of incarceration and insufficient food and water, her will propelled her forward as she hopped between the tracks. She stared down at the wooden ties in order to maintain her footing until she passed the old Scarborough Post Office on her left and a tiny parking lot squeezed between the train tracks and the river on her right. The lot was empty except for a red SUV sitting alone in the dark.

Andy hopped off the tracks and ran to the vehicle, out of breath, and reached into her pocket to retrieve the key. Within a minute, she was steering the SUV east across a small bridge that ran over the train tracks. She drove for a few miles to distance herself from the prison before pulling over along a quiet residential street. She opened the glove compartment and retrieved three different maps and a short handwritten note. After reading the note, she poured over the maps and spotted her final destination, marked with a red X on the third map. The location surprised her.

In the back of the car, she found the food and water, nearly frozen, beneath a winter coat, a hat, and gloves. Also in the trunk were three five-gallon cans filled with gasoline. Now armed with warmth and sustenance, she read over the maps once more and used the route highlighted by her friends.

An hour and two bottles of water later, she pulled off the highway and into a strip mall with a drugstore. She went inside the drugstore and began to scour the shelves with her flashlight. Her bladder was about to burst, but she did her best to ignore the intense discomfort until she found what she was looking for.

When she finally found the right shelf, it was empty. Desperate, she got down on all fours and flashed the light underneath. To her surprise, not one but two boxes of what she wanted were beneath the shelf. After removing her gloves, she pressed her cheek against the dirty carpet and strained her left arm under the shelf until her fingertips barely brushed the first box. With her insides screaming for relief, she freed the box and strained once more for the second, and just as she thought she couldn't take anymore, her hand achieved a precarious hold on the second box. With a grunt, she finally secured it and scrambled to her feet.

The bathroom door of the drugstore was locked and there was no time to find the key. She ran back outside and turned on the SUV's ignition. After flicking on the headlights, she glanced once at her surroundings before squatting down in front of the vehicle. Her bare hands struggled in the cold to open the two boxes. Inside each were two sticks wrapped in plastic. After tearing apart the plastic from each stick, she gathered all four exposed sticks in her left hand and yanked her filthy jeans and underwear down around her ankles with her right.

Though air chilled her bare skin, the urge to relieve her bladder was far greater. After adjusting her position, she carefully aimed the stream of urine on each stick before tossing them aside on the ground. After pulling her pants back on, she paced around the parking lot and waited.

As the minutes ticked by, she grabbed one of the empty boxes and read over the instructions on the back. Then she picked up the first stick.

The pregnancy indicator in the middle displayed an unmistakable symbol.

END OF BOOK ONE

Epilogue

January 2024

With an average of a quarter-million vehicles crossing between Virginia and Maryland daily, the Woodrow Wilson Bridge was once a traffic nightmare for residents of the Washington DC Metropolitan area. More than a mile long, the bridge spanned the Potomac River at the southern end of the Capital Beltway.

Riding a motorcycle, Chad's was the only moving vehicle in sight as he headed east from Virginia into Maryland. The rusted-out skeletons of dozens of abandoned cars, trucks, and SUVs still littered the highway in both directions of the bridge; permanent reminders of a past that would never return.

Chad zoomed ahead a few more miles beyond the bridge as a cold, winter rain pelted his helmet and jacket. He exited the Beltway and made his way onto Andrews Air Force Base. After parking his bike within a particular hangar, he walked beneath the canopy before stopping directly in front of a UH-1N Iroquois twin-engine helicopter. Daunting in size and scope, the helicopter stood in the same position as it had for over six years, seemingly frozen in time. As he stared up at the impressive machine, a rare emotion stirred in Chad: fear.

The aircraft seemed to be taunting him, almost daring him or anyone who gazed at it to give it a spin. Without realizing it, he took a step backward. He'd never flown in an airplane before, let alone a helicopter. The sound of an approaching vehicle pulled his attention away, and he glanced at his watch.

Five minutes early.

Resorting to habit, Chad reached into his back pocket and pulled out his knife. He began flipping it back and forth between his hands as three people exited the SUV and approached. Two were boys, Brandon and Calvin, each around sixteen or seventeen and both Infantry officers reassigned to Chad. The third individual was a tough-looking girl about the same age. She had shorter, dark hair and wide brown eyes, and she seemed to wear a permanent smirk.

"Megan?" Chad asked as the girl drew closer.

The girl gave a half-hearted nod. "Yeah, that's me." She didn't regard Chad, or anything else except the helicopter towering before her. She walked around it slowly, touching a few rivets and joints here and there, her eyes examining the aircraft studiously. "It's not in terrible shape, but it'll take some time to fix," she declared after completing a lap. "I should have it running again in…a month. Two, at most."

Chad raised his eyebrows skeptically. "A month? You better not be messing with me."

"Maybe two," she quickly repeated before turning back to the aircraft. "You got someone who can fly this thing?"

Chad looked at the two boys, one of whom nodded. "Let me worry about that."

Megan shrugged. "Whatever, but I can't be a hundred percent sure that everything's working without a pilot. Got it?"

Chad took a deep breath. She was right, but instead of relenting, he forced a smile. "This is one of Sean's highest priorities right now, so let's just get it done fast."

Acknowledgments

There are a few people who have helped me out during this whole process that I'd like to thank:

Katrina, for supporting me from the very beginning.
Buzz, for your watchful eye and attention to detail.
Ally, for working through all the tough spots with me.
And my parents, for always supporting me...no matter what.

A Conversation with Britt Holewinski

❧ **When did you start writing? Why?**

I began writing when I was seventeen, beginning with the story that would eventually become *Schism*. I had just finished reading *Lord of the Flies*, and my mind became fascinated with the idea of a world without adults and only children to figure out how to live and survive. Then the characters of Andy and Ben began to form in my mind, and I couldn't let the idea go. I had to write it down. Before then, I had never attempted to write even a short story. I jumped right into the notion of writing a book...and more.

❧ **What is your favorite dystopian movie or book? Favorite book turned into a movie?**

While *Lord of the Flies* may have inspired *Schism*, my favorite dystopian book is *Fahrenheit 451* by Ray Bradbury. Books and words are the foundation of modern human history, and to imagine them being erased from our daily lives is terrifying. Bradbury captured this fear perfectly.

Though not a movie, the 1995 television adaptation of *Pride and Prejudice* with Colin Firth and Jennifer Ehle is something I watch at least once a year. Not only is it one of my favorite books, but the series remains faithful to the novel while still allowing for some interpretation and creative license. If a book is loved by its readers, why change the story for film? Viewers want to see a director's own vision of the book, and changing the plot is always confusing to me.

❧ **How did your background in working for the CIA help you** come up with the premise of a government-engineered virus outbreak in Schism?

I joined the CIA a few months after September 11, 2001. The focus of my work for the majority of my career was helping to counter global terrorism. Almost all terrorists are adult-aged males. The idea that the US government—or any government—would try to create a virus that quickly killed adult males was inspired by my experience working in Iraq and Afghanistan.

⁊ **What will happen next for Andy? Will Ben survive?**

Andy has very difficult times ahead, even more so than what she experienced in the first book. She will need to rely on her friends and her own internal strength and doggedness to not only keep her alive, but also to keep her sane.

Ben's future looks bleak, doesn't it? Drugs take a terrible toll on both the body and the mind, and it remains unknown how much more he can withstand this forced addiction. But this is Ben, after all, and he's survived tragedy before. His chances of pulling through are better than most.

About the Author

Britt Holewinski was inspired to write *Schism* more than twenty years ago after reading William Golding's *Lord of the Flies* in high school. After studying mechanical engineering at the University of Notre Dame and Pennsylvania State University, she joined the CIA during the months following 9/11. Besides traveling for her job, she has visited nearly every location she has written about for current and future works, to include Bermuda, Paris, and the Channel Islands.

Britt is currently working on the next book in her *Schism* series.

31901059547937